AN ANGEL'S FURY

Angel smacked the water with her fist and shrieked when it sprayed in her own face instead. Holt laughed huskily and held her firmly in place against his chest.

"Don't be so ornery," he whispered against her ear. "I just want to get to know my new partner a little better."

"The devil you do," Angel gritted out through clenched teeth, trying to drive her elbow back into his rock-hard stomach. "I know all about men like you!"

"Do you?" Holt mused, easily deflecting her elbow and then nibbling suggestively at her earlobe. "I wonder."

"Stop it." Angel struggled harder to get free, and only succeeded in getting wetter and more snugly ensconced in his embrace. "I don't want this anymore!"

"Little liar. It's all you've wanted from me since you came here, and you know it." Holt twisted her chin to one side and forced her to look into his quicksilver eyes. "You can't deny you're attracted to me."

"Oh! You are the most impossible, arrogant—"

Holt cut off Angel's tirade with a fierce kiss, breaching her soft lips with his tongue. Then he pulled back and murmured softly, "You know we want each other, Angel. Why fight nature? And don't forget, in the eyes of the law you belong to me now."

PATRICIA McALLISTER

MOUNTAIN ANGEL

ZEBRA BOOKS
KENSINGTON PUBLISHING CORP.

ZEBRA BOOKS are published by

Kensington Publishing Corp.
850 Third Avenue
New York, NY 10022

First Printing: January, 1995

Printed in the United States of America

Dedicated to three very special women . . .

Jennifer, who helped make the dream a reality;
Anna-Louise, for her unconditional love;
and Lalene, for raising her son to the right kind of hero.

O LYRIC Love, half angel and half bird,
And all a wonder and a wild desire . . .

—Robert Browning

Chapter One

Independence, Missouri
1875

"There must be some mistake."

Angel heard her own anxious voice echo through the room, and she leaned forward in the damask chair to emphasize her words.

Across the gleaming expanse of his huge mahogany desk, her father's solicitor gravely shook his iron-gray head.

"I wish I could tell you there was, Miss McCloud, but I'm afraid figures don't lie." Henry Fraser's soft Missouri drawl had never sounded more ominous. He was an old family friend, and he knew better than to try to pull the wool over Angel's eyes. She was an intelligent young woman and would learn the truth eventually. He sighed and decided to be brutally honest with her, no matter how much it tried him.

"Your father was many thousands of dollars in debt when he died. It seems he made some very poor investments over the years, and, of course . . . there were the gaming tables."

Fraser cleared his throat apologetically and went on. "Unfortunately, once he ran out of funds, Royce used various McCloud properties as collateral." He pushed a ream of paper across the desk with another grim shake of his head. "Everything is spelled out here in black and white, I'm afraid. I don't see any alternative but for you to sell everything in order to satisfy these obligations."

Angel briefly closed her sky-blue eyes, but when she opened them again they flashed with resolution. Even dressed in black taffeta she was a beautiful young woman. Her heart-shaped face was framed by loose wisps of golden hair that had escaped the neat confines of a chignon. Her skin was flawless and creamy, like the single strand of pearls fastened around her throat. That mouth alone would tempt a man to treason, Fraser thought. It was no wonder there had been dozens of offers for her hand before Royce's death.

It was a good thing Angel McCloud was as strong, or stronger, than most men Fraser could name, and, like the walls around them, could weather the worst of storms. She would need to call upon a miracle to survive the days to come, he realized. But when she spoke again, there was no doubt left in his mind that she was Royce McCloud's daughter.

"What sort of price will the horses fetch?"

"Not enough to make a difference. I understand Royce had a contract with the U.S. Army to supply mounts, but they've never been known to pay well, or on time."

Angel nodded tersely. "Sell them anyway, Henry. I can't afford to feed them anymore." She was determined not to let the lawyer hear her heart breaking, and kept her tone brisk and businesslike. "What about the extra land?"

"I've already figured that in. You're still thousands short. I included the stables, the house furnishings, even the kitchen sink." His poor attempt at humor was lost on Angel. She looked as wretched as he himself felt. "However we look at it, you'll barely make a dent in these debts."

"What about the mine? Didn't my father own shares in a mine somewhere out west?"

Fraser pursed his lips and quickly reviewed his papers. "Why, yes, he did, but it never produced and the claim is almost certainly worthless. You'd never find a buyer for such a chancy enterprise anyway."

Angel gave a weary sigh, pressing a slim white hand to her temple. "At least I have the house."

Fraser made a move to speak and then hesitated, and she looked sharply across the desk at him.

"I still have the house, don't I, Henry?"

He shook his head apologetically. "I don't intend to lie to you, Angel, and I'm afraid there's no way to soften this blow. . . . Among these papers is a promissory note deeding Belle Montagne, house and all, to Willard Craddock."

"Craddock!" Angel shot to her feet at the name, her blue eyes wide with horror. "Are you absolutely certain?"

"I'm sorry, but the first thing I did was verify your father's signature. Apparently he lost the estate to Mr. Craddock in a—er—game of five-card stud."

Angel began to pace the lawyer's office, the mourning gown swirling around her slender ankles. It was obvious she was searching for a solution.

Fraser put in tentatively, "Perhaps you're aware that Mr. Craddock has offered for your hand . . . ?"

"Yes." Her curt reply indicated her decision. Of all men, why Craddock? The lecherous old widower had pursued Angel for the past two years to the point of embarrassment. The fact that he should be the one to own Belle Montagne now made her seethe with helpless rage.

Fraser cleared his throat. "Maybe you should reconsider his offer, Angel. He's promised to deed back Belle Montagne for your dowry—"

"No! Never, Henry. Never will I marry that disgusting swine." He saw the passionate conviction in her voice confirmed in her beautiful eyes. It was obvious she didn't intend to give Craddock another thought.

Calming herself, Angel picked up the black kid gloves resting on the arm of the chair and tugged them back on her hands. "How much time do I have?"

"Mr. Craddock has allowed you a month, in view of your state of mourning." Fraser picked up the cigar resting in a silver tray and took a brief puff. He was amazed by Angel's dignity in the face of losing all she had. Though it had clearly shocked her to learn she had lost Belle Montagne, she was already planning for a future that didn't exist.

"Very well. I shall review these papers tonight and contact you later in the week." Angel picked up the sheaf of documents from his desk, and he hastened to see her to the door.

She managed to exchange a few more pleasantries with Fraser before they parted company. But once outside the lawyer's office, Angel's shoulders slumped with defeat. She had never imagined her father would be so foolish as to use their family home as collateral! Royce McCloud had been so proud of Belle Montagne and the fine horses they had raised there.

Angel had known her father's major weakness had been gambling, but she had never imagined the extent of the debt they were in. Royce had kept his problems carefully hidden from his only living child. His daughter's sole concern, he had always said, should be finding a wealthy husband who could take care of her in the style to which she was accustomed.

She released a bitter little laugh at the memory. Her father's high-brow friends had quickly disappeared once they heard of the debts and his subsequent suicide. The note Royce had left his daughter had begged her to forgive him, but those words were scant comfort now. Someday there would be tears, but for now all Angel could summon was bitterness. How much had her father wagered on a few rolls of the dice or a single turn of a card?

She shook her head in dismay as she hurried down the boardwalk to the waiting coach. She got no farther than a few steps when a wide shadow suddenly fell across her path.

"Miss McCloud."

Angel reacted with alarm to the familiar nasal voice. Willard Craddock quickly doffed his black felt bowler hat and gave her a formal bow. As his watery eyes rose, they fixed on Angel's breasts and lingered. She tried not to shiver at the horrible sensation that glance engendered.

Will Craddock was twice her age, a wealthy widower with an excess of flesh always hanging over his trousers. Today he had squeezed his considerable girth into a pair of plaid knickerbockers. His satin waistcoat was stained and unevenly buttoned. An attempt had been made to tame his graying hair with oil, but his bushy Dundreary whiskers sprouted out like small wings on either side of his round, sweaty face.

"I wish to express my condolences on the death of your father," Craddock said, licking his thick lips while his eyes continued to roam up and down Angel's body.

"Thank you," she murmured reluctantly, gathering up the folds of her gown to move around him. For a man of his size, Craddock moved with surprising speed to cut her off.

"Surely you must reconsider my proposal now."

His assumption infuriated Angel. She informed him in an icy voice, "I am still in mourning, Mr. Craddock. I am therefore considering nothing of the sort. Now kindly step out of my way!"

Craddock only chuckled, daring to brush lewdly against Angel before she could escape to the safety of her carriage. She promptly yanked down the shade over the view of his leering face outside the window and sank back against the velvet cushions. Her hands rose to cover her face. "Oh, Papa," she whispered, "what have you done?"

Angel watched in mute agony as the last horses were led away from the auction ring. It had taken every ounce of her strength to sit and watch the very soul of Belle Montagne being sold to strangers. The McCloud estate had always been known for the best horseflesh west of the Mississippi, and almost everyone attending the auction cast her mixed looks of pity and sympathy as the stable doors shut for the last time.

Everyone except Willard Craddock, who lurked, hat in hand, just outside the arena, waiting for another opportunity to accost Angel. She shuddered and turned away from the sight of the old widower. Her eyes moved instead to Elsa Loring, and softened on the stout German woman who had raised her from a child.

"Mein Gott!" Elsa exclaimed as she hurried to Angel's side. "Is that old vulture still trying to win your hand?"

Even in her grief Angel had to laugh at the indignation of the older woman. Elsa was short and plump with apple cheeks and a hearty, booming laugh. She had been the only mother Angel had known, after the death of Theresa McCloud when she was only two years old.

Elsa and Hans Loring had seven children of their own, and Angel had always felt a part of their big, happy family. Until now. Now she was reminded just how far apart their worlds really were, for the Lorings would be leaving Belle Montagne soon. Angel could not afford to pay the servants now, and though the Lorings were like family, they could ill afford to continue to work for her out of charity.

Angel clung to the older woman for a moment and bravely checked her tears. "It's so unfair, Elsa!"

"Ach, I know." The housekeeper patted Angel's back consolingly. "But you know you are welcome to live with us, *madchen*. Hans and I would gladly make room."

Angel stepped back and dabbed at her eyes with a lace-edged handkerchief. "Thank you, Elsa. I know it comes from your heart, but you and Hans have too many mouths to feed. It wouldn't be fair of me to impose like that."

"But what will you do? Where will you go?" the elderly woman fretted.

"I have a plan; don't worry. Do you remember what Papa always told me? He said if I was ever in trouble, I should write to his partner at the Lucky Devil Mine in the Colorado Territory. Papa said Mr. Murphy would be able to help me. He apparently owed my father a great debt of some kind."

Elsa nodded reluctantly. "But you have less than a month, child. Will you be able to hear from Herr Murphy before then?"

"I sold some of Mother's silver to pay a man to take Mr. Murphy a message," Angel began.

The German housekeeper released a heartbroken cry. "Your mother's silver! It was her pride and joy."

"I know, Elsa, but there was nothing else left after I settled Father's overdue accounts in town. I was lucky the man agreed to take it as payment. He promised to ride night and day until he reaches the Territory, and he'll give my letter only to Mr. Murphy himself. He said he would bring a reply back to Belle Montagne. If all goes well, I should hear something in a few weeks."

After reading the note, Angel crumpled the paper in her hand and flung it into the corner of the room. It was yet another of Willard Craddock's warnings, this one even worse than the last. Craddock apparently considered her fair game now that her father was gone, for he no longer even offered marriage.

In his latest proposal the widower had suggested Angel take him as her "protector." Which, she knew, meant no more than being his mistress. He had promised to deed back Belle Montagne to her if she agreed. He knew how desperate she was. But not that desperate, Angel thought. Not yet!

She whirled to pace the empty conservatory, which just days before had contained a magnificent grand piano and many other elegant furnishings. She had sold everything, but as Fraser had warned, the funds had barely touched the mountain of debts.

And so far there had been only silence from Mr. Murphy. Angel was forced to wonder if her message had reached him. Three weeks had passed now, and the creditors were beginning to circle her. Henry Fraser had held them off as long as he could, but even the lawyer could not prevent them from riding out to Belle Montagne and delivering various threats.

If not for Hans and Elsa Loring, Angel would have been completely defenseless. The big German man ran off intruders on a daily basis, some of whom were thugs who had heard that Royce's beautiful daughter was alone now. Hans taught Angel how to load and fire a revolver and rifle, for he was not always around to guard against strangers.

What a turn her life had taken! Angel McCloud, who had once been toasted as the reigning belle of Independence, was now reduced to defending her very virtue with weapons. She desperately wished her older brother, Matthew, had not died in the war. Matt would have protected her, and he would have known what to do now.

A short time later Angel heard the rapid clatter of horse's hooves on the lane leading to the house, and she rushed to the window with trepidation. Hans had gone to town and Elsa was down at the river, doing the laundry. Would she be forced to draw a gun for the first time?

When she recognized the rider swinging down from a rangy bay Angel let out a relieved cry and gathered up her skirts. She ran outside to meet the man she had hired to ride all the way to Colorado Territory.

"Miss." He tipped his filthy hat at her, ogling the lovely young woman who faced him with anxiety written all over her face.

"Did you give Mr. Murphy my letter? Did he send one back?"

"Yep and yep," he said, pausing to spit a wad of juicy tobacco at her feet.

"Give it to me, please." Angel held out her hand.

"It's gonna cost ya, missy."

"I already gave you all of the family silver!" she cried, outraged.

The man shrugged and spat again. "You kin pay however you want, but you're gonna hafta pay," he repeated, roaming his crude gaze up and down her trembling body.

"Wait here!" With an exasperated noise, Angel rushed back into the house and grabbed one of the few things that remained. She returned and thrust an ivory figurine at the man, waiting impatiently while he carefully tucked it into his saddlebag and retrieved a worn, dirt-smudged envelope.

Angel snatched it from him and returned to the house. Shutting and bolting the door behind her, she tore open the travel-stained envelope and began to read. A small cry of relief escaped her as she deciphered the bold male scrawl. Then her brow furrowed in disbelief, re-reading the words. Surely he couldn't be serious!

Mr. Murphy proposed that she marry him by proxy and come out to Colorado Territory. He assured her that it would be in name only, and for just long enough to protect Angel from other men, especially Willard Craddock. A single woman would risk a great deal traveling so far alone, he had written. And he could not leave the mine at the present time to escort her west. Enclosed in the letter were several banknotes, enough to pay her passage on the train.

The letter also said Royce McCloud still had an interest in the Lucky Devil Mine, and Murphy expected a big strike any day now. It might provide enough money to buy back Belle Montagne from Willard Craddock.

What Murphy said made sense, but Angel was hesitant. What if the mine didn't produce as expected? Would she be stuck in Colorado Territory, never to see her beloved home again?

Of course, she still had a choice. She could always agree to become Craddock's mistress. With a sigh of quiet despair, Angel went upstairs and began to assemble her trousseau.

"Don't forget to write!" Elsa Loring chugged alongside the train, waving frantically at the young woman sitting in the window seat. A final word of wisdom trailed Angel out of the station. "Watch out for men!"

Angel smiled and waved back, returning her attention to the book in her lap once the train was well on its way. She was reading all she could about the Colorado Territory, especially the mines. It was little surprise her father had invested in gold-mining, for it had appealed to his gambler's soul. Royce McCloud had been a wonderful father, but he had been sadly shortsighted. He had failed to provide properly for his daughter, and now she was forced to improvise.

Soon Angel shut the book with a sigh. She could barely concentrate upon the script dancing before her weary eyes. She had gotten very little sleep since the night she had made her decision to head west. And no doubt she had made an unsightly bride, garbed in black bombazine and deathly pale.

Henry Fraser had stood in for the groom at the ceremony, and the judge had also worn black. When he had pronounced them man and wife Angel had nearly giggled, realizing they resembled more of a funeral procession than a wedding when they left the courthouse.

But she was legally Mrs. Holt Murphy now, as the gleaming gold band on her left hand attested. Willard Craddock had been furious when he heard Angel was married, and even more so when he learned she was leaving Missouri. It had given her great delight to saunter past the scowling Craddock one last time before she caught the train west. He hadn't dared to say anything to a properly married woman, and Angel had almost blown him a mischievous kiss before she departed.

Safe at last! Now all that remained was to secure a quick annulment from Mr. Murphy and claim her share of the Lucky Devil's profits. Maybe by this time next month she would be setting foot on Belle Montagne land again.

With a relieved sigh, Angel closed her eyes and drifted off to sleep, lulled by the clickety-clack of the wheels and the rocking motion of the train.

* * *

Every jolt of the stagecoach carried Angel closer to her bridegroom. The train service had ended at Denver and she had been forced to take the stage, an outdated mode of travel that was uncomfortable at best and outright merciless on the tender portions of one's anatomy.

But Angel temporarily forgot the bumps and bruises when she gazed awestruck at a mighty snow-flocked peak soaring up into the fluffy clouds. She had never seen anything so beautiful, and when the coach lurched again, she didn't even feel her seat mate's elbow jabbing into her side.

"It's purty, ain't it?" cackled the old woman next to her. "Pritner right next to God, least that's what I always say."

"You mean, that's what Preacher Murphy says," corrected a bespectacled man across from them. He gave a disapproving sniff and returned to his paper.

Angel's mouth nearly dropped open. "Holt Murphy is a preacher?" she exclaimed.

The old woman cackled again. " 'Course not, child. His brother Neal runs the little parish over in Oro."

"Oh." Angel exhaled with relief. She didn't think she would make a very good preacher's wife. Not even for one day!

The tiny town of Clear Creek, Colorado, lay snuggled between two peaks in the Sawatch Range, like a jewel set on a lady's bosom. It had sprung up overnight during the Gold Rush of '58, and though the boom had long since died, a handful of hangers-on still populated the high mountain town.

Angel's first glimpse of the sagging, clapboard buildings and the equally sorry-looking inhabitants wasn't encouraging. She stared with shock at the obvious desolation of the place; the burned schoolhouse, a churchyard nearly returned to dust itself, a creaky door to an abandoned stable that swung and banged forlornly in the wind. There had obviously been some mistake! Angel had expected something primitive, but nothing like this.

The stage came to a rolling halt in the middle of town, and the passengers began to disembark. Angel gathered up her wide skirts and stepped down into the dusty street. Out of respect for Mr. Murphy she had chosen not to don mourning any longer, but wore a deep sapphire-blue silk gown. Her golden hair was coiled neatly under her velvet-trimmed bonnet, tied with matching ribbons. Since it was cool Angel had draped a lace shawl over her shoulders, but at once she felt out of place.

Within moments Angel sensed the eyes of a passing man assessing her, and she turned in slight distress to search for Mr. Murphy. But the grizzled old prospector weaving along the boardwalk reeked of whiskey and something worse, and she exhaled with relief when he belched and stumbled on by, obviously not there to meet the stage. With a little shiver Angel turned around again just as her bags landed in a cloud of dust at her feet. When the stage driver made no move to assist her further she realized she was going to have to forge on by herself.

She picked up the nearest bag and began to struggle toward a fading signboard that read CLEAR CREEK HOTEL. It looked slightly disreputable, but she had little choice. She only hoped her remaining bags would be safe until she could retrieve them.

"Excuse me," Angel panted as she approached the wide-eyed clerk standing behind a dusty desk inside the hotel, "can you tell me where I will find Mr. Murphy?"

"The preacher?" He gaped at her openly through grimy spectacles perched on the end of his narrow nose.

"No, the other one."

"I see." Now the clerk looked even more curious. He jabbed his thumb in the direction of Mount Elbert as he peered suspiciously at Angel. "Up at the mine."

"Oh, of course." She nodded with a mixture of relief and worry. How would she get up there to let Mr. Murphy know she'd arrived?

"I'd like a room, please. Could you send someone outside for my other bags?"

"Of course." The clerk rang a bell on the desk, and a seedy-looking porter appeared to take on the task.

"Will you be staying long, miss?" The clerk pushed the registration book towards her. It was ominously blank.

"I—I don't know yet." Quickly, Angel signed *Mrs. Murphy* under the day's date and handed back the pen.

Angel noticed the clerk's pursed lips as he read over her signature. And when his eyes rose and narrowed on her she wondered what he knew that she didn't.

Angel strolled down the boardwalk, greeting everyone she passed. At best she elicited a grunt from the men, or an outright leer. The few women she saw wouldn't speak at all. In fact, they pointedly turned their faces aside, and Angel soon gave up trying to make new acquaintances.

What was wrong? She had been here three days now and was no closer to solving her problems than when she had been in Missouri. The note she had sent up to the mine had gone unanswered. Was it possible Holt Murphy had left the area for some reason?

Even if he had, it didn't explain the townspeople's reaction to her. She rightly assumed that the nosy hotel clerk had spread who she was all over town by now, but it still didn't excuse their behavior. Angel was being treated like a pariah, and it didn't make any sense.

She paused warily on the streetcorner across from the Prospector Saloon, the only place in Clear Creek that seemed busy. A second later shots rang out, and the sound of breaking glass echoed down the alley. She had no chance to flee before the tavern doors burst open, spewing two men into the street.

One was ugly and scarred and wildly waving a gun. Angel let out a soft screech and ducked behind a tall post, but not before he had seen her.

"If it ain't the yeller-haired doxy!" the man crowed drunkenly, drawing attention to Angel.

Her eyes moved to focus on the second man, who wore buckskin trousers and a fringed shirt. He was lean but muscular, and as he spun around to stare at Angel she unconsciously noted the felinelike grace of the movement.

The younger man's black hair glistened like a raven's wing under the sun, reflecting bluish highlights. At first Angel thought he was Indian, but when he stared directly at her she saw that his eyes were light.

The gunmetal-gray eyes suddenly narrowed, and his square jaw clenched in a savage frown. Angel wondered what she'd done to incur his wrath, but the scarred man unwittingly supplied the answer when he pointed at her.

"Thas' the one who calls herself Missus Murphy!" He

doubled over in a drunken fit of laughter, all thoughts of a brawl apparently forgotten.

Angel suddenly saw the younger man start toward her, each stride a furious one. Strapped to his lean waist, a long Bowie knife flashed ominously in the sunlight, and too late she turned to flee.

The man caught her by the arm, yanking Angel back hard against his fringed chest. Her bonnet tumbled off into the dust, unfurling a banner of long blond hair. His nostrils flared angrily as he drank in Angel's fresh young beauty up close, and his silver eyes narrowed suspiciously.

"What hell game are you playing?" he growled.

Angel was shocked for some reason to hear English spill from his lips. And even more surprised to find herself intrigued by his savage good looks, the proud posture of his powerful body, his burning steely gaze.

"I don't know what you mean," she flared, struggling in vain to free herself.

"You're the woman claiming to be Murphy's wife, aren't you?" His lips curled back, exposing even white teeth. Cold fury laced his every word. He shook Angel until she answered him.

"Yes!"

He set his teeth, obviously enraged by her reply. Then he sent her reeling back from him, and Angel caught the post just in time to avoid falling on the boardwalk.

"How dare you treat a lady this way!" she cried.

The man stared at her incredulously for a moment, then threw back his head and let out a loud whoop of laughter. "Did you hear that, Jack?" he asked the other fellow, who was still snickering in the street. Then he turned back to Angel and said dryly, "I've heard some fancy lines coming from whores in my day, but I reckon that isn't one of them."

Angel let out an outraged screech and flew back at him. He barely avoided the nails slashing dangerously near his face. With a blur of hands he captured her wrists, hauling her up on her tiptoes while Angel twisted about helplessly.

"Who the hell are you?" he demanded.

"My name is Angel," she began breathlessly. She got no farther than that when his deep laughter rang out, mocking her from head to toe.

"Angel, hmm? And you still expect me to believe you're not a lady of the evening?"

"Mr. Murphy will make you rue the day you called me a trollop!"

"I doubt that," the handsome stranger chuckled, slowly lowering her back to her feet. "Arthur Murphy's dead."

Angel shook her head, her outrage momentarily forgotten. "Not Arthur," she gasped out. "Holt Murphy. I'm his wife."

The gray-eyed man stared at her for a moment. "Well, you don't say. What a damned interesting coincidence."

"Why is that?"

"Because," he drawled, "I'm Holt Murphy!"

Chapter Two

Angel felt a bright flush creeping up her cheeks. There had to be some mistake! She couldn't possibly be married to this . . . this ruffian! But even as she stared back horrified into his silvery eyes, she remembered the name neatly typed on the legal wedding documents in her trunk.

Holt Murphy. Not Arthur. There was simply no question about it. She opened her mouth to inform him of it when he suddenly pulled her around the side of the building, flat against the wall.

"What is it?" she asked breathlessly.

Holt only shook his head, holding Angel tightly against him until two horses plodded on by, ridden by a pair of hard-looking men scouring the streets. After they disappeared around another bend he gradually released her, apparently as surprised as Angel to discover how closely they were standing together.

"Now," he demanded, "you're going to explain what this is all about."

"Gladly," Angel agreed tersely, "if you'll be so kind as to release my arm!"

Holt glanced down to see his hand still clamped hard around Angel's wrist. The pressure of his grip had drained all the color from her fingers. Her delicate bone structure was evident; he could easily circle her wrist twice over. With a soft oath he let her go.

She chafed her wrist as she explained, "My name is— or rather, was—Angel McCloud. I was recently married by proxy in Missouri to a Holt Murphy."

"Are you sure?" he asked, searching her blue eyes for the slightest hint of treachery. "Not Arthur Murphy?"

Angel nodded. "I remember thinking Holt was such a strong name. And I . . . I thought it was perfect, because he agreed to help me out."

"Who?"

"Holt Murphy! He sent me a letter explaining why it would be wiser for me to be married on the trip west. He offered to wed me by proxy, so I would have safe passage to Clear Creek."

Holt frowned, his gray eyes stormy. "I don't know why you dreamed up this wild story, or who helped you to do it, but I'm the only Holt Murphy in Clear Creek, and I most certainly never agreed to marry anyone purely out of the goodness of my heart."

"I'm not surprised," Angel snapped back, "because you haven't got one! Please stop looking at me as if I'm lying. I'm not. And I have the papers to prove it!"

"Good." He nodded shortly. "I want you to show me that letter first."

She hesitated. "I haven't got it anymore. I didn't think it necessary to keep it."

"How convenient, Miss McCloud. And I suppose it's also central to your plan that my father has died."

"Your father?" Angel looked genuinely bewildered, and Holt frowned down at her savagely.

"You're a good actress, I'll give you that, but it won't save your hide if you're lying to me. I intend to escort you back to the hotel where you're staying so you can show me those documents."

Angel matched glares with him. "Certainly, Mr. Murphy. But how did you know I'm staying at the hotel?"

"Since I came down off the mountain all I've heard about is the doxy posing as Mrs. Murphy. I figured it was just another chippie trying to get a cut of the mine." He paused to give her an insolent up-and-down look. "And I'm not so sure I'm wrong."

Angel gasped and raised her hand to slap him, but he knocked it aside easily.

"There's a regular little she-devil hiding under that sweet little name." Holt chuckled unexpectedly. "Maybe I'll keep you after all."

"Not for a day!" Angel declared. "I'll be on the next stage to Denver. There's obviously been a terrible mistake."

"There sure has," Holt agreed, a devilish sparkle in his gray eyes. "But until it's all straightened out, I intend to enjoy every minute of your angelic company."

Later Angel watched those same gray eyes visibly widen as they scanned the copy of the wedding banns.

"Now do you believe me?" she asked.

Holt tossed the paper aside. "It could be forged." He

moved to stalk the confines of her hotel room, the taut male strength evident in every line of his body.

For a moment Angel just drank in the sight of him, the fringes of his jacket swaying gently as he moved, the blue-black sheen of his hair under the soft gas lamps.

Holt Murphy was incredibly handsome, the high cheekbones of his face blending with his square jaw in perfect symmetry. He was clean-shaven; not even a faint razor stubble showed on his deeply tanned skin. She studied him thoughtfully, wondering if he was possibly part Indian. But she was afraid to ask. If nothing else, his temper was savage enough to discourage polite conversation.

When Holt glanced at Angel, sitting there so demurely with her hands folded in her lap, he almost laughed. It seemed incredible now that he had mistaken her for a whore. Good breeding always showed, his brother said. Although Neal had meant it disparagingly, of course, for Holt's benefit.

"Well?" Angel prompted him anxiously. "Do you believe me now?"

"I believe something happened," Holt replied, "only because it's impossible for either of us to prove otherwise. But it's hard for me to believe we could be husband and wife, especially without my knowledge or consent."

"As far as I knew, it was your idea," Angel reminded him curtly. She rose to pace the other side of the room, her lavender gown swishing as she moved. Silk Parma violets had been artfully arranged in the golden tresses, and Holt was struck anew by how lovely she was. Beautiful and innocent-looking, just like her namesake. Dammit, how come he always got himself in such messes? First thing tomorrow, he was putting Angel McCloud right back on the stage. The mystery of their supposed marriage would just have to wait.

"You don't believe me, do you?" Angel challenged him as she looked back over her shoulder. Unexpectedly, her tone changed to a soft plea. "I wouldn't have come all this way just to play a joke on you. I swear it!"

"Don't swear," Holt said huskily, and slanted her a wry smile. "It doesn't suit a lady."

So he believed some of her story, at least. "Thank you," Angel murmured.

"But we still have to figure a way out of this mess. Obviously we'll have to file for divorce."

"Annulment," she corrected him. "The marriage was never consummated."

Holt's smile was transformed into a predatory one. "That could change."

Too late Angel read the intent in his smoky gray eyes and took a hasty step backwards. She bumped against a chair and found herself trapped on the other side by the dresser.

As if he had all the time in the world, Holt sauntered up to Angel and gazed down at her upturned face, into beautiful blue eyes darkening with apprehension.

"Don't be afraid of me," he said softly. "I won't hurt you."

Holt's hands gently gripped her shoulders, drawing her slowly toward him. Angel was mesmerized by his silvery smouldering gaze, the black pupils large in the dim light. She caught the male scent of him, of leather and horses and fresh tobacco. It was not an unpleasant smell, but it made her stomach churn in a disconcerting way.

"Please," she whispered.

"Please what?" Holt murmured. "Kiss you? After all, Mrs. Murphy, if I'm really your husband, then it's certainly my right, isn't it?"

His mouth moved to capture hers, so swiftly Angel was unable to protest. She jerked slightly with the impact, but her lips parted of their own accord and she moaned at the unfamiliar sensations. Holt's hands tightened on her, and he pressed his hard male body firmly against her while he made leisurely love to her mouth.

Fire! An image of all-consuming flame blossomed in Angel's mind. She was burning, engulfed in Holt's smouldering gaze and the long, flamelike strokes of his hands upon her back. Angel felt an answering shudder course through his frame when her own hands settled on his narrow hips. Under her fingertips the buttery softness of his buckskin trousers seemed incredibly sensual.

A shattered gasp escaped Angel's lips when he finally withdrew his mouth. She pressed a hand to her wildly fluttering heart, and stared up at him with wide eyes.

"Don't look at me like that," Holt warned, "or I'll forget my promise not to take advantage of the situation."

Angel hastily looked down, the dark sweep of her lashes like tiny crescents against her rosy skin. She hoped Holt hadn't sensed her burgeoning response to his caresses, or felt the shameless way she'd leaned into him. She could hardly believe it herself. Nobody had ever affected her in the way this quiet, mysterious man did. Holt had told her nothing of himself or his life, yet she felt compelled to trust him. Her instincts were all she had to go on, and though Angel realized how foolish she had been, letting a stranger into her hotel room, it had never occurred to her to worry. She had been so determined to prove herself right!

Angel swallowed as Holt simply looked at her for an endlessly tense moment. "You're not safe in Clear Creek," he announced abruptly.

"I'm putting you on the stage first thing tomorrow," he added, and his silver eyes visibly hardened on her. Gone was the burning moment they had shared, the flare of unexpected passion that had nearly consumed her. Angel felt a curious mixture of relief and disappointment, and she couldn't speak.

"I'll call for you in the morning and see you to the stage," Holt finished. He paused by the door and gave her a long, unfathomable look. "Can you stay out of trouble till then?"

Angel nodded shakily. The moment he was gone she walked in a daze to the bed and sat there staring out the window until darkness fell.

A sharp rapping sound jolted Angel from a deep sleep. She sat bolt upright in bed, her long braid falling over one shoulder. It was still dark outside. She wondered if she had been having a nightmare when the knocking came again.

"Who is it?" she called out warily.

"Holt Murphy."

The curt announcement instantly launched Angel from the bed. Hastily drawing a wrapper over her cambric nightgown, she moved toward the door.

"Are you ready to leave?" he demanded.

Angel hesitated. "I'm afraid I haven't packed yet, Mr. Murphy. It's early morning and I thought . . ."

From the other side of the door she heard Holt make an exasperated sound. "This is not New Orleans! Here ladies don't sleep till noon unless they entertain all night!"

Angel flushed at the reminder of what he had first thought she was. It also explained the townfolk's reaction to her, especially the snubs from the women.

"Give me five minutes," she requested.

There was no reply but the sharp chinking sound of spurs as Holt turned and stomped down the stairs.

Angel moved to light a lamp and gazed over her trousseau, spread over half of the room. How proud she had once been of her gowns! Some were a bit frayed now, others completely out of fashion, but here in Clear Creek she would have been the reigning fashion plate. She hastily donned lacy underthings, a plain yellow skirt and white blouse, and cinched a wide leather belt around her waist. It was her most practical traveling outfit, and she slipped on bronze kid boots to match.

Afraid Holt would give up waiting on her, she swept up a woolen mantle and hurried from the room. The hall was dark, the only light coming from her room and the downstairs lobby. The hotel itself was eerily quiet; she seemed to be the only occupant.

Taking a deep breath, Angel navigated the gloomy stairs. She was almost to the landing when a dark shadow glided up to meet her, and she released a small shriek.

Holt quickly steadied her with a broad hand. "Ssh, we don't want to wake the clerk!"

Angel nodded and let him guide her down the last steps outside into the frosty morning air, just in time to see the first rosy blush of dawn peeking above the Rocky Mountains.

"Why did you fetch me so early?" she grumbled as she rubbed her eyes.

"I didn't want you to miss the stage."

His hard, quick answer hurt a little, but she waited on the boardwalk while he departed to retrieve her bags from her room. A smug smile teased at Angel's lips when Holt stormed back outside with an angry accusation.

"You didn't pack!"

"Of course not. I'm staying," she announced.

The broad shoulders tightened as he frowned. Then Holt reached into a fringed pocket and withdrew a few coins. He grudgingly held them out to her. "Here, then. Fare for the stage."

"No, thank you!" Angel's eyes snapped blue sparks as she knocked his hand aside, and the coins scattered in the dusty street. "I have enough money when—or if—I ever choose to return to Denver. But I've been doing some thinking, Mr. Murphy. I've decided to stay."

By the look on Holt's face Angel knew she had struck a raw nerve.

"That's out of the question," he growled, rubbing his smooth-shaven jaw with the back of his hand.

She gave him a brilliant, insincere smile. "Impossible is all in the mind, Mr. Murphy. And don't waste your time trying to talk me out of staying. I'm not some silly-headed southern belle who can be scared off so easily. Don't think for a minute that you're deceiving me."

Holt's gray eyes darkened to the color of thunderclouds. "What do you mean?"

"Why, it's obvious as sauce on the goose that you're just trying to get rid of me in order to claim my share of the Lucky Devil mine." Much to her satisfaction, Angel saw him redden slightly at her accusation. "Since my father has died I happen to know his half of the mine now belongs to me, and I'm going to claim my share."

"Why, you little——" Holt began, but he fell abruptly silent as the nearby door of the apothecary cracked open an inch and slowly closed again. Lowering his voice, he hissed at Angel, "I told you I have no patience for games. But if you want to play, sweetheart, just remember . . . according to your own story, you're not a McCloud anymore. And anything you own now belongs to your husband."

Angel gulped. She'd completely forgotten that niggling little detail. "But you still don't believe we're really married," she added desperately.

"No, I don't. But until we can get to a court of law and settle this properly, I choose to operate under the assumption we're man and wife." Holt's silver gaze raked over her figure with slow relish. "Which means I can legally demand my rights."

"Your . . . rights?" Angel stammered, staring up at him with shocked disbelief as Holt chuckled low in his throat.

"Precisely, sweetheart. All of which has very little to do with the mine."

Heaven forbid! Angel hadn't counted on this at all. While her mind frantically sought for a way out, she kept one eye trained for the stage. Perhaps Holt was only teasing her. Yet the deep warm thread that ran through his voice told her he wasn't.

"Maybe I wouldn't complain too much if you stayed," Holt continued, reaching out to twine a golden curl, which had escaped her braid, around his callused finger. "It gets mighty cold in the winter up on the mountain, and I could use another body to keep me warm."

"Sleep with your horse, then!" Angel suggested tartly, pointing at the sleepy buckskin that stood hitched to a wagon at the hotel post.

"I don't think so," Holt mused, slowly drawing the tendril of golden hair over his upper lip. "Old Buck smells like horse. You smell like roses."

"Don't touch me!" Angel batted away his hand, gaining a yank on her own scalp for the effort. "I declare, sir, you are the rudest man I have ever met! I wish I had never left Missouri!"

"So that explains your charming accent, if not your manners," Holt said dryly. "What town are you from?"

"Independence."

"I should've guessed."

Angel ignored his comment and plunged on. "I'm completely serious. I have no intention of leaving until I get my share of the Lucky Devil's profits. I have to save Belle Montagne!"

At Holt's quizzical look she reluctantly explained. "It's the family estate back in Missouri. All that's left of my heritage now, except for the mine."

"Belle Montagne? What kind of a name is that? Sounds like a cheap French wine."

Angel sniffed at his remark. "Yes, it's French. It means 'beautiful mountain.' The house is in a little valley, surrounded by rolling green hills and a river. It's the most beautiful place in the world."

Her look dared him to deny it. Holt threw up his hands, unimpressed. "Then go back if it's so wonderful!"

"I can't go back, not until I have the money to buy it!"

As they argued, dawn heralded a slow but increasing activity in Clear Creek, and with an uneasy glance down the street Holt finally sighed and nodded. "All right. You can have your share of the mine, Angel."

Shocked, she stared up at him, hardly believing he had capitulated so quickly and easily. "What's the catch?" she demanded suspiciously.

"You have to work up at the mine for a month. Not by proxy this time, sweetheart, but with your own lily-white little hands." He gave her a slow, infuriating smile that burned all the way to her tingling toes. "You can keep whatever you find and I'll throw in your half when you leave. Take it or leave it."

Angel hesitated. "One week."

"Three and not a day less."

"Two?"

"Two-and-a-half."

"Deal." She stuck out her hand in a businesslike fashion her father would have approved of, and felt Holt's fingers close around it, rough and warm. He looked as surprised as she herself felt, but Angel had never shirked hard work or a challenge. And this qualified as both.

"When do we leave?" she asked him cheerfully.

"Damn."

Perched so ladylike up on the wagon seat, Angel looked like a fancy porcelain doll shipped in from back east. Holt kept his sour thoughts to himself as he tossed her bags in the rear of the buckboard, but he was already fuming and the day wasn't even warm.

He still couldn't believe she had accepted his offer. He had tried to think of the most repulsive, appalling, compromising scenario to scare her off, and even thrown in a rude grope or two for good measure. But instead of clearing out of Clear Creek like any respectable woman, Angel McCloud had cleverly negotiated her stay.

Double damn. Holt glanced up from heaving luggage in the wagon bed and saw a familiar horse and rider making their way down the main road.

As the man got closer, he waved at them. He didn't seem to notice Holt's scowl as he brought his mount up beside the wagon, but he did doff his bowler hat when Angel looked his way.

"Miss. Holt."

The young man's hair was fair and wavy, combed carefully back over his ears. His sandy lashes were almost invisible and made his pale blue eyes all the more startling. While he wasn't strikingly handsome in the sense that Holt was, he was certainly pleasant-looking. His coat and trousers were black wool, and the unrelieved color made his fairness all the more pronounced. Angel couldn't imagine who he was or why Holt looked so angry until the other man spoke again.

"I'm here in Clear Creek on the Lord's work today, brother. I hope you will offer me succor."

"Sorry, Neal, but I've been your 'sucker' one too many time," Holt retorted as he hurled the last of Angel's bags into the wagon with a loud thud. He ignored her gasp of outrage for both his comment and the abuse of her bag, and stalked around to the front of the wagon to climb up beside her.

The older man quickly nudged his horse up beside their wagon. He was closest to Angel, and he smiled winningly as he leaned over and spoke softly to her.

"You'll have to forgive my little brother, miss. Sometimes he forgets himself. But the good Lord can work miracles, even with hardened souls like Holt."

Angel saw that Neal Murphy had a Bible clutched in his free hand. She felt acutely uncomfortable sandwiched between his gentle smile and Holt's dark scowl. Neal must be the preacher she had heard about, but it had never occurred to her that they might be brothers; they looked and acted as different as night and day.

"Aren't you going to introduce us, Holt?" Neal pressed. "Surely Father taught you better manners than this."

"You leave Arthur out of this," Holt snapped, but after a taut silence he grudgingly introduced Angel. "Neal, this is my wife." He appeared to enjoy shocking the other man, and after a long silence he added only the briefest facts. Holt admitted her maiden name was McCloud, which caused a flicker of surprise to cross the preacher's face.

"Royce McCloud's daughter?"

"Yes. You knew my father?" Angel exclaimed eagerly, leaning toward Neal, to her seatmate's dismay. Her heart-shaped face was now framed by a poke bonnet, and Holt tensed when he saw his brother drinking in her beauty like a parched man.

"I didn't know Royce personally, I regret to say, but I'd heard from Father what a fine man he was." Neal Murphy hesitated, seeing Angel's lovely eyes suddenly darken. "Has something happened?"

"H-he died," Angel choked out, pressing a small hand to her lips for a moment. She blinked rapidly and saw Neal's kindly face swimming through her tears. "It was very sudden. I'm afraid there was nothing anyone could do."

"You have my sincerest condolences."

"Thank you," she whispered.

"And belated congratulations on your wedding." Neal looked almost as uncomfortable as Angel felt, and it was obvious he could sense something amiss with the couple.

"Are you two finished?" Holt inquired tersely.

Startled by the harshness in his voice, Angel merely nodded. She was appalled that he would be so rude to his own brother, especially in public. And Neal Murphy was a preacher!

"Where are you headed?" Neal asked Holt.

"Back to the mine. Not much of a honeymoon, but I've got a lot of work to do."

There was a brief silence while Neal observed Angel's rosy cheeks and obviously toyed with the notion of asking more questions. But eventually, and probably wisely, he decided not to provoke Holt any further and said good-bye.

As Neal rode off, a somber figure garbed in black, Angel couldn't resist voicing her displeasure.

"You are insufferable! If that's how you treat your family, I certainly got off lucky being a stranger!"

Holt's steely eyes swung on her. "You don't know what you're talking about. Just thank your lucky stars, sweetheart, that you're prettier than Neal. Or believe me, you'd be riding the rail out of town right after him."

Angel opened her mouth to speak, then clamped it firmly shut again. Oh, what a despicable man Holt Murphy was! Perhaps she was mad to toy with him and his precious mine. Well, it was too late now. The wagon shot forward with a hard jolt, headed out of town. While she clung to the post with a vengeance, Angel set her teeth and her mind to hang on. The Lucky Devil was half hers. She would not give it up, not for a madman or a minister!

Chapter Three

"What do you have against Neal?"

Angel saw Holt's frown close on the heels of her question. His long callused fingers tightened on the reins, yet he kept his gaze trained fiercely on the twisting, rutted road stretching up the side of the mountain.

"He's your brother," she pressed. "And if I'm truly your wife, then I have a right to know."

"Nosy woman," Holt muttered, and spared her an irritated glance.

"I'm not being nosy; I'm merely curious. I can't help wondering why you resent him so much. He seemed perfectly pleasant to me."

Holt snorted. "Maybe your blue blood mingles well."

Under the wide brow of the cowboy hat Holt had clamped down hard over his glistening black hair, his features were hidden in shadow. But Angel could sense the thundercloud crossing the high planes of his face, and she steeled herself for the storm.

Holt finally sighed. "If you really must know, Neal and

I are only half-brothers. We had different mothers. Not that it's any of your business."

Of course, it certainly explained the lack of resemblance between the two. But the one-sided animosity. . . . ? Angel's silence served as a question.

Holt reluctantly explained. "Neal's mother, Virginia, was married to Arthur Murphy for some fifteen years. Neal was their only child. Virginia died of consumption when I was ten. I remember her funeral."

"You remember . . . but how?" Angel was puzzled.

"I was there." Holt's voice lowered an octave. "Arthur forced me to go out of respect. It was the first time I saw Neal. He's just a year older than me."

Suddenly Angel understood. She went bright pink, and then flushed a dull red. "But . . . but you're a Murphy, too," she stammered.

"Oh, Arthur never denied I was his son." Holt's voice was barely above a growl now. "I'll admit it takes a pretty big man to claim a half-breed. And in his own way I think he loved my mother, Soft Snow. But she could never fit into his world, just as I could never fully fit into his."

Angel swallowed, feeling guilty over rousing such sad memories and Holt's obvious ire. But she was pleased with herself for discovering Holt was indeed part Indian, as if it might explain the aura of mystery about him.

Suddenly he chuckled, throwing her off guard. "You can see why I wasn't too surprised to think Arthur might have yet a third wife tucked away somewhere."

She straightened on the seat beside him. "I have more pride than that!"

"Do you?" Holt slanted her a silver glance, narrow and mocking. "My father was very suave with the ladies in his day, and Neal is his spitting image. Even if he is a Holy Roller."

"Just because your brother has manners doesn't mean he's a womanizer!" Angel bristled. "I think you would do well to take a few lessons from Neal yourself. Obviously he holds nothing against you personally, even though he easily could. He has found peace and acceptance in his own way, and now it's your turn."

"How do you expect me to find any peace with you here?" Holt grumbled. He slapped the reins to urge his horse faster, and they ascended the rough road at an amazing speed.

Angel fell silent, tilting back her face to gaze up at the solitary splendor of Mount Elbert, soaring up into the white clouds. Somewhere up there was her mine, and the fortune necessary to save Belle Montagne. She shivered with the mixed sensations of the crisp, clean breeze blowing across her face, hinting at the winter to come, and the icy silence of the man beside her. What had ever possessed her to come to Colorado Territory? It didn't matter now. She was here, and whether Holt liked it or not, she was going to stay.

"Whoa, boy."

The buckboard shuddered to a stop on the steep incline halfway from the top, and Angel looked at Holt in alarm.

"Why are we stopping?"

"Because the wagon won't go any farther. We'll have to walk the rest of the way up." He gestured up the road, where several large pines had fallen, blocking the final leg of the journey.

"There must be some other way," Angel began, with a rueful glance at her thin-soled boots.

"Nope. Not unless you intend to fly."

Angel set her lips and climbed carefully down from the wagon, smoothing out her skirts. It felt good to have a break from the jarring transportation, but she didn't relish the idea of walking up the mountain.

"How far is it?" She shaded her eyes and peered up into the thick growth of trees, seeing nothing but green.

Holt shrugged, busy undoing the harness on the horse. "A few miles. Don't worry; you'll make it. You don't have much choice."

"But what about my bags? I can't just leave them here!"

"Who's going to steal them? A bear? Don't be ridiculous, woman. They'll have to stay in the wagon until I can make another trip down."

"I don't think so. That could be days." Angel marched to the rear of the wagon and grabbed the handle of her portmanteau. "I'm not leaving them here."

Holt cocked an eyebrow at her while she struggled to pull her luggage out of the buckboard. The bags fell with heavy thuds to the ground, one by one. Angel took a handle in each hand and heaved. She got only a few feet and dropped them both, panting with dismay.

"You could at least offer to help!"

"Why?" Holt countered. "You're doing fine. Just a few more miles and you'll be there."

Hands on her hips, Angel narrowed her eyes at him. "Nothing was said about leaving my luggage on the side of the mountain. By the looks of it, those trees have been there quite awhile. You knew we wouldn't be able to ride all the way up!"

He shrugged, his buckskin jacket gripping the broad planes of his shoulders for a moment. "You wanted to work the mine, Angel McCloud. It means accepting the hardships as well as the profits. There won't be any fancy tea parties up there. You can spare a few yards of lace."

"For your information, Mr. Murphy, this bag contains necessary feminine underthings!" Angel gasped after blurting out such intimate details about her wardrobe, and to her further mortification Holt grinned. "Are you suggesting I just leave it behind?" she shrilled furiously.

"Please, spare me the female hysterics." He sighed. "Take one bag, then. But you'll have to carry it yourself."

"Certainly." Angel forced herself to pick up the bag on her right and staggered up the deeply rutted road to meet him. Holt unhitched the horse completely, replaced the wagon tracings with a saddle and bridle, and easily swung up on the buckskin.

She gaped up at him. "You're going to ride?"

"It's my horse, remember? I'll go slow."

Holt hid a devilish grin as he nudged the buckskin gelding around her and headed up the trail. He didn't miss Angel's angry mutterings as she followed, dragging the heavy portmanteau behind her, and he smiled to himself. She'd give up this ridiculous notion of mining long before the day was out. Before she knew it, she'd be begging to go back to the ballrooms in Missouri. It was only a matter of minutes now. With that comforting thought, Holt began to whistle a spritely Irish air, deliberately ignoring the very unladylike curses and grunts that punctuated his cheerful tune.

* * *

"Wait . . . just . . . a . . . darned . . . moment. . . ."

Angel gasped out the words, but Holt didn't hear her. He had disappeared around the bend of the trail up ahead.

Her head roared and her lungs burned every time she inhaled the thin mountain air. Angel was in shape, at least as good a shape as any society woman who rode on a regular basis and waltzed across ballroom floors, but the high altitude was quickly taking its toll. They had only gone a few hundred feet and already she was sweating and struggling to keep up.

Holt, the unrepentant rogue, had made no move to help her the times she had fallen. She knew he had heard her tripping and stumbling like a drunken fool over broken roots and fallen branches, but other than an occasional chuckle, he showed no sign of sympathy for her plight.

Angel was ready to swear—and had already done so quite proficiently—that Holt was actually enjoying this. Did he think he could scare her off so easily? Well, McCloud women were made of sterner stuff.

Just as she raised her chin a notch, Angel staggered into a large boulder in her path, painfully bruising her hip. The portmanteau also bounced off the rock and its latch broke, dumping frilly white petticoats across the dirty ground. To her own surprise, Angel burst into tears. It was the final straw.

All she had gone through to save this one bag had been for naught. She was convinced her luggage back in the wagon would be pilfered by some unscrupulous person like Holt Murphy, and now there was no way to pick up her remaining lingerie.

Sliding down in a sorry heap beside her portmanteau, Angel examined the latch. It was broken and would not hold even long enough for her to cart it the rest of the way. She fiercely wiped the tears from her cheeks and got fleeting satisfaction from getting up again and kicking the empty box down the steep mountainside.

It bounced and rolled for some way before she lost sight of it. With a self-righteous sniff, Angel bent to scoop up the white mound of underthings. A burning pain suddenly shot through both her calves, and her legs buckled. She landed face-first in the snowy sea of her intimate articles just as Holt reappeared around the bend.

"What the—" he began, choking off his laughter when Angel struggled back on her heels and threw a pair of lacy drawers at him.

"Not one word!" she sputtered furiously, getting to her feet and snapping the folds of her skirts out from around her legs. "I'm coming."

"Angel—" he began, ready and resigned now to hop down from his horse and offer her a ride, but she shook her head emphatically.

"You go on. I'll catch up."

Her voice was barely a whisper, her cheeks flushed rosy from exertion. Holt knew when enough was enough. He began to dismount.

"Go on!" Angel's fury lashed out at him along with a whaleboned corset, which ricocheted off the buckskin's rump and sent the horse bolting up the trail. Holt held on for dear life, ducking as pine branches whipped across his face.

Damn the proud little priss, anyway! If she wanted to walk, then she could damn well do it. Holt finally got

control of his horse just as they rounded the last hairpin
turn in the high valley. He drew the fractious gelding to
a prancing halt and gazed out over rippling meadow.

Home again. Holt would never grow tired of the lush
little valley where he had carved out a living from the very
bosom of Mount Elbert. Sheltered by rising peaks on
every side, the Lucky Devil Mine was located in a hidden
paradise. He had lived here alone for the last five years,
going into town only for necessary supplies or occasional
nightly comfort.

Holt sighed with pleasure just to be back. Then he
stiffened in the saddle, hearing a woman's curses loudly
echoing off the mountainside behind him. Had he mistak-
enly believed Angel's story? After all, his well-bred "wife"
apparently had the vocabulary of a miner! Holt started to
laugh again. Then he heard the scream.

Pine needles crunched beneath his high-topped moccasins, releasing a pungent scent as Holt knelt beside the
fallen woman. Angel's eyes were closed, and except for
the fresh tears streaking down her grimy cheeks, she
looked to Holt as if she'd found a permanent resting place.

He gently lifted and touched her right foot. Angel
winced and cried out at the stabbing pain.

"Dear God," Holt rasped. "You little fool."

He stared down at the bloody inch-deep gash in her
sole where a sharp rock had penetrated the flimsy boot.
Her other foot wasn't in much better shape. The kid soles
had worn completely through, leaving her tender skin to
be mercilessly abused and torn on the steep hike.

Angel lay in a patch of slushy early snow between two

gigantic boulders. Her forehead had grazed one of them and was dotted with blood. The fall had clearly stunned her. She only moaned softly when Holt slid his arm under her and lifted her against his chest.

Angel smelled buckskin. That, and something tickling her skin. Feathers? She slitted her eyes against the sunlight and saw a silky black strand of hair brushing her cheek. Holt had come back for her. She felt dizzy relief at the realization before she cried out in pain.

"Quit fighting me," Holt ordered. He carried Angel to his horse and settled her on the saddle before he quickly and carefully mounted behind her. Leaning Angel back against him, Holt steadied her with one hand and held the reins with the other. He clicked to the horse until it lapsed into a smooth canter.

Angel's head lolled sideways against his chest, and she found her eyes opening again on Holt. Right now he had three faces instead of one, but he was just as handsome. She giggled at the thought, and all three Holts simultaneously frowned down at her.

"Fool woman," they all said.

It was not the most romantic thing a man had ever said to her, but it was a start, Angel thought. She had to close her eyes again as an overwhelming urge to retch rose in her throat.

"Not on me you don't," Holt growled, and held her just far enough over the side of the horse for clearance. When Angel was through being sick, he pulled her briskly back in place and hardened his heart against her soft groans.

Angel remembered nothing of what followed. When she finally awoke she found herself stark naked in a narrow bed with suspicious-smelling patchwork blankets tucked up to her chin. She tried to lift her throbbing head and moaned as splinters of pain shot through her brow. Above her, a rough-hewn log ceiling spun in crazy circles. She swallowed hard, closed her eyes, and tried to fight the nausea.

"That was a nasty fall you took," someone said.

She opened her eyes again and gradually focused on Holt. Just one face this time, but as annoyed as ever. He hunkered down beside the bed and pressed something cool and wet on her forehead.

"I underestimated you, Angel McCloud. You have more damn pride than a whole boatload of Irishmen. And not one single drop of common sense!"

"What happened?" she croaked.

"I heard you cry out and rode back to find you had bounced halfway back down the mountain. Those ridiculous dancing shoes you wore probably slipped on an icy spot."

Weakly she shook her head. "I remember now. I was trying to climb a big boulder."

"Trying to climb a—what the hell for?"

"It was so beautiful." Her soft voice startled Holt, and for a moment he was simply absorbed in watching her blue eyes shine. "The clouds parted and the sun came out, and I could see the valley below just peeking above the pines. It was like nothing I'd ever seen before. I had to get a better look. . . ."

"And almost lost your life in the process," he reminded her sternly. Then Holt rose from her bedside and moved away, and Angel noticed he was shirtless. His deeply tanned skin gleamed bronze in a patch of sunlight as he passed a window. The fringed buckskin trousers rode low on his hips, snugly emphasizing his narrow waist and muscled thighs. She took a deep breath when she felt suddenly light-headed and caught the heavenly whiff of something cooking.

"Where am I?" she asked, struggling to get up on her elbows. She was forced to move quickly to salvage her modesty when the blankets suddenly slipped. "And—oh dear—where are my clothes?"

"Drying." Holt gestured to the limp clothing hanging from wooden pegs on the cabin wall. Her outfit looked as sorry as Angel felt. He moved to stir a black cauldron simmering on the stove. "You were soaked to the bone and shivering. I didn't want to tempt a fever."

As Holt sampled the beans, Angel slid down under the evil-smelling blankets until only her eyes showed, round as two pie plates. Holt Murphy had undressed her? He had seen her . . . her female parts? Bright color washed up Angel's cheeks as she imagined the scene. Husband or not, she couldn't bear the thought of those lazy gray eyes examining her every inch.

"Did you . . . look?" she whispered.

"Ah-um." Holt made an approving noise over the mouthful of beans and raised one black eyebrow at her.

"Is that a yes or a no? You are the most maddening man!"

"And you are acting like a spinster." He returned the spoon to the pot with an audible splash. "What does it matter if I looked or not? You claim we're man and wife."

Angel inched down under the blankets just far enough for him to see she was scowling. "I resent the fact that you brought me here to this—this pigsty and proceeded to divest me of all my clothing without my knowledge!"

"This pigsty, woman, is your new home," Holt responded tautly. His silvery gaze pinned her to the bed. "This is the cabin Arthur and your father built to live in while they worked the mine. We've both inherited it now. It serves its purpose well enough, I think, especially since it is now sheltering your sorry little—"

"All right!" Angel interrupted tersely. "You've made your point."

"And as for removing your clothes, it was necessary in order for me to get you warm and dry. And made it a damn sight easier to bandage your delicate little feet."

With surprise, Angel lifted the blanket and peeked down at her linen-wrapped limbs. She realized that while they still smarted, the pain was nothing like it had been before.

"Thank you," she muttered reluctantly.

Holt didn't respond. He stalked with feline grace across the sod cabin floor and right on out the door.

"Sorehead," Angel sniffed. Once he was out of view from the tiny double-paned window she sat up and ruefully examined her injuries. She was bruised from her toes on up, with approximately one scratch or dent per limb. It was a wonder she hadn't broken her neck. Her palms were raw and scraped from trying to break her fall, yet as she examined them more closely Angel saw a greenish ointment had been worked into the cuts. She sniffed each palm suspiciously. Yech! She was the source of that vile smell, not the blankets! If it was the last thing she ever did, she would have a bath.

Inching gingerly from the bed, Angel rose wobbly and

tried to get her bearings. Her feet were so thickly wrapped, she was thrown off balance. She took a single step toward her clothes and felt her knees give way. Holt entered just as she nearly stumbled into the hot stove.

"Watch out!" He caught Angel by the waist, reflexively swinging her free of danger, and she erupted like a wildcat, mortified and furious to find Holt manhandling her. Her golden hair lashed around them both, just barely concealing her nudity.

Holt was too absorbed in subduing Angel to stare at the vision of loveliness in his arms, but he could feel her ivory skin moving like raw silk under his callused hands. A shudder rippled through his frame as he remembered how long it had been since he had had a woman. Especially one as beautiful as her . . .

"Angel," he said thickly, "get back in the bed. Right now."

"Why?" she argued, struggling to free her arms so she could slap that odd look right off Holt's face. "I want to get dressed."

"If you don't get under those covers, I'll—"

"What?" she taunted him furiously. "What could you possibly do to humiliate me more?"

"This," he muttered, crushing her lips beneath his.

Angel swayed and clutched his shoulders, too startled to fight. Holt's kiss was hard at first, angry and punishing, but his lips soon softened to an incredibly sensual rhythm as they branded hers with sweet desperation. Angel moaned and Holt made a throaty noise, raising a hand to caress her.

Chills rippled through her body as his fingers found and toyed with the pink tip of a breast. Angel gasped, tearing her mouth free only to watch his descend and capture the proud nipple. Breath hissed slowly from her lips as her head fell back, her long hair touching the floor. His tongue circled and teased at her until she cried out, and then his hand moved to cup the silky triangle between her thighs.

Angel arched against him, one leg pressed tightly against his buckskin-clad thighs. Holt's fingers parted the pale down, touching the most intimate part of her. She whimpered as invisible white lightning streaked clear up to her tingling breasts. Gently, slowly, his fingers breached her. Just as she cried out, his mouth found hers again.

Holt's kisses were like wildfire, burning down Angel's every inhibition. She didn't fight when he suddenly withdrew his hand and lifted her in his arms. She looped her hands around his neck, stroking the length of his blue-black hair as he carried her to the bed.

Holt laid her down gently, drawing the blankets back in place. Angel waited with bated breath for him to shed his trousers.

"Please," she whispered, not knowing herself if it was a plea for him to cease or to continue.

The word seemed to reach him, for the hand that had been tracing the curve of her cheek slowly withdrew. Then Holt stiffened and rose to his full height above the bed.

"Nice try," he said hoarsely as he looked down into her passion-glazed eyes. "You really should be an actress, Angel. But if you want a share of the Lucky Devil, you'll still have to work a pick and shovel as well as you act. There's no free ride on this mountain."

Stunned, she stared up into Holt's hard gray eyes. "But in the eyes of the law we're married. I thought—"

"I know what you thought, sweetheart. But I'd have to be a complete idiot to fall for your obvious ploy. I don't intend to consummate this mock marriage just so you can claim to be my wife and get your claws on the whole mine."

Her illusions shattered, Angel felt a burning rage rising in her throat. She felt even more furious when Holt turned to nonchalantly walk away. "I hate you!" she screamed after him, every nerve in her body teetering on razor's edge and still painfully aflame with passion.

She threw her pillow after his departing figure. It bounced harmlessly off the doorjamb. Then Angel buried her hot face in her hands. What had she done? Holt apparently thought she was a tease, trying to get him to consummate the marriage in order to claim the entire mine. It was true the thought had occurred to her once, but she had swiftly dismissed it, just as she had once dismissed the idea of ever wanting a man as much as she wanted Holt Murphy.

He was her husband, but he didn't want her. Angel realized how much it hurt when she waited on tenterhooks all night for Holt to return, but he never did.

Chapter Four

It was so cold in the early morning hours of the dawn that Angel's teeth chattered as she lay huddled under the mound of blankets. When she stuck her head up for air at last her breath emerged in frosty little puffs that drifted across the cabin.

Had Holt left her up here to freeze to death? It wasn't entirely illogical. He'd been furious when he'd left the night before, and Angel had been so upset herself she hadn't even been able to touch the beans he'd left behind.

They sat congealed in the kettle on the cold stove, but she was so hungry now, she didn't think twice about getting up. She tucked one of the blankets sarong-style around her body, and tiptoed across the floor to fetch the cauldron.

After Angel had eaten some of the sticky beans, which tasted remarkably good, she took a good long look around the little cabin Royce and Arthur had built. It was purely functional, small and square, but so well built, she didn't even feel a draft through the log walls. There were no curtains, which she'd certainly have to do something about. She could ply a needle reasonably well; assuming Holt would be kind enough to ride down to Clear Creek to buy her some material, she could set about improving their lot.

Angel frowned. Knowing Holt, though, he'd be neither sympathetic nor sensitive to her request. And where was he? Out at the mine already? It wouldn't surprise her if he'd completely forgotten her up here!

Well, she didn't intend to stay cooped up in the cabin all day. Her head still throbbed dully, but at least she could function, and she wanted to see just what she had gotten herself into. Her immediate problem was one of clothing. Her gown from the day before was still damp, and she shuddered at the thought of tugging the cold, clammy material over her skin. Looking around the cabin, Angel found an old trunk strapped shut with cracked leather bonds and decided to see what it held.

It took her some time to undo the straps, which had gotten wet and tightened up. But at last her fingers coaxed the leather knots apart, and she threw back the heavy lid with a resounding bang and a cloud of dust.

Sneezing, Angel knelt to examine the contents of the trunk. She set aside several sheets of crumbling yellow newsprint to reveal cream-colored, soft doeskin, elaborately decorated with porcupine quills and sky-blue beads.

Angel carefully lifted out her find. It unfolded into a woman's dress, simply but strikingly designed. She dropped the coarse blanket and held the butter-soft doeskin dress up against her body. It looked like it would fit, and it certainly felt heavenly against her bare skin. Excited by her discovery, she continued looking through the old chest and also found a pair of matching moccasins and leggings.

To whom did these things belong? She dismissed her first thought that Holt had an Indian mistress hidden away somewhere. The outfit was carefully preserved but obviously old. Even the newsprint that had protected the contents of the trunk was dated over twenty years ago.

Angel didn't puzzle further but slipped into the dress. It stretched snugly across her breasts, emphasizing their fullness, and was a trifle short. Otherwise it was perfect. The doeskin would stretch further to accommodate her more generous curves after she wore it awhile.

Feeling immeasurably better, Angel removed some of the bandages on her feet and slipped on the moccasins, then braided her hair into two equal plaits. Now she could go outside and look around. She only wished she could thank the unknown woman who had left the outfit behind.

She opened the cabin door to a misty meadow surrounded by soaring gray peaks. Awestruck, she simply stared for a moment before venturing outside. Angel gasped softly when she startled a pair of deer not ten feet from the cabin. Before bounding gracefully away, the doe and her fawn paused for a long moment to fearlessly regard the young woman.

The mountain morning air was invigorating but distinctly icy. Angel was grateful for the heavy leather dress, and hugged her arms around herself as she walked around the cabin in the knee-high dewy grass. In every direction there were thick stands of blue-green pines and rising slate-gray peaks. The sky was piercingly clear; it seemed she could look straight up to heaven.

A sturdy corral and outhouse lay north of the cabin; Angel gratefully used the latter before moving on. Twenty yards from the cabin, a snow-fed stream trickled by. She knelt and watched some tiny fingerling trout struggling to get upstream. Angel rose and walked along the water for a time, appreciating its pure crystalline beauty. She soon discovered that it led directly to the mine itself.

The mine shaft was unmarked, but the claim Arthur and Royce had staked was obvious. Yawning deep into the throat of Mount Elbert, the tunnel disappeared into total blackness. Angel shivered. She wasn't sure she'd get used to working underground, even with lanterns. But it was the only way she would get enough gold to buy back Belle Montagne.

Angel heard the distant whicker of a horse. Turning around, she saw a strange man dismount from a piebald horse and approach the cabin. Not knowing why, she slipped behind a concealing stand of pines. There was something about the scruffy look of the man she didn't like.

He pounded on the door several times, his blows echoing through the little valley. Then he cupped his hands around his unshaven face and peered through a window. Was he one of Holt's cronies? He looked about the right age but was much more unkempt and dirty.

Angel held her breath when he turned in her direction and scrutinized the mine shaft. She gulped and tried to make herself as small as possible behind the trees as he started to move toward the mine. When he glanced furtively around himself the stranger's actions told Angel he wasn't welcome at the Lucky Devil. But where could she hide?

Trapped behind the pine trees, Angel was only a few feet away from the man as he stepped into the mine shaft.

She could hear his harsh breathing echoing down the dark tunnel. The moment he left the mine, he was sure to see her. Perhaps she could slip back into the cabin while he was in the shaft. There she could hide under the bed until he left.

Making a quick decision, Angel moved to flee. Her moccasins were silent, but the fringe of her dress snagged on a tree limb. The branch snapped crisply in half before she could free the material.

The man came bursting out of the mine, a pistol clutched in his hand. He stared at Angel in confusion for a moment, and then with mounting lust. His beard was filthy and matted to his jutting jaw, and his bloodshot eyes roamed over her greedily.

"Squaw, huh?" he said, and squirted a wad of tobacco off to one side.

Angel shook her head, slowly backing away from him. "Please, I don't want any trouble."

"You speak English purty good. Half-breed, heh?" He considered her shining golden hair with obvious relish. His approach was slow but steady, like a lumbering bear. He was about the size of one, too. Angel knew she didn't stand a chance unless she could catch him off guard.

"My husband is nearby. Leave now and I won't scream."

He snorted, spraying spittle in every direction. "I don' see yer man anywheres, squaw. Ain't no reason whys we cain't make a little deal of our own, eh?"

Angel could scarcely understand his slurred speech, but she understood the look in his eyes. It was exactly how Willard Craddock had always stared at her!

"What are you doing here?" she demanded, trying to stall for time.

"Jest came up for a little look-see at the mine, honey. T'ain't no laws against that, far as I knows. Name's Stokes. Heard you got gold up heres on the moun'tin."

"It's not true. The mine's gone dry." Angel tried to delay his approach. "But there's word of a good strike over in Oro. Why don't you ride on over there and take a . . . a look-see."

Stokes considered for a long moment and then smiled, exposing blackened, rotted teeth. "Nah. I likes the company here better."

Suddenly his long hairy arm shot out, catching Angel. She screamed as he yanked her against his huge chest, and she almost gagged on the noxious fumes of sweat and alcohol wafting from his body. She fought wildly until Stokes pressed the cold barrel of his pistol against her temple.

"Settle down, little lady. You and I gonna have some fun. I hear Injun wimin knows all sorts of tricks, and yer man won't mind sharin'. Bet you even done that a'fore, eh?" He sniggered lewdly in her ear.

"Filthy pig!" Angel tried to drive her elbow into his big gut. Instead Stokes tumbled her around as easily as he would a barrel, and she found herself pinned under his arm. He proceeded to half-carry, half-drag her back toward the cabin.

"I ain't got no qualms 'bout killin' no Injun, so you jest simmer down and you won't get hurt," Stokes panted as he hauled a struggling Angel across the meadow.

She tried to plant her feet, but the moccasins were too slippery in the wet grass, and her soles still burned from the day before. When Stokes tried to heave her through the open door she caught the jamb in her fingers and held on for dear life. He grunted and shoved, but Angel clung as hard as barnacle to a rock. Finally he smacked her knuckles with the pistol, and with a wail of pain Angel let go of the doorjamb. Stokes kicked the door shut and hurled her onto the bed.

Just after Stokes dropped his trousers, the sound of horse's hooves thundered up to the cabin. Angel's attacker hesitated, a look of confusion on his ugly face, and then he moved to flee. He tripped over his dirty drawers in the process and lurched for freedom just as the cabin door flew open with a crash. Holt came hurtling in. The two men collided in midair and went down with a hard thud.

Angel scrambled off the bed and watched in terror as their bodies rolled across the floor. Holt ended up on top, punching his fists down in rapid succession into Stokes's face. But the bigger man squawled like a sore bear and lopped a meaty fist against Holt's temple. Angel cried out when Holt toppled over, dazed and groaning. Stokes heaved himself up onto all fours and crawled for his gun.

Without thinking, Angel beat him to it. She snatched up the pistol with surprisingly steady hands and leveled it at Stokes.

"I'll shoot!" she vowed, remembering everything Hans had taught her. With both thumbs she drew back the hammer.

Stokes's eyes went wide. So did Holt's. It was clear neither one believed her.

"I know how to use this," Angel assured them both. Then, with perfect precision, she lowered the sight to

Stokes's dirty drawers and pulled off a shot. The bullet winged through the narrow space between his manhood and the cabin floor and buried itself deep in the sod.

"Gawd, please!" Stokes cast an urgent plea to Holt as he protectively clutched his crotch. "Call yer squaw off!"

Holt chuckled, both for Stokes's predicament and in amazement over Angel's cool trigger finger. He held out his hand as he got to to his feet. "Give me the gun, Angel."

Reluctantly, she surrendered it to him. Holt prodded Stokes with the weapon and herded him out the door. Outside, Holt spoke quietly to the hairy stranger for a few minutes, and then Stokes ran to his own horse, leapt up in the saddle, and rode away without his trousers.

Angel dashed from the cabin with a cry of outrage. "You let him go!"

" 'Course I did. What better way to spread the word about the dangers of crossing Holt Murphy . . . or his squaw." Holt blew down the hot barrel of the pistol and grinned at her.

"It's not funny! That man could have killed me." Angel shuddered as she watched Stokes vanish through the trees. "Who was he, anyway?"

"A claim-jumper. Dime a dozen here in mining country." Holt suddenly noticed her unusual attire and frowned. "Where did you find that outfit?"

"In the trunk." She pointed back at the cabin. "I didn't think you'd mind."

Holt fell silent, scrutinizing her with those steely eyes until Angel grew uneasy. He was clearly displeased about something, but she couldn't imagine why he would care if she chose to wear Indian garb or not. He did so himself, so what was the problem?

"You mean to tell me I went all the way back down to the wagon for nothing?" he finally grumbled, gesturing to the two large bags strapped to his buckskin's saddle. "I was foolish enough to feel sorry for you not having any clothes."

"Oh, Holt!" Angel's face lit up as she hurried over to his horse. Stroking the gelding's velvet nose, she murmured, "So that's where you were. I wasn't sure if you were coming back."

"Of course I had to come back. The mine is getting close to having a big strike." Holt nodded in the direction in which Stokes had disappeared. "And it seems the word is getting around."

"He seemed to be looking for something," Angel agreed. "Do you think more will follow?"

"There've been a handful of jumpers up here since word leaked out that I was getting closer to the big vein. I've been finding nuggets this size for several months now." Holt picked up a small pebble and showed it to her.

"Then it could be any day," Angel breathed. The thought of so much gold sent shivers of excitement through her. Not only would she buy back Belle Montagne, but she would build an even bigger and better stable so she could raise and sell the famous McCloud trotters again.

Holt tore off a big hunk of corn bread and chewed with obvious relish. "I didn't know you could cook," he said around a mouthful, looking a little suspiciously at Angel, sitting on the other side of the plank table.

She smiled back winningly. "I'm more useful than you

think. You see, I can make life much more pleasant for both of us up here."

He grunted doubtfully at that and took a long swallow of coffee from his tin cup. "You're more trouble than you're worth."

After Holt chased every last crumb from his plate Angel got up to take the dishes to the stream. Before she left he said, "Don't get that dress wet. It'll ruin the material."

Angel paused and turned to look at him. "Do you know who this dress belonged to?"

His look was brooding. He didn't answer her for a long moment. Finally he said, "It was my mother's. She wore it on her wedding day to Arthur Murphy."

"But Arthur was already married to Virginia."

"Arapaho tradition lets a man take more than one wife if he can afford it," Holt explained. "Soft Snow didn't have a problem with being Arthur's second wife. But Virginia did."

Angel saw the pain in his eyes. "She knew about your mother, then?"

"Yes. She tried to get Arthur to disown us both. For some crazy reason she thought I was a threat to her own son. And it goes without saying . . . she was also jealous."

Angel decided to probe cautiously for more information. She wanted to know more about Holt, about what had made him the inscrutable, angry man he was today. She understood what the resentment of Virginia Murphy must have done to him as a boy, but she still didn't comprehend his own coldness toward his half-brother.

"Virginia's gone now," she said softly, "and so is the past. Can't you settle your differences with Neal?"

Holt shrugged. "We'll never see eye to eye. He's dedicated to saving men's souls. I'm obsessed with making a fortune. That's too wide a chasm to cross."

"But you could at least be civil to each other." Angel didn't add that Holt was the one who needed to make the effort, not Neal.

He abruptly rose from the chair. "Why don't you worry about the mine instead? After all, that's why you're here."

Angel opened her mouth to make a sharp retort and then sighed. It wasn't worth the effort. "When can we start working?"

"Right now is as good a time as any. Pay dirt won't come to us without some work. Leave the dishes for now. I'll take you down to the mine." Holt paused and suggested, "You'll want to change your clothes. Do you have anything practical in all those bags I brought up?"

She had to shake her head. She only had dresses, which would be awkward and uncomfortable to work in.

"Then I suggest you try on some of my clothing. I have a few trousers and shirts you could roll up. We'll have to get you some real boots on the next trip to town."

Holt tossed out some old clothing on the bed for her to try and went outside. Angel took off the doeskin dress, treating it with extra-loving care now that she knew where it had come from. She folded it carefully and placed it back in the trunk with the moccasins. Then she tried on one of the shirts Holt had given her. It was comfortably worn and still smelled faintly of him. She rolled up the sleeves and tucked the shirt into a pair of trousers. The pants were comically huge around her waist, but a piece of hemp rope kept them from falling down.

Angel dug through her bags until she found the sturdiest pair of shoes she owned. They were black patent leather and brand-new. After today they would likely be ruined, she thought with a sigh, and tugged them on over her bandages.

Lastly, her braids went up under an old hat hanging from a peg on the wall. She walked outside only to be greeted by Holt's peal of laughter.

"You look like a boy trying on his pa's breeches!"

"Thanks a lot," Angel said sourly. She stomped after him and frowned when he turned and thrust a pick in her hands.

"Try this one today. Don't you have any gloves that will protect your hands?"

She shook her head and he gave an exasperated sigh. "You don't have the faintest idea of what mining involves, sweetheart. But you'll find out," he added ominously.

They reached the shaft, and Angel suppressed a shiver as she peered into the inky blackness below them. Holt paused to light two lanterns, handing one to Angel. She tried not to let her hands tremble as she followed him down into the chilly tunnel.

The lanterns cast wavering light across broken rock as they went deeper and deeper into the mine. Angel could hear a ceaseless dripping of water somewhere on the rock floors. It echoed endlessly, as did her voice when she whispered, "How deep is the mine?"

"I don't know. There are so many tunnels now, it's hard to tell for sure." She noticed Holt was stringing a ball of twine behind them.

"What's that for?"

"In case we get lost, we can follow it out."

Holt's voice echoed against the cold rock walls. An icy

draft blew against them, and Angel stepped closer to his comforting warmth. The lantern light was scarcely adequate.

She whispered, "How long will our light last?"

"An hour at the most. I don't like to stay much longer than that. The fire uses up the oxygen pretty quick, and a man could go crazy down here without light."

Or a woman, Angel thought. She shuddered as the tunnel narrowed abruptly, squeezing them in on both sides. She resisted the claustrophic urge to turn and run back up the shaft. She mustn't let Holt see her so afraid.

"You're trembling," he said.

"It's so c-cold down here." Angel was surprised when Holt stopped and set down his lantern, wrapping an impersonal arm around her shoulders.

"Better?" he murmured.

"Yes." Her voice was muffled as she turned and briefly pressed her cold face against his flannel-covered chest. She decided she could happily stay like this forever.

"Good." Holt set her back from him and lifted his pick. "We'll start here."

Angel quelled her disappointment, set down her lantern, and hefted her own pick. It was surprisingly heavy, and her shoulders ached with the effort. Holt pointed out the veins of quartz running through the rock.

"That's a good sign. Gold is almost always in the same vicinity as quartz deposits." He swung his pick almost effortlessly, and a fist-sized chunk fell at their feet.

Following his example, Angel grunted and swung. Her first try missed completely, and her second chipped off only a tiny flake of rock. "It will take forever like this!" she cried with disappointment.

"That's why I've been down here five years, honey." Holt chuckled as he continued working. "Did you think the gold was simply waiting down here for us to pick it up?"

She flushed rosy in the dim light. "No. But I thought it was going to be easier than this!"

"It's not bad once you get used to it. A little company sure helps. Do you know any songs?"

"Songs?" Angel stared at him in disbelief.

"Sure. Helps the time go faster and sets a rhythm."

"Oh, I see. How about 'Frere Jacques' for starters?"

Holt shrugged. "Anything's fine."

In a tiny, wavering voice, Angel began to sing. She was a passable soprano, and Holt nodded approvingly as he worked. After a while he peeled off his shirt, and his bronzed muscles gleamed with sweat by the lantern light. He picked up an amazing rhythm and speed, and Angel gave up trying to match his skill and just kept singing instead.

She couldn't help but admire the bunching and stretching of Holt's sinewy muscles, or the bulging of his biceps as he swung the pick up high. She was so absorbed in studying Holt that she didn't even react when he suddenly hooted and yanked something shiny from the wall.

"Pay dirt!" he crowed, showing Angel the fingernail-sized, gleaming bit of gold. "There's bound to be more where this came from!"

"Our light's getting low," she put in tentatively.

Holt nodded with disappointment. "We can come back down later. I want to get my other pick anyway." He picked up his shirt and both lanterns and waited for her to follow. Angel scurried to retrieve the pick she had dropped and almost cried out at the pain that sliced through her arms.

"You'll get used to it," he promised her again. Then, whistling cheerfully, he led them up and out of the mine.

Outside in the fresh air, Angel collapsed on the ground. She hated mining and everything associated with it, but she wouldn't dare admit it to Holt. He would be only too happy to boot her off the mountain, clear back to Missouri, and claim her share of the Lucky Devil.

Holt paused to look down at the young woman and hid a triumphant grin. He'd deliberately exposed Angel to the hardest and most unpleasant part of mining in order to make her reconsider her plans. She hadn't cried uncle yet. But she would.

"Come on," he urged her. "There's no time to rest. We have to get some more kerosene and head back down."

"Oh, for heaven's sake!" Angel dragged herself to her feet and braced herself on the pick. "Isn't that enough for one day?"

"Do you want to save Belle Montagne or not?" Holt goaded her, and headed on back toward the cabin. Angel made a frustrated noise and started to follow him. But the pick was stuck deep in the ground and she was forced to stop and tug on it. It didn't budge. She kicked at it a few times and eventually ended up leaving it.

Glancing over his shoulder, Holt resisted the urge to laugh out loud. He didn't want to provoke Angel's pride any more than he already had. Was it remotely possible this stubborn, exasperating woman was really his wife? He didn't even dare consider the possibility.

Angel hurried after him, clutching her pants in place as she ran. Her hat flew off and her blond braids tumbled down, giving her the look of a dirt-smudged scarecrow.

"I want a bath first!" Angel begged when she caught up with Holt just outside the cabin.

He slanted her a teasing look. "You know where the stream is."

"No, a real bath. With hot water and soap and everything!" Angel clasped her hands together in an eloquent plea. "If you'll haul me in some water to boil on the stove, I'll make you dinner."

"You will anyway. As I said, everyone pulls his weight around here." But Holt appeared to seriously consider her request. "What's in it for me?"

She hesitated. His tone hinted at something a little racier than corn bread. Was it possible he was only teasing her?

"Whatever you want," she said breathlessly, recklessly.

Those silver eyes narrowed on hers. For a long moment they simply stared at one another. Holt felt his loins stir.

"Damn your blue eyes," he finally muttered. "I'll get you your water."

Angel didn't question her good fortune but went into the cabin. There she impatiently waited while Holt hauled pail after pail of water for her to heat on the stove and dump into the wooden tub in the corner.

When the tub was finally filled to the brim and steaming deliciously, Angel shooed Holt out and hung some old shirts over the windows so she could disrobe. She stripped and gingerly lowered herself into the hot water with a bar of lavender soap retrieved from her luggage. Gooseflesh rose on her bare arms, and she quickly soaped and rinsed her hair free of grime first.

Then Angel sank down and luxuriated, letting the hot water melt away her aches and pains. She sighed with pleasure just to feel clean again. Her bandages floated off and she scooped them out of the tub, examining her injured soles. They seemed much better, thanks to Holt's doctoring efforts. She really ought to thank him . . .

A whisper of cold air stole across her bare shoulders. Angel sat up abruptly, sloshing water over the edge of the tub. She looked over in alarm to see a grinning Holt leaning in the doorway.

"I'm here to collect on your offer," he announced lazily. "Anything, I believe you said?"

"Get out!" Angel picked up her discarded shoe from the side of the tub and threw it at him. It landed just short, and she quickly searched the floor for the other one.

Holt slammed the door behind him. "Don't make me mad, Angel. You don't want to do that."

She glared over the edge of the tub. By strategically draping her wet hair over her breasts, she barely avoided total humiliation. "You're just trying to scare me," she accused him. "It won't work."

"Honey, I don't want you to tremble with anything except plain, old-fashioned desire." Holt sat on the bed and began to tug off his fringed boots. He sent them spinning, one by one, to land across the room with ominous thumps.

Angel said desperately, "I'll be done in a minute. You can have the tub then."

"No, sweetheart, that isn't the deal. You said *anything*. And what I want more than anything right now is to join you in that tub."

"You're mad!" Angel sputtered, tossing damp strands of hair out of her eyes.

"Where's your sense of adventure, Angel?" he taunted her softly.

"O-ooh!" She tried to reach for her clothing from the tub, but it was just out of reach. Holt chuckled as he skimmed his trousers down over taut brown thighs, and Angel quickly looked away. He wasn't wearing any long underwear, just a very tiny Indian breechclout.

She could sense Holt coming closer even though she didn't hear his stealthy footsteps. She sat frozen in the tub, her hands balled into tight, defensive fists. Her heart was pounding like a drum and her mouth was cotton-dry.

"Scoot forward," Holt ordered. His voice was deep and rolled like soft thunder off the cabin walls. Angel gulped, crossed her arms over her breasts, and inched forward. The hot water surged and rose as Holt settled in behind her.

She gasped as his bare legs slid under hers. The tub was barely big enough for two. Holt drew her back to sit on his thighs, and she felt his hard maleness prodding against her buttocks. The steam rose and curled around them, like a thick curtain of mist. Holt drew her back in his arms.

"Mmm," he said, pushing her hair aside and planting tiny kisses on her right shoulder, "you smell like a meadow full of wildflowers."

"And you smell like a randy goat!"

Angel smacked the water with her fist and shrieked when it sprayed in her own face instead. Holt laughed huskily and held her firmly in place against his chest.

"Don't be so ornery," he whispered against her ear. "I just want to get to know my new partner a little better."

"The devil you do," Angel gritted out through clenched

teeth, trying to drive her elbow back into his rock-hard stomach. "I know all about men like you!"

"Do you?" Holt mused, easily deflecting her elbow and then nibbling suggestively at her earlobe. "I wonder."

"Stop it." Angel struggled harder to get free and only succeeded in getting wetter and more snugly ensconced in his embrace. "I don't want this anymore!"

"Little liar. It's all you've wanted from me since you came here, and you know it." Holt twisted her chin to one side and forced her to look into his quicksilver eyes. "You can't deny you're attracted to me."

"Oh! You are the most impossible, arrogant—"

Holt cut off Angel's tirade with a fierce kiss, breaching her soft lips with his tongue. At the same time his hand dipped beneath the water and found a nipple, teasing it to a hard, throbbing peak. Angel arched and moaned, still trying to fight the unfamiliar sensation of mingled desire and longing that swept through her trembling body.

Holt murmured softly, "You know we want each other, Angel. Why fight nature? And don't forget, in the eyes of the law you belong to me now."

Chapter Five

Angel quivered as Holt's work-roughened hands slid slowly down her upper arms, banishing the cold and the goose pimples. She gasped softly when he paused at the fullness of her breasts, cupping the slick globes gently in his palms.

"Beautiful," he said huskily, nuzzling her neck beneath the damp waterfall of her silken hair. "Every inch of you fits so perfectly in my hands, like clay."

"I—I'm not a statue," Angel stammered, and he laughed low in her ear.

"No, you're not. What you are is a warm, loving woman, whose husband wants to show her how beautiful she is."

Holt's quiet suggestion was followed by a shift in their positions as he carefully rose and stepped out of the tub. Looking down at Angel, he extended a darkly bronzed hand, and she saw her own smaller, whiter fingers reach out and lace snugly with his a second later.

Holt's eyes were like warm gray flannel in the dusky light, enfolding her as she rose. He watched her frankly as she stood there, dripping with water. He shook his head when she made a move to cover herself.

"Don't, sweetheart. You shouldn't be ashamed. You're just as lovely as nature intended you to be."

Angel's hands slowly fell to her sides. Holt took a leisurely moment to study her. Her skin, creamy ivory in some places and palest gold in others, was as flawless as her heart-shaped face. Angel's hair, slightly darker when it was wet, fell to her waist in gleaming, golden waves. Her hips were gently flared, her waist tiny. And her breasts, perfectly proportioned, were only a part of the luscious, totally unexpected package he had received a few days ago.

Just as eagerly, though more reserved, Angel studied him in return. Unconsciously she touched her tongue to her lips as her gaze roamed over Holt's powerful shoulders, tapering to a broad chest and a narrow waist completely devoid of hair. Slowly, tentatively, she reached out to touch his skin; she found it surprisingly silky. She trailed her fingers over his collarbone and up to his strong jaw, pausing at the corner of his lips.

He bent his head to kiss her fingers and said, "It's completely up to you, Angel. I've never forced a woman before, and I don't intend to start now. We'll stop now if you say the word. But say no quickly, because I can't stand much more of this—"

His husky words halted as she laid a finger directly across his lips. Holt's burning silver eyes asked the question; her heart gave the answer. Slowly, easily, she came to him, Holt's skin adhering to hers like wet silk.

For a moment they simply stood there, swaying slightly in a mutual embrace, each hearing the pounding of his own heart, and that of the other.

Holt threaded a hand through the damp hair at the nape of Angel's neck, tilting her head back to gaze directly into her dark blue eyes.

"I never wanted a wife," he confessed a little roughly.

But Angel heard the hesitation in his voice. "And now?" she asked.

"Now I don't know. Now I wonder what I've missed— and if I can ever make up for it."

"What do you mean?"

He looked directly into her face. "I don't have anything to offer you, Angel. This is no life for a woman, especially a woman like you." She felt his fingers shaking slightly as they traced her lips. "Lord, you're so fair and soft, so fragile—"

"No," Angel said, gently but firmly, "what I am is your wife. And I'm not fragile, Holt. I'm not afraid of hard work or of living here in the wilderness. And I'm not afraid of you."

The words hung between them, frank and heartfelt words that reflected what Angel believed with all her might. She had come here out of necessity, in order to reclaim Belle Montagne. She hadn't ever expected to find herself falling in love with an inscrutable, mysterious man like Holt Murphy, or wanting to be his wife in every sense of the word. But there it was now, staring her in the face so intently, she couldn't deny it. And she didn't want to.

"Please," she whispered, and her hands rose to frame Holt's face, his midnight hair feathery soft against her skin.

He didn't ask what she wanted. He didn't have to. Holt lifted her up in his arms, imprisoning her in an embrace so strong and yet achingly tender that Angel could have cried. She clung to his neck as he carried her to the bed, and he followed her down as lightly as a cat. She whimpered softly, unable to deny the sensual feelings his hard male body evoked as it slid against hers. He brushed a damp lock from her forehead and lightly kissed her there.

"You're like a board, woman. Relax." Holt trailed his tongue down to the satiny globes of her breasts, licking the beads of water from her skin, one by one. Slowly he proceeeded to her quivering stomach, then lower still. At that she gasped and cried out, for he had parted the pale curls between her legs and lightly teased her in the most intimate area of all.

Angel bit her knuckle. But she couldn't stop her hips from rolling sensuously from side to side, thrusting up to meet his probing tongue. She simultaneously loved and feared what he was doing to her, and in her own confusion she felt her body beginning to respond.

"You taste like honey," Holt rasped.

"Please, Holt . . ."

"That's it. Say my name. I like to hear it on your lips."

"Holt . . . please stop!"

"No, little one. I don't intend to stop for a very long time."

Angel tightly clutched the blankets beneath her as Holt took her to trembling, unbelievable heights of ecstasy. She had never dreamed lovemaking could be so powerful, or that her mind was so weak when confronted with her body's needs.

As she rose higher and higher, like the mountains around them, Angel stopped fighting. Instead she let the passion roll over her like thunder, and keened hungrily for more.

"Yes," Holt muttered, sliding his lean frame over hers, "Yes!"

Angel felt his maleness probing for entrance between her soft thighs. She moaned, and her breasts arched against him, moving wetly over his chest. She opened her legs to him. Holt bit her neck gently as he pressed his hips into hers.

"Oh-h!" Her startled cry of pain was cut off by his mouth sliding quickly over hers. Angel felt him ease farther into her, and she inadvertently tightened around him.

"Ssh, love," Holt murmured. "Just relax."

Easier said than done. Still, Angel tried to let the tension flow from her rigid frame as he began to move slowly and sensuously against her. He was so big, he filled her up completely, and still there was more. She couldn't understand how her woman's body compensated for his size, but maybe Holt did.

"Sweet Angel," he murmured against her cheek. The sound of her name on his lips sent a strange feeling through her. Tentatively, she moved her hands up around his neck. She could feel his muscles bunch and relax as he thrust into her. His damp hair fell over his shoulders, gleaming like black silk. And his eyes were molten silver when he opened them again.

"You see, sweetheart, it can be good between us," he whispered hoarsely.

Good? Oh, yes, it was very good, but obviously very dangerous, too, which Angel understood when Holt quickly withdrew to spill his warm seed on her belly.

"Had to—protect you," he gasped, rolling up on his side next to her. His large hand moved a corner of the blanket to tenderly cleanse her skin.

Angel resisted the urge to snuggle against his chest. She was so confused and weakened by her own feelings, she didn't even feel slighted when Holt soon fell asleep. Instead, she inched out from under his arm and moved on jellied legs to fetch her clothing. Her skirt, blouse, and underthings were dry now, and she quickly slipped them on, wrapping her arms around herself to ward off a sudden chill.

How had it happened? No, that wasn't the question. The question was really *why*. Angel sank down in a nearby chair and trembled as she watched Holt Murphy sleep. She was afraid she knew the answer why, and it frightened her to the core.

"Good morning!"

Angel kept her voice deliberately cheerful and casual as she shoved a tin plate full of steaming homemade biscuits and gravy under Holt's nose. He opened sleepy gray eyes and sniffed. Then he sat bolt upright in bed.

"Food. Real food." He looked over at Angel in outright amazement. Then he grabbed the plate and greedily wolfed the food down.

"You're welcome," she said a little tartly when he'd finished and still sat there in the bed, looking for all the world like a little boy, with his hair all rumpled.

"I'm sorry. That was delicious." Holt looked sheepish. "I'm still surprised you can really cook."

"I said I could. Didn't you believe me?"

He didn't answer her directly. "I haven't had a meal like this since my mother was alive."

"It's only biscuits and gravy."

"And it's only heaven on earth to a man who's been forced to eat his own cooking for over a decade." He slid from the covers, and Angel carefully kept her gaze averted while he dressed. Then Holt came over and dropped a stray kiss on the back of her neck. "About last night—"

"Not now, Holt. We've so much to do." Angel worked hard at keeping her voice bright and preoccupied as she wriggled from his embrace and sprinted across the room. "Ready for another day in the mine?"

"All right." He looked a little grumpy at the prospect of facing the new day. "Lead on."

Holt stayed silent as they gathered up the equipment and headed outside.

Halfway down to the mine, she stopped and exclaimed, "I forgot my pick!" It was still snugly buried in the ground near the corral.

"Better go back and get it," Holt said. "I'll go on ahead, if you don't mind."

Angel nodded and went back to the cabin. Even a minute more in the fresh air was bound to be better than a single second in the mine.

She was tugging uselessly on the pick when a horse and rider emerged from the trees. Looking up, Angel froze, and then relaxed when she recognized Neal Murphy.

Waving, she waited until he caught sight of her and turned in her direction. Her greeting was a rueful one.

"Know how to get a pick out of the ground?"

Neal laughed at her predicament. It made him look years younger even garbed in the grim black cloth of a minister.

"Hello, Mrs. Murphy. You certainly look happy today."

Angel flushed a little, though whether from his use of her married name or the way his light eyes admired her, she wasn't sure. But his tone was friendly, and she forced herself to relax.

"Holt is down at the mine," she told him. "I assume you came up to talk to him."

"Actually, I came to talk to you instead. Is that all right?" Neal waited until she nodded and then he dismounted, tying his horse to the corral.

"Would you care for some coffee?" Angel offered shyly. "There's some on the stove and it's still fresh."

"That sounds divine." Neal grinned. "I'll wait out here."

He seemed sensitive to her discomfort, and Angel sighed with relief as she quickly fetched two clean tin cups full of coffee and joined the young minister outside.

He sampled the hot brew. "Thank you. It's delicious."

There was a brief silence while each waited for the other to speak. Angel nervously twisted the wedding ring on her left finger until she saw Neal's eyes drop to her hand.

She flinched guiltily. Did he possibly guess the marriage might not be legitimate? If he did, Neal Murphy was tactful enough not to say anything.

"May I call you Angel?" At her nod he smiled. "And of course you can call me Neal. After all, you shall be my sister in spirit as well as in name now." He hesitated, obviously wanting to talk to her about something else.

"Angel, I'm not sure how much Holt has told you about the mine. You've been married such a short time."

"I know a little," she said.

"Fine. That's what I wanted to talk about. I'm very

concerned about Holt . . . and you, too. I've been ministering down in Clear Creek for the past few days. And in that time I've heard some rather disquieting rumors."

Angel swallowed hard. Her first guilty assumption was, of course, that Neal had heard she was only a doxy scheming to get the mine by fair means or foul.

"Word about town is that Holt has started finding some sizable nuggets," Neal continued, not seeming to notice when Angel visibly relaxed. "And I don't need to tell you it's starting to give some of the men down there gold fever. There's even talk of running him off and splitting shares."

Angel gasped. "How could that happen? The Lucky Devil is mine—and his, of course!"

Neal gave her a curious look. "On paper, naturally. But that means little to hard-bitten men like Red Garrett."

"Red Garrett?"

"I'm surprised Holt hasn't mentioned him. Red considers himself the law in Clear Creek, insomuch as there is any. And he demands a cut of most profitable ventures in the area to preserve the peace."

Angel shrugged. "We haven't seen hide nor hair of him. Anyway, the Lucky Devil is out of the jurisdiction of Clear Creek. What would Mr. Garrett want up here?"

"Gold, of course. And I'm afraid he'll stop at nothing to get it."

Neal's ominous words had barely sunk in when Holt's angry voice boomed at them across the meadow.

"Did you come all this way just to preach at Angel about the follies of marrying me?"

"I'm sorry." Neal shot Angel an apologetic look. "I'm afraid it's time for me to leave."

"Don't be ridiculous," she snapped, turning to confront Holt as he stormed up to them. His bronzed chest and arms glistened with sweat, and he wiped a stray black lock off his brow in order to glare more effectively at his half-brother.

"This is my house, too, and you're not going to be rude to our guest," Angel informed Holt. "Neal came up here to congratulate us."

"I thought he already gave us his felicitations in town," Holt drawled sarcastically.

"I'm on my way back to Oro today," Neal said.

"Good. See that you stay there."

"Holt!" Angel gasped.

But the younger Murphy stalked off to the cabin, leaving a scandalized Angel to deal with Neal.

"Oh, Neal, I'm sorry." She flushed bright pink with embarrassment. "I don't understand why he's being so rude!"

"Never mind, Angel. Sometimes it's just the Lord's way of testing a person. By the way, I also came to invite you to the ladies' social in Oro this Sunday evening. They're all eager to meet my new sister-in-law."

Angel thought longingly of wearing a pretty dress again, and sipping tea and nibbling tiny sandwiches, if only for a day. "I'd love to," she began eagerly, and then hesitated. "But Holt—"

"I'm sure he wouldn't begrudge you female companionship, Angel. You might approach him with it that way."

"Yes, of course. It would be lovely." Self-consciously, she studied the ground. "I'll try to come."

"Fine. Holt knows the way. Or, if you like, I could come again and drive you over in my wagon."

She shook her head. "You'd never make it up the pass. There are fallen trees blocking the road."

Neal looked surprised. "Oh, but there are several different roads to the mine. The other two are gradual inclines, and much quicker as well. You're referring to the old trapper trail, I think. It hasn't been used for years."

Angel stared at him for a moment and then blinked. "I see," she said slowly. "Let me talk to Holt first. I'm sure he'll let me go."

"Very well. Well, goodbye for now, Angel. Sorry to disrupt your day."

With a friendly smile, Neal untied his horse and swung up on the saddle. He tipped his hat at her before he rode off at a brisk trot. Angel waited until he was out of range and then stalked into the cabin. Holt looked up from the table without a word.

"How dare you!" she sputtered, waving her arms for emphasis. She was so angry, she could hardly speak. "You knew full well it was the worst road up the mountain and you deliberately took me that way!"

"And you deliberately provoked me into doing so," he responded flatly. "Since you wanted to come up here so badly, I figured you ought to be exposed to the rougher edges of this kind of life."

"Well, thank you very much! You nearly got me killed and without so much as a by-your-leave!"

Holt only shrugged, which was as much an apology as she'd ever get, Angel knew.

"By the way, I'm going to a ladies' social in Oro this

Sunday," she tossed out at him. "I'll thank you to drive me there."

"All right."

Expecting a heated argument, Angel was disarmed. She stood and stared at Holt until he finally asked irritably, "Now are you ready to go back to work?"

Sunday arrived quicker than she expected. Angel nervously smoothed the elaborate black ruching on her best rust-colored taffeta. The underskirt was black silk and piped with jet rosettes. She wished she had more than a hand mirror to view the final results, but she had to be satisfied with Holt's opinion.

"You'll make the old biddies jealous."

"Oh, Holt, don't be unkind." Angel finished sliding a hairpin into her elaborate chignon, coiled in black netting. "There. That's as much as I can do without a maid." She picked up a matching rust hat with a jaunty black ostrich feather and pinned it on as well.

"Enough already!" Holt said when she began to fret about wearing gloves as well. "You're already overdressed for Oro. It's a mining town, for God's sake."

She frowned unhappily at him. "But I do want to make a good impression!"

"Angel, your beauty is impression enough." Holt gave her a lazy smile, and she was forced to smile back. "Every man in the Territory is going to envy me. Now, get your wrap and let's go. It's a long drive and I don't want to be gone for more than a night."

As they settled into the wagon Holt had brought up,

Angel ventured softly, "Thank you. This means a lot to me."

"It ought to. I don't understand why we have to take all your bags along, too." He flung a glance to the wagon bed, where Angel had neatly arranged her luggage.

"In my experience it's wise to be prepared for delays," she replied tartly as she tossed the black wrap around her shoulders and tied it in place. "And heaven knows I don't like leaving my things in the cabin while we're not here. Someone like Stokes could steal them."

"What he'd want with a woman's petticoats I'd rather not guess," Holt grumbled, but he obligingly slapped the reins and Buck started forward.

The wagon rolled slowly toward Oro City, and further conversation wasn't necessary. The beauty of nature held Angel completely enthralled. It was a full hour's drive to the thriving town of Oro, where silver-lead ore had recently been discovered after a gold-mining drought in the early '70's. She enjoyed the view and the peaceful scenery, and found herself a little disappointed when the busy boom town suddenly sprouted into view below them.

Unlike Clear Creek, this place was clearly thriving. There were throngs of people in the streets, raucous noise, and even an occasional gunshot as they came off the mountain.

Angel was surprised and disconcerted by all the stares cast their way when Holt and she drove down the main street. A few men made ludicrous bows in her direction and then snickered among themselves. The older ladies and young women walking by pointedly looked in every direction but at the passing couple. Angel colored with confused embarrassment and flashed a quick glance at

Holt. His entire body was taut with anger and his free
hand unconsciously dropped to the gleaming Bowie knife
at his side.

"I'll take you to the parsonage," he muttered, giving a
black look to everyone who crossed their path or made a
rude remark. Angel tried not to absorb the impact of the
stares and whispers but was unsuccessful. Her confidence
was shaken. Heavens, what were the townfolk thinking?

The answer came from an unexpected source. Leaning
from a second-story window, a heavily rouged blonde
waved a lacy handkerchief at them.

"Holt, luv, I see you found you another doxy! Is she
better n'me?"

Her laughter tittered down at them before the window
hastily slammed shut. Angel reddened with fury and
quickly tugged the black netting from her hat down over
her face.

"Angel, I'm sorry—" Holt began.

"Don't apologize! Just drive." Though she managed to
keep her head high, Angel's hands, tightly clutched in her
lap, showed how distressed she was. So everyone here
thought she was Holt's whore! And why not? A man like
Holt Murphy was no more likely to marry than . . . than
a priest!

After forever, it seemed, they reached the tiny parish
over which Neal Murphy resided. The whitewashed
church was stark and simple in design, with a wooden
crucifix tilted slightly off center over the double doors. To
the rear of the church was the small parsonage. Holt
swiftly dismounted and led Angel inside, where she was
sheltered from the stares and sniggers. There she
promptly lost her composure.

"This is horrible!" she cried. "I never imagined it would be like this. I want to leave!"

Neal overheard the noise and hurried out from the adjoining rectory. "Angel . . . Holt . . . you're early." He looked a little distraught himself. "The social doesn't begin for another hour." Then he saw Angel's face. "What happened?"

"Apparently the good folk of Oro seem to think I keep public company with fallen women!" Holt snapped. "They did everything but hurl rocks when we rode into town."

Neal had the grace to look embarrassed. "Oh, dear. I never imagined—"

"Imagined what?"

"Well, I had heard some rumors, of course, but . . ." He shook his head, apparently unwilling to say more. "Of course it's out of the question to subject Angel to a social now."

"We'll be heading straight back," Holt confirmed.

"Holt?" Angel spoke quietly. "I don't want to go."

"Of course you don't. We'll head right home."

"No, I mean I don't want to leave Oro. I want to go to the ladies' social as planned."

He frowned at her. "Angel, I don't think that's a very good idea. . . ."

"But how else will I prove to them that I'm not what they think? No doxy is this refined or educated!"

Neal grinned. "She has a point, Holt. When they meet her in person I'm sure the good ladies of Oro will be a little chagrined by their behavior."

Holt considered it for a moment but still frowned. "I don't like it. Angel's my wife, and I won't stand for her being treated badly."

The words rolled so easily off his tongue that even Holt himself looked surprised. Then he winked at Angel when Neal wasn't watching, and she flashed a small grin back.

"Don't worry, Holt," Neal continued. "I'll watch over Angel tonight. And you can come pick her up in the morning."

Holt raised an inquiring brow and Neal flushed. "I just meant, of course, that the social will run late, and I imagine you have work to do up at the mine. I'd be happy to drive Angel back tomorrow if you prefer."

"No, I don't think so. With your permission I'll stay the night here as well."

Neal inclined his head. "Very well. I'll show you two to the guest room."

As he fell into stride ahead of them, Angel glanced over at Holt and saw that he was still looking at her with a conspiratorial little grin on his lips. She flushed, almost able to read his mind. Here in a House of God, they would be living openly as man and wife. Somehow it almost seemed to carve the fact of their marriage in stone.

A sudden idea occurred to Angel. They could trust Neal, couldn't they? She would ask him in confidence if he could find out how authentic her marriage to Holt was. Was it any less legal because it had been accomplished by proxy, without Holt's actual signature? These were things she had never hoped to answer until she returned to Missouri. But a minister would surely know, no matter the size of the parish over which he presided.

"Are you ready, Angel?"

"As ready as I'll ever be," she told Neal breathlessly,

giving him a brilliant white smile. Inside she was churning with doubt, already reconsidering her bold move to throw the ladies of Oro off guard. Once she walked into the den of wolves there would be no turning back. Neal's grim expression served to remind her of that.

"You don't have to do this, Angel," he said quietly before they left the parsonage. "I know Holt would be relieved if you didn't."

"But I have to do it!" she exclaimed. "For him as much as myself. It's the Murphy name they're soiling. Don't you care about that?"

"Of course I do, Angel. But I don't want to see you hurt." Suddenly Neal seemed almost timid. "I've grown very fond of you in the short time we've been acquainted."

"Thank you." She patted his arm in passing when he moved to hold open the heavy wooden door for her. "I just hope I won't disappoint you tonight."

Outside, Angel took a deep, steadying breath of the cool, crisp air before taking Neal's arm and letting him walk her to the Triumph Hall, where the ladies' social was being held. Her legs felt like jelly. Thankfully, it was already dusk; if there were further stares, she couldn't see them.

Holt had departed earlier, after the couple had shared a quiet meal with Neal. Angel suspected he had merely crossed the street to avail himself of the nearest saloon, but as long as he was close, she didn't care. Suddenly they were standing before Triumph Hall and Neal was giving her last-minute bits of advice.

"Just be yourself. Don't offer any advice or excuses."

There was a warning beneath his forced cheer, Angel saw.

"I'll be fine. Will you walk me back when it's over?"

"With pleasure." Neal opened the door for her with a flourish, gently ushering Angel into the lion's den.

Chapter Six

As one body, conversation ceased. Heads turned, muslin rustled, bright eyes pierced. Angel faltered briefly. Then, with a determined smile wide enough to span the Colorado River itself, she swept into the hall.

"Good evening, ladies." Gracefully she removed her black lace shawl and hung it on a peg beside the others'. There was a moment of supreme silence in the hall. Angel glanced up from beneath lowered lashes and saw stark outrage, amusement, and various other emotions reflected on the faces around her.

The ladies had formed a circle with their chairs, so as to better display their Sunday best as well as to make gossip easier. A table bearing a crystal punch bowl and slivers of iced cake stood nearby. Angel glided toward it, to fetch the only chair remaining as yet unoccupied. Her heart was in her throat and she could feel dozens of eyes measuring, appraising, and otherwise gauging her worth and mettle.

"The nerve," she overheard one matron whispering to another, "the absolute nerve!"

"What did you expect?" retorted the other, sotto voce, just loud enough for Angel to appreciate. "She's a Murphy, after all."

Suddenly Angel wanted to laugh. The gall of these supposed Christian ladies! It wasn't enough that they criticized her. No, they were holding the entire Murphy family responsible for her "brazenness"!

"You don't want any of that cake." A soft voice at the refreshment table startled Angel. "It's terribly dry and not particularly tasty."

Angel looked into the twinkling hazel eyes belonging to a brown-haired, thin young woman assigned to a straight, hard chair behind the cake. She was garbed in brown calico and blended in so well with the plain wooden decor of the hall that Angel hadn't seen her sitting there at first.

"How do you do," the churchmouse said. Her voice was still almost at a whisper. "I'm Rachel Maxwell, Prudence Maxwell's daughter. You must be Mrs. Murphy."

"Was there any doubt in your mind?" Angel murmured, tilting her head back toward the bristling, outraged matrons. Rachel giggled. She sounded like a young girl but had to be at least as old as Angel.

"I've so wanted to meet you," Rachel continued. "Ever since Pastor Murphy mentioned you had married Holt. It makes you sort of a mystery, you know."

To stall the inquisition and get to know Rachel better, Angel picked up a crystal plate and pretended to look over the refreshments. "A mystery?"

Rachel looked surprised. "Why, of course. Nobody could believe Holt had actually married . . ."

"And some still don't," Angel finished, with another glance at the storm gathering behind her. She wanted to continue her conversation with Rachel, but she realized she had better avert a scene before it began. With a quick wink to Miss Maxwell, Angel smoothly pivoted about. She was just in time to hear another hiss, this one coming from the huge woman who obviously occupied the throne in Triumph Hall.

"Bold as brass, the little thing. I wonder if she dragged Holt Murphy to the altar all by herself!"

Angel knew the woman fully intended to be overheard. In a sweet, clear voice, she said, "Actually, I used a lasso. It's particularly effective on those tougher bachelor types."

There was a moment of breathless silence while all the other ladies anxiously watched Prudence Maxwell for her reaction. Then, seeing the lines around her eyes crinkle with amusement, they began to titter in quiet accompaniment.

"I don't believe I've had the pleasure," Prudence said after a brief, grudging smile. She introduced herself and waited regally for her latest petitioner to respond.

Angel complied with grace and saw a growing respect in Prudence's eyes. While the matron of Oro City was enough to frighten any newcomer, Angel had cut her teeth on social etiquette. She enjoyed stunning those who had expected her to prattle on like an uneducated tart.

Before she knew it, Angel had been invited to sit on Prudence's right, displacing a weasel-faced woman named Justine Garrett who was obviously displeased by the turn of events. Angel didn't pay much attention to Mrs. Garrett's pinched expression before she stiffly moved off to the refreshment table. She had to concentrate fully on Prudence's nosy questions instead.

"What a delightful accent you have, Mrs. Murphy. Are you from the south?"

Angel nodded cautiously. "Missouri."

"Of course. I should have recognized it. I myself have a cousin in St. Louis. Do you know the Harpers?"

Angel started to explain that St. Louis was on the other side of Missouri from Independence, but Prudence wasn't listening anyway. Her sharp eyes had fixed on someone else entering the Hall.

"Harlot," she suddenly hissed under her breath.

Angel felt a wave of relief when she realized the word wasn't meant for her. She looked over and stared with the other ladies as a particularly striking redhead in pale blue silk breached the unwritten law of Triumph Hall and entered without invitation.

"Why . . . it's Miss Valentine," the church lady on Angel's right gasped softly.

Everyone looked to Prudence for a cue. Rachel's mother drew herself up like a rattlesnake prepared to strike. Angel watched with silent fascination, feeling pity for the unsuspecting Miss Valentine and a mixture of shock and amusement over Prudence's reaction.

Why, everyone's acting like I'm a regular saint now, and poor Miss Valentine's the harlot, Angel thought. Then she reddened when she remembered it was exactly the word Prudence had used. Mrs. Maxwell came to her feet with another hiss of righteous indignation, and regally swept forward to confront the intruder.

Angel did a quick reevaluation of "poor Miss Valentine" in the next few moments. Not only did the woman refuse to meet Prudence halfway, but a mischievous smile teased at her dark red lips. Her throat and wrists sparkled with a vulgar display of diamonds or what were excellent paste fakes, and Angel saw the woman's silk dress was so thin as to lend credit to every sleek curve beneath. Her cat-green eyes roamed leisurely and insolently over the assembled ladies, lighting for a fraction of a second on Angel herself.

Like everyone else, Angel waited with baited breath to see what Prudence would do. Rachel glided up behind Angel's chair and placed a tense hand on the backrest.

"Who is she?" Angel murmured.

"You don't know who Lily Valentine is? Oh, she's merely the most infamous singer in these parts. Or, as some maintain, she really gets her living from another trade—"

Rachel's whisper brought disapproving looks from the other ladies. They all wanted to hear what Prudence had to say to the most notorious woman in Oro City.

"Jezebel!" Prudence dramatically leveled a plump finger at the obviously amused Lily. "How dare you enter a House of God where decent ladies reside!"

Lily inclined her head, and her bright auburn hair glittered beneath the gas lamps in the hall. "I apologize for disrupting your evening, ladies," she said in a polite, throaty voice, as if Prudence had never called her a whore. "But I'm looking for Holt's wife. It's important."

Angel came slowly to her feet, too surprised to be offended by Miss Valentine's casual use of her husband's name. "I'm Mrs. Murphy. What is it?"

The green eyes inspected Angel from head to toe and betrayed a flicker of surprise. Then Lily's voice echoed endlessly through the hall. "You and I have something rather urgent to settle between us, Mrs. Murphy. May I suggest we step outside?"

"You don't have to go anywhere with her!" Prudence Maxwell told Angel indignantly. Her bristling outrage echoed the consensus in the room.

Though Angel was chagrined by the other woman's announcement, she was also admittedly curious. She answered the challenge in Lily's bold green gaze.

"All right," she said. "Let me get my shawl."

Angel was immune to further whispers and stares as she moved to drape the black lace over her shoulders. Rachel would have followed willingly, but Angel shook her head at her new friend as she reached the door. "What is this all about?" she asked the singer.

Lily just shook her head, unwilling or unable to explain. "So you're Mrs. Murphy," she murmured. "Funny, but I expected something a little different."

Angel didn't know how to take the dry remark, and she was equally surprised when Lily took her impatiently by the arm. "Come on. I haven't got all night."

Just outside the hall, Lily paused before the windows, where the church ladies were now rushing to get a first-hand view of what would surely be the fight of the season. Lily waited a few more moments to let them all get settled, then released Angel's arm and turned to face her.

"Hit me, honey."

"What?" Angel stared at the woman.

"You heard me right," Lily said in a low, quick voice. "Right now, while they're still watching." She gave Angel a mocking little smile for the benefit of their eager audience. "But not too hard. I just had my teeth fixed," she added under her breath.

"You're crazy. Why, I'd no more hit you than—"

"I've slept with Holt, you know."

Crack! Before she could stop herself, Angel saw the palm of her hand leave a bright red imprint on Lily's rouged and powdered face. She gasped.

"Perfect. You'd make a damned good actress yourself," Lily said ruefully as she touched her burning cheek. "Now listen hard and fast, chick. Holt'd want me to protect your reputation, so on the count of three I'm going to turn and run down the street like all the proverbial hounds of hell are at my heels. You follow. Yell out a few bad words to make it look good. But don't stop for anything. Holt's life is at stake."

Angel stared at the redhead, feeling apprehension jolt through her. Whatever this was all about, it didn't sound good. The mere mention of Holt's name made her go stiff and wary.

"What happened?"

"Holt was ambushed," Lily said succinctly. "He was shot just outside of Jake's tonight."

Angel's soft cry and anxious questions went unanswered.

"Just chase me," Lily said before she turned and sprinted down the street, "and make it a good one!"

Angel remembered little of the cold or the dark or the stares as she thundered across the town on the skirts of the town tart, shouting lively words for the benefit of any passersby.

Lily rounded a corner around the town barber shop and stopped at the back door of a narrow two-story building that looked vaguely familiar. Angel was too worried about Holt to be shocked when she realized it was Oro's cathouse.

"This was the one place I knew he'd be safe," Lily said briskly in answer to any unspoken criticism. She pushed open the door and steered Angel inside.

The muted sound of spunky piano music came through some velvet-padded doors to their right, and husky feminine laughter rippled from somewhere high above. Lily ignored both as she pulled Angel after her up a narrow set of stairs. She knocked softly at a closed chamber draped with red tassels before she opened it. Then she stepped out of the way so Angel could see the man in the bed.

"Holt!" she cried, as if the words ripped from her very heart. Angel went to the bed and felt herself falter at the sight of him so pale and unmoving in the velvet-draped canopy bed. She whirled on Lily. "Where in heaven's name is the doctor?"

"Doc's come and gone," the singer replied. "Nothing he could do once he got Holt patched up."

Angel's eyes flew back to the blood-soaked bandages wrapped around Holt's upper left arm and shoulder. He moaned softly and shifted in the bed, and she felt a flood of relief to know he was alive. But also a keen frustration at being unable to help him herself.

"If it's any comfort," Lily put in, "I knew a man who was hit by a stray bullet once and bounced right back."

"But this wasn't a stray bullet, was it?" Angel looked once more to Lily for the answers. "You told me he was 'ambushed.' "

"Did I?" Lily mused. "A poor choice of words. Let's just say it was a lively night at Jake's."

The saloon where Holt must have gone. Angel bit her lip and turned back to the man in the bed. She wanted to hover over him but was uncomfortable with Lily watching.

"Go on," Lily urged her. "He needs you."

Angel moved to obey. She had never felt more desperate than when she took his limp hand tightly in her own. "Oh, Holt," she whispered.

His eyelashes flickered. Then the familiar steel-gray eyes opened and he made a wry, pained face up at her.

"I should have gone to the ladies' social instead," he murmured hoarsely.

Lily chuckled, but Angel could find no humor in his words. "What happened, Holt? Please tell me."

"Jumped." He licked his dry lips and tried again. "Some yellow-livered coward jumped me outside of Jake's."

"But why?" Angel burst out.

"Why, indeed?" Lily interposed almost sarcastically, and in that moment Angel truly disliked the woman. "When a man has a gold mine on the verge of a strike what more reason does there need to be?"

Angel couldn't bite her tongue any longer. She turned on Lily. "He only owns part of the mine. The other half belongs to me. They could have shot me just as easily."

The singer looked surprised, and Angel felt a brief flare of satisfaction before she turned back to Holt. He was trying to grin up at her but looked for all the world like he'd tasted something nasty.

"My scrappy little squaw," he murmured, wincing when his arm moved inadvertently. "The best of claim-jumpers couldn't get a jump on you."

Angel wasn't sure if it was a compliment or not, but she could sense unspoken questions in the air. Before Lily could get bossy again she told Holt, "I'm going back to the parsonage. I've got to tell Neal what happened."

It was as if she'd dashed saltwater on his wound.

"No!"

Holt sat halfway up in bed, and she had to grab his uninjured arm to keep him there.

"Neal mustn't know," he hissed through clenched teeth.

"That's the most ridiculous thing I've ever heard. Of course Neal needs to know what happened to you and where I am now. Holt, when will you let go of that silly grudge?"

He was mutinously silent and Angel sighed. "All right. But how do I explain to him how I ended up in a—a fancy house like this?"

"You leave that to me," Lily interrupted briskly. "I'll escort you back to Preacher Murphy's place. And don't worry; Holt and I already figured out a story about how he got shot."

Holt and I? Angel's eyebrows raised while the beautiful redhead exchanged a sly wink with her bedridden husband. It was obvious they knew each other from somewhere, not that it was any of her business.

"Thanks, Lil," Holt said wearily before the two women left. "I don't know what I'd do without you."

"Don't mention it. You know I'd do anything for you."

Which left Angel wondering just what *anything* might include.

* * *

"You might as well wipe those thoughts right out of your mind, honey," Lily said before she accompanied a silent Angel back to the parsonage. The two women faced each other in a downstairs receiving parlor, decorated in lush claret-red velvet and gold brocade.

"I don't know what you mean," Angel replied, softly and defensively. But she heard the censuring note in Lily's low voice.

"You know perfectly well. If you married Holt Murphy, it was for better or worse. And if you expect it to be better most of the time, you're going to be sorely disappointed."

Angel glanced at the singer's profile as Lily moved to pour herself a shot of warm golden liquor at the leather-padded bar. She was slightly surprised by the ring of familiarity in the words. Hadn't Elsa Loring also warned her not to expect too much from men? But the stout German woman had meant something entirely different than Lily did now.

"Holt lives dangerously," Lily added, "and sooner or later you're going to get caught in the cross fire. If he's busy looking after you, too, he's not going to be as alert as he needs to be."

Angel heard a definite note of disapproval in Lily's smooth dialogue. She began to bristle. Just who was this Valentine woman, anyway, to be making judgments about her? No better than a doxy, according to Prudence Maxwell.

"I'd like to know why you're so concerned about Holt," Angel blurted out.

Lily's slim eyebrows arched. "I was wondering when you would get around to that. You're certainly more patient than most wives I know." After a brief, disarming smile at the younger woman she said, "Holt and I go back a long way. I met him when I was coming west on a wagon train with my parents. They were poor Irish immigrants looking for a better life. But the tickets they bought were one way, to a couple of unmarked graves high in the Rockies."

When Lily gave a low sigh Angel momentarily felt confused. Her emotions warred between sympathy for the woman and jealousy for what Lily meant to Holt.

"I didn't plan to stay here," Lily continued. "Fact is, I was looking for a way out of these backwoods, to someplace fancy like New York or San Francisco. But that takes money. A lot of it. So when someone offered to pay me for singing in a saloon I said why not. Didn't realize one job would label me from there on out."

"As a singer, you mean?"

"No. A whore." Lily's voice held, strangely enough, not even the tiniest trace of bitterness. "Oh, don't get me wrong, Mrs. Murphy. I understand how most folks here jumped to that conclusion, seeing as how I have to confine my talent to the saloons. And a woman like me can't get lodging in a proper hotel for all the money in the world. But that's where Holt came in. He saw through the spangles and the rouge to the real me. We've had plenty of opportunity to help each other out in the past."

"Oh," Angel said in a small voice.

"And now you need to help him, chick. He won't be up and about for a while . . . and it's too dangerous to spread word of him being down all around town. We'll have to cover for him, you and me. If that means tearing out each other's hair and screaming like a couple of harpies in public, so be it. Until he's on his feet again Holt needs a safe haven. And believe me, this is about as safe as it gets in Oro City."

Angel glanced around the garish parlor with dismay. Lily was obviously insisting that Holt remain here for a while, but were her reasons based on his best interests or her own?

"I don't know," she hedged. "What about the mine?"

The beautiful singer shrugged. "Holt can run off any jumpers when he's feeling lively again. Not much damage they can do in just a few days. And maybe it'll flush out the rats who tried to take him down at Jake's tonight."

Angel felt a shudder course through her. "I don't see how you can be so calm after all this."

"Simple, honey." Lily raised her liquor glass with a cynical smile. "This is all it takes to dull even the worst pain. You might want to try it yourself."

"No, thank you." Angel remembered Royce McCloud's drunken binges and gambling streaks, and a sadness descended over her like a dark cloud. Though Holt was seriously hurt, she almost resented him putting her in this position. And Lily Valentine wasn't helping much, either.

"I'd like to go back to the parsonage now," she said quietly.

"Of course. If you agree, Mrs. Murphy, the story will be that you and I had a quarrel over Holt. The good church ladies will confirm that much with pleasure. And then you followed me here and I threw you out. Holt's whereabouts can be safely left up to their imaginations, I think."

"But how will I be able to visit him?"

"You won't. Just trust that I'll keep an eye out and see he's taken proper care of. I'd suggest you stay with Preacher Murphy for a few more days. Then Holt can suddenly reappear and make amends, and keep the town-folk happy."

But what about my happiness? Angel wanted to argue. She had to fight the desire to run back upstairs and take care of Holt herself. It was galling to have to accept the hospitality of a soiled dove like Lily, even though the woman appeared to be doing the sensible thing. If someone truly wanted Holt dead so they could claim the mine, it would be foolish to expose him to unnecessary danger.

"I'm asking you to play a role," Lily said softly. "Possibly the greatest role you've ever played in this life, Mrs. Murphy. Holt's life may depend on your ability to act. Trust me. He's in grave danger. The less folks know of what happened tonight, the better. I don't want his enemies to think they've won a single round."

"Enemies?" Angel exclaimed. "Are there more than one?"

Lily was silent a fraction too long. "For your own sake I'd better keep quiet. Just go back to the parsonage and play the role of the outraged wife."

Play? Angel almost laughed out loud. It was easy enough for her to feel wounded and embittered at the mere thought of Holt with another woman.

Neal looked very pale and grave after Angel finished imparting the news to him later that night. *Why, Lily's right, I could be an actress,* she thought, as she watched his expression change from concern to upset and then out-rage for her situation.

"Angel, I never imagined . . . I knew Holt had a wild streak, but . . ." he sputtered, growing bright pink as she continued to regard him with huge tear-filled eyes.

It wasn't hard to summon a few crocodile tears, be-cause she really was worried about Holt. And Lily. And what the two of them meant to each other.

Wiping her eyes, she asked huskily, "What do you know about that . . . singer?"

For a moment Neal didn't look inclined to answer. Then he released a low, tense sigh. "Not much. Of course, she's not received in any of my parishioner's homes."

"She's very beautiful."

"Angel, don't torment yourself—"

"Isn't she?" she pressed him, turning to stare out the rectory window into the darkness, as if it held the answer she sought. "So sophisticated and poised."

"She's a fallen woman," he said with distaste.

"No wonder Holt was smitten," Angel murmured as if he hadn't spoken. "What man wouldn't be?"

"My dear, you need to get some rest. In the morning we can talk further and decide what to do."

A sudden idea popped into Angel's head. "Neal," she continued, "do you perform marriages?"

He looked surprised. "Why, yes, of course."

"Good. Then you know all the rules, I presume. Do—do you know if marriage by proxy is legally binding?"

He seemed perplexed by this question. "I suppose so," he said at last, slowly and carefully, as he considered her fidgeting posture. "If the documentation is all there, legally signed, I don't see why it wouldn't be completely legitimate."

"Oh. I see." Angel didn't know whether to be relieved or distraught. Right now she just felt frustrated. "Neal," she burst out, unable to bear his concerned silence any longer, "I don't know if Holt and I are really married!"

As the story tumbled out, Angel was relieved to share the burdensome secret with someone who cared. And it was obvious Neal did, by the way he kept nodding kindly when she began to tremble.

"It is certainly strange," he mused when she had finished and nervously awaited his reply. "I find it most peculiar that someone should go to the trouble of getting Holt married. Unless . . ." he hesitated, giving Angel a regretful look, "unless, of course, my brother is lying for some reason."

"But why would he do that?" Angel wondered. "What does he have to gain?"

The moment the question shot out, she felt the answer scald her heart. The mine! It was half hers by law. If Holt had somehow found out about that and wanted the mine for himself, the most convenient way was by marriage. And if Angel proved difficult . . . accidents in the mountains were so easy to explain away.

A cold shiver ran lightly over her skin and Neal saw it. He made reassuring noises, repeating once again that she needed to get some rest. Things would be clearer in the morning, he said again. Yes, indeed! The fog was already lifting from Angel's mind. The reason why Holt had married her seemed to be getting clearer all the time.

Chapter Seven

Three days passed slowly by, days Angel would have gladly forgotten rather than ever lived again. Unfortunately, there seemed to be no escaping the fact that she and Holt were the talk of Oro City, in every residence from churches to bordellos.

What would she have done without Neal? Instead of letting her hide her head behind closed doors he made a point of drawing her outside and making the townsfolk acknowledge her publicly. Accompanied by the stiff-necked preacher, none dared cut the questionable Mrs. Murphy. Although the good ladies of Oro were sympathetic to her plight over Holt, they all agreed she had behaved quite scandalously, shrieking like a fishwife as she chased the town tart down Main Street.

Only Rachel Maxwell dared to speak to Angel, when they met by chance one day inside Lane's Mercantile. Angel had slipped inside to indulge her sweet tooth while Neal was busy in the rectory, and she only hoped she wouldn't receive yet another cold shoulder. But the other girl put a mischievous finger to her lips, cautioning Angel to silence, until the proprietor went out back to load some bags of grain for another customer.

"Mrs. Murphy!" Rachel exclaimed then with real pleasure. "How are you? I haven't seen you since—since—" Words failed her, but a bright blush didn't, and Rachel scolded herself while Angel smiled in understanding. "Oh, I'm such a tactless goose! I hope you won't take offense, but I've longed ever so much to meet you again. There aren't many young ladies my age about town, and—"

Rachel abruptly ceased chattering as the beetle-browed Mr. Lane reappeared and suspiciously eyed the two women who were suddenly absorbed in examining his bolts of calico.

"I don't see a thing I like," Rachel declared loudly, flipping the cut edge of the material aside. "I do believe I'll walk over to Caxton's to see if he has any nicer cloth in stock."

While Mr. Lane drew himself up with silent indignation, Rachel shot Angel a conspiratorial look from beneath lowered lashes. Taking the hint, Angel waited a moment more after the other young woman had left, then bought a few pieces of hard candy from Mr. Lane to soothe his ego, and proceeded down the street to Caxton's. She caught up with Rachel just outside the second store.

"Why did you act so oddly back there?"

"Oh, it's just that Lane is such an old gossip, worse even than the church biddies."

Angel couldn't restrain a peal of laughter at Rachel's frankness, and they exchanged looks of understanding and instant friendship.

"I'm not my mother's daughter, as you can probably see," Rachel confessed frankly. "I'm nothing like Mother, and I admit it doesn't bother me. Let her be content with those dull church socials. I'm looking for adventure!"

"And you're certainly courting it now," Angel said. "By associating with me you risk being ostracized."

"Oh, no, not really. Nobody would dare cut Prudence Maxwell's daughter, even if I wore red pantalets on the Lord's Day!"

Angel chuckled. "You seem determined to make your own adventure if you can't find one, Miss Maxwell."

"Rachel, please. I can't abide formality." And suddenly she slipped her arm through Angel's as if they had been great friends for many years and led her down the walk.

Angel was relieved that she'd chosen to wear her dove-gray dress, the plainest she owned, and so far nobody had spared them another glance. More likely it was because the town was too busy with the rumor of another silver strike up on the hill. Men were pouring out of town like tea from a kettle.

"Back to the mines!" Rachel exclaimed, her eyes bright with envy as they watched a pair of whooping old prospectors kicking their mules for more speed on the way out of town. "I declare, it's gotten to be like a fever of some sort! How I wish I was a man so I could take off these silly old skirts and go mining with the rest of them!"

"Why, Rachel!" Angel feigned shock, though there was an amused twinkle in her eyes. "There's an echo of the suffragettes in that! I should report you to your mother . . . though, of course, I would then be forced to admit I wear men's trousers when I mine beside Holt."

"When you—" Rachel began, stunned, as she turned

to face Angel; then she let out a soft cry of envy. "Truly? But how exciting! Mr. Murphy lets you? He doesn't mind?"

"Mind? On the contrary, he quite insists," Angel said dryly, remembering Holt's slave-driving ways. "But, Rachel, it's not quite so glamorous as it seems—"

"Oh, but to really work your own mine, looking for the mother lode!" Rachel's rapturous expression probably mirrored that of her virtuous mother, presently attending the Ladies' Aid Society meeting, and Angel laughed again.

"Goodness, is it really so exciting to you? Well, I shall ask your mother if you might come visit for a day . . . and we'll even nip a pair of Holt's trousers for you to wear!"

She was only teasing, of course, but Rachel's eyes began to shine. A dreamy look stole across her freckled features as she murmured, "If you promise not to tell Pastor Murphy . . ."

"Neal? Of course not." Angel was confused until she saw the pink stain on the girl's cheeks. Oh dear, did it mean what she thought it did? What a pickle! She knew Neal hadn't the faintest idea of Rachel's idolization, for he had mentioned her only briefly and with brotherly fondness.

"I'd best be getting back to the rectory," she said into the brief silence, after which Rachel visibly snapped back into order. "Would you like to walk back with me?"

"Oh, yes . . . I would."

Obviously Rachel was hoping to catch a glimpse of the elusive young preacher. Now, why was love so fickle? Neither of the Murphy brothers had the vaguest notion of the secret agony they were causing the two women who loved them.

* * *

Tap! Tap! Tap!

Angel stirred groggily in the chair where she had fallen asleep over a dusty copy of Shakespeare. The tapping came again, only more insistently, and she shook herself awake and rubbed her tired eyes. Where was she? Oh, yes, the parsonage. She had borrowed a book from Neal to read before bed, and the only work he possessed that was not evangelical in nature was *Macbeth*.

A cold chill ran over her when she sensed someone was watching her. The curtains were slightly agape at the guest bedroom window, and she rose to pull them shut. Just as she moved, a dark shadow scratched the glass again.

Angel swallowed a scream when she saw the moonlight reflect off auburn hair. She recognized the pale oval face framed by the night and reluctantly opened the window.

"About time," Lily Valentine snorted softly as she leaned halfway over the sill. "You sleep like the dead!"

"What is it?" Angel knew the woman wouldn't have come if it weren't urgent, and dread pierced her like a red-hot needle. "Is it Holt?"

Lily raised a hand to warn Angel to keep her voice low. "He's ornery as a sore-headed bear right now. Doc won't let him leave my place, much less the bed. The wound isn't healing like it should."

Angel's eyes went wide, and she saw a flash of concern mirrored in Lily's gaze. "Don't worry, chick. He'll make it. He's lived through worse than this, God knows. But I'm having a hel——a cuss of a time keeping him calm and quiet like he's supposed to be."

Angel frowned. "Then what's wrong?"

With obvious reluctance the woman shrugged and admitted, "He wants to see you. Won't tell me why. Not that it's any of my business—"

"That's right," Angel echoed with a faint air of triumph. Never mind Lily's disgust when Holt was finally coming round to her! Could it be he missed her after all? Did she dare hope she'd come to mean something more to him than a mining partner or a millstone around his neck?

"I'll get my cloak," she breathed, reaching to the wardrobe nearby. Thank goodness she was still dressed and ready to go. Then she hesitated. "Neal—"

"Blast the preacher!" Lily hissed. "You'll have to slip out the window here. Make your bed to look like you're in it first. Then come on. It's too dangerous for Holt to risk anyone else knowing the truth."

Reluctantly, Angel moved to comply, stuffing a spare pillow in her night rail to make it appear like a huddled sleeper before she shoved it under the blankets. She turned the lamp down low. Then she grabbed her cloak and, with Lily's aid, climbed through the narrow window. They left it open so she could sneak back in later the same way.

Out in the chill air Angel drew up a concealing hood around her face and followed Lily's swift figure through the night. Minutes later she was at Holt's side. And oh, how she had missed him! Her heart ached, seeing him thrashing restlessly in the grip of a fever. She looked accusingly at Lily, who just shrugged and said the doc had done what he could.

How could she have left him to the other woman's

haphazard care? Angel should be here nursing him herself. But she shelved her anger and regrets to pull up a chair to his side. There she sponged his sweaty brow with wet cloths from a basin of tepid water left on the ruffled nightstand.

"Angel?" Holt licked his dry lips and spoke her name through the haze of delirium. She leaned forward eagerly, wanting to press her cheek against his but restrained by Lily's disapproving presence in the background.

"I'm here, Holt."

His eyes opened on hers, feverishly bright but with an unwavering gaze that made her uneasy. He spoke clearly and distinctly.

"The mine, Angel. We've got to protect it." He winced and visibly struggled with the pain, and with horror Angel saw his injury was crisscrossed with faint red lines. Gangrene!

Lily read her mind. She moved forward and in the lull of Holt's silence murmured against Angel's ear, "The doc thinks it should come off. Of course Holt won't hear of it."

Angel brushed off the woman's ominous words and took her husband's other hand. She felt Holt's strong brown fingers tighten on hers, and a wave of protectiveness swept over her.

"Holt," she said, evenly and calmly, "tell me what to do."

He seemed to sag with relief. She knew then with a burst of triumph that he trusted her—even if he didn't love her. For now, it was enough. It had to be.

"Hire a man to ride up and watch the place," he said, and though his voice wavered now it was still strong with insistence. "Lily can recommend one . . ."

"Holt, I haven't any money."

"I'll take care of it," Lily put in sharply. She coolly returned Angel's outraged look.

"Too—important," Holt gasped out, biting the inside of his cheek to quell the rising pain. "Can't have my girls fighting now . . ."

His weak smile was just as devastating as ever, even though Angel flinched inwardly at his words. His "girls"? How dare he put her in the same category as a . . . a harlot!

But Lily chuckled long and low at the joke, leaning over Angel to pat his uninjured arm. "Don't worry, love. We can handle it."

He nodded briefly and closed his eyes. The effort had exhausted him to the point of passing out. Angel reluctantly surrendered his limp hand and rose from the chair. Her face was a study in misery as she turned toward Lily.

"He trusts me to carry out his orders," she said. "But how can I worry about the mine when his life is in danger?"

Something akin to sympathy flashed briefly in Lily's green eyes. "You're his wife, chick. You promised Holt your loyalty. Love, honor and obey, remember?"

Angel didn't care to remember the proxy marriage. She only nodded disconsolately and twisted her hands together until they were strained white with tension.

"There must be some other way!" she burst out.

"Way?"

"To guard the mine. I don't want some town drunk sent up to the Lucky Devil. Heaven knows all the able-bodied men are already up at the silver mines! So what would that leave us to hire? Drunks and thieves!"

A measure of grudging respect showed in Lily's expression. "You're right," she said. "So what do you suggest?"

Angel thought for a moment. "I know the way," she said, and a brief smile teased at her lips as she thought of Rachel and remembered her promise to show the other girl the mine. "And I have a friend just begging to come along. Surely a couple of women could hold down the fort for just a few days."

"A couple?" Lily looked indignant at the idea. "Better make it three!"

Angel's jaw dropped as understanding dawned. "You?"

"Why not? I can pack a pistol cleaner than most and I'm a crack shot when it warrants. Besides, I'm sure you and your lady friend have confined yourselves to more genteel pursuits . . . like church socials and gossiping around town."

Lily's smirk made Angel want nothing so much as to slap the woman, but she remembered Holt's plea and gritted her teeth. So, she was to be saddled with a church-mouse and a notorious woman. Maybe someday she would cease to be surprised by the wild cards life dealt her.

"Are you sure you want to go, Angel?"

Looking past Neal's worried expression to the core of genuine concern underneath, Angel was touched and more than ever wanted to tell him the truth. But Lily had been insistent that she reveal their plan to nobody. So she and Rachel had concocted the tale of driving over to Clear Creek to visit an elderly aunt of Rachel's. It had satisfied Prudence Maxwell and Neal, too. If either of them had even suspected the truth, Angel knew they would have restrained both young women physically.

With a dazzling smile, she lied, "Of course I want to go! There's no use hanging about here, waiting for Holt to return, and I have no intention of being pitied any longer. I'll stay at Rachel's Aunt Clara's until he comes crawling back!"

Neal's expression clearly indicated what he thought of that likelihood, but he was too tactful to say anything. "Are you sure you wouldn't like me to come along? There could be some rough characters along the way."

"Nonsense. It's only a few measly miles on a good road, and besides, where would you stay in a maiden lady's home? Even a preacher doesn't need that sort of gossip."

"I suppose you're right," he said, but there was a puzzled light in his eyes that Angel carefully ignored.

"Thank you for bringing out my things. Here's Rachel now." Angel gave him a sisterly peck on the cheek, standing on tiptoe. Out of the corner of her eye she caught Rachel's wistful expression as the wagon drew near.

While Neal loaded her bags, Angel climbed up beside Rachel and tied on her bonnet. She felt something hard bump her hip and glanced down in surprise to see a heavy pistol hidden in the folds of Rachel's skirts. The other girl gave her a fleeting, devilish grin before turning to say goodbye to Neal Murphy.

As they drove off in a roiling cloud of dust, Rachel with a competent hand on the team of mules, Angel let her amusement bubble over.

"You're certainly expecting your adventure!"

"I'd be disappointed with anything less," Rachel admitted, patting the cracked leather holster at her side. "This was Pa's before he was killed in the War. The army sent it home, along with a note telling how much he prized it. Mother kept it even though there were no boys to give it to. Later I nabbed it and hid it in my room. I always fancied myself a Martha Jane Burke of sorts."

"Who?"

"Calamity Jane. Haven't you heard of her?" Rachel's face took on a dreamy look again. "She's the equal of any man at guns, and doesn't apologize for it. Why, she brings dire calamity down on any man who crosses her!"

Amazed at the quick, quiet revelation, Angel saw her new friend in a different light. She would have imagined Prudence Maxwell's daughter to be a prissy, self-righteous soul if she hadn't seen evidence of Rachel's pluck up front. Somehow it didn't seem so shocking when Rachel evidenced curiosity rather than outrage when Lily joined up with them on the road just out of town.

Seated atop a prancing white mare, Lily looked dressed for a day in the park. Her split-skirt riding habit was of green velvet and ostrich feathers sprouted from her rakish hat. Her hair was coiffed and dressed to one side, spilling in auburn curls all the way to her waist. If it was false hair she didn't bat an eyelash at wearing it, and she returned their wide-eyed gazes with a toothy white grin.

"Ready, ladies?" She tapped her spirited mare with a gold-tasseled quirt and fell into a brisk trot beside them.

Rachel leaned over to Angel and whispered excitedly, "I've never talked to a fancy lady before!"

"You haven't, eh?" Lily interrupted unabashedly and winked at Rachel's shock. "Well, chick, now's your chance. We've got a few hours to kill before reaching the mine. Might as well exchange our life stories."

Angel sensed the sarcasm, but Rachel didn't. "Oh, I've got ever so many questions!" she burst out, then bit her lip in consternation when Lily began to hoot and slap her thigh.

Angel only hoped they wouldn't run into anyone they knew along the way to the mine, because it certainly would prove difficult trying to explain both Lily's presence and why they were going the wrong way!

As the miles fell behind them, all three gradually relaxed and enjoyed the unusually warm fall day. Lily regaled the younger women with what she swore were true stories of some of her more interesting customers. Without mentioning names, she talked about the rich and famous who had heard her sing, and how she had once received a gold sovereign from a real European monarch.

Angel was skeptical, but Rachel oohed and aahed appreciatively when Lily produced the sovereign from her bodice, neatly drilled to fit on a gold chain around her neck.

"It's real," she told them, and bit the coin to prove it. She then removed her treasure and let Rachel inspect it at her leisure while Angel took over the reins for a time.

"How romantic!" Rachel gushed, thrilled with the thought of a king enamored of anybody, even a singer with a questionable history. Angel thought with amusement that her friend wasn't half so worldly as she pretended to be, Martha Jane Burke stories or not.

By the time Lily finished up her most dramatic tale, of how she had hidden an infamous pair of bank robbers in her bedroom and brazenly lied to the authorities about their whereabouts, they had reached the little valley.

Half rising from the wagon seat, Angel released a stricken cry. A blowing pile of ashes and a few chimney bricks were all that remained of the little cabin. It had been burned to the ground! And obviously quite recently, as the smoking pile of rubble attested.

"There's a warning if ever I saw one," Lily remarked grimly as she reined in her horse.

Angel felt tears stinging her eyes. The cabin was one thing that could be replaced, but not the memories or the precious Indian dress Holt's mother had owned. And suddenly her tears were those of rage, not misery. The other two glanced at her in alarm when she jumped down from the wagon and ran across the meadow toward the ruins.

All Angel found of the chest was a melted lump of iron that had been the lock. She started to pick it up and cried out when it scorched her fingers. Then Lily came rushing over and physically hauled her out from the ashes. The singer took off her expensive hat and crushed it as she beat at the smoldering hem of Angel's skirt.

Rachel met them halfway back to the wagon. "Oh, Angel, I'm so sorry!"

Dazed, Angel only looked at her helplessly until the dam broke. She fell into her friend's arms and quietly sobbed. It was like losing a part of her soul.

Finally the tears passed. "Who did it?" she cried, too angry and miserable to be consoled by Rachel's pats on her back. "Who would do something so hateful?"

Lily produced a battered but recognizable tin star she had found lying in the grass. "Not just anyone. Sometimes the law's the worst offender of all."

Angel turned and snatched it from her. She stared

red-eyed down at the badge and what it represented and let out a colorful oath. Rachel squeaked and Lily chuckled.

"He won't get away with it," Angel vowed.

"Who?" The others spoke in unison.

"Red Garrett. Of course he's behind this. He wants a cut of the mine, but by God, he's going to have to come through me to get it!"

Even Lily was startled by this revelation. "Honey, I never said—"

"Never mind how I know. I understand you can't risk crossing him yourself. I don't expect either of you to stand behind me on this one. I'll have to do it myself."

Suddenly Angel remembered the mine. She looked across the clearing in alarm, but the shaft appeared undisturbed. Of course, Garrett couldn't jump a claim if he sealed off the only means of getting the profits.

"Well, what now?" Rachel asked uneasily.

"I'm going to stay," Angel said. "It won't hurt me to sleep on the hard ground for one night."

"I reckon it won't at that," Lily agreed, moving to her horse's saddle, where she withdrew a rifle from the silver-chased scabbard.

Rachel hesitated only briefly. Then she also went to retrieve her trusty pistol from the wagon. "Just in case the adventure isn't over yet," she told the other two grimly before they began setting up camp for their stay.

Chapter Eight

Somewhere in the trees, a horned owl hooted low and deep. Angel muttered and drew the blankets farther up and rolled over onto one side, trying to get comfortable. A rock dug into her spine and another into her thigh. She thrashed a moment to reposition herself. What had woken her up? She blinked sleepily against the white glare of a full moon, then froze as she happened to glance across the moonlit meadow.

A few feet away Rachel snored softly. Lily had volunteered to take first watch, but Angel could see the other woman's figure slumped back unconscious against a boulder. She stiffened when she saw a dark shadow gliding from the trees.

"Lily," she hissed. But her voice choked off in her tight throat. The shadow hesitated, a big black figure, and Angel felt her skin go clammy with fear. It was a man, not an animal. It moved upright, and too stealthily to be anything else.

Lily's rifle lay propped up against the boulder at her side. Angel was lying a good ten feet away. She eyed the gun and the creeping shadow and decided to take the chance. But for a moment her limbs wouldn't move. She was so scared, her body had frozen in place.

But she had to do something. The other two women were fast asleep and she couldn't wake them without catching the man's attention. Numbly, Angel forced her body to obey her mind. She began to crawl across the cold ground, a lump of wriggling blankets, pausing occasionally to gauge her chances as the shadow advanced.

A few feet more and she'd be safe. Dry-mouthed, she felt a spasm of terror clench her stomach as the intruder drew ever closer. Both of them apparently had the same goal: Lily's rifle. Angel didn't know if he'd seen her or not; she was mostly hidden by the boulder. But if it was Red Garrett, he was about to get the surprise of his life.

Her fingers inched over the boulder to grasp the barrel of the gun. They closed home just as Lily stirred. Quick as a cat, the singer's hand shot out and jerked the weapon from Angel's grasp. Then Lily whirled and leveled the rifle on the other woman.

"Not me!" Angel croaked. "Him!"

She gestured desperately at the shadow that suddenly materialized into a man. Lily spun back around, but a trifle too late. A huge fist contacted with her jaw, and the singer slumped back against the boulder.

"Rachel!" Angel screamed.

The moonlight threw the ugly, scarred face of the intruder into sharp relief as he whirled toward her. Angel struggled out from the imprisoning blankets and lurched out of his reach. She heard his muttered oath as he swiped at her and missed. She forgot about everything but the need to save herself.

Angel only made it a few pitiful few feet. His foul breath came hard and fast in her ear when he grabbed a handful of her hair and yanked her backwards, lifting her off the ground. White-hot pain lanced her scalp, and her scream was cut off as his big hand began to squeeze her windpipe shut.

Then she heard an explosion just as stars behind her eyelids blossomed. She fell, jarring both elbows on the ground. Choking and gasping, Angel rolled out of the way just as the man's body crumpled to the earth beside her.

Angel lay wheezing for several moments as the world slowly righted itself. Her hands on her bruised neck, she struggled to her knees and and saw the trembling figure of Rachel Maxwell standing there.

Rachel's shaking white hands held her father's pistol in a death grip. Her eyes were huge, glistening pools as she stared at the unmoving man.

Lily groaned and stirred. The other two women's eyes met at last, and Angel managed a weak croak.

"Thanks, Calamity."

They buried the body in the morning in a shallow grave just inside the forest's edge. Angel turned away the moment the deed was done, letting Lily tamp down the moist earth with a shiny black patent leather shoe.

"There," the redhead said briskly, gingerly touching her bruised jaw. "That'll do. No need to go to a lot of trouble just so the animals can dig him up again."

Rachel shuddered visibly. Angel went to her friend and offered quiet words of comfort.

"You saved our lives, Rachel. He was up to no good. I'm glad you were here."

"But . . . but I killed a man." Rachel's teeth were chattering.

"Don't be a ninny," Lily said in a strident tone. "He would have been happily shoveling us three under instead, given the chance." Her words were blunt but well-meant. "I have the damndest feeling we were followed up here."

"Me, too," Angel said. In full daylight she had studied the features of the stranger and wondered why he seemed faintly familiar. Then it had come to her with a rush of shock. The pitted scars supplied the answer. He had been the man quarreling with Holt when she had first arrived in Clear Creek.

Jack Olsen was his name. Lily knew him. She said he was a no-good weasel, a tough who could be hired by anyone for the right price. She showed no remorse when she helped the other two drag him into the forest, and even less when they buried him.

Rachel went to place stones around the shallow grave. "Even a criminal deserves a marker," she whispered as the tears streamed freely down her freckled cheeks.

Lily made an irritated noise and stomped off. Angel followed her, catching up to the other woman as Lily moved to saddle her horse.

Lily was shaking her head in disgust. "It's hard to believe that's the same girl who had the gumption to pull the trigger last night."

"Everyone has a soft spot," Angel said. "Even you."

"That so?" Lily jeered. "What's mine?"

"Holt."

Angel felt a rush of jealousy when the other woman didn't deny it. She watched Lily plunge a fist into her mare's belly to force the animal to exhale, and then draw up the cinch with more force than necessary.

"You little fool," Lily muttered. "You don't know the first thing about me and Holt. So I suggest you keep your mouth shut."

"Then why are you so defensive? You love him, don't you?"

Lily threw down the stirrups and whirled around. "Listen, chick, I only came up here to watch the mine because Holt asked me to. That doesn't include answering questions from his nosy little wife."

Angel saw the high color in the woman's cheeks and was even more convinced the singer was in love with Holt, and probably had been for a very long time. She felt sorry for Lily and for herself, because she suspected no woman would ever own Holt Murphy's heart.

"I'm sorry," Angel said quietly.

Lily only stared at her with hard green eyes for a long moment, then swung up into the saddle. As she briskly arranged her velvet skirts, she said, "I'm going back to Oro. You ladies better wait awhile before following me in."

"We're not going to Oro. We'll visit Rachel's aunt over in Clear Creek as planned."

Lily gave a curt nod and rode off. Angel could sense the animosity lingering in the air long after the other woman had left.

* * *

Rachel finally wandered out of the woods. Her skirts were stained with mud and grass, and bright tears still dotted her cheeks. "I put some flowers on the grave."

"I take it you don't care much for adventure now."

Swallowing hard, Rachel shook her head. "I'm sorry I ever wanted to come up here. No wonder it's called the Devil Mine."

"Lucky Devil," Angel corrected her automatically, and then paused. Why had her father and Arthur Murphy chosen such an ominous name for their mine? Why not Lady Luck or Annie Mae or something relatively amusing and harmless?

There was something very dark and frightening about that endless tunnel delving into the heart of the earth. Angel tore her eyes from the dark hole and shivered.

"Let's get going, Rachel. It's a long drive to Clear Creek."

She didn't have to suggest it twice. Both women gratefully climbed into the wagon, and Angel cast one sorrowful look over the ruins of the little cabin. Then, with a brisk click to the team of mules, she pointed the wagon north.

Rachel's hands shook noticeably as she poured the tea into eggshell-thin porcelain cups for three.

"What's the matter with you, Rachel?" Clara Maxwell's querulous voice cut through the silence like a finely honed knife. "I declare, you're spilling priceless Earl Grey all over my fine lace tablecloth."

"Sorry, Auntie." Rachel set down the silver teapot but didn't raise her eyes to meet her relative's.

Angel smoothly intervened, distributing the cups and overlooking the fact that all three saucers had their share of tea, as well.

"I've never known you to have a case of the nerves, my girl," Clara continued. She was an older lady, all the more imposing in glistening black bombazine. Her neatly rolled white hair resembled two fat sausages dangling on either side of her head, and they danced about as she shook her head. "I want you to take a dose of Mrs. Carter's Nerve Tonic in your tea, Rachel."

Brooking no argument, Clara Maxwell poured a healthy dollop into her niece's teacup and nodded with satisfaction. "That will buck you right up, child. Would you care to try some, Mrs. Murphy?"

"No, thank you." Angel hid a smile. "I feel quite recovered from our journey already."

She gazed around the cozy little parlor, admiring the Victorian decor and old-world atmosphere of Clara Maxwell's home. Clara's tart voice still held an English accent, a little faded by living on American soil but distinguishable just the same. She wondered why the old lady had chosen to stay in Colorado Territory after her husband's death and asked why.

Clara's lips curved in a faint smile at the question. "Mercy, it never occurred to me to leave. A woman's place is at her husband's side, no matter if he's six feet under."

At the mention of death Rachel made a choking sound and set her saucer down with a clatter.

Angel looked at her friend with alarm and reached out to touch Rachel's tightly clenched hands.

"My niece obviously doesn't approve of widow's

weeds," Clara sniffed. "But a lady has no place gallivanting about after her husband dies, and I'm quite content
with my lot."

"You have a lovely home," Angel said, hoping to
change the subject.

"Indeed. James had it built for me on our twentieth
anniversary. He didn't want me to be homesick for England, you see. Now, there was a considerate man." The
old woman's eyes softened in memory. "Perhaps you'll be
fortunate enough to have a home of your own someday,
Mrs. Murphy."

So Clara Maxwell already knew about Holt and the
cabin. Angel forced a smile to curve her lips.

"Perhaps. Actually, I find I am a bit fatigued after all.
I think Rachel and I would do well to take a short nap."

"Of course." Clara approved of women having delicate
constitutions, and seemed relieved to find an excuse for
Rachel's odd behavior. "Dulcie will show you to your
rooms."

Dulcibel, Aunt Clara's ancient maidservant, had come
over from England with her mistress eons ago. She was a
stooped and wrinkled little creature, who openly scowled
in disapproval at their guests' soiled gowns.

"Best be giving those frights to me," she told Angel
gruffly. "It'll be a day-long chore to get out those grass
stains, it will."

Angel obliged by changing into a borrowed dressing
gown and handing Dulcie her dress. Rachel did the same,
and for a long time it was quiet in the house, except for
the tick-tock of the old grandfather clock in the hall.

Sitting on the edge of the guest bed, Angel let out a long
sigh. She was tired but not sleepy and didn't wish to lie

down. Then she heard a muffled sob through the wall. Rachel! Her heart went out to the young woman, and she quietly slipped out of her room and padded down the hall.

Opening the door to Rachel's room, she went inside. The shades had been pulled and in the dusky gloom Rachel Maxwell sat curled up in a rocker, crying her eyes out.

"Rachel, what's wrong?" Angel hurried over to comfort her friend.

"I k-killed a man and my soul is forfeit now! Oh, Angel, you don't understand! I'm lost!"

"Nonsense!" Angel spoke more sharply than she'd intended. "You know he meant us harm. You did what you had to do."

Angel waited until Rachel's sobs quieted, then reached out and drew the hands down from the freckled face.

"Listen to me. You saved my life. Anyone could see that."

"E-even Pastor Murphy?"

So that's what this was all about! "Yes, even Neal," Angel said firmly. "Now dry your eyes and get some rest. We'll head back to Oro tomorrow, and nobody will be the wiser."

"But I won't forget," Rachel sniffled. "And every time Pastor Murphy looks at me I'll remember and feel guilty all over again."

Angel sighed with momentary defeat. "Then perhaps you should tell him."

"No, never!"

"Rachel, I think Neal would understand. And I wouldn't be a bit surprised if he absolved you completely. Isn't it worth a try?"

There was a brief silence while Rachel struggled with

her conscience. Then, in a tiny voice, she asked, "Will you come with me to tell him?"

"Of course." Angel patted her on the shoulder. "Now, I'll turn down the covers and you hop into bed for a spell. You don't want that old virago Dulcie to catch us and tell Aunt Clara, do you?"

Rachel giggled a little. "No."

"Then into bed with you." Angel tucked her in and smiled at the sudden silence. Rachel had fallen asleep instantly from sheer exhaustion. She tiptoed back to her own room and crawled under the covers with a sigh. Maybe it wasn't such a bad idea to take a little nap after all. Right after the thought went through her head, Angel fell fast asleep.

Angel stared at Lily in disbelief. "Holt is gone? Where? How?"

The other woman shrugged a little defensively. "He slipped out the back way last night when I was working. I came up after the show and the room was empty."

"How could you leave him alone?"

The green eyes flashed. "Listen, honey, he wasn't going anywhere. Doc said the laudanum would keep him down. I never thought he would leave while his arm was still so sore."

Angel felt frustration claw at her as she gazed at the actress. Lily looked just as worried as she was. Angel's first priority had been to check on Holt when she had gotten back to Oro. She hadn't cared who saw her slip into the alley leading to the whorehouse. Concern for Holt superseded everything, even her own reputation.

"Where do you think he went?"

Lily shrugged. "He could be anywhere. But chances are pretty good he went up to the mine."

Angel bit her lower lip, worrying it between her teeth. "I have to find him."

"Don't be a fool. You've already risked his life enough!" The angry words escaped before Lily could stop them, and she pressed a hand to her red lips.

"What do you know that I don't?" Angel demanded, taking a single step toward the other woman. "What did Holt tell you?"

Lily raised her chin a notch. "He didn't have to tell me anything. When you said you owned half the mine I put it together myself. He's so busy trying to protect you that he's forgotten all about himself. And sooner or later it's going to get him killed."

"He doesn't care that much about me."

"Keep lying to yourself if it keeps you happy," Lily retorted.

"What do you mean?"

"I mean he loves you, and you're too much the fool to see it! He found out you rode up to guard the mine and I'm sure he went after you."

"Who told him?"

"The stupid girl I sent to take him dinner didn't think it was a secret. She blabbed everything." Lily let loose an angry sigh and turned to pace the velvet-flocked parlor. She twisted a sparkling ring on her finger as she spoke. "I'll admit I tried to turn him against you, chick. When Holt told me he was married I imagined some overblown hussy trying to worm her way inside his pockets. And I was bound and determined to see it didn't happen."

Lily paused and took a deep breath. "But when I saw you at the ladies' social I knew why Holt had married you. You're young and beautiful and . . . acceptable."

"Acceptable?"

"Of course. You don't think he'd ever marry a madam, do you?" Lily laughed bitterly. Her hand shook as she brushed back a loose tendril of auburn hair. "Even a half-breed has better taste than that."

"Stop it, Lily." Angel saw the tortured light in the woman's eyes and put her own private pain aside. "I know Holt cares for you. It's in his voice, his eyes."

"But not his touch. Never his touch," the other woman whispered. "I lied to you, Angel. Holt hasn't ever slept with me. Hell, it's not that I haven't tried."

The silence was broken by an explosive burst of laughter in the other room. Someone started to pound a lusty tune on the piano and the clinking of glasses could be heard.

"Saloon's open," Lily said with a twist of her lips. "I've got to get backstage."

"Where's Valentine?" A man shouted as if on cue. "We wanna hear our own Irish Nightingale sing!"

"Hold on to your britches," another voice said as the music reached a crescendo. "Ya ain't gonna believe this."

"Aw, come on, Sheriff. No woman can be *that* talented."

Hearing the male sniggers through the thin wall, Angel stiffened. Lily had left to don her costume for the night. Angel felt her blood begin to boil, listening to Red Garrett brag about his male prowess in a loud, coarse voice. Just hearing his voice made her tremble with outrage. She remembered Neal's warning not to cross the man, and

Lily's wariness when Angel had threatened to bring Garrett to his knees. Now was her perfect chance. Angel didn't think Garrett knew her by sight, and even if he did, he'd never see past spangles and sequins to the woman beneath.

A slow smile curved Angel's lips and a vengeful gleam lit her eyes as she left the parlor in the direction Lily had taken. She would make this one night the sheriff of Oro City would never forget.

Chapter Nine

Angel swirled a finger in the pot of rouge and raised it to her cheek. She applied the makeup with a heavy hand in a sweeping round circle, as she had seen the other girls do. A puff of powder removed the perspiration on her brow. She stepped back and studied herself in the cheval mirror. Perfect!

The gown she had found in a dressing-room closet backstage was brassy enough to satisfy Angel. Made of pink taffeta with black sequins and lace, it was shockingly low-cut, nearly baring the entire upper half of her breasts. She couldn't wear her stays under it, either, and it felt strange being able to breathe so freely.

Hairpins rained everywhere as Angel shook out her hair into a soft golden cloud. Her reddened lips parted in a smile. Yes, it would do. The sheriff would be too busy gaping at her body to see the calculating gleam in her eye.

Angel didn't pause to consider the consequences as she sailed boldly out into the saloon, balancing a tray on her right hand. She was immediately aware of mens' stares from around the crowded room, and a rustle of interest.

A new girl was always welcome. Several men tried to catch her eye as she crossed over to the bar, but Angel ignored them.

The bartender was a taciturn old-timer Lily had referred to as Joe. In her most cajoling voice, Angel asked Joe to fill her tray with drinks. The old man looked at her with rheumy eyes and squinted a little. Angel let out a low breath of relief when he didn't question her request.

"New 'un, huh? Well, put it up here." He slapped the velvet-padded bar and Angel obligingly set down the tray so he could fill it with shot glasses of whiskey. She glanced around the milling saloon, then reddened when she saw several men staring at her openly. Hurriedly she tore her gaze away and was forced to eye the figure of a nude woman stretched out on the huge painting behind Joe.

"Here ya go, missy." The bartender slapped down the last glass and turned to fill someone else's. Angel took a deep breath and lifted the tray. It was surprisingly heavy. She waited a moment to balance it, then started off. She got no farther than a few feet when she got her first pinch.

Cheeks flaming, Angel nearly dropped the tray. She bit down an outraged cry as she spun about. The prospector only winked at her and chuckled. She bumped into another table and nearly upset her drinks in the lap of a well-to-do gent garbed in black.

"Sit and stay awhile," the gambler invited in a dangerously silky voice. Angel mumbled something and scurried off.

Where was Red Garrett? Her eyes scanned the crowded saloon desperately. He must be against the wall somewhere. Then she spied a table in the back of the saloon with three men. One of them wore a badge.

Maybe they issued more than one, Angel thought bitterly. So when a lawman lost one while burning a homestead he could pick up another when he got back to town.

Forcing down her fear, Angel made a beeline for Garrett's table. Behind her the lights dimmed, and the noise trailed off as a spotlight fell on the stage. She had to stop and get her bearings in the sudden darkness. She turned to face the stage when a husky contralto began to sing.

Lily stood on stage, wearing a red spangled dress and a feather boa. Shivers ran down Angel's bare arms at the aching beauty of the song. It was a sad ballad, but the audience seemed to eat it up. It was obvious Lily had a rare talent. The words said something about unrequited love, and Angel studied the woman's face as she sang. Lily's eyes sparkled as brightly as the diamond collar around her throat.

Why, she's crying, Angel thought with some concern as the song ended. The next selection was more upbeat and raucous, and the men began to cheer and beat the tables with their fists as a piano player with garters around both arms pounded gleefully in double time. After it was over, Angel started off again, musing over Lily's plight. *She loves Holt as much as I do and neither one of us can win.*

Soon Angel was staring down into the heavy-jowled face of Red Garrett. There was no mistaking the man, whose rusty banner of hair was neatly slicked back over his scalp. The sheriff saw her then and gave Angel a wink.

"See somethin' you like, sugar?" Garrett drawled, and behind the wide handlebar mustache his broken and yellowed teeth were bared at her in a grin.

Now it was up to Angel to soothe his ego and lull him into trusting her. With her blue eyes appropriately wide, she cooed, "Why, Sheriff, fancy you dropping in like this. We sure are honored. This here's just a little thank-you from the house."

She plunked down a whiskey glass in front of the man, hoping he didn't notice her trembling hand. Quick as dry lightning, Garrett snagged her arm and held it fast.

"I'd rather have the house special," he leered, letting his bloodshot eyes travel up and down her body. "I don't reckon I've seen you a'fore. And you look like a right nice tasty piece to me."

Angel forced a giggle into her voice. "Forgive me, Sheriff. I'm a little bit nervous tonight. I'm new here."

Garrett sniggered, jabbing the hard-bitten man on his right. "Hear that, O'Shea? The new girl's got the jitters. Hell, honey, if all you need is to be broke in, I'm your man."

Disgusting pig, Angel thought, as his sour whiskeybreath floated up to her. *I'm not some filly you can break to your hand!* Keeping her voice light and cajoling, she said, "I can't do anything without asking Miss Valentine first. I'll just tiptoe backstage and get her permission."

Eyeing her a bit suspiciously, Garrett countered, "Lily knows better than to send out her girls without teachin' them the ropes first. What did you say your name was, honey?"

Without thinking, she blurted out the truth. "Angel."

Garrett started to rise from his chair. "I'll just have a little talk with Miss Valentine. 'Less this is just a shy act on your part . . . *Angel.*"

At his brief hesitation Angel seized her only chance. With a pout, she said, "Why, Sheriff, you're just too smart for little ole me. I thought you'd like something fresh and innocent to go with your hard old liquor tonight."

With a suggestive wink and shimmy, Angel stopped the man from alerting Lily in the nick of time. Garrett licked his chops like a hungry dog and drew her closer to him.

"Kind of excitin', gettin' picked by the law, ain't it?"

"It sure is," Angel agreed readily, trying not to gag on the whiskey fumes spewing from him.

Garrett made an absent gesture to the other two men at the table. "I'll be back later." He slid a thick arm around Angel's waist and drew her toward the stairs.

Now that her plan had clicked so easily into place, Angel panicked. She'd counted on Garrett being intrigued by her, but never expected him to be so outright aggressive. Now what was she going to do?

All she wanted was a chance to loosen Garrett up enough so that he'd confess to burning the cabin, and then . . . then she'd figure some way to make him pay. But she'd certainly done it this time! The sheriff made Willard Craddock seem like a prude.

At the bottom of the staircase Angel snagged the passing post with one arm and hung on. Garrett shot her a surprised look.

"What's the matter, Angel?"

"Why, I never go upstairs without a bottle of my favorite Confederate whiskey," Angel lisped in her most seductive southern drawl. "Let me wheedle old Joe for a pint and I'll join you upstairs in a minute, lover."

She felt Garrett's eyes scouring her carefully for a full minute before he said gruffly, "You don't need likker when you're with a real man, sugar."

"But I get real . . . interesting with a little firewater in my veins," she breathed against his ear, holding her own breath so she didn't have to smell the rank combination of unwashed man and malt liquor. "I guess you could say I'm even a little bit . . . dangerous."

Garrett's eyes nearly popped from his head at the sultry promise in her voice. "Go git your bottle, sweetie. I'll just make myself comfy upstairs."

Watching to make sure he went up the stairs, Angel lingered just long enough to buy some time. What a foolish idea! She had almost gotten herself in hot water too deep to swim across.

A deep breath of relief escaped Angel as she slipped past the bar and melted into the shadows of the saloon. She avoided the bright lights and activity and headed for the stage, where the velvet curtains were now closed. She prayed there was a rear exit from backstage.

As she fumbled to find the opening in the curtains, Angel was startled when someone seized her flailing hand and jerked her roughly through.

"Are you trying to get yourself killed?" Holt demanded furiously, his silver eyes raking up and down Angel with barely concealed rage.

"Holt!"

She cried out in mingled relief and surprise, but he only made an angry noise and clamped a broad hand over her mouth.

"I'm sure I'll regret this, but you're coming with me. I don't have any choice now."

There was annoyance in his low voice as he hauled Angel through the darkened corridors that led from the stage entrance to an unmarked rear door.

"If you have any sense at all, you won't scream." He released her just outside, where the cloak of darkness provided a temporary respite.

"Of course I won't scream." Angel saw the silent criticism in his silver gaze. "I just can't believe you're up and about . . . and in one piece."

She eyed his left arm and saw that it had been thickly and carefully bandaged so he could use it again. He released a low chuckle as he read her thoughts.

"It was necessary to sneak out a little earlier than you two ladies planned."

"But Lily—"

"Oh, Lily knew what I had to do. She didn't like it much, but her line of business calls for common sense. After I proved to her I could get around without that damned laudanum, she finally agreed to let me out of that fancy hospital of hers."

Angel's temper suddenly flared. "You deceived me! You let me think you were fighting gangrene and fever, and I made a fool out of myself over you!"

"Oh, the fever was real enough, sweetheart. But for your benefit I'll repeat myself once again. I had to fake a more serious injury in order to draw out my enemies. They wouldn't have moved so openly if they thought I still could hold a gun. And by the way, rouge looks better in the pot than on your face. You look like a cheap dance-hall girl."

"You ought to know," Angel muttered. She added, "That was the plan. I wanted Garrett to fall for my act."

"Why?"

She was silent for a moment, and then countered with a question of her own.

"Holt, why did you trust Lily, and not me?"

He didn't seem to hear the genuine hurt and quiet bewilderment in her voice. "Believe me, it was safer this way for everyone concerned. As soon as I find out for sure who's behind all this, I can show my hand. But right now I need to lay low."

Angel was silent, drinking in his nearness and his strength. It hurt more than it should, knowing Holt had taken Lily into his confidence and not her. Of course, she was glad he wasn't seriously injured, but the fact that he had deceived her in the first place stung.

Holt continued, "Speaking of laying low, you sure risked a lot tonight. Just what were you hoping to prove?"

The disapproval in his tone pushed Angel to the edge. "Nothing. I wanted to get a confession from Garrett, that's all. Holt, someone burned the cabin to the ground, and—"

"I know," he cut in wryly. "Lily told me."

Lily again! Was that all she would ever hear?

With an exasperated noise, Angel snapped, "Is there anything that singer hasn't told you yet?"

"Only what you're doing here, and why you're dressed like that."

"Lily doesn't know. I filched a dress and did it all myself." Angel's chin lifted a notch as she considered his handsome face half hidden in the shadows. Holt's smirk was really too much. "It seemed the most expedient way to get the sheriff to admit he burned our cabin."

"Expedient?" Holt laughed as he looked at her incredulously. "Sweetheart, only you would describe luring the law to your bed as 'expedient'!"

His mocking laughter didn't go over well. "I didn't plan to go to bed with him!" she hissed. "It was only a ploy to loosen him up and—then—uhm—"

"Yes?" Holt quirked an interested brow at her.

"Well, I would have figured out something!"

Angel's hurt pride was obviously lost on Holt.

"It's the thought that counts, I suppose. I know you were upset over losing the cabin."

"Upset? I suppose Lily told you that, too." Angel sniffed. "I'm your wife, but you don't trust me half as much as you trust that . . . that 'singer.'"

"I happen to have known that 'singer' for nearly fifteen years, while you, my sweet Angel, I've known far less than a month. Who do you think I would trust?"

The corners of his eyes crinkled in a wry smile and Angel had to admit defeat. She couldn't stay angry at Holt, not when she was so very relieved he was even alive.

"What now?" she asked him softly.

"We're going to Denver tonight."

"Denver?" she exclaimed. "Why?"

"Two reasons. One, to secure my rights to the mine. I need everything spelled out in black and white in order to make sure there are no legal loopholes." Holt hesitated, then looked at her with steady gray eyes. "And two . . . I'm sending you home."

Home! There was no home but with Holt now. Angel started to speak, but he cautioned her to silence when a sudden burst of noise erupted from the saloon behind them.

"Bar fight," Holt said succinctly, looking a bit regretful to be missing out on the fun. But he took Angel by the arm and steered her ahead of him. "There's a stagecoach waiting at the end of the alley. Get in and wait for me."

"Where are you going?"

"Back to the saloon for a minute. I need to tie up some loose ends."

Lily again. Angel felt the bitter bile of jealousy rising in her throat but quickly swallowed it down. "What about Neal?"

"What about him?" Holt was exasperated. "We don't need his permission to come and go!" He gave her a gentle push in the direction of the street. "Go quickly and don't stop for anything. Dressed like that you're a natural target."

Angel reluctantly moved to obey. When Holt had disappeared behind her she paused on the street corner and glanced around warily. The streets were empty and the parsonage was only a few blocks away. What would it hurt to go and get a few clothes? She certainly couldn't go to Denver dressed like this!

With a self-righteous little nod Angel hurried past the waiting stagecoach and down the boardwalk. She felt the cold keenly through the thin taffeta of the saloon gown and clutched at the tiny wisps that served as shoulder straps to keep the bodice from shifting and fully exposing her charms. She was halfway there when she heard a hoarse male shout behind her. Oh, Lord, don't let it be Sheriff Garrett!

Angel quickened her pace, but the rapid patter of hoofbeats gained on her as she fled into the dark.

"Hey, you there, Angel!"

Angel lapsed into a run along the boardwalk, paced by the ugly roan Garrett rode. He tossed out a few ominous threats about what he would do when he caught her, and Angel's only chance was to stay off the road. Her heart pounding and her breath coming in gasps,

Angel nearly wept with relief when she finally reached the church.

She threw herself at the door and tugged. Her horror grew when she found it locked. Behind her, Garrett snarled a particularly colorful oath and began to dismount from his horse. Luckily for Angel, he was so drunk it gave her the precious seconds needed to bolt around the rear of the building to the window of Neal's room.

Her urgent tapping on the glass and Garrett's growing bellows finally brought a light on in the rectory.

"Hurry, oh, please hurry!" Angel whispered, trying to melt into the shadows when the sheriff suddenly lurched around the corner. At last she heard the door on the street side opening.

"Neal!" Angel cried, taking the risk she would be caught when Garrett turned and lunged in her direction.

Further cries were cut off as the sheriff caught her and yanked her into his arms. "Like to play games, huh, Angel?" he snarled, squeezing Angel so tightly, she thought she would faint.

A flare of light fell over them. "Unhand the lady, Sheriff," Neal Murphy said quietly.

Angel saw a lantern bobbing in Neal's left hand, a gun in his right. So did Red Garrett.

With a cold smile, the lawman asked, "Now, why you wanna stir up trouble, Preacher? This ain't none of your business, so why don't you just crawl back in your hidey-hole, pin on your collar, and pretend you don't hear nothin'?"

"Because you are on church property, sir, and therefore it is my business. The young lady is requesting asylum. By God's Law, I must give it to her."

"God's Law, hell! I'm the only law here!" Garrett snarled, thrusting Angel aside to confront Neal instead. "You high-and-mighty Murphys forget your place now and then, but I'm sure as shootin' gonna remind you now, boy. Put down that piece a'fore I have you arrested for tamperin' with justice."

"Justice? I don't see how molesting this young woman is contributing to the safety of Oro."

"Young woman, my eye! She's one of Valentine's whores and deserves whatever she gets."

If Neal was wondering why Angel was dressed like a saloon girl, he gave no indication. He merely inclined his head toward Garrett.

"It's your choice, Sheriff. Either you let the girl come safely into my custody or I will be forced to take dire action against you."

Garrett snorted in disbelief. "You'd never shoot."

"Perhaps not, but I have no qualms about discussing this matter with Mrs. Garrett."

At the mere mention of his wife something miraculous happened to the sheriff. He whitened and then purpled with outrage, opened his beefy jowls to say something else, and then apparently thought better of it.

"I wonder if Justine would be as understanding of your plight as I am," Neal goaded him softly.

"Damn you, preacher." Garrett spoke through clenched teeth. "If you wasn't wearin' that collar, I'd—"

Neal merely smiled. Angel was surprised at the cool head he'd kept.

"Good night, Sheriff. Give my regards to Mrs. Garrett."

After Red Garrett stomped off, muttering, Angel found

her breath and rushed toward Neal. She stopped just short of embracing him from sheer gratitude.

"I can explain everything—"

"Don't." Neal sighed wearily as he turned and led the way back to the open door. "I'm quickly learning not to be surprised by anything you or Holt do."

Angel felt like a chastened child and wanted badly to make amends. "Holt's back," she blurted, noticing it gave Neal slight pause as he turned and bolted the rectory door behind them. "He's taking me to Denver tonight. Or, rather, he was." She glanced ruefully to the window, wondering if the stagecoach had left without her.

"Then he's—ah—moved out of Miss Valentine's?"

Angel nodded vigorously. "It wasn't anything like I thought, Neal. We've made amends. I don't know if I'll ever understand him, but . . . I care for him." Her voice was quiet as she confessed her feelings, but Neal seemed preoccupied.

"Is it wise, Angel? Going to Denver when winter could strike anytime?"

She shrugged. "There are too many important things to do there." She remembered Holt's vow to send her back to Missouri. If it was at all in her power, she'd stop him.

"Besides, we're going in a stagecoach. It won't be like we're exposed to the elements." Angel took a deep breath. "I suppose you're wondering why I'm dressed like this."

Neal gave her an indulgent smile. "Not really. But I'll listen if you want to tell me."

"It's a long story. I slipped into Lily's to try to lure the sheriff into confessing something."

"Lily's?" Neal frowned at the obvious familiarity.

Angel hesitated. What could it hurt to tell Holt's own brother about the woman?

"She and Holt are just old friends—really," she said, wondering why she was trying so hard to convince herself as well as Neal. "Holt explained everything to me, and I was being rather a ninny about the whole thing."

"Most wives wouldn't be so understanding."

"Oh, but there's nothing to understand . . ."

Just as she finished speaking, a loud, angry pounding came at the door, startling them both. Garrett again?

"Damn you, Angel," Holt Murphy said evenly when Neal finally answered the summons. "I told you to wait for me."

"I couldn't go in these clothes! And the church was just a short skip away." Actually, that wasn't true. It had seemed more like a thousand miles when she had been chased all the way!

Without acknowledging Neal, Holt came halfway in, his broad shoulders filling the entire doorframe. "Go on and change then," he said grudgingly. "We've got to leave."

The two brothers matched silent gazes as Angel briefly disappeared down the hall. Finally Neal inquired softly, "Does it have to be like this, Holt?"

"You know it does. We have nothing in common but our last name."

Holt's terse retort didn't faze Neal. He said quietly, "There's Angel now. She's found a place in her heart for me, even if you haven't."

At his words Holt jerked slightly. Then his square jaw hardened, and his eyes were chips of ice as he stared the older man down. "I don't forget a wrong, Neal."

"I was young. We both were. Before I found the Lord—"

"A leopard can't change its spots," Holt interrupted flatly. "And a snake remains a snake, even after it sheds its skin."

Neal blanched just as Angel reappeared, hastily dressed in a dark blue serge gown, her cheeks bright pink where she'd scrubbed them free of rouge.

Reaching up to buss Neal's cheek, she murmured, "Thank you. I won't forget what you've done."

"Will you be gone long?" the young preacher asked.

"Long enough," Holt said curtly. "Come on, Angel."

"I need to pack my bags—"

"I'll buy you a new dress in Denver. A dozen if you want." His unexpected generosity wasn't entirely for her benefit, she saw. Holt's hard gray gaze was fixed on Neal instead.

Chapter Ten

The stagecoach rumbled off into the darkness before Angel remembered her promise to Rachel. In all of the excitement she had forgotten to ease her friend's confession to Neal. She reached over and urgently touched Holt's arm.

"We've got to go back! I need to talk to Neal."

Even though it was dark inside the coach she could sense his scowl. "That's impossible now. I wouldn't turn back if the Devil himself asked me to."

"But it will only take a few minutes. I promised to intervene on a friend's behalf with your brother."

"Good Lord, woman, what are you meddling in now?" Holt sighed with exasperation and neatly plucked her beseeching hand off his sleeve. "I told you to stay clear of Neal. And especially his parishioners. Now there's a sorry lot of folks if ever I've seen one."

"How would you know?" Angel asked indignantly. "I doubt you've so much as darkened the doorway of a church!"

The rising moon cast sharp relief on Holt's features,

and she saw he was silently laughing at her. It made her angry, and even more determined to return to Oro.

Angel turned and reached for the window. Lifting the leather flap, she quickly stuck her head out and hollered, "Driver, stop!"

The words were barely out when Holt yanked her back in, to land with a jarring thump on the seat beside him.

"What are you doing?" he demanded, and there was an aggravated tone to his deep voice she couldn't miss.

Angel struggled to free herself from Holt's strong grip, but the powerful hands encircling each of her wrists didn't relent in the slightest. With an inspiration born of desperation, she bent her head and bit his right knuckle.

It worked. Holt let out an oath and let her go, just as the stagecoach lurched to a stop and spun her to the seat across from him. Angel wasn't hurt, but her hastily pinned hair tumbled down to her waist, and they matched glares as the driver climbed down and walked back to see what was going on.

Holt reached out and threw open the door with a resounding bang. He cradled his injured hand out of view as he snapped, "Drive on, Gil. There's no reason to stop."

"But I heard someone call out—"

"That was me," Angel said huffily. She immediately regretted it when the driver, a huge bearded man, swung in her direction and eyed her loosened hair.

There was a twinkle in his tone when he spoke. "I won't interrupt again," he said meaningfully to Holt, then he winked and walked back to the team.

Angel released her breath in a long, slow hiss. "What a horrible man! I could almost read his mind."

"No, I think he read mine." At Holt's low chuckle,

Angel's eyes flew to his face. A roguish grin was spreading over his handsome features, and he added softly, "You look beautiful by Colorado moonlight. Beautiful, and you're all mine."

"Holt—" she began warily.

"There's nobody to hear us out here, Angel." He pulled the door shut, letting the darkness seal them off. The stagecoach was soon underway again. "I won't lie about what I want. I want to make love to you."

"Here?" she squeaked in surprise.

"Why not?"

She refused to let the silky promise in his voice sway her. "I wouldn't make love to you again if you were the last man on earth!"

Holt chuckled. "It's a long drive to Denver, sweet-heart."

Tingles raced up her arms as Angel fidgeted on the seat across from him. She brushed back her mass of tangled blond hair and saw him watching her intently, like a hawk trained on its prey.

"Come here, Angel."

"No."

"You're going to get mighty cold over there all by yourself."

She hesitated, her eyes searching the coach for any refuge beyond his arms. There didn't seem to be any. And she did intend to change his mind about putting her on a stage for home. She wasn't going anywhere until she had her half of the mine in gold and could buy back Belle Montagne.

Letting Holt think he'd won, she cautiously rejoined him on the other seat. His arm immediately reached out and curled around her shoulder, drawing her against his warmth. Angel sighed as she snuggled against his broad chest. His buckskin jacket was soft against her cheek, and she didn't begrudge Holt gently stroking her hair.

"There now," he crooned in her ear. "That's better, isn't it?"

Angel nodded sleepily. She hadn't realized just how exhausted she was after all the excitement of the past few days. "I really do need to write a letter to Neal right away," she murmured. "It's very important."

There was a long silence. "All right," Holt said at last, "we'll stop at the first town come morning and you can send a telegram back to him."

"Thank you."

Angel's gratitude was punctuated with a hug that she felt him return. But, over her head, Holt's gray eyes hardened as he stared off across the moonlit landscape.

Morning found Angel tightly snuggled in Holt's arms. Her even breathing matched the rhythm of his heartbeat, and they were pressed together so tightly that when the stage came to a halt, they slid to the floor.

It was a rude awakening. Angel heard Holt's low oath before she felt the hard floor hit her backside. She scrambled up beside him and ruefully rubbed her eyes.

"What now?" Holt grumbled, opening the door to peer out into the settling dust. The cool morning air hit Angel like an icy blast, and she shivered.

"Gil?" Holt called out warily, seeing no sign of the burly driver. He absently pushed Angel back a bit. "Stay here. I want to see what's going on."

He left the stagecoach and Angel sank back down on the creaky seat. She was only half awake, though the cold air was doing its best to revive her. She heard the men's voices outside a moment later and relaxed enough to yawn. Obviously nothing was wrong.

But outside the coach Holt hunkered down and stared in dismay at the front foreleg of the horse Gil was showing him.

"She's got a bad leg. Can't push her no more," Gil said, and spat a juicy wad of tobacco out of the side of his stubbled cheek.

"How far are we from Denver?"

"Shoot, 'least thirty miles. Mebbe forty." The driver shook his head to discourage Holt from any crazy ideas about walking. "An' a bad storm headed this way, that's for sure." He jabbed a callused thumb in the direction of some heavy gray clouds in the west.

"Maybe it'll pass us by," Holt said hopefully.

"Nope. We'll have snow a'fore morning."

Holt had known Gil for years and trusted his judgment. "Could we keep going with just one horse?"

Gil squinted and considered the suggestion. "Without the coach, sure. But not with all those whatnots you've got stored under there."

"I can't leave those behind," Holt muttered, with a glance at his precious cargo, securely wrapped and stored beneath the stagecoach. He rose and dusted off his buckskin trousers with a thoughtful expression on his face.

"Is there a place we could shelter for a few nights?"

Gil chewed deliberately a moment more and then grunted, "I passed an old prospector's dig on the creek a few miles back. Looked deserted, but the cabin was still standin'."

Holt nodded. "Then here's what I want you to do."

He briefly explained his plan, pressed a few coins on Gil with the promise of more to come, and then returned to the coach to inform Angel of his decision.

She stared at him in disbelief and mounting suspicion. "Walk a 'few' miles? This isn't anything like walking up Mount Elbert, I suppose?"

Holt chuckled at the memory she evoked; of a very straitlaced, genteel young lady struggling up the side of a rugged peak, determined to save every last frilly underthing she owned. "I promise you won't even get blisters this time," he replied with a grin. "But we'd better hurry, because snow's on the way."

Angel reluctantly joined him outside the coach, and didn't turn down the offer of his jacket to keep her warm. Gil was busy unhitching the horses and saddling the uninjured mare.

"What's going on?" she asked the men.

Holt answered as he looped a piece of rope in a slipknot around the other animal's neck. "This mare hit a chuck hole just before dawn. She's too crippled to go on. I'm sending Gil on ahead to fetch help. You and I will take shelter in a cabin we passed a ways back."

"Are there settlers there?" she asked hopefully, with wistful thoughts of a hot breakfast and wool blankets.

" 'Fraid not," Gil answered. "Looked empty to me."

Angel set her shoulders, determined to make the best of a very discouraging situation. "Are we just going to leave the stagecoach here?"

The men exchanged long looks. Then Holt said evenly,

"I'll be taking a few things with us for safekeeping. Likely nobody will bother the coach. Not many travelers out this time of year, right, Gil?"

The driver grunted, which apparently indicated an answer in the affirmative.

Angel walked a bit to stretch her cramped leg muscles while the men busied themselves with something under the coach. She was too busy gazing at the incredible landscape to pay much attention to the cargo they hauled out and strapped to the back of the injured horse.

The pale morning sun revealed a lush green valley ablaze with wildflowers. Larkspur, mariposa, and blue columbine dotted the mountains as far as the eye could see. Lodgepole pine rippled along the rim of the valley like blue-green flame. A nearby cluster of firs reminded her of soldiers in green uniforms, waving a welcome in the brisk morning breeze.

Angel knew she should be frightened, but she wasn't. The cold air was invigorating and her blood pumped faster with the excitement of the challenge they faced. Suddenly the gentle hills of Belle Montagne seemed very far away.

When Holt joined her a short time later there was a tender tone in his voice that surprised her. "Are you sure you're up to this?"

Angel gave him a wry smile. "What are my choices?"

He looked a little abashed. "I'll make it up to you somehow. No lady should have to endure conditions like this."

Something was definitely amiss, Angel thought. He'd

had no qualms about forcing her to work the mine or live in a crude cabin. Now for some reason he was trying to please her. And it was working.

Angel was silent and thoughtful after Gil said a brisk farewell and rode ahead on the other horse. She and Holt turned southwest and started to follow the tracks left by the stage.

They had to go slowly to accommodate the limping horse and stopped several times for Holt to examine the animal's leg. Each time he rose with a grimmer expression than the last. Finally he said, "It's bad. I'm afraid I'll have to put her down."

"Oh, no. Let me look at it first." Angel stilled his hand as it moved to the holster at his waist. She knelt, heedless of her skirts pooling across the dirty ground.

"Easy, girl." Angel spoke soothingly when the mare shuddered at her touch. "I just want to feel you a little."

Angel's slim white fingers moved expertly inch by inch up the sorrel's leg. She located the injury at the joint and gently felt the swelling.

"I don't think it's a fracture," she said after a moment of examination. "More likely a bad sprain. Some cold compresses would work wonders."

She rose, her gaze fixed on the shady ground beneath the firs, where patches of early snow still lingered. "If we can get her to the cabin, I think I can do something for her."

Holt gazed at her in frank amazement. "I didn't know you knew anything about horses."

"My father raised trotters. I grew up around them," she answered absently, already looking ahead to see how far away the cabin was that Gil had seen. "This load on the mare's back doesn't help any, either. Let's take it off and ease her burden."

Her hand was intercepted as it moved to uncinch a strap. Holt's palm came down on hers with just enough finality to make Angel uneasy.

"No. We have to keep my cargo safe, and it's too heavy for either of us to carry."

"Now what's so important you'd ruin a fine horse to protect?" Angel demanded, reaching with her other hand to try and pluck up the tarpaulin covering the mysterious box.

He swiftly captured her other hand as well. "Don't try it, sweetheart," Holt said in a low voice, made even more ominous by the sudden narrowing of his gray eyes. "It's better for everyone if you don't know."

Angel drew herself up to explode. "You could very well permanently cripple this poor creature! I won't allow it."

"Then we'll go slowly, even if it takes all day to get to the cabin." He cast a glance skyward. "But I'm afraid Mother Nature intends to push us a little."

Holt was right. By the time they spotted the abandoned homestead lazy white flakes had begun to fall. The small log dwelling had been built in a grove of quaking aspen, beside a gurgling creek. Fall had turned the aspen leaves to various beautiful shades of red, gold, and orange, and whenever the wind gusted the leaves rustled softly like starched petticoats.

But Angel was soon too busy to admire the scenery. She had Holt secure the horse underneath the sheltering trees while she tore off a loose piece of the canvas tarpaulin to use as a wrap. Within a few hundred yards she found a patch of old snow and, as new flakes began to fall ever faster, she scooped up handfuls and made a crude cold pack.

While Holt steadied the mare's leg, Angel wrapped the injury and tied the canvas pack in place. She rose and stepped back with a slight frown. "It's the best I can do."

"Where did you learn to do that?" Holt asked.

"I told you, I was practically raised with horses. I liked to hang around the stables and watch my father work. I'd give anything to have him here now."

For a moment they were both silent, while the snow fell and melted in their eyes and hair. Then Holt turned toward the cabin, extending a hand to her.

"Come on. Let's see what we've gotten ourselves into."

The dwelling was little more than basic shelter. Unlike the cabin Arthur and Royce had built, this one had been hastily and sloppily constructed, and huge chinks in the logs allowed a cold draft to flow through the room. Oil tarps served as glass for the windows, flapping forlornly in the wind. A few small animals had burrowed in for the coming winter, and the place had a musty, unpleasant smell.

Angel shivered and drew Holt's warm jacket closer around her as she inspected their lodgings for the night. A lumpy, mouse-ridden mattress had been left behind, as well as a rough chair made from a piece of tree trunk. Filth dominated the place, and she couldn't bring herself to stay inside. Holt looked like he felt the same way.

"Well," he said as he joined her back outside, "let's see if there's anything better nearby."

They found an old covered wagon as well, but it offered little more in the way of shelter than the cabin. Together they walked down to the creek and along the shore for a while, but they didn't go too far. The snow started to fall even faster, blanketing the landscape with a harsh white that warned of a devilish winter to come.

Angel was shivering, even with Holt's coat. Her black patent leather shoes weren't made for walking in snow-storms. "I suppose it's that awful old cabin or sleep out-side," she bemoaned their fate with a little shudder.

"Wait." Holt stopped and peered ahead through the snow flurry. "Do you see something over there?"

At first she saw nothing against the blinding snow. Then, gradually, Angel could make out another cabin, half hidden by a row of stately pines. And as they watched, a lazy curl of smoke rose from its chimney and drifted away in the wind.

Holt had to restrain her from bolting ahead. "We don't know who's living there."

"It's worth the risk. We'll freeze and starve out here if we don't find some decent shelter soon."

Angel's argument soon won him over. Holt was cold and hungry, too. They trudged on with hope in their hearts and wariness in their eyes.

Both were somewhat reassured upon seeing a single mule tethered under a shelter near the cabin. It was probably just a prospector working the creek for gold. Just the same, Holt took the lead and approached the cabin. He decided to be forthright and boldly knocked upon the door.

For a long time there was only silence. Then they heard the soft tread of footsteps behind the door. Holt knocked again. Finally the door swung halfway open.

Angel gasped softly. A young Indian girl looked out at them, her huge onyx eyes glittering with apprehension.

She couldn't be over fifteen or sixteen years old. Her dusky skin was like rich cream, and her oval face was framed by two oiled black braids. She wore a doeskin dress similar to the one Holt's mother had owned, only this one was golden-buff in color and relatively plain.

Holt's gaze fell to the bone choker around the Indian girl's neck. And then he began to speak softly to her in her native tongue, in a soothing singsong rhythm that caused the girl to relax and begin to nod.

She hastily gabbled something to Holt and pointed off in the direction of the mountains. Then she looked at Angel, and the two young women studied each other curiously for a moment.

"What did she say?" Angel asked Holt.

"She says her man has gone hunting. She's worried about him in this storm."

"Her man? An Indian?"

Holt shook his head. "No. A white. She's his squaw, his Indian wife."

Angel concealed her surprise and dismay, aware of the girl's keen black eyes watching her. "She isn't old enough!"

A rich chuckle escaped him. "Tell that to her. She looks pretty mature to me."

"Yes, but—" Angel trailed off, feeling a sense of outrage for the young girl and her own plight. "Would she let us take shelter here?"

"She's already invited us inside. I told her we were lost in the storm."

With relief Angel followed him across the threshold, studying the clean and cozy lodgings, where a fire blazed merrily in an open hearth and the delicious smell of something cooking wafted through the cabin. A cradleboard had been propped against one wall, and Angel let out a soft cry when she spied the black tuft of an infant peeking above the blankets.

"Why, she has a baby, too." Angel glanced at the Indian girl again and returned the tentative smile she was offered. Then the girl babbled something more to Holt, and he quickly interpreted.

"She wants to know if you like babies."

"Oh, yes. I love children!" Angel's enthusiasm escaped her in a rush, and her cheeks grew warm when she felt Holt studying her.

The girl gravely listened to his response and then asked something else.

This time Holt gave Angel a mischievous wink. "She also wants to know where your children are."

"Where my—oh, dear. Can't you tell her we've just been married a short while?"

"I'm afraid she still won't understand." Holt was laughing at her openly now. "She'll only assume that means you're barren, and pity us both."

A slow flush rose on Angel's cheeks. "Tell her they're staying with my mother while we travel."

This was quickly relayed and the girl nodded, as if accepting the explanation. Then she invited Angel with handmotions to come over and admire her baby boy.

It wasn't hard to delight in the chubby infant, who curled a little finger around the larger one Angel offered him. Then he yawned hugely and snuggled back to sleep in his blankets. He seemed perfectly content to remain strapped in the cradleboard.

The Indian girl was fairly beaming with pride. Angel asked Holt to find out her name and the baby's.

A moment later he told her. "She says her name is Okoka. It means 'raven' in Cheyenne. Her little baby is called Nahqui—'bear.' "

"Tell her he's beautiful," Angel said. "And so is she."

When this was translated Okoka reached out and touched Angel's hand. The two women exchanged open smiles.

"I wish I could talk to her!" Angel said.

"She probably knows a few words of English. Why don't you work on it while I go back and check on the horse."

Angel was too intrigued by her new friend to argue. She kept both herself and Okoka busy for an hour trying to find a common word between them. Whenever Angel would point at an object in the cabin and say its English name, Okoka would shake her head, her black eyes dancing with mischief, and substitute the Cheyenne word.

Finally they agreed upon one thing. Angel made as if to touch the burning coals in the hearth, and like a little mother Okoka snatched her hand back from the flame.

"No," she scolded clearly, in English. "No fire!"

The two of them laughed happily at the tiny bridge of communication they had made. They sat facing each other on the sod floor and gabbled back and forth in their respective tongues. Angel didn't understand a word of what the Indian girl was saying, but she understood the contentment in Okoka's lovely doelike eyes, the happiness in her voice. Maybe her white husband wasn't so bad. Okoka didn't seem to have any complaints.

Holt returned just as Okoka was dishing up big bowls of a thick, meaty stew. They joined her, eating Indian-style on the floor, instead of at the small plank table, where an empty bowl still awaited her husband.

The meal was simple but delicious. Angel had two big helpings and then sat back enjoying the warmth of her insides. Outside it continued to snow, building up a thick barrier around the cabin. Holt had brought the horse up to the cabin, where he could check on its leg more easily, and it had the mule for company. He reported that the swelling seemed to have gone down a little. Both animals had sufficient graze for a few days underneath the shelter, and it took one burden of worry off Angel's mind.

But now there was the matter of Okoka's missing husband. She said he had been gone three days now, and he had intended to return in two. She had enough firewood and food for several weeks. But with the baby, she couldn't leave to look for him.

After the meal the Indian girl departed for a moment to feed her baby. Holt and Angel quietly discussed the problem.

"Tomorrow morning I'll take the mule and go look for him," Holt said. "It's the least I can do to repay her hospitality."

Angel agreed. "But what if the snow doesn't stop?"

"Then we'll be stuck here for the winter. It could be worse. We could be back at the inn down the road, you know."

She shuddered at the thought of the other dilapidated old cabin. "I wonder who lived there."

"I'll ask Okoka. Maybe she knows."

It turned out that the other cabin had belonged to a lone prospector who had died a year ago. Okoka and her husband had buried him up on the mountainside. She told Holt that he had gotten sick with the "white throat."

"What's that?" Angel asked, after he translated the girl's reply for her.

"Diphtheria." Holt looked grim. "Sometimes it runs like wildfire through the settlers. Especially children."

Angel's eyes flew to little Nahqui, now back in his cradleboard and gurgling contentedly. She shivered. "I knew there was something about that place I didn't like."

"It's just a sorry old cabin, Angel. Places don't have memories."

She bit her lip to keep from telling him otherwise. The Irish half of her was always tuned to places as well as people, and she had sensed bleak despair and hopelessness in her single foray into the old miner's abode.

Now she forced herself to concentrate on her new friend and the baby instead. She stayed up a few more hours, oohing and aahing appreciatively over garments Okoka had made and now proudly displayed, and trying to communicate with hand gestures about the long journey she had made from Missouri.

Finally the sun slipped behind the mountains, and sheer exhaustion took its toll. Angel gratefully slid into the furs and blankets Okoka offered for their use. The Indian girl also slept on the floor in a pile of furs. Holt stayed up for a while longer, going outside periodically to check the animals and return with more firewood.

Angel slept heavily, awakening only once when Holt slipped into the makeshift bed beside her and curled an arm around her. She finally woke in the morning to the sound of the baby's hungry whimpers. She climbed out of the furs, noticing with dismay that Holt had already gone. She went to the window and saw the mule was gone as well.

Okoka soon came up beside her. Together the two young women looked out at the falling snow, which was already several feet deep in every direction.

"Snow," the Indian girl announced gravely in perfect English.

Angel clapped her hands in delight. "That's right!"

"Snow," Okoka repeated, and this time the word was ominous. "No good snow."

Chapter Eleven

By late afternoon the cabin was the centerpiece of a huge Rocky Mountain blizzard, and Angel and her new friends virtual prisoners inside. The snow was blowing so hard that it came in through the cracks of the walls and drifted up against the door nearly to the eaves.

Angel fought her rising panic and tried to stay calm. By comparison, Okoka seemed relatively unconcerned, but who knew what thoughts drifted behind her dark eyes? At least she was sensitive to Angel's discomfort, for she insisted with hand gestures and many nods for the other woman to accept the heavy buffalo robe she offered. Angel had to admit that even though the robe smelled slightly gamey, it was deliciously warm against the bitter chill of the coming night.

Night fell quickly, and with it Angel's hopes. At best, Holt must be lost in the storm, and at worst . . . she didn't even want to finish the thought. A shiver coursed through her frame as she imagined him lying frozen or dying somewhere in the deep snow. She simply couldn't accept the possibility. He had beaten worse odds before, hadn't he?

Angel's pensive mood increased as the night wore on. The baby, as if sensing her restlessness, woke almost every hour and quietly fussed while his mother rocked him in her arms and crooned a soft, soothing chant. Even though Angel didn't understand the words, the peaceful melody soaked gradually into her conscious mind and she found herself relaxing almost against her will. When morning came both Angel and the baby were fast asleep. Okoka rose and quietly set about preparing breakfast, retrieving pemmican cakes and dried fruit from storage. Her moccasins made no noise upon the sod floor, and Angel slept later than she had expected. When she finally awoke she was angry with herself for sleeping so blissfully when Holt was in grave danger.

Okoka coaxed Angel to eat, even though she wasn't hungry. Her stomach was in instant knots upon seeing that instead of lessening, the storm had worsened overnight. The wind howled around the little cabin, and Okoka was hard-pressed to keep a fire going. Snow fell down the chimney and hissed as it met with the pitiful little fire. The Indian woman hunkered down by the hearth, steadily feeding a stream of dry tinder and wood into the coals. Angel relieved her for a while, glad to be able to huddle near their only source of warmth, while Okoka fed her baby.

So passed the second day, and the third. Okoka ventured outside only to feed the horse and return with more firewood. Angel awoke with a violent start on the fourth night and found the fur robe wrapped around her drenched with her tears. She had been crying soundlessly in her sleep, too cold to sob aloud and too grief-stricken to voice her fears. Okoka wouldn't understand anyway, she thought miserably. But Angel found she was wrong. Moments after she awoke, the Indian woman padded over to the bed where Angel lay and sat beside her, taking Angel's ice-cold hand in her own.

Sandwiching it gently between her warm palms, Okoka held Angel's hand until she went back to sleep. When Angel woke again she found Okoka gone from her side, but the sun had appeared in her place.

Throwing off the buffalo robe, Angel hurried to the window to stare out at the vast, glittering white. The storm was over! As if the previous days had never existed, the sky was clear and glacier-blue, and not a hint of breeze stirred the drifts that reached the lower boughs of the snow-flocked pines.

"Okoka!" she called out, wanting to share her excitement with the other woman. Angel motioned the Indian woman up beside her and chucked the baby under his chin as she spoke in careful English. "Look. Snow stopped. Good, yes?"

Okoka nodded, but she didn't smile. There was something troubled about her expression, but Angel didn't question the other woman.

This morning Angel was too anxious to eat, no matter how delicious the biscuits tasted when slathered with wild honey. Even the normally taciturn baby crowed and waved his chubby little fists in the air, and Angel communicated her wish to carry Nahqui to the window to show him the new day, too.

Okoka suggested something even better by going to fetch the buffalo robes and two pairs of snowshoes for the women. While Angel strapped on the additional footwear, Okoka bundled the baby up so snugly that only his little face showed and tucked him in the cradleboard, easing it onto her own back by means of two loops over her shoulders.

Soon the little expedition bravely forged outside. Angel gazed around with quiet wonder at the frozen stillness surrounding them. In the distance white-capped peaks soared to a sky of blazing blue, and in every direction the snow sparkled and glistened beneath the warming sun. Even the stream nearby had been temporarily silenced. Angel glanced back at the tiny cabin and realized how insignificant it seemed against the stark backdrop of nature's majesty. How much smaller was Holt against the brutal reality the blizzard had left behind?

A shiver sliced through her, and she turned in slight distress to find Okoka watching her with knowing eyes. The two women exchanged sober looks. Now Angel understood why the Indian woman wasn't jubilant about the ending of the storm. It might only mean the beginning of even more problems.

Seeking to distract herself, Angel moved toward the lean-to where the horse was sheltered. The mare had been adequately watered and fed, thanks to Okoka, but Angel knew it was time to check the leg again. She soothed the animal while she ran her hands up and down the injury. To her relief, there was no sign of swollenness now, and the mare didn't flinch at her touch. It had only been a bad sprain after all.

Angel rose and shook out her damp skirts with a sigh. If only she had more confidence about directions, she might go in search of Holt herself. Of course that would leave Okoka alone, and though the Indian girl was doubtlessly quite capable of looking after herself, Angel didn't think it would be very wise for them to part company until the men were found. In case neither man returned, the two women would be completely dependent on each other.

Worrying her lower lip between her teeth, Angel turned to head back to the cabin. She was the first to spot the distant figure struggling through the snow, halfway up the nearest mountainside.

"Okoka!" she cried, and pointed at her discovery. The Indian girl echoed her excitement. But there was something very wrong. Both of them sensed it immediately, and as the man gradually neared they could see the shape of another figure slung across his back.

Angel pressed her hand to her mouth. The man was too far away yet to tell if it was Holt or Okoka's husband. But in either case one of them was seriously hurt or dead. Chills of foreboding washed over Angel. Don't let it be Holt, she prayed. Then she felt guilty for Okoka's sake.

The Indian girl had quickly moved to the lean-to where the horse was sheltered and was wrestling with something on the ground. Angel turned back to help her, not understanding until Okoka unfolded a rectangular piece of frozen hide upon the ground.

"Travois," Okoka said, this time speaking clearly. She motioned to the man struggling down the mountainside with his human burden, and then indicated the sorrel. "Horse pull travois."

Angel nodded eagerly. "I'll help you." She steadied the mare while Okoka slipped the crude harness in place. The horse seemed a bit jittery at first, dragging something behind it, but eventually calmed enough for Angel to lead it forward. Her heart began to beat faster when she saw the approaching man stumble, fall, and slide a few feet down the mountain. Luckily, he didn't drop his burden, but Angel could sense his exhaustion even from a distance.

She clicked to the horse for more speed, pulling it by the cheek strap, careful to keep her clumsy snowshoes from being crushed. Okoka trailed behind them, having stopped at the cabin to deposit Nahqui and retrieve some blankets.

The snow was so white, it hurt Angel's eyes. She paused to wave her arm vigorously to catch the man's attention and then resumed her slow, clumping walk across the snow. *If Holt is dead, I don't want to live.* The thought struck her with surprising force. She briefly scrunched her eyes shut, feeling the tracks of frozen tears drying tight on her cheeks, and pushed on.

Finally she could hear the man's harsh breathing ahead of her. Angel looked up just as the hood of his buffalo robe fell back to expose his agonized, wind-burned face.

"Holt!" she cried, surging forward and falling to her knees in the snow. The horse stopped and didn't move. She threw herself forward at the deep barrier of snow again and sank down beside Holt.

"Got to . . . get him inside," Holt gasped, stopping to shift the burden of the man he carried over his shoulders. His knees threatened to buckle and take them all down in the deep snow.

"Of course." Angel realized now was not the time for tearful reunions. She got up clumsily and managed to retrieve the horse again. "Okoka made a travois."

Holt carried the unconscious man to the makeshift sling and lowered him in place. He had wrapped strips of buffalo hide around his hands earlier, but now they shook with the cold as he tried to tie the other man in place.

Angel hurried over to his side. "Here. I'll do it." Her own gloveless fingers were already blue from exposure, but she had been outside for far less time. She forced herself to secure the leather thongs around the unknown man's wrists and ankles without looking at his face. Was he dead?

As if reading her mind, Holt rasped, "I found him shortly after I left. But the storm hit and I was forced to take shelter with him in a cave. I managed to keep a fire going and find some food, but I couldn't do much for his injuries."

Okoka reached them now and let out a strangled cry. She hurried forward to the man stretched out on the travois, her hands reaching out to tenderly touch his bearded face.

Angel picked up the pile of blankets the Indian girl had dropped. While Okoka hovered over her husband, Angel quickly covered the unconscious man. She was relieved to see the man's eyelids tremble a little in his unconscious state; he was not dead after all.

Holt himself looked ready to drop where he stood. Angel went to him and pulled the snowshoes from her feet. "Here. Put these on."

He started to protest, but she silenced him with a finger across his lips. "Put them on, Holt Murphy. It'll make the walk back to the cabin that much easier for you."

For once Holt didn't argue. He slipped on the snowshoes and Angel adjusted them around his larger feet. She saw the soaked condition of his boots and rightly suspected his feet were numb with the cold, too. If they didn't hurry, frostbite could make things even worse.

Angel urged Okoka to lead the horse back while she brought up the rear of the little party. The going was slow in knee-deep snow, and she had to struggle to drag her skirts free of the heavy stuff. She slipped several times but managed to save herself from falling. Thankfully, it was only a few hundred yards back to the cabin.

Okoka drew the travois up before the cabin door, and both she and Angel untied it from the horse, each of them taking one end in order to drag the man in the sling inside.

Holt tried to help, but Angel ordered him out of the way. Then she and Okoka finished hauling the other man to a choice spot before the crackling fire. Both of the woman gasped for breath and straightened at the same time. Just then Holt stepped across the threshold.

"So c-cold," was all he said, and the word was uttered so strangely that Angel's head turned with alarm in his direction. She was just in time to cushion the fall of his body with her own.

The jarring impact sent them both tumbling to the floor. Angel felt her elbow slam against the sod as she attempted to break her fall, but all she gained for the effort was a pain that sent her senses spinning. Seconds later that agony doubled when Holt's fur-clad figure knocked her flat. He landed just next to her, his outstetched arm flung across her body.

Angel forgot her own problems and struggled to her knees. "Holt!" she cried, bending over him and only faintly reassured to find he was still breathing. She looked frantically toward Okoka, but after seeing the other couple was all right the Indian girl had quickly turned to tending her own injured husband. Angel could expect no help from that quarter; she was on her own.

"Oh, Holt," she repeated, framing his cold jaw with trembling hands, "what can I do?" Again she looked around the cabin for answers. Extra furs and blankets remained on the floor where she had slept during the last few days.

Rising as quickly as she could manage, Angel unfurled her tangled skirts and hurried to retrieve an armful of coverings. She returned to drape them over Holt's prone figure, and then peeled off her own buffalo robe to cushion his head.

Kneeling beside him again, she took his hand this time. It was still wrapped in old hide, which she unwrapped and set aside. Working with precise strokes, she sandwiched his icy palm in her own and briskly rubbed it back to life. Holt made no protest. He didn't so much as stir.

When his first hand was a healthy pink again, and her own were warm from the friction, Angel repeated the action on his other one. Then she eased off his frozen boots and did the same for his feet. His toes were literally blue from the cold, and she hoped it wasn't too late for them. Finally she decided she had done all she could and tucked him all around with the furs and blankets and stood up.

Angel saw Okoka had gone a step further for her man. The Indian girl had unobtrusively stripped and slipped naked beneath the furs beside her husband, in order to warm his entire body. She had also settled little Nahqui on the other side, and the baby gurgled happily and played with his unconscious father's beard. When Okoka met Angel's surprised gaze, she gestured for the other girl to do the same.

Angel quickly shook her head. She wouldn't dream of

doing such a thing, and not merely for modesty's sake. As if sensing her thoughts, Okoka frowned sternly at Angel. Her dark eyes seemed to be saying that in a crisis you must do everything to save the one you love.

Biting her lip, Angel glanced back to Holt. He did look terribly cold, and he had begun shivering violently in his unconscious state. A moment more of indecision passed before Angel started to unbutton the bodice of her gown with shaking fingers. A swift glance around assured her that no one was watching. She turned her back as the dress puddled at her feet, and she was reduced to her chemise and petticoats. Angel decided that was good enough; she had gotten rid of the damp clothing that would only chill him more. Tentatively, she knelt and lifted a corner of the blankets, then slid beneath the edge, as close to Holt as she could manage. She ruefully realized she would have to undress him, as well.

The buckskin ties were frozen stiff, and Angel struggled for a long time to pull off his shirt and trousers. Holt's skin, when she inadvertently brushed it, was ice-cold. She could hardly bring herself to press against him in order to transmit some of her meager warmth.

Holt groaned softly, and Angel wondered if she was helping or hurting him. The ice crystals on his hair and eyelashes melted as she anxiously watched his face. Almost shyly she reached up to brush a damp lock from his forehead. He shifted in his sleep, rolling lengthwise against her.

For a long time Angel heard nothing but the sound of breathing in the little cabin, and the rising howl of the wind outside. Cold drafts seeped beneath the furs, and she huddled closer to Holt, surprised when his arm curled around her waist and pinned her close. He was definitely warming up now. She was curled up tightly against Holt, her back curved against his hard stomach and lean thighs. She was nearly asleep when she felt his hands begin to wander.

Angel bolted awake, eyes huge in the darkness. Was Holt conscious? She felt a callused palm casually inching up her thigh, then slowly rucking up her petticoats to expose the bare flesh underneath.

"Holt!" she whispered, reaching back to tug down the petticoats but instead encountering the silky-smooth hardness of his male member. He had somehow pinned her petticoats beneath his leg, and Angel's frantic squirming only served to encourage him further.

"Wake up!" she hissed, but Holt didn't reply. Instead he neatly cleaved her thighs apart with a knee, and his hips picked up a rhythm that was insidiously familiar to her panicked brain.

Dear heavens, not now! Angel thought, wildly shooting a glance across the room, where the trapper and his family slept peacefully in their furs. Holt's other hand moved to toy with a nipple through her chemise, and she stifled a groan at the piercingly sweet sensations that slammed through her.

So much for keeping him warm! Holt didn't have any problems his hot-blooded body couldn't handle. Angel quickly discovered that struggling was useless, so she concentrated on keeping her legs clamped shut and her arms folded across her breasts. She was sure she could frustrate him eventually.

But Holt had different ideas. Angel was on her back a moment later. She opened her mouth to protest and his mouth swiftly captured hers, staking a fierce claim of its own. She saw Holt wasn't asleep. His silvery irises reflected the moonlight from the window. He straddled Angel so that his hard male flesh pressed into the softness of her belly, and his need for her was unmistakably clear.

Angel tried to shake her head, to indicate that they weren't alone, but he cut off her anxious whisper with a kiss that left her mind whirling and her lips slightly swollen. She moved to shelter her torso, but Holt captured her wrists with a single hand, holding her still as he briskly dispensed with the tiny ribbons securing her chemise.

Night air swept across her flesh like cold silk, and Angel shivered. Holt pressed himself slowly upon her until she was wrapped in a cocoon of warmth. He cupped her breast in one hand, lightly rubbing a callused finger over the tip until she shuddered in surrender.

She could sense his wolflike smile in the dark, and there was animalistic triumph in the way he lowered his head to swiftly capture the aching bud. He worried it gently between his teeth, and Angel closed her eyes and felt the piercing, sweet sensation tumbling over her like a waterfall.

Suddenly nothing mattered but their mutual need and the means to satisfy it. Holt released her wrists, sensing that she would not deny him. When Angel arched against him he drove deeply into her moist warmth.

The silence of the night wrapped around them both as she locked her ankles around his, moving with him to the ancient rhythm of her woman's blood. She felt his lips claim her again, leaving a fiery brand of kisses down her throat and bare shoulders, pausing to nip at a tender earlobe until she gasped with silent delight. He drove a hand into her tumbled golden hair, holding her still as he lightly, teasingly raked his teeth and tongue over the fullness of her lower lip. Her whimper was silenced when his mouth slid quickly over hers, coaxing her tongue to fence with his as their bodies ebbed and surged together like a mighty ocean.

Angel's cry was drowned by the force of his need, as Holt buried his seed deep within her woman's core. Higher and higher she spiraled, until Holt's ragged whisper of her name was enough to bring her plunging back to earth, to find herself clutched securely in his arms.

For several minutes the mingled sound of their harsh breathing echoed through the room, and Angel resisted the urge to succumb to the languorous relaxation stealing over her limbs. Weakly, she pried herself free from Holt's grasp, but further resolve fled when he threw a leg possessively over her, keeping her at his side.

Very softly, he kissed her shoulder, and though he didn't speak, she could sense a quiet apology within the act. Then a shudder rippled through his frame, and she glanced over to see his dark head bowed beside her.

Without hesitation, Angel reached over, offering the comfort words could not. Then, quietly, she lay back down beside him, holding him close against her pounding heart until the peace of the night lulled them both to sleep again.

Chapter Twelve

Angel felt something tugging at her hair. She moaned sleepily and rolled over, opening her eyes just in time to receive the full impact of Nahqui's raspberry in her face. She couldn't help but smile at the baby as he wriggled by on his belly, waving his arms in his first attempt at a crawl.

Angel glanced over and saw Okoka stirring a kettle over the fire. It smelled like meat broth, and it was a heavenly odor. Then her smile faded abruptly as she remembered Holt. He was nowhere to be seen. Had it been only a dream?

She sat up in the pile of cold blankets and furs and found her underclothing slightly askew. She felt every ache and pain from sleeping on the hard floor, and there was a sticky dampness between her thighs that couldn't be explained away.

Carefully shielding her body with a blanket, she rose a little unsteadily and approached Okoka. The Indian woman seemed to smile a little knowingly, or maybe it was only Angel's guilt that made her suspect Okoka knew more than her bland gaze betrayed.

"Hungry?" the other woman motioned, indicating the steaming black pot. Angel nodded and offered a sheepish smile. Now was one time she wished she could communicate better with her new friend. How much had Okoka heard and seen last night?

Angel looked across the room to the trapper still buried snugly in the furs. She indicated her question to Okoka with her eyes and hands.

"Hurt," Okoka confirmed, but there was no indication of how badly by her expression.

"I'm sorry," Angel said, knowing the Indian woman would understand her concern by her tone, if not her words.

Okoka nodded and returned to her cooking. Angel looked around the cabin for Holt, but other than the strips of rawhide that had bound his hands, there was no indication he had ever been there.

Angel wanted to ask Okoka where he was, but she wasn't sure the Indian girl would understand. And there was something embarrassing about having to ask where your own husband was, especially after last night.

A short time later Angel had her answer. Holt came into the cabin with a grim set to his features that didn't bode well for anyone. He had been outside assessing the snow situation, balancing the risks of travel against the very real need to get the other man to a doctor.

He looked at Angel, and when their eyes met she felt a warm glow that had nothing to do with the fire Okoka was tending.

"We'll have to chance it," he said, with a gesture to the

unconscious man. "Either we get Jean-Claude to Denver or he'll probably die."

"Jean-Claude?" Angel repeated, with a curious glance at the injured man. "He's French?"

Holt nodded. "A fur trapper, Okoka told me. They've lived here for several years, trapping beaver up and down the river. He met and married Okoka two years ago, after his first wife died."

"How did you find him?"

"Luck, I think," Holt answered grimly. "There weren't many tracks left after that storm, but I took a chance he was smart enough to seek shelter. I found him in a cave about two miles from here. By then he was already delirious with fever."

"What happened to him?"

Holt shrugged. "The most I could get out of him was that he'd gotten kicked in the head by his mule, and by the time he came around the wound was festering. He's got a concussion as well as a bad case of frostbite."

"He's in no condition to travel!" Angel exclaimed with a shocked glance to the bed.

"No," Holt agreed quietly, "but the alternative is worse. Even Indians can't treat head injuries as serious as his."

"What are you going to do?" she asked.

"I'm going to hitch up the horse and wagon and set out for Denver this morning."

Angel was alarmed. "Can't you just ride out for a doctor and bring him back here?"

Holt shook his head. "It'll take too long. By the time I got back, assuming I could even persuade a doctor to ride out with me, the man would probably be dead. We've got to take the chance."

"I'm going with you," Angel said quickly.

"No. I want you to stay here with Okoka and the baby."

"You'll need someone to steady him on the journey," Angel argued reasonably. "He'll have to be kept warm and quiet, and fed somehow. All that bouncing around won't be easy on his head."

Their stubborn gazes met. Finally Holt sighed. "All right. I don't like it, but you're right; I can't drive and take care of him at the same time. But it'll be a long, cold journey, Angel. Are you up to it?"

"Yes. Even if I wasn't, I owe Okoka this much."

Holt's glance was surprised but approving. "Then I suggest you start rounding up all the blankets she can spare, and figure out a way to carry some food and water."

"Does Okoka know what you plan to do?"

Holt nodded soberly. "She understands it's his only chance. She told me about an old buckboard stored out back. We'll have to rig a shelter of some sort over the top."

Angel bit her lip, thinking hard for a moment. "What about the covered wagon down at the old miner's cabin? It looked like it still had some life left in it."

He looked at her in outright admiration. "You're right. That would be much better. It's sturdier and probably rolled through a few snowstorms in its day. I'll walk down with the horse and see if I can't get it going again. You'd better have some breakfast before we leave."

"Not to mention clothes," Angel said, inadvertently reminding them both of the passionate night they'd shared. She blushed. Holt cleared his throat and made a hasty departure, and Okoka glanced up from her cooking and smiled.

"It's the best we can do," Holt said after they had carefully moved Jean-Claude to the rear of the covered wagon, bundled him snugly in furs, and cushioned his head with several blankets. The man still hadn't stirred or spoken. Angel thought he looked worse by the hour, but she didn't want to frighten Okoka any further.

Before they took their leave of the woman and her child Holt saw to it that plenty of firewood was stacked close to the cabin. In turn, the young woman gave them packages of pemmican and dried strips of meat for the journey, and insisted that Angel take her buffalo robe and snowshoes.

As Holt made final preparations outside, Angel returned to the doorway of the cabin to thank the Indian woman again. There were tears in her eyes, but Okoka shook her head and smiled.

"No," she said, her fingers making the motion of tears rolling down her cheeks. "See—Hoah." Her palms came together in a parody of a handshake. "Hoah—friend." Then she pointed at Nahqui, still happily exploring the floor. She made a cradle with her arms this time, and then pointed at Angel's abdomen. "Baby."

"Okoka!" Angel blushed beet red and glanced after Holt to make sure he hadn't overheard. "That can't be true," she whispered. "It . . . just can't be."

"Oto ke," the Indian girl said, gesturing with both hands up at the sky. Puzzled, Angel watched closely as Okoka held up all five fingers and wiggled them in a starlike fashion. *"Oto-ke* before Nahqui come. See?"

"No," Angel responded a little forcefully. "I don't understand, Okoka. You're wrong."

Stubbornly, the girl held up nine fingers. "*Soto* moons," was all she said.

Angel blanched. Unconsciously, her hands dropped to cradle her stomach. Was there even a remote possibility that the girl could be right? She shook her head to deny the ominous words. Okoka merely smiled again.

It was hard for Angel to leave the security of the little cabin, but harder still to meet the Indian girl's knowing eyes. She took her place in the back of the wagon with Jean-Claude and steadied him as the wagon broke through fresh snow with a jarring start-and-stop motion.

Their progress would be agonizingly slow, Angel realized. She felt every rock and rut they encountered, and the old wagon shuddered with protest as they made their way across the snowy passes and deep ravines. Within an hour she was thoroughly chilled, but she realized Holt was in more danger since he was directly exposed to the winds and snow.

The first short day of winter quickly passed, and they were forced to stop when it became dark. Holt joined the others in the rear of the wagon, and when Angel lit their single lantern she was shocked by the haggard look of him.

He gazed at her directly across the unconscious body of Jean-Claude. "I'll be honest with you; I don't know if we can make it."

"Can we turn back?"

He shook his head. "Morning will show us what we're up against. It's starting to snow again. Best turn down the lantern now. We need to conserve our kerosene."

Wish You Were Here?

*You can be, every month, with Zebra
Historical Romance Novels.*

AND TO GET YOU STARTED, ALLOW US TO SEND YOU

Historical Romances Free

A \$19.96 VALUE!
With absolutely no obligation to buy anything.

YOU ARE CORDIALLY INVITED TO GE
SWEPT AWAY INTO NEW WORLDS OF
PASSION AND ADVENTURE.

AND IT WON'T COST YOU A PENNY!

Receive 4 Zebra
Historical Romances,
Absolutely Free!
(A $19.96 value)

Now you can have your pick of
handsome, noble adventurers with
romance in their hearts and you on
their minds. Zebra publishes Historical
Romances That Burn With The Fire
Of History by the world's finest
romance authors.

This very special FREE offer
entitles you to 4 Zebra novels at absolutely no
cost, with no obligation to buy anything, ever. It's an offer designed
to excite your most vivid dreams and desires...and save you almost $20!
And that's not all you get...

Your Home Subscription Saves You Money Every Month.

After you've enjoyed your initial FREE package of 4 books, you'll begin
receive monthly shipments of new Zebra titles. These novels are delivered
direct to your home as soon as they are published...sometimes even before the
bookstores get them! Each monthly shipment of 4 books will be yours to
examine for 10 days. Then if you decide to keep the books, you'll pay the pre
ferred subscriber's price of just $4.00 per title. That's $16 for all 4 books...a
savings of almost $4 off the publisher's price! (A nominal shipping and han-
dling charge of $1.50 per shipment will be added.)

There Is No Minimum Purchase. And Your Continued Satisfaction Is Guarantee

We're so sure that you'll appreciate the money-saving convenience of
home delivery that we guarantee your complete satisfaction. You may return
any shipment...for any reason...within 10 days and pay nothing that month.
And if you want us to stop sending books, just say the word. There is no mini
mum number of books you must buy.
It's a no-lose proposition, so send for your 4 FREE books today!

YOU'RE GOING TO LOVE GETTING
4 FREE BOOKS

These books worth almost $20, are yours without cost or obligation when you fill out and mail this certificate.
(If the certificate is missing below, write to: Zebra Home Subscription Service, Inc., 120 Brighton Road, P.O. Box 5214, Clifton, New Jersey 07015-5214

Complete and mail this card to receive 4 Free books!

Yes! Please send me 4 Zebra Historical Romances without cost or obligation. I understand that each month thereafter I will be able to preview 4 new Zebra Historical Romances FREE for 10 days. Then, if I should decide to keep them, I will pay the money-saving preferred publisher's price of just $4.00 each...a total of $16. That's almost $4 less than the publisher's price. (A nominal shipping and handling charge of $1.50 per shipment will be added.) I may return any shipment within 10 days and owe nothing, and I may cancel this subscription at any time. The 4 FREE books will be mine to keep in any case.

Name _____

Address _____ Apt. _____

City _____ State _____ Zip _____

Telephone ( ) _____

Signature _____ LP0195
(If under 18, parent or guardian must sign.)

Terms, offer and prices subject to change without notice. Subscription subject to acceptance by Zebra Books.
Zebra Books reserves the right to reject any order or cancel any subscription

Angel turned down the wick until darkness and cold enveloped them like a thick, icy dome. She lay down beside Holt and tried not to think of what lay ahead. Later she was certain she only dreamed about the sound of horse's hooves in the night, and the rich aroma of chickory coffee.

But she knew she wasn't dreaming when she awoke with a start to a trio of unsmiling, unshaven faces looking in the back of the wagon.

"Holt!" she cried with alarm, but her husband didn't respond. He didn't dare. He just sat there gazing with burning silver eyes at the man who held a rifle snugly pressed against his heart.

"Thought you could outsmart me, Murphy?" Sheriff Garrett asked with a nasty laugh as he sharply poked the rifle into Holt's chest several times. With a swift move, Holt grabbed the barrel and wrenched it upwards. Garrett looked surprised, but Holt merely knocked it aside.

"Don't ever do that again," he said, softly and dangerously.

Red Garrett's beady eyes flew to Angel instead. "I thought there was somethin' a little cockeyed 'bout Valentine's new whore," he snarled. "Sure 'nuff, 'cause she's an Injun lover."

"What do you want, Sheriff?" Angel demanded, refusing to let her fear show in the face of danger. She sensed that cringing and whimpering would only stroke the lawman's already huge ego, and she had no intention of giving him that satisfaction.

"What do I want?" Ugly laughter burst from the man's

chapped lips. "Why don't you ask your Injun stud here, 'cause he surely knows."

Angel looked at Holt, but his face was carefully blank. His silver eyes remained fixed on the sheriff's face as Garrett ordered them out of the wagon, all except Jean-Claude, whom he had determined was no threat.

Garrett chewed on his wad of tobacco for a moment as he studied the couple, apparently plotting his next move. Angel glanced at the little makeshift camp they had blundered into in the middle of the night. There were five rough-bitten men there besides Garrett. She had the sinking feeling they were well and truly trapped.

Holt stated calmly, "We're taking this man to Denver, Garrett. It's his only chance."

"Pshaw, son, when did you ever care 'bout anyone's behind 'cept your own?" the sheriff sniggered. "You Murphys seem to think you're a cut above everyone else in this world. Even a half-breed like yourself is puttin' on airs nowadays."

Holt's eyes flashed, but he didn't react to the man's goading. Angel stepped forward in the snow, her chin held high.

"I demand to know on what grounds you are detaining us, Sheriff," she said coldly. "A man's life is at stake here, and I'd hate to have to report your conduct to your superiors in Denver."

Garrett eyed her with surprise and then mounting anger. "Mouthy little thing, ain't ya? All high and mighty now, jest as if you'd never wiggled your hindsight a'fore all the men in Valentine's—"

"Garrett," Holt interrupted mildly, "shut up."

"You gotta lot of nerve, boy!" The sheriff's expression

was ugly. He resumed jabbing the gun at them as if he relished the thought of pulling the trigger. "You know why I'm here, so you better talk fast and sweet, 'less you want the little lady to get hurt."

"Holt, what's he raving about?"

Holt didn't answer. He kept an even smile pasted to his features as he said, "Come on, Garrett, be reasonable. You know I didn't have anything to do with those uprisings. I'm too busy with the mine to even pay my respects at Valentine's anymore."

"There's a re-ward on your head, son, and I'll be damned if I'm gonna let it slip away," Garrett smirked in reply. "You might of tore down all those wanted posters in Oro and Clear Creek, but you sure as shootin' didn't cover all of the Territory."

"Holt Murphy," Angel repeated crisply, "what on earth is he jawing about?"

Holt shot her a quick and apologetic glance. "Sheriff here seems to think I had something to do with those Indian troubles down south."

"Did you?" she blurted.

He hesitated a fraction too long before he turned back to the older man. "Like I said, Sheriff, the mine and my new bride here have kept me too busy to go gallivanting around. Anyway, Garrett, you haven't got any proof."

Garrett cackled. "Proof? When it comes to proof in a court 'round here nobody's gonna believe a 'breed like you. 'Sides, you know who the judge is."

"Felton Garrett." Holt uttered the name with contempt. "Your brother stinks of corruption as strongly as you do, Sheriff."

"Now, just a damn minute—" Red began to snarl.

Angel stepped between them, gambling that the sheriff wouldn't shoot her. She'd seen the lust rekindled in his bloodshot eyes whenever he looked at her, and she was right.

Trying a new tactic, Angel scolded them in her sweetest tone. "We aren't getting anywhere with this, boys. Now, let's be reasonable and work something out over a cup of coffee. That is coffee I smell, isn't it?" Dumbfounded, Garrett nodded. Angel rewarded him with a bright smile and, as all the men stared in open-mouthed amazement, she sauntered over to the campfire and reached for the tin pot that hung over the flames.

The two men had no choice but to obey when Angel briskly handed out a tin cup to each. With a calm air she poured for Holt, ignoring his murderous glare, and then turned to the sheriff. With one swift movement she deposited the remainder of the boiling-hot coffee in Garrett's lap, and as he howled in agony Holt neatly plucked the rifle from his hands.

"I wouldn't try that," he advised the other five men, who all made moves to grab for their guns. He chuckled as he observed Angel primly picking up the dropped coffee tins. Casually, she finished cleaning up, and then at Holt's quiet instruction removed the weapons from the other men and put them in the wagon. Meanwhile the sheriff continued to curse and hop around, grabbing up handfuls of snow to press to his injured area.

"Angel," Holt asked, "can you drive a wagon?"

She nodded. "And I can drive one even faster with a few more horses."

Holt grinned. "I think that can be arranged." He motioned to the posse men to fetch their mounts. "Nice and easy now, boys. I'd hate for any of you to end up like old Red here, all burned up before his time."

None of them doubted Holt's finesse with a gun, for they'd heard enough of the Murphy family. They all moved, swiftly, if sullenly, to do his bidding.

Holt kept the gun trained on Garrett and his men from the rear of the wagon after Angel hitched up the remaining horses. They set off again, Holt chuckling over the memory of Angel's resourcefulness in a pinch. Well, he couldn't deny the young lady had gumption. He just might reconsider that vow of his to send her home, after all.

"We made it, Holt!"

Angel could have wept with relief when she gazed down into the snow-flocked valley where the frontier town of Denver lay slumbering peacefully.

Suddenly she forgot the cold and hunger and impulsively reached out to hug the man beside her. Absentmindedly, Holt hugged her back. "How's Jean-Claude doing?" he asked.

Angel turned to look back into the wagon bed. "He's still sleeping," she said. "I can see him breathing."

"Good. Let's see if we can't get him squared away. He's made it this far, and I'll kill him if he dies on us now." The threat was empty and Angel knew it; she exchanged a quick grin with Holt before he urged the team on down the mountain. It was amazing how much faster they'd gone with six horses to pull the wagon and a spare behind, and she grinned at the mental picture she had of Sheriff Garrett and his cronies struggling on foot to reach Denver.

With any luck, all their important parts would freeze right off, she thought mischievously. And by the time they reached town, she and Holt would be long gone . . . together.

It was midmorning when they arrived in Denver, and by then considerable activity was underway. Horse-drawn carriages and coaches clogged the narrow streets, and paperboys hawked the latest headlines in loud, ringing voices.

Holt stopped to ask someone directions to the nearest doctor, and it was another hour before they negotiated the busy streets and found the clapboard hospital.

There was some question about Jean-Claude's admittance until Holt produced a handful of coins, and a short while later a doctor appeared to assess the situation. He was a thin, stooped-over old man with a shuffling gait and rheumy eyes. Neither one of them were reassured by his appearance.

"This man has concussion," Dr. Phineas Bunker pronounced after examining Jean-Claude, and paused.

Angel and Holt exchanged quick looks.

Doc Bunker clucked his tongue. "You said he never regained consciousness?"

Holt shook his head.

"His chances are poor. Perhaps if we bleed him—"

Angel gasped. "Bleed him? Why, he's lost a gallon of his own blood already. And it won't help his head injury in the slightest."

The doctor frowned and looked at Holt. "Your wife?"

Holt cleared his throat and nodded reluctantly.

"She's very outspoken." Doc Bunker sniffed disapprovingly. "I'd remind her that I'm the doctor here." He waited, as if expecting Holt to do just that.

"Maybe someone else should look at him, sir."

Bunker was obviously insulted, but he snapped for a passing colleague to take a look. The younger doctor was clean-cut, enthusiastic, and quite obviously fresh out of medical school. But he was interested in the case, and agreed with Angel that bleeding Jean-Claude wasn't the answer. The two physicians began to argue.

Strangely enough, it was Jean-Claude himself who saved the day. He groaned faintly and moved just a bit.

"Well!" Doc Bunker exclaimed grudgingly. "Maybe there's some small chance for his recovery, after all. You're welcome to him, Jorgensen."

While Holt and the younger doctor saw to Jean-Claude's removal to a hospital ward, Angel looked down at her sorry attire and dirty hands and wondered how she might straighten herself up. Holt returned shortly and read her mind.

"We'll take a room at the nearest hotel."

She didn't argue, not even over the issue of sharing a room. All that mattered now was getting clean, and the quicker the better.

They registered at the Henderson House, an elegant establishment that would obviously cost a bit more than its equivalent in Clear Creek. An anemic-looking desk clerk pursed his lips over the signature, as if doubting they were truly married. Holt dared the man to dispute the issue with a hard stare, and the clerk swiftly turned over the key to their room.

A short time later Angel had a bath, a brush, and a new set of clothes. Holt had gone out and seen to her needs, for which she was very grateful. She was testing the bed when he returned, but he didn't notice her embarrassment at being caught in such a childish act. He strode over to the window and stood scowling down at the street.

"What's wrong?" she asked, a little piqued that he'd failed to notice how smart the blue alpaca gown looked, and how she'd neatly plaited her hair with the matching ribbons he'd bought.

"There's a man down there," Holt answered at last, his hands tightening on the windowsill, "and I'm half convinced he's been watching me. Only I've never seen him before."

"Is he one of Garrett's men?"

"No. I'd never forget someone that looked like this. He's across the street now, pretending to read a newspaper. But he keeps looking up to our room."

Angel rose and went to peer through the lace curtains. She let out an involuntary gasp. Holt seized her by the arms.

"You know him, don't you? Who is he?"

He gave her a little shake, his eyes suddenly hard and suspicious.

"You don't understand!" Angel cried. "I don't really know him, but—I'm almost sure it's the man I paid to bring you my letter."

"Almost?" Holt growled, still not releasing her.

"I never looked at him that closely, but . . . yes, he does look familiar." She shivered, hating the way Holt lingered suspiciously over every word, taking close measure of her expression. "But I can't imagine why he'd be watching us."

"There's more to this than meets the eye," Holt said.

She nodded, pulling him away from the window. "Please believe me, Holt, I'd never do anything to hurt you. Why, when I hired that man I only told him to give my letter to Mr. Murphy. I never knew your father had died, or that there was more than one Murphy." She paused and bit her lip, trying to remember her exact words to the man. She had been too frantic to reason back then.

"How did you find him?" Holt asked.

She shook her head. "I didn't. He came around asking for odd jobs, offering to do anything, muck stalls, handle the horses . . . or ride." Angel suddenly realized the too-convenient circumstances of the man's arrival at Belle Montagne. "Now that I think of it, he claimed to be from Colorado Territory, and he knew about my father's death before I told him."

"Kind of coincidental, don't you think?"

She flushed. "I was too distraught to find it unusual. He seemed God-sent at the time. So I paid him to ride west and give my message to Mr. Murphy—to you."

"Only I never knew anything about it, now or then," Holt finished as he stared down at her. He wanted to believe Angel, but beautiful blue eyes had betrayed many a man before this. He couldn't risk everything now.

"You're staying here," he said in a hard, quick voice, steering Angel back toward the bed. "I'll have them send up a tray for you. But you're not to leave this room, understand?"

Angel nodded miserably. She realized Holt didn't trust her. "Where are you going?" she asked him softly.

His silvery gaze pinned her to the wall. "Just for now, Angel, I think it's for the best if you don't know."

She tried not to feel the ache in her heart too keenly when he left her without another word.

Holt had been gone for three hours. Afternoon had come and gone, and Angel paced the room fitfully, impatient to know what was going on. She had barely picked at the luncheon that had been brought up to her, and there was nothing of interest to be seen from the window. Even the man who had been watching them was gone. Quite likely he had followed Holt when he had left.

What harm could there be in going downstairs for supper? For all she knew Holt had intended to return before now, and nobody was going to remember her up here. She was registered as a married woman, and she wore the plain gold band that had been her mother's. There didn't seem to be any danger in having a nice, quiet meal in the hotel restaurant.

Angel brightened up considerably as she checked her appearance one last time in the mirror before she left. It felt good to be fashionably dressed again. She must remember to ask Holt where he had learned about female sizes and fashion. Then again, maybe she didn't want to know.

She went downstairs feeling almost guilty for disobeying Holt's orders, but surely even Holt wouldn't expect her to starve for a good cause. At the entrance to the dining room Angel sensed the desk clerk giving her a dubious look, so she blinded him with her southern-belle smile and left the poor man standing flabbergasted as she sauntered past.

The small French restaurant situated in the hotel was

decent and well-kept, and presently occupied by a small number of couples. Angel was heartened and so was the maître d' when he appeared and took note of such a beauty prepared to dine alone.

"Eh bien! Perhaps you seek someone, mademoiselle?" he inquired with a toothy smile.

Angel responded graciously. She clearly shocked him when she replied in perfect French, *"Oui, mon mari. Il n'est pas encore la."*

He was suddenly respectful. "Would you like to wait for your husband at a table, madame?"

Angel said she would, and the maître d' escorted her to a prime table reserved for guests of worth. She thanked him, and her warm smile promised a hefty tip. After handing her the menu the maître d' literally rubbed his hands together in anticipation and hurried off.

So her tiresome French lessons with Madame Faunt had not gone to waste, after all. Angel hid a smile behind the menu as she remembered her father's insistence that she be properly versed in French, Latin, and the classics in order to snare a rich husband. She had the distinct feeling that Holt Murphy wouldn't give a fig for Chaucer or *Macbeth* and, what's more, she was tempted to agree with him.

Angel chose a consommé, followed by veal fricassee and a frothy syllabub for dessert. She was ravenous and had almost forgotten how good real food could taste after a diet of hardtack and dried meat. The maître d' hovered over her, making sure everything was in perfect order and reporting periodically that her husband had not yet arrived.

Finally he was called away to some dispute in the

kitchen, and Angel was left in peace to finish her dessert.
She lingered over the last spoonful of the rich syllabub
and then touched a linen napkin to her lips. She'd better
be getting back upstairs before Holt appeared. She had
told the maître d' to bill her dinner to their room, so there
would be no problem if she quietly slipped away now.

Just then Angel happened to glance out the dining-
room window and got a closeup, unexpected view of the
man who had been tailing Holt. It was the rider she'd
hired, all right, and he was just moving into position
across the street near the barber shop. Holt was definitely
headed back this way, then. Angel felt a quick wave of
panic and started to rise from her chair. The maître d' was
just exiting the kitchens when he saw her setting aside her
napkin.

"Madame!" The little Frenchman hurried over, concern creasing his sweaty brow, and rushed to assist her
with the chair. "Did you find everything to your satisfaction?"

"Excellent," Angel assured him hastily. "But I must be
going now. My husband is due to arrive soon."

"Surely he will be hungry as well?" the maître d' asked
hopefully. "Will you not wait for him here?"

"I-I think not," she said hesitantly. "I am sure he has
already dined elsewhere this evening."

"*Vraiment?* What a pity, madame. But I trust you will
recommend our establishment?"

"Most definitely."

He gave her a grateful nod. "Send all your friends to
Pierre, madame. I shall take great care of them."

"I'm sure you shall." Angel was getting impatient.

Fortunately, Pierre's attentions were quickly removed

to another customer waiting at the entrance. He hurried off as Angel prepared to make a quick escape. She was gathering up her skirts when she heard Pierre's high-pitched voice saying obsequiously, "Right this way, monsieur. Your lovely wife awaits you at our finest table."

Angel looked up with surprise, expecting to see Holt. She made a choked sound of disbelief and revulsion when she recognized the florid-faced man looming over her table.

"Surely you can do better than that, my dear." Willard Craddock laughed dryly as the color drained from Angel's face. He waited until Pierre had plopped down a menu and scurried away, and then he placed his fat knuckles on the table and leaned toward her ominously.

"Did you think you could escape me so easily, girl? No, don't leave. You'll hear me out."

"I don't care to hear anything you have to say," Angel said stiffly, every nerve in her body tense with fear.

"I think you'll listen well enough when you know the subject involved. You still want Belle Montagne, don't you?"

When she made no further move to depart, Will Craddock cackled softly with triumph. He pulled out a chair and eased his huge girth down beside her. Angel could smell the grease on his hair and the noxious odor of onions on his breath as he leaned close. When she looked at him with outright hatred he only waggled a fat finger at her.

"Tsk, tsk, my girl. None of that, now! You'd do well to thank me for saving your family home." His small eyes fell with interest on the dessert bowl, and he pursed his plump lips with disappointment when he saw the dish was already scraped clean. He realized Angel was staring at him in shock, and he decided to feast on her instead. His eyes rose to leer at her. "The price is the same, my dear. You can have your family home back if you agree to my original proposal."

"This is absurd." She angrily tossed aside her napkin. "We've been over this before. I'm not interested in making any deals with you."

Craddock rasped, "You're ravishing when you're vexed, my dear. Simply ravishing! Of course I couldn't get you out of my mind after you left. It took but a few inquiries to find out where you'd gone and when you'd come to Denver."

His words frightened her. Who had given Craddock such information?

"I'll buy back Belle Montagne from you shortly," Angel stated rashly. "I'll have the funds to buy it twice over; you'll see!"

"But there's one problem, my dear," Craddock sniggered as he reached out and pressed his sweaty palm down on hers. "I'm not selling."

Angel snatched her hand away. "And I'm not buying on those terms, Mr. Craddock! I'll thank you to remember I'm a married woman now."

He sniffed disdainfully. "Married to a half-breed wanted by the law? A small inconvenience, I'm sure. Merely say the word, my dear, and your—ah—husband can meet with an unfortunate accident. . . ."

"I've heard enough." Angel rose and ordered the old man fiercely, "Stay away from me! If I see you lurking about or following me, I'll go straight to the law!"

Craddock merely smirked. "Shall we start with Sheriff

Garrett? Or perhaps his brother, Judge Felton Garrett? Both of them are old acquaintances of mine."

"You're bluffing, Craddock." But Angel couldn't stop the tremor of fear that coursed through her body.

"Your father was someone who knew all about bluffing, Angel. Why, he lost everything to me in five-card stud, except for you. I suggested he wager his delectable daughter as well, but McCloud was a stubborn man. He refused."

Angel whirled and ran from the dining room, denying his ominous words. Behind her, Craddock chuckled slyly and made no move to follow. He had plenty of time and opportunity to force her to his hand. All that remained was to dispose of Angel's half-breed husband, and make sure she had no refuge left but Will Craddock's arms.

Chapter Thirteen

Angel's heart was pounding as she slipped into the hotel room and closed the door, leaning against it briefly to catch her breath. She was not a moment too soon; just as she stepped away the door opened again and Holt entered.

He stopped on the threshold, and Angel whirled around and stared, her hands going to her mouth. She didn't recognize him at first, and the transformation was almost more than she could absorb.

Gone entirely was the buckskin outfit Holt always wore, replaced by dark-striped trousers and a black swallow-tailed dinner jacket. The jacket was unbuttoned and she caught a glimpse of a white pleated shirt and a tie. But even more surprising was his hair. It was cropped short, glistening blue-black wherever it caught the light. He looked handsome and debonair, and for a moment she just gaped at him.

"Sorry. Didn't mean to startle you." Holt gave her a rakish grin. His teeth flashed white against the darker bronze of his skin. He shut the door and casually spun a gold-handled walking stick in his gloved hand. "Like my new look?"

Angel nodded. She was glad he mistook her breathlessness for surprise and not guilt. "But your hair . . ."

"It'll grow back. Time I took you out to dinner in the high style you deserve, Angel."

"I'm not hungry now, Holt. Maybe later . . ."

He frowned, suddenly noticing her flushed cheeks and trembling hands. "Did something happen while I was gone?"

Angel shook her head too quickly. Holt tossed aside the stick and the top hat he was holding and rapidly crossed the room toward her.

"You've never been a very good liar, Angel. Tell me what happened."

She forced herself to meet his gaze as she told him about Willard Craddock in a quivering voice. Holt listened until she had finished and then let out a soft oath.

"Why didn't you tell me all this before?"

"It didn't seem important. I thought Craddock was part of my past . . . someone I'd rather not remember."

"You're telling me this old man has Belle Montagne now?"

She nodded miserably. "He refused to sell it back to me. He has a different idea about how I can save my family home."

Holt snorted. "Every man has his price, Angel. We just have to find out what his is."

"I know what Craddock's price is. He wants me to be his mistress. Nothing more, nothing less."

"That's ridiculous. Doesn't he know you're married?"

"Of course. He's made it his business to know everything I do. He even threatened to hurt you, Holt. I couldn't bear it if you were in danger because of me."

Holt tipped up her chin with his hand so that he could look directly into her anxious eyes.

"It'll take more than an old lecher like Craddock to scare me away from you, sweetheart." Very gently his lips found hers, teasing them apart until he could touch her tongue with his own. Angel shivered and clung to his broad shoulders, awash with emotion for the man who held her now. The only man she had ever loved.

Regretfully, Holt broke off the kiss a moment later. "I'm afraid I have some business to settle before we can continue. And I need to check on Jean-Claude."

"Let me go with you, Holt. Please." Angel laid a hand on his arm, her face upturned with a plea. "I feel I owe it to Okoka and the baby to make sure he's all right."

He nodded. "Get your wrap then. It's chilly outside."

Angel slipped on the jacket he had bought her to go with the gown, and together they left the hotel to walk to the hospital. Both were aware of the man watching them leave, and when he fell into stride several paces behind them Angel glanced up and saw Holt's eyes narrow.

"He can't follow us into the hospital," he murmured with some satisfaction. "He'll have to take his best guess as to what we're doing in there."

"Why do you think he's interested in us?"

"Probably Craddock's man. It would certainly explain a lot."

Angel found it hard to believe the widower would go to such lengths to track her movements, but then, Craddock did seem to be obsessed with her. Well, his crony would just have to go back and report that they had visited the hospital and let old Craddock make of it what he would. She found the thought amusing.

"What are you giggling about, woman?"

Angel shot a mischievous glance at her dandified escort. "Holt, what if we were to enter the hospital and never come out?"

His gray eyes flashed back at her with admiration. "How come I didn't think of that? I do believe there's an alley conveniently situated behind the place," he said in a low voice.

They finally reached the clapboard building. A quick glance confirmed the idea.

"After we visit Jean-Claude we'll make good use of the back window."

Angel's heart began to race with anticipation as she mounted the wooden steps beside Holt.

"Slowly, now," he cautioned her with a grin. "We don't want our new friend to get suspicious."

She slanted a glance over her shoulder at the shadowy figure pausing beneath a lamp post, ostensibly to light a cigar. It was definitely cold out, and the poor fellow was likely to get quite chilled before his night was through.

Holt held open the door and Angel went in first, to be greeted by the resident nurse on duty. The doctor had gone home for the evening. The couple exchanged quick looks.

"How's Jean-Claude?" Holt inquired, as he stripped off his dinner gloves and stuffed them in his coat pocket. The nurse was respectful to the well-dressed pair and invited them to see for themselves.

"Your brother awoke several times this afternoon," the nurse said as she led them down the hall, and Angel looked at Holt with surprise. He shrugged and winked, then stepped into the small room where Jean-Claude had been settled.

There was a narrow iron bed upon which the patient rested, a wooden chair, and a nightstand with a pitcher. Other than that, the chamber was quite plain. It was, however, spanking clean, and so was the patient. Someone had taken the time to shave Jean-Claude, and without the heavy growth of beard the Frenchman looked very young and vulnerable.

"He keeps asking for someone named Anne-Marie," the nurse said, looking curiously at Angel.

"Ah, yes, our sainted mother," Holt quickly supplied, with a dazzling smile at the nurse that clearly rocked the poor woman back on her heels. "He was always her favorite, you know."

"I see . . . well, you may stay a few minutes," the nurse said, backing slowly out of the room. "He mustn't be upset, though. I'm sure you understand."

Holt nodded. Angel smiled sweetly at the woman as well. Soon they were alone with the patient.

"Your 'sainted mother'?" Angel giggled, pressing a hand to her lips.

Holt scowled. "It was the best I could do on such short notice." He walked over to the bed and looked down at Jean-Claude. "Looks like Doc has done the best he can. Time will tell."

"Poor man. He looks so young!"

Holt nodded grimly. "But old enough to have a family depending on him. If he doesn't recover, who will look after his wife and child?"

"We will," Angel said promptly, and at his surprised

look she stammered, "I mean, I'd hope you would check in on them from time to time."

"I fully intend to, but what about you?"

"Me?" Angel's voice was barely a whisper. "What do you mean?"

"Are you up to staying in the Territory a little longer? Or do you want to take Craddock up on his offer?"

"Of course not . . . Holt, are you saying what I think you're saying?"

He shrugged a little defensively. "It's entirely up to you. There's still the question of our marriage—"

"And the mine," Angel finished. She moved closer to him, trying to read his impenetrable gray eyes. "Yes," she said softly, "I'd like to stay, Holt."

"All right. We'll try to work something out . . ."

Jean-Claude suddenly groaned. Both of them leaned toward the bed anxiously.

The young man's lips moved soundlessly for a moment, and then a name escaped him, very distinctly in the taut silence of the room.

"Anne-Marie!"

The couple looked at each other in faint alarm when he began to roll his injured head from side to side, calling the name louder and more plaintively with each passing second.

Angel moved quickly, taking his limp hand in her own. *"Taisez-vous!* Hush, Jean-Claude."

"Anne-Marie?" The delirious man struggled to lift his head. "Is it you?"

She hesitated only briefly. *"C'est moi.* Lie quietly, now. You've been hurt."

"Ah, *cherie* . . ."

Angel exchanged a surprised glance with Holt. Anne-Marie was definitely not his mother!

The trapper suddenly gripped Angel's hand so hard it turned white. She gasped softly.

"Espouser moi . . ." Jean-Claude muttered.

Angel paled, and Holt demanded, "What's he saying?"

"He just asked me—I mean, Anne-Marie—to marry him!"

"What the devil?" Holt didn't like that one bit. He asked skeptically, "Are you sure the man's out cold?"

"Oui—y-yes." Angel stammered.

In vain Angel tried to tug her hand free, but Jean-Claude's grip was so intense, it almost brought tears to her eyes.

"Anne-Marie?" he repeated anxiously.

"J'y pense." I'm thinking about it. And if Holt's glare was any indication, she'd better think fast!

Suddenly Jean-Claude's grip went slack. Angel lowered his hand gently to the bed. "He's unconscious again," she said with relief, massaging her aching fingers.

Holt still wasn't smiling. "What was that all about?"

"I think Anne-Marie must have been his fiancée. Maybe his first wife. Obviously he loved her dearly."

"Obviously," Holt growled, tapping his shoe a little impatiently.

"He's doing better, I think," Angel said. "He has a chance now."

"And in his imagination he has a chance with you."

"Oh, Holt, don't be foolish. The poor man is delirious. He wouldn't be at all interested in me if he were awake."

He slanted her a wry glance. "Don't be so sure. It suddenly seems I'm being challenged on all sides for you."

"That's nonsense and you know it. We'd better leave him to rest now. I hope the nurse didn't hear any of that."

The nurse hadn't, and was nowhere to be seen as they stepped out into the hall.

"Now's our chance," Holt said, leading Angel swiftly to the rear of the building, where he hefted open a large window. It was a good drop to the alley, and Holt helped Angel onto the sill and lowered her down first, dangling her briefly until she could get her legs in position for the drop.

A musty pile of straw cushioned her fall, and Angel brushed loose strands from her skirts and hair as she stepped back out of Holt's way. He dropped catlike from the sill, landing a few feet away. They both looked to the end of the alley, where they could just see the man who had followed them still smoking his cigar, watching the hospital entrance.

"What now?" Angel whispered.

"We find a new hotel." Holt took her by the hand, tugging her along. "Or better yet, a boardinghouse."

"There's still a tab at the front desk where we were!"

"I'll stop in and pay it later. Let's give Craddock some time to cool his heels."

"And Jean-Claude?"

"We can check on him again. Right now we need to find a safe haven for a few days."

A safe haven, as it turned out, was a seedy boarding-house close to the railroad tracks. Holt insisted that they'd be safer there, but Angel didn't relish the view or the mouse-infested room they rented for a night.

She insisted on accompanying Holt to the mining claim office the following morning, if only to get out of the boardinghouse. She'd never imagined the confusion that would follow once they arrived at the government building to check the status of their claim.

Holt supplied the name of his father and the mine, and they waited a half hour for the clerk to research the deed. When the fellow returned shaking his head both Holt and Angel stared at him in disbelief.

"Sorry; can't find anything. You sure it's under the name Murphy? Spelled M-u-r-p-h-y?"

"Yes—or the Lucky Devil Mine. Did you check all the records?"

The elderly clerk squinted at Holt indignantly over his pince-nez. "I always do, young man. 'Fraid I checked everything there was."

"Then I suggest you check again—" Holt began hotly, but Angel placed a restraining hand on his arm.

"Sir, what about McCloud? Royce McCloud. Try that name."

Grumbling resentfully, the clerk wandered back to his dusty files, only to return a short time later with a thick sheaf of papers.

"Yep, it's here, all right," he announced. "You could of saved me a lot of time by giving me the right name in the first place—"

"Yes, yes, but what does it say about the Lucky Devil?" Holt interrupted impatiently.

"That's another thing, son. T'ain't called the Lucky Devil. It's spelled out clear right here." He opened the file and jabbed an ink-stained thumb on the deed. "A-n-g-e-l. Lucky Angel. Odd name for a mine," he mused.

" 'Pears there's been some misunderstandin' on your end."

Angel and Holt exchanged shocked glances.

"Are you sure?" they asked in unison.

The clerk shoved the file at them. "See for yourself."

They did, and it was. Angel shook her head over that revelation, as much as another paper Holt read aloud a second later.

"I hereby deed over all my claim in aforesaid mine to my partner, Royce McCloud . . ."

It was signed by Arthur Murphy and dated several months before his death.

Holt slammed the file shut with a poof of dust. His face was white. Suddenly Angel understood. She alone, not she and Holt, had inherited the mine. It had been named for her in the beginning, and it belonged to her now. Holt had nothing . . .

"There must be some mistake," she began faintly.

"No mistake." Holt spoke curtly. "It's Arthur's signature, all right. What I don't understand is why the old bastard didn't bother to tell me he'd sold out—"

"Holt, please." Angel could understand his rage and disappointment, and placed her hand over his balled fist on the counter. "It doesn't change anything—"

He jerked his hand away. "The hell it doesn't. All my life I've sweated, broken my back in that hellhole, for Arthur and his dreams, and he led me to believe I'd have a stake in it someday. What have I got to show for it now?"

She faltered, trying to rally them both. "You can still work the mine. I'll deed you back your half—"

"No. Spare me any favors, sweetheart. Murphy men

have more pride than to take the leavings of a woman."

The words stung, but Angel knew how devastated he was. "Let's reason this out," she suggested gently. "Maybe we're missing something here—"

"A hell of a lot, I'd say." Holt shoved the file back at the clerk and stalked out of the claims office. Angel picked up her skirts and hurried after him, calling his name. She finally got him to stop on the boardwalk, but the silver eyes were resentful as they swung back to focus on her.

"I know you're angry, Holt, but I didn't have anything to do with this," she pleaded. "How could either of us know what our fathers would do?"

"I feel like such a damned fool," he growled, furiously raking a hand through his newly cropped black hair.

Angel shook her head. "You're not. Neither of us had any inkling that Arthur might have sold out. My father certainly never mentioned it. He always referred to Arthur Murphy as his partner."

Holt briefly closed his eyes. When he opened them again they were dark with anguish. "Everything," he rasped at last, "everything I've ever done and been and had was wrapped up in that mine. There's nothing left now."

Angel started to protest, but he savagely cut her off.

"I don't want your pity. And I'll be damned if I'll take your charity, Angel McCloud. You should be happy now. You have the whole mine to yourself and now you can buy back your precious Belle Montagne."

Her blue eyes flashed. "I told you, Craddock won't sell. Even if he would, I wouldn't use your half of the mine to pay for it." She paused for a long moment. "And one more thing: The name's Angel Murphy now. What I have is yours."

"The marriage isn't legal!" Holt almost shouted at her. Several passersby looked at them with alarm and hurried past.

"Prove it." Hands on her hips, Angel squared off with the glowering Holt, her chin jutting out stubbornly. "Go ahead, Mr. Murphy; prove I'm not your wife."

"Prove that you are!" he hurled back.

"Fine. I'll just head on back to Oro and get those papers from Neal—"

"What did you say?" Holt's voice was suddenly quiet and almost dangerous. He stepped closer to her, his brows low. "What the hell does he have to do with this?"

Angel flushed under his hard stare. "I asked Neal if the marriage was legitimate. I showed him the papers . . . he said it was." She raised her chin a notch. "Your brother ought to know. He's a minister, after all!"

"He's a base opportunist, and a liar to boot," Holt snarled. "I might have known he was in on this with you."

"What do you mean?"

"I mean you two probably cooked up this whole clever scheme together." He sneered as she took a step backwards. "What's the matter, Mrs. Murphy? Did that strike a little too close for comfort?"

"No, of course not. You're being ridiculous. Neal and I—"

"That's right, Neal and you. I wonder why I didn't see it before. Those pretty blue eyes of yours could entrap any man, even a man of God."

"Holt, you're making a big mistake!"

He chuckled mirthlessly. "No, lady, you are." He tilted up her chin and, as Angel's eyes flashed dangerously at him, he taunted her a final time. "But there's one thing I know for sure, sweetheart. Even my paragon of a brother can't kiss like this."

Hard and quick, Holt's lips slanted down across hers, jolting her to the core like summer lightning. Angel gasped and grabbed his lapels for support, weaving unsteadily for a second while she absorbed the impact of his barely leashed anger. Finally he set her away from him, his eyes even harder than before.

"There. A souvenir of our sweet, short honeymoon."

Angel lightly touched her bruised and throbbing lips. "You don't mean that, Holt."

"Don't I?" Without another word he turned and briskly strode away through the milling traffic of carts and horses.

Watching him vanish into the hubbub of the city, Angel felt the pain of loss so sharply, she almost doubled over from it. She crossed an arm across her waist and managed to make it to a wooden bench.

There she sat and collected herself, ignoring the rush and press of humanity around her, too stunned to even consider her options.

"Miss? Ticket, miss?"

A whiskered man wearing the railroad insignia on his cap stopped to hold out his hand.

"I'm not waiting for a train."

"Then you'd best move. This bench here's for folks waitin' to ride the rail."

"Oh, I see. I'm sorry." She rose and he quickly steadied her.

"There now. You sure you're all right?" He looked at her a little suspiciously, as if suspecting she might be intoxicated.

Angel nodded. "Yes, thank you. I was just disoriented for a second. I'm not familiar with Denver . . ." She hurried off before he could ask further questions.

Back at the boardinghouse, Angel collected her few things, hesitating when she found the cache of coins Holt had left there, knotted in a silk kerchief. She did need a means of survival, after all, and a way to get back to Oro.

Thoughts of Rachel and Neal heartened her, so she didn't feel quite so guilty when she took a few coins and slipped them into her bodice for safekeeping.

Maybe Holt only needed some time to come around. When he found Angel gone he might be persuaded to look for her and make amends.

She only wished she could believe that as certainly as she wished it.

Chapter Fourteen

Angel was waiting for the last stagecoach to Oro City when she saw a familiar figure coming down the boardwalk. There would be no more stages west until spring, so she was forced to stand her ground. But it wasn't easy, especially when Craddock halted right before her.

Hooking a hand into the waistcoat barely buttoned over his huge stomach, Craddock rocked back on his heels with glib satisfaction.

"So we meet again, m'dear." He grinned triumphantly at her. "Really, you're wasting your time trying to escape me."

"Don't flatter yourself," Angel snapped, turning the other way.

Craddock moved to her other side, forcing a confrontation. "I know everything you do, everywhere you go. I even know your half-breed abandoned you." He clucked his tongue sympathetically. "I told you he wasn't a reliable sort."

"You know nothing of Holt or me," Angel said flatly.

She waved to get the stagemaster's attention. "This man is harassing me," she complained when he came over.

The stagemaster looked at Craddock. "Afternoon, Will."

"Percy." The rich widower nodded dismissingly at the man, and that was that. The stagemaster quickly moved off, avoiding Angel's angry stare. She bristled with outrage. She should not be forced to suffer Craddock's attentions!

"I wasn't aware you had so many connections in the Territory," Angel told Craddock coldly.

He took her sarcasm as a compliment. "There are few places where the almighty dollar doesn't reach."

Angel sighed. "What would it cost me to be left alone?"

"Very amusing, my dear."

"I'm completely serious." Her candid blue eyes turned on him, a new spark in their depths as a wild idea dawned. "You're a gambling man, Craddock. You drove my father to deliberate ruin. You must be very clever to have done that."

He preened, not sensing the cutting edge beneath her words. "Well, it's not my fault McCloud was a poor cardplayer."

"Indeed," Angel murmured. She watched him closely beneath lowered lashes. "What would you say to one last game of five-card stud?"

He looked surprised. "With whom?"

"Me, of course."

Craddock laughed so hard he began to wheeze. "You? But you're a woman!"

"Thank you for noticing, Will." She deliberately used his nickname in a seductive manner that left Craddock gaping at her.

"But—" he sputtered, waving his arms about, "ladies don't draw poker!"

Angel tossed her head. "I wasn't under the impression you wanted a *lady* to warm your bed."

He stared long and hard at her, but there was definite interest blossoming in his beady little eyes.

"What are the stakes?" he asked a second later.

"Let's keep it simple. Your word as a gentleman—and on the Craddock family honor—that you'll leave me alone for good if I win. And deed me back Belle Montagne."

Craddock considered. He didn't really want the place; it had been merely a means to entice Angel back to Missouri.

"And what do I get?" he asked.

This was the hard part. Angel swallowed, realizing she would be bound to keep her word. "You get me," she said.

"Deal." Craddock stuck out his fleshy hand, his big belly shaking with laughter. This was not only going to be easy, he thought—it was going to be damn fun, too.

Even the old-timers hadn't seen such a crowd at Pike's Peak Saloon since the first gold rush. Word spread quickly around the gambling district that a young lady was willing to bet her body in exchange for a hunk of ground back east. It was not only unheard of but exciting enough to draw the attention of folks from every walk of life.

Outside the saloon, the Oro City stagecoach sat ready and empty, well paid by Craddock to change their schedule. He didn't believe for a minute that Angel would win, but nobody could accuse him of not being a good sport. Will sat awaiting the young woman he'd lusted after for almost three years and discreetly wiped the saliva from the corners of his mouth with a handkerchief his first wife, Edna, had embroidered with his initials.

A short time later Angel walked in and took her place amid the raucous crowd of betting men. She'd undone her tightly plaited hair to massage her aching temples, and her golden hair rippled over her shoulders and back nearly to her waist. There wasn't a man there who wouldn't have given his eyeteeth to be in Will Craddock's place once they saw the flesh-and-blood stakes sit down across from him.

Watching from the bar, Holt Murphy nearly inhaled his whiskey. He coughed and choked, but nobody noticed except the bartender, who obligingly gave him a hard slap on the back.

"Right nice looker, ain't she?" the barkeep agreed.

Holt couldn't believe his eyes. Angel—*his* Angel—was sitting down calmly at a poker table, rolling up her sleeves and briskly shuffling a deck of cards. And it was obvious she knew what she was about.

She looked up once, and Holt could have sworn she stared right at him. But the blue eyes didn't betray so much as a flicker of recognition before she turned away and slapped down the deck in front of Craddock.

"Your cut, Will," she said, folding her hands beneath her chin and propping her elbows on the table to watch.

Craddock picked up the deck a little suspiciously, shuffled it a few more times for good measure, and then cut the cards. It was agreed a third party would deal the hand to make it fair.

The first cards were dealt facedown. The rest would be revealed after the bets were placed. Tallies were taken and money exchanged hands in a flurry, almost everyone agreeing that the young lady wouldn't stand a chance. That included Holt.

He asked the bartender in a strangled voice, "What the hell is going on?"

"That sweet thing done bet ol' Craddock he can't beat her at five-card stud. She bet herself against some ol' house she wants. Craddock'll be a lucky coot tonight."

Holt stiffened. What on earth was Angel doing, gambling with her life like that? The little fool had no more sense than a chicken!

Holt left the bar and pushed his way through the knot of yelling, cheering men just as Angel and Craddock revealed their first cards. His was a queen, hers a seven. Those who had bet on Angel groaned.

"Buck up, girlie," one old-timer hollered. "T'ain't over yet!"

"Oh yes, it is," Holt growled, squeezing through to the table, where he slapped down a hand over Angel's before she turned over her next card.

"What do you think you're doing?" he demanded.

Her frosty blue eyes rose and met his without a waver. The golden brows raised. "What difference does it make to you, Holt Murphy?"

"You don't know the first thing about poker!"

She smiled a little cynically. "I watched my father enough when I was growing up. I think I can muddle through."

"Dammit, woman, you're playing with fire!"

"But it's my choice, isn't it? I've no husband to tell me

otherwise." Her steady gaze mocked him. So, too, did the disappointed men all around them.

"C'mon, son, let 'em play!"

"Get outta the way, feller."

Rough male hands literally removed Holt from the arena. He thought about grabbing her anyway and dragging her out of the saloon but decided it wasn't worth it. Angel wasn't worth it, he told himself. He pretended to ignore the hoots of derision and cackles of glee when the next round gave Craddock an ace and Angel a six.

Angel wasn't as cool as she appeared. Her mouth was cotton dry and her ears roared with the blood pounding in her head. And Holt's appearance had definitely thrown her for a moment. She stared down at her measly six and seven and said a quick little prayer.

Craddock was grinning ear to ear. "Not long now, darlin'," he breathed, and almost everyone leaned back as the strong smell of onions wafted across the table.

Angel glanced past Craddock to Holt's lean, taut figure, poised against the bar. His arms were folded, his expression fixed. What did he care if she sold herself to an old lecher? He didn't seem to have much use for her himself.

Everyone held their breath, due as much to Craddock's foul odor as the flip of the next card. A ragged cheer arose from Angel's loyal handful of supporters. She had a pair of sevens now. They quickly quieted, though. Craddock still had a queen, and now another ace.

"Pretty bird, why put yourself through this?" Craddock gloated as he leaned across to Angel, unsuccessfully trying to grab her hand. "I can promise you your cage will be a nice one."

Angel responded by turning over her fourth card: another six. Two pair. She smiled. Craddock started to sweat, mopping his streaming brow as he stared down at the card before him.

A sigh left him with a huge whoosh. Another queen.

"Royalty," he said. "We'll live like royalty, m'dear."

"In a pig's eye," Angel replied. Her fingers trembled as she reached for the last card. Her eyes rose and drifted to Holt. He stared at her unsmilingly across the smoky saloon.

Craddock noisily licked his lips, bringing her attention back to the table. "Go ahead; ladies first," he goaded her.

Slowly, Angel turned over the last card. She slapped it down under Craddock's nose and rose from the table with dignity.

"Full house, gentlemen."

The saloon erupted. Craddock purpled. "Sit down!" he bellowed. "It isn't over yet!"

He cast a contemptuous glance at her motley array of three sevens and sixes as he fingered his last card. He moved his arm slightly as he flipped it over.

"Well, well," he announced, "it seems I have a full house also. Only mine now includes the very desirable young woman sitting across from me."

Angel whirled back as the surge of congratulations died. She stared in horror at the third ace on the table. "No!" she cried, and the saloon went silent.

Craddock's chair scraped backwards as he rose heavily and held out his fleshy hand to her. "Be a good sport, my dear. You've had your fun."

"I—no, it can't be," Angel whispered, her shock-filled eyes still fixed on the table.

"Come along. The eastbound train is waiting."

"It'll wait a little longer," a third voice drawled.

Craddock flicked a dismissing glance at Holt Murphy. "This doesn't concern you, boy."

" 'Fraid it does, mister." Holt pushed off from the bar and strolled slowly toward the older man. "See, it concerns me whenever I see a worthless old lecher taking advantage of a sweet and innocent thing like Miss Angel here."

Craddock's lip curled. He snorted. "Sweet? Innocent? She's hardly in either class anymore, after living with a 'breed like you."

Holt halted barely a foot away from the other man. His gray eyes were hard as flint. "I also take exception to a man who wears long sleeves during a game of cards," he stated.

A brief flash of panic lit the old man's eyes. "You're babbling nonsense, boy. Get out of my way."

Craddock moved, but Holt cut him off, grabbing the older man by the lapels to hold him fast.

"I'm sure you won't have any objections to having me shake you down, then," he gritted out, and gave Craddock a good hard shake. A fistful of cards tumbled out from the old man's jacket, and there was an audible gasp across the room.

All were aces. Angel knelt and picked one up, bending it in half as she stared at Craddock.

"You did the same thing to my father, didn't you?" Her voice shook, and she hurled the card at him. It bounced off his waistcoat and fell to the floor. "You cheated him, and because of what you did he killed himself!"

Craddock snarled back, "I didn't have to cheat! Royce McCloud was a worthless bum, a drunken sot! If he couldn't hold on to his land or his daughter any better than he played cards, then he deserved to lose both to me!"

"Shut up!" Holt ordered the man, shaking him by the collar until Craddock was bright red and wheezing. With a disgusted noise, Holt threw Craddock back against the wall. He didn't need to do anything more. The angry crowd mobbed Craddock of its own accord as Holt followed Angel out of the saloon.

Tears spurted down her cheeks as she hurried down the boardwalk. Fiercely, she wiped them away.

Holt caught up to her, grabbing her hands in his and pulling her around to face him. The tears sparkled on her cheeks like diamonds in the sunlight.

"The old man's a liar," he said.

"No, Holt, I am. I lied to myself all those years. I even helped my father live a lie." She looked up at him with eyes that tore at his soul. "I knew Royce drank. I knew he gambled. I didn't try hard enough to stop him."

He enfolded her gently in his arms. "It wasn't your place to stop him. You were just a child."

"B-but I could have t-tried harder," she whispered, closing her eyes as fresh tears slipped down her cheeks. "I hid the bottles sometimes, and even slipped him a dose of laudanum from time to time to keep him home, but it never worked long enough to make a difference. And after a while I stopped trying. Maybe if I'd kept up I could have protected him from Craddock . . ."

"Your father was a grown man, Angel. He made his choice. I know it hurts, but you can't take responsibility for someone else's life, no matter who they are." Tenderly, Holt stroked her shining golden head until she released a low, shuddering sigh.

"I know you're right. But I just can't stop thinking about Belle Montagne . . ."

"It's yours now, Angel. We've got fifty witnesses if Craddock tries to back out on his word. You can go home now," he said softly. She looked up at him with surprise when she heard the quiet pain in his voice.

"I'm not going," she whispered.

"Don't be ridiculous," Holt suddenly exploded. "That house is everything you've wanted, woman. All you've waited for and talked about since I met you!"

"Exactly," Angel said. "That 'house,' Holt. It's nothing more than that now. It's been stripped of furniture, decoration, even its dignity. I've no funds to set it up properly. I still have to wait for our mine to produce."

He hesitated, as if debating the truth of her words, then bluntly corrected her. "*Your* mine."

Angel shook her head with sudden exasperation. "Holt, listen to me! I need you. You know about mining; I don't. Nothing will be accomplished if we continue to fight like cats and dogs over a legal technicality. Don't deny you still want to work the mine."

"All right, I want to. But you'd better realize, Angel, it may never produce. If we don't strike it rich by spring, we probably won't find anything at all. I've exhausted almost all the tunnels."

She nodded, accepting the risk. "I don't have anything to lose."

He gave her a wry grin. "And the only thing you're gaining is a penniless partner."

"I meant what I said earlier, Holt. I still consider you

half-owner of the mine. I don't want things to change now. Besides, I know next to nothing about mining."

"I won't dispute that. But I don't think I've ever seen anyone quite so determined as you."

"It's a McCloud trait, I'm afraid." A hint of a smile curved her lips for the first time, and she added, "And it's every bit as maddening as Murphy pride."

"I'm sorry I lost my temper earlier, Angel. I said some things I shouldn't have," Holt admitted. "But our time apart gave me time to think. I also made arrangements for Jean-Claude. He regained consciousness for a short time when I visited him today. I explained what happened, and he was very grateful to us both. The doctor said Jean-Claude's head injury is healing well. He'll be able to rejoin his family when he's fully recovered."

"I'm so glad. But will he have enough money to pay the doctor bills?"

Holt nodded. "Actually, I used the last of my own money to take care of that. Jean-Claude said he'd pay me back, and I think his word is good. I told him he could contact me at the mine. Maybe that was a little presumptuous of me."

Angel smiled and touched his smooth-shaven chin. "No, it wasn't. You belong there, and so do I. I want you to take me home now, Holt."

He hesitated only briefly. "Are you sure that's what you want?"

"It's all I've ever wanted," Angel softly confirmed.

Angel slept all the way back to Oro, and even the worst bumps and jolts of the stage didn't cause her to stir. She awoke yawning when Holt opened the door and hopped down to give her a hand.

She eyed the three feet of snow awaiting her with some surprise. "My goodness! It looks like winter beat us back."

"It does, doesn't it?" Holt agreed as he helped her down. "Watch your step; it's slippery here."

She steadied herself on his arm and looked up just as a couple moved forward to greet them.

"Rachel! Neal! What a nice surprise." Angel was genuinely surprised to see the minister there with Rachel on his arm, but the warm glow on Rachel's cheeks told a story of its own.

"We heard the stage was coming in, and I had a feeling you'd be on it," Rachel said as she returned Angel's quick hug. "Gracious, you look exhausted!"

"I am," Angel admitted ruefully, then caught sight of Neal and Holt exchanging their usual wary looks. She quickly stepped between the two men. "Maybe I need some of your Aunt Clara's nerve tonic," she said gaily as she turned to face Rachel again.

Rachel laughed. "I daresay I'll get a few bottles at our wedding."

"Wedding?" Suddenly Angel understood Rachel's pink cheeks and the merry secret in her eyes. "Oh, my goodness! You're engaged?"

Rachel drew her left hand from the fur muff and thrust it out to be admired. "Do you like the ring? Neal said I look so good in gold!"

"It's beautiful, Rachel. Congratulations, both of you." Angel looked to the man beside her. "Here we've been gone only a few weeks and look what's happened. Isn't it amazing, Holt?"

"Amazing," he agreed dryly, putting a different emphasis entirely on the word.

Angel quickly changed the subject. "Tell me everything that's happened," she ordered Rachel, linking arms with the other woman as they moved down the street toward the parsonage. "I want you to fill me in on all the gossip!"

Rachel delightedly complied. She told Angel about the latest social, the latest scandals, and the mysterious recent appearance of Sheriff Garrett out of nowhere, with frostbite on various parts of his body.

"He wouldn't tell anyone what happened," Rachel said, "and Mrs. Garrett took after him with a frying pan!"

Angel choked down her laughter. "Whatever for?"

"Justine was just sure he'd been fooling around at Valentine's again, got too drunk, and wandered out in the snow. He's done it before. She's always managed to cover it up till now, but this time he walked right down Main Street, howling for old Doc to come out and check his crotch."

Angel couldn't restrain the peals of laughter. She chuckled until her sides hurt, and by then they were back at the parsonage. Rachel thought it was funny, too, but couldn't fully appreciate Angel's hilarity over the story.

Finally Angel wiped her streaming eyes and composed herself for the benefit of the two men behind them. Holt and Neal had obviously been having a long discussion, and the topic was serious enough that neither one was smiling. She looked back and forth between them and felt a prickle of foreboding at their expressions.

"There's been trouble up at the mine again," Holt said.

"What kind of trouble?" Angel instantly sobered, and Neal proceeded to explain.

"A couple of U.S. Marshals came poking around, asking a lot of questions of the locals here and in Clear Creek. They even came to the parsonage and quizzed me."

"What did they want?" Angel asked.

"They seemed to be looking for something up at the mine. I don't know what it was. They wouldn't tell me. But it doesn't sound good."

Angel moved closer to Holt. She touched his arm and murmured, "Was that what Garrett was rambling about?"

He shrugged. "Maybe. None of it makes any sense to me." His gaze shifted back to Neal. "Did they ask you where I was?"

The minister nodded. "Yes. I told them only that you'd left the area some time ago. They said something about an inquiry."

Holt stiffened. "They'll have to catch me first."

"Now, let's not get all upset," Rachel said cheerily, moving toward the kitchen in the parsonage. "Why don't I warm up some nice hot cocoa for us?"

"Sounds good," Angel agreed. "I'll help you."

They left the two men to talk and moved out of hearing range to exchange some quick words of their own.

"Is it that serious?" Angel asked her friend in the kitchen. "Did you see the marshals?"

"No, I didn't see them, but the town was all abuzz with the news. Angel, I almost didn't recognize Holt with short hair and a suit! I know he can be a bit of a scoundrel, but he isn't dangerous, is he?"

"No," Angel replied firmly. "There's been some awful mistake. I think Garrett's behind it. He followed us from Oro and ambushed us halfway to Denver."

"Gracious! What happened?"

Angel told her, and Rachel looked a little envious of their adventures. Then Angel remembered something else.

"Did you tell Neal about shooting that Olsen man?"

"Ssh!" Rachel cautioned her. "He mustn't overhear us. No, I didn't tell him."

"But, Rachel—"

"Don't you understand, Angel?" her friend pleaded. "I couldn't risk it. Not after he proposed to me at long last, and when I'm about to have everything I've ever wanted. That was a stupid, foolish thing to do, going up to the mine, and I don't ever want to talk about it again."

Rachel's tone was fierce. Tears had sprung to her eyes.

"Of course," Angel said soothingly. "We'll say no more about it."

But inside she was troubled. If Neal loved Rachel enough to marry her, wouldn't he understand what had happened, and absolve his bride-to-be of her painful burden of guilt?

The flames in the grate crackled and popped merrily in the silence that reigned in the parsonage study. Angel sat on the sofa across from the grate, extending her cold hands toward the warmth of the orange flames. Holt leaned against the mantel, halfheartedly smoking a thin cheroot. Neither of them could find words just yet, not after the announcement Holt had made.

Angel's eyes were still swimming with tears. Holt was leaving her again! And nothing had swayed him this time, not her arguments, not her sweet wheedling, and certainly not her curt reminder that she was the legal owner of the mine and thus had every right to go with him.

She raised her gaze to study the handsome man lounging across the room from her, wondering if anything ever reached that steely heart. How terribly Holt must have been hurt as a child, to maintain that blank facade toward her now. Her pleas had fallen on deaf ears, and what was worse, he didn't even seem to regret his going.

The silence had drawn on longer than she could bear. Swallowing hard, Angel glanced at the clock on the mantel. "Neal should be back any minute. He said he was walking Rachel home and coming straight back to the parsonage."

"Maybe he ran into some of his do-gooders."

Holt's tone was harsh. He still hadn't accepted Neal or the possibility that his brother could care for him, or want to make amends for the past.

Angel realized she had lost the battle, but the war wasn't over yet. She said softly, "You should reconsider, Holt. Nobody will bother the mine now that winter has hit. And you could be stuck up there for days, maybe weeks. There's no shelter there anymore. What if you got sick?"

"Dammit, Angel, we've been over this a dozen times. Somebody has to guard the mine, even in winter. Otherwise it could be milked dry by spring."

"Then take me with you." Her eyes beseeched his, but he tore his gaze away with an irritated noise. "Or hire someone else to watch the place. Just don't go alone."

"I don't trust anybody in this one-horse town, and besides, you wouldn't survive a winter in the mountains. Not without the cabin. Hell, maybe I'm crazy, but if the mine isn't guarded day and night, summer and winter, I have a feeling we'll lose it altogether."

"There's no chance of that, Holt. We checked on the claim in Denver. Unless I sell—which I have no intention of doing—the Lucky Angel is legally mine."

"Laws and lawyers don't mean anything out here, sweetheart." Holt clamped down on the end of the cheroot and spoke through clenched teeth. "The law of the land prevails, which means scum like Garrett and his men are like little kings. They could string either one of us up and nobody would stop them."

Angel gasped softly. "Surely even Garrett is answerable to someone, somewhere!"

Holt shook his head. "Nope. The only fellow to ever question our good sheriff was a man by the name of Burl. Harlow Burl, I believe it was. Anyway, Burl was some fancy eastern lawyer with some pretty fancy ideas about justice and the law." He paused to puff a smoke ring from his lips and it drifted lazily across the room. "Burl threatened to report Garrett's activities to some senator back east, as I recall. But he never did, of course."

"What happened to him?" Angel asked apprehensively.

"Burl was found a couple of miles up Clear Creek, with a bullet lodged in his brain. All that book-learning crammed in there didn't so much as slow the shell." Holt looked at her directly to emphasize his story. "Needless to say, Garrett's friends confirmed that the sheriff was in the Oro saloon all day. Only I happen to know differently."

"Lily?"

Holt nodded slightly. "Garrett wasn't within a mile of the place. When he heard about Burl's death all Garrett said was, 'Well, there's a lot of wilderness around here, ain't there? A city boy can get hurt purty easy.' "

Angel shuddered, even though the warmth of the fire had finally soaked into her bones. "But now you want to go up and guard the mine alone. Don't you see how crazy that is?"

"No crazier than letting you talk me into working it with you again. The mine is yours, Angel, from top to bottom. Don't think that doesn't gall me every time I think about it. But without the mine you can't restore Belle Montagne. Craddock promised to deed it back, but a man's word is only as good as the man. You have a long, hard fight ahead of you. You'll need a few lawyers of your own to get back your land. The least I can do is provide the means."

Angel shook her head and rose from the sofa, approaching him with her hands outstretched. Reluctantly Holt sandwiched those small hands in his own, forced to listen as she quietly extended her final plea.

"If you won't take me with you, then at least hire someone else to go along. You'll be an easy target all alone up there. I can't bear to think of you being injured or sick without any help at all. There must be someone you could trust to help you guard the mine."

"There is," said a third voice from the doorway. The couple glanced over in surprise at Neal Murphy, briskly brushing off his snow-flecked coat and hat. He hung them on a stand and came into the study. "I'd like to go with you, Holt."

The announcement obviously caught the younger man off guard. Holt looked at the preacher with mixed emotions, not the least of which was obviously suspicion.

"This isn't your fight, Neal."

"No, but you're my brother, and it's high time we both accepted that fact, don't you agree?" Neal's calm blue gaze met an icy gray one and was just as steady. "Now's the perfect chance for me to prove to you that I've always been and continue to be sincere about making amends. Father made his mistakes, but he was just a man. So am I. It's obvious you still hold a grudge against us both. While it's too late for Arthur, I hope I might have a chance to kindle some sort of relationship with you."

"Impossible," Holt muttered angrily, confronted by Neal's proposal on one side and Angel's pleading eyes on the other. "You don't know anything about mining, and besides, there's that church of yours."

"What's to learn, Holt? I can fire a gun as well as anyone else when the occasion warrants. And as for the church, my parishioners would understand. Their former minister was a miner, as well. He had to leave from time to time, and the elders substituted for his sermons quite well."

Angel could almost hear Holt's teeth grinding. "No!" he said bluntly.

She saw her chance and took it. She still held his hands, and now she squeezed them tightly as she murmured, "For me, Holt. Do it for me. I swear I'll ride after you if you go up there alone. Take Neal with you. It's past time you two got to know each other. I know it's hard, but as you told me once yourself, you can't accept responsibility for someone else's mistakes. You have to look within yourself for the answers, and for forgiveness." Her eyes darkened with tears at the memory of her own father.

"Please, Holt," she continued huskily, "don't let the

bitterness consume you both. Let the past go . . . let the future begin."

Holt saw the love and pain behind those beautiful blue eyes and realized she didn't have the slightest idea of how much she asked of him. But knowing Angel, she would, indeed, round up a horse and chase after him, no doubt end up frozen to death before she made it halfway up to the mine.

"All right," he finally growled. "I'll take Neal along, but only if you'll have Rachel come and stay here at the parsonage. And one of us will ride down each week to check on you. You're not to go anywhere after dark, and you'll keep the doors and windows bolted at all times."

"Of course," Angel agreed as she impulsively flung her arms around his rigid frame. "Oh, Holt, I'm so happy you agreed. It's the perfect solution, you'll see."

But Holt had already fixed Neal with his stony stare.

"And as for you . . . no more preaching at me, understand? I don't intend to listen to the Sermon on the Mount all winter long."

Neal didn't dare crack a smile. He knew he stood on perilous ground, and that the inch he had gained today was far too precious to quibble over.

"You have my word, brother. For the next few months I intend to adopt the complete garb and tongue of a layman."

"Good. See that you do," Holt warned as he turned and left the room in a few brisk strides.

Angel looked after him for a moment, then turned her hopeful gaze on Neal.

"It's a start, isn't it?"

"Yes, indeed. One I wouldn't have dreamed of without

your help, Angel." But Neal didn't look particularly jubilant.

"Is something wrong?" she asked.

"No. Yes. I'm not sure." He hesitated, as if wondering
if he dared complain. "It's Rachel, I guess."

"You're worried about her reaction to the news?"

He shook his head. "It's more than that, Angel. There's
something wrong with her. I can't put my finger on it—"
he gestured helplessly "—but she's acting differently. I
think something is weighing very heavy on her mind. I
wanted to ask, since you're her closest friend, if you could
possibly find out what it is."

Angel carefully controlled her reaction. She only hoped
she hadn't paled at his words. "Why, Neal, of course I'll
speak with her. I'm sure it's nothing serious . . . bridal
nerves, perhaps."

"Perhaps," he agreed thoughtfully, before he retired
for the night. Angel waited until he had gone to let out her
breath in a long, slow hiss. There would be no keeping
Rachel's secret forever; Neal was too perceptive a man.
She would have a word with her friend again tomorrow.
Rachel must come to realize that such a burdensome
secret would only erode the foundations of her marriage
over time.

Chapter Fifteen

Bells on sleigh harnesses jingled to a stop outside the parsonage doors, and with apprehension Angel went to the window and peered out into a snow flurry that had struck just before dusk. The wintry glow of the fading sun cast the yard of glistening white, and the smart red sleigh parked outside, into sharp relief.

Angel smiled when she recognized the slight figure stepping down from the sleigh, and hurried to open the door. Rachel was back from her weekend visit with Prudence Maxwell, who lived across town.

"Mercy!" Rachel cried as the door swung open and the two women briefly embraced, "I thought we'd never get here! Mother says it's the deepest snow since '68."

"I'm just glad you arrived safely," Angel replied. "I was getting worried." Following Rachel's lead, she turned to wave goodbye to Mrs. Maxwell until the sleigh was underway again. Shutting the door against the bitter chill, Angel helped Rachel unwind her scarf and took her friend's damp woolen mantle to hang before the fire.

Rachel followed Angel into the study, briskly rubbing

her freckled hands together. "It'll certainly be a white Christmas. I wonder how the men are holding out up on the mountain."

"Holt stopped by briefly yesterday," Angel said, her tone carefully neutral as she remembered the tense scene that had taken place in this same study not so many hours ago. She had begged him to stay for Christmas, only a week away, and he hadn't even hesitated in giving his answer. No. An unequivocal, unapologetic no. Neal would come for the holidays, but not Holt. No, the mine was too precious to take time out for the rest of the world, Angel thought bitterly. It was her mine, and she reasoned it could go along just fine for a few days. After all, even outlaws took time out for Christmas, Angel argued. But it was a waste of breath. He and Neal had been up on the mountain for three weeks, and in that span of time she had hardly seen either of them. If not for Rachel, she knew she would have gone crazy.

The two women had cemented what had been at first a tentative friendship. Rachel stayed in town during the week, returning to the little country home of Prudence Maxwell only on the weekends. It gave all of them their breathing space, and even though Prudence had initially disapproved of her daughter leaving home, she couldn't fault Angel as a pillar of respectability the town of Oro so sorely lacked.

In fact, if not for the shocking incident of Angel's quarrel with Lily Valentine, Mrs. Maxwell would have had no concerns at all. But the church ladies' favorite topic of conversation at Triumph Hall was still the night Angel had chased the town strumpet right back into her own saloon. It was enough to make Mrs. Maxwell hesitate slightly at the idea of her precious daughter associating with such a libertine.

Rachel was saying, "Mother and I argued again. She thinks I should move home, at least until the wedding."

"But that's not until spring, Rachel. Surely she doesn't expect you to be without benefit of female company that long."

Rachel made a wry face. "No, she doesn't. But she thinks Justine Garrett or Sally Wilson would be better company for an 'innocent' like me. Mother thinks you're just a bit too worldly to be wise."

Angel chuckled at the notion, moving to pick up the sampler she had left on the arm of the chair and comfortably rearranging herself before the fire. "Maybe she's right. Perhaps I'm unduly influencing you, hmm?"

"Only for the better. I've never had a friend like you, Angel. Someone I could talk to heart-to-heart, without any need for pretenses. And someone who will actually answer my very un-innocent questions!"

They laughed softly together as Rachel reclined on the sofa, taking off her snow boots and propping up her stockinged feet on an ottoman. "Oh, I don't know," she sighed. "I suppose Mother's got a right to put in her two-cents' worth. But after a weekend with her I wonder why I didn't leave home years ago. Do this, don't do that, dress like this . . . why, it's utterly maddening. Do you know, if I was just a teensy bit braver, I might even run off and become a saloon singer myself!"

Angel smiled a little uncertainly at the unbidden reminder of Lily Valentine. She knew that Holt had gone to visit the woman each time he was in town; he made no move to deny it. In fact, he'd been quite open about the entire affair, even inquiring if Angel wanted to come along. Of course she hadn't. The mere idea was ridiculous. Word would have quickly filtered back to Prudence Maxwell if she had, and Angel never would have gained another ounce of respectability in Oro. So Holt had gone alone. And Angel had been left to wonder if their reunion had been more poignant than hers and Holt's.

". . . don't you agree, Angel?" Rachel was asking.

"What? Oh, I'm sorry, I was woolgathering again. This storm must have upset me more than I thought."

"It's true the roads are treacherous; why, the horses slipped twice on the way here. But I wouldn't worry about Holt and Neal if I were you. They're both strong, sensible sorts. They wouldn't risk leaving the mountain in weather like this."

"It's possible we'll be spending Christmas alone," Angel said. "Or, more likely, I will. Neal did promise to come down."

"Still no luck persuading Holt to be reasonable?" At Angel's headshake, Rachel threw up her hands. "Men! As if that blooming mine couldn't be left unattended in the middle of a bloody blizzard!"

Angel laughed. "You sound like Aunt Clara! English accent and all."

"I do, don't I? Well, Auntie's promised to come over for the holidays, and of course you'll have to come too. I'll make Mr. Brindle take us all for a ride in his fancy new sleigh."

"Mr. Brindle?" Angel inquired curiously as she poked her needle through the embroidery hoop.

"Oh, did I forget to tell you?" Rachel bounced up and down on the sofa and clapped her hands with glee.

"Mother has an honest-to-goodness beau! And a rich one at that. It's his sleigh we were riding in tonight."

"I didn't see a man with you."

"That's because he had business. Or so he said." Rachel lowered her voice conspiratorially. "If you want my opinion, I think he's entertaining more prospects than just my mother, if you know what I mean."

Angel almost sputtered. "Rachel! You mean to say he's a fortune hunter?"

The other young woman shrugged. "Well, my mother may be many things, but she isn't a beauty and she isn't really very nice." She ignored Angel's little gasp, continuing calmly, "But Mother is relatively wealthy. Pa saw she'd lack for nothing before he left for the war. And she invested most of it wisely. Yes, she'd make some fellow a nice ripe plum. I think this Brindle chap is just trying to get her to land in his lap."

"If it's true, don't you think you should warn her?"

Rachel shrugged again. "Mother's a grown woman, capable of making her own decisions, however foolish. I don't care to follow in her footsteps and be forever lecturing everyone else about propriety and appearances. For heaven's sake, Angel, I almost became an old maid because of her! She chased all my suitors off before they could even screw up the courage to approach me."

Rachel smiled at the memory, then continued, "Neal is the first man she's taken a liking to, though she despairs over his 'humble calling' and lack of ambition. Actually, I think I would rather like it if she were taken down a peg or two."

Rachel looked smug, and Angel wisely refrained from comment, thinking to herself that poor Mrs. Maxwell had no idea of the revolution that had been brewing right there beneath her own roof.

Two days before Christmas, Angel was shopping in the Oro General Store, busily absorbed in comparing an emerald-green bolt of muslin with a more practical gray wool. She had already decided on yard goods for Rachel's present, as well as several lengths of lace and dress collars, which she had already embroidered for her friend. She'd also purchased a bag of peppermints and horehound candy to titillate Rachel's sweet tooth, and a small bottle of lavender water. For Neal, she had chosen a pair of simple cuff links and plain white handkerchiefs. And for Holt, though the effort would surely be wasted, Angel had sewn shirts of heavy winter flannel, in both red and green. Neal could take the presents back to his brother when he left, she supposed. But she would never see the expression on Holt's face when he opened her gifts.

With a nod to herself, Angel finally decided on the green cloth. Rachel needed something springlike to cheer her up, and the color would complement her. For too long she had worn the grays and browns dictated by Prudence Maxwell. Rachel was only a mouse because she let others see her that way. It was time she showed her pretty skin and eyes to advantage. This beautiful material would do just that.

Feeling elated herself at the thought of Rachel's impending delight, Angel moved to lift the bolt and carry it to the front of the store. She first caught a whiff of attar of roses. Then she felt the nudge of an elbow and whirled around to look into a pair of twinkling green eyes.

"Lily." Angel spoke without thinking, forgetting everything but the woman leaning across the bolts of fabric.

"Hello, chick. Making yourself a new dress?"

Angel shook her head. "It's for Rachel." She was surprised to see nobody else in the store was minding their exchange. But then, it was crowded just before Christmas as everyone anxiously sought gifts for loved ones. Nobody paid attention to two young women apparently comparing cloth in low voices. Too, Lily was dressed more conservatively than usual, in a dark green gown buttoned all the way up to her neck. Her red hair was drawn back in a sleek chignon, emphasizing her classic cheekbones.

Angel suddenly felt unaccountably dowdy, though she knew her blue merino walking suit was one of the smartest she owned and brought her own blond hair to vibrant life. There was just no comparing herself to Lily, she thought. No wonder Holt wasn't apologetic about continuing his old association.

In that musical lilt of hers, Lily mused, "I'd have thought to find you and Holt all snuggled up in this foul weather. Don't tell me he booted you out of bed to go Christmas shopping!"

Angel fought the blush threatening to steal over her cheeks. Really, the woman was entirely too brazen!

She said coolly, "Holt is up at the mine. He won't be down for the holidays."

"Oh?" Lily's green eyes went wide with interest. She looked as if she would ask something more, then apparently thought better of it. "Well, chick, it was nice to see you again." She briefly pressed a gloved hand down on Angel's. "You have a Merry Christmas, now."

The words were as insincere as Lily's smile, Angel

thought. But she nodded politely and, clutching her bolt of fabric like a drowning woman, hurried into line to escape the knowing eyes of Holt's "old friend."

Glass shattered explosively, leaving a dark trail of liquor down the velvet-flocked walls. Red Garrett was in an ugly mood. Nobody watching the sheriff in the saloon dared dispute that, as another shot glass prepared to meet its end.

"That's enough, Red."

Lily's silky voice rang out with just enough authority to cause the man's aim to waver. He spun around, eyeing the madam of the house with narrowed, bloodshot eyes.

"No whore tells me what to do."

To her credit, Lily didn't flinch. "In my house, with my liquor, I'll damn well tell you what to do," she retorted calmly.

The others watching let out a collective sigh of relief as Lily strode forward in her low-cut silver gown and pried the glass from Garrett's clutched fist. Setting it down with a thud on the nearby bar, she said, "Now, Sheriff, I've heard of starting off the holidays with a bang, but this surely takes the cake. What's the problem?"

Red snorted, but the fight seemed to have gone out of him as he faced the singer. Her steady gaze offered understanding, which was something he wasn't accustomed to.

"Aw, hell, Lil. Justine done threw me out again. On Christmas Eve, no less, right in front of my own kin."

The barest hint of amusement flickered in the green eyes across from him, but Lily was careful not to let him see it.

"What happened this time?"

Red rubbed his bristly jaw. "She found out somehow 'bout that little sweety I keep over to Clear Creek. 'Tina weren't very amused."

"No, I imagine not," Lily said dryly, imagining that poker-faced woman's reaction to her husband's public infidelity. Of course, Red had been stepping out on Justine for years and everyone in Oro knew it, but everyone was also wise enough to look the other way—or, in Lily's case, keep her mouth shut.

The sheriff looked closer to defeat than ever she had seen him. Why, the old coot was almost crying, Lily thought with surprise. He actually loved that viper he was married to!

"Now, Red," she began in her most sympathetic tone, companionably slinging an arm around the man's shoulders and steering him toward the stairs, "there's nothing so bad a little tumble can't cure. Why, my Celia's been asking about you. You haven't favored her in a mighty long time, you know."

Red immediately stopped sniffling, evidencing the true depth of his emotions. "Ya don't say, Lil? Where's the little sweety now?"

Lily smiled, patting his arm. "All tucked away upstairs, just waiting for you. I declare, Red, you must of spoiled Celia for other men. She won't have a thing to do with any of those ol' cowpokes but you."

Red gave Lily's waist a squeeze of thanks, then released her and began his uneven ascent up the stairs. She watched long enough to make sure he wouldn't fall back down them, then motioned for Joe to send a pint of her "special" up to Celia's room.

When Sheriff Garrett was in a melancholy mood he was at his most dangerous. He was also inclined to talk a lot. With her special brew, and the help of the warm and understanding young woman upstairs, Lily was fairly certain she could get the necessary information on Garrett's latest activities and turn a nice profit at the same time.

A light tap came at Lily's stage door at close to midnight. Distracted, the singer called out, "Come in!" as she fussed with the neckline of her hostess gown. Lily was changing costumes after her performance, preparing to move out and mingle with the customers. She was in a reasonably good mood. Her bawdy rendition of "God Rest Ye Merry, Gentlemen" had resulted in a standing ovation. The only regret she had was having to spend the holidays alone.

Lily's dressing-room door opened and a young woman slipped in. She was wearing a nearly sheer white wrapper and her dark hair was tangled wildly around her shoulders. She was trembling so badly she couldn't speak at first.

"Celia!" Lily rushed to the girl, anxiously searching for bruises. "Did that jackass hurt you?"

Wordlessly, the girl shook her head, grabbing the hand that was offered to her and gripping it fiercely until she could find her breath. "Mr. Murphy," she finally gasped out.

Lily felt a cold chill grip her at the name. She felt like shaking Celia but, realizing it wouldn't help in the slightest, she gritted her teeth and tried gentle persuasion instead. "Did the sheriff talk? Was it about Holt?"

Celia nodded shakily. With a soft oath, Lily released the girl and grabbed a nearby bottle of gin and a shot glass. Filling it rapidly, she shoved it at the girl.

"Here. This'll loosen your tongue, honey."

Celia held the glass and looked at Lily uncertainly. "B-but we're not supposed to d-drink on the j-job . . ." she began.

Lily was beginning to see this could take all night. "I'll make an exception this time, Celia," she said briskly, urging the young woman to down it all in one gulp. Celia complied, and several more minutes passed as she choked and gasped and stamped her feet.

Lily pounded her on the back, then decided enough was enough and demanded, "What has Red got up his sleeve for Holt now?"

"Ambush," Celia wheezed, then finally caught her breath and continued, "Sheriff said his men are gonna jump Holt up on the mountain. Everyone knows Holt isn't leaving the mine for the holidays. They figure it's the best time to bump him off once and for all. He'll be outnumbered . . ."

Lily cursed soundly and crossed the room to retrieve her hooded cloak and gloves. "Damn fool!" she raged, and Celia wondered if Lily referred to the sheriff or Holt Murphy. As she shrugged on her outerwear and exchanged her satin shoes for riding boots, Lily asked briskly, "Did you drug Red like I told you?"

Celia nodded. "He's snorin' like an ol' billy goat."

"Good. Make sure he stays down. Hopefully when he doesn't show up later, Red's boys will be a little too cold and confused to carry out his orders tonight." Lily smiled as she opened a closet and pulled out a heavy, sawed-off shotgun.

Celia's eyes bulged. "Lordy!"

"Now, Celia, you know I don't tolerate using the Lord's name in vain," Lily scolded her lightly. "If you have to cuss, girl, there's plenty better language than that. Now get back upstairs and make double sure our good sheriff is indisposed for the night. If you have to, tie him down. Poor old Red likely won't remember anything in the morning, and you can tell him things just got a bit rambunctious, understand?"

The younger woman nodded, then bit her lower lip. "Miz Valentine, you gonna try and hold off all those bad men on your own?"

Lily laughed huskily. " 'Course not, Celia. But there's an old saying . . . half the advantage in a fight is the advantage of surprise. I want to find out if it's true."

"Oh, Lordy—I mean, gracious, Miz Lily, you will be careful, won't you?"

Celia, like all the girls at Valentine's, liked Lily immensely. She was firm but fair with them, and was more of a mother than most of them had known.

Lily smiled kindly at the worried young girl. "Of course I'll be careful, chick. Now get upstairs and back under those covers. You don't want to catch a chill just before Christmas, do you?"

Chapter Sixteen

In the wee hours of Christmas dawn, Angel hugged her happy little secret to herself. She would never forget the shock and uncertainty that had roiled throughout her body just the day before, but in the meantime she had come to accept and even rejoice over the news.

She chuckled softly at the thought of telling Rachel when her friend awoke, but then she didn't want to overshadow everyone else's Christmas. Besides, Rachel had avoided her since she thought Angel had the stomach flu, and it might prove quite a feat to convince both her and Mrs. Maxwell that the illness she had wasn't at all the contagious type, and would likely lessen in a few months, anyway.

Those were the doctor's words, near as Angel recalled, though it was hard to remember much of anything past the initial announcement.

"Congratulations, Mrs. Murphy, you're going to be a mother."

A mother . . . a mother . . . the phrase rang over and over in Angel's mind now, ominous and exciting, echoed faintly by the prophetic words Okoka had spoken just over a month ago. Nine moons, she had said. Now less than eight moons to go.

Why did Angel ever suppose she could sleep? With soft laughter she rolled over and lit the kerosene lamp beside the bed. The warm orange glow soon filled the guest room, and she sat up and rubbed her eyes. Then she tentatively touched her stomach again. It was still deceptively flat, but soon it would blossom with life. The life of hers and Holt's child.

Humming softly, Angel threw back the covers and found her robe and slippers. She was ravenously hungry and could already detect the aroma of cooking downstairs. Mrs. Maxwell had hired a cook for the holidays, at a dear price, no doubt, but she was determined to impress her new beau, Mr. Brindle, when he arrived for the noonday meal.

As she quickly dressed in a ruffled white blouse and a festive red wool skirt, Angel glanced over the neatly wrapped packages she had hidden in her portmanteau. Everything was in order, including a last-minute gift for Mrs. Maxwell and her male guest. She imagined Prudence's appreciation of the gold-stamped Bible Preacher Murphy had autographed, and no matter his own religious background, Angel suspected the bottle of rare sherry would be appreciated by Mrs. Maxwell's gentleman friend. Angel had especially enjoyed choosing a present for Rachel's feisty Aunt Clara. The mercantile had a goodly supply of tonics and liquid remedies, and she'd chosen several that would no doubt come in handy whenever Aunt Clara felt "puny," as the old woman was wont to say.

Almost giddy with excitement, Angel finished dressing and slipped down the hall to knock on Rachel's door. Her friend was still abed but awake, and regarded Angel a little warily when she started to come close.

"Goodness, Angel, shouldn't you be resting? The flu is nothing to toy with!"

"Oh, Rachel, I'm simply bursting! I couldn't wait any longer to share my news. I wanted to tell Holt first, but since he isn't coming down for Christmas . . . I had to tell someone."

Rachel looked alarmed. "You aren't leaving, are you?"

Angel shook her head, a merry smile teasing her lips as she sat down in a wooden rocker beside Rachel's bed. "No, I daresay I'll be staying as long as the Territory will have me. I'm going to have a baby, Rachel!"

"A . . ." Comprehension slowly flooded her friend's hazel eyes. Rachel flung back the covers and squealed with glee. "Truly? Oh, you goose! You had us all so worried. What with Mother fretting you were seriously ill, and all the guests coming . . . why, it's wonderful news, Angel! I can't wait to tell everyone!"

Angel shook her head vigorously. "Not a peep, Rachel! Not until Holt knows first. He'll be furious if he finds out from someone else."

Her friend pouted a little. "Can't I even tell Neal?"

"Especially not him. With those two working so closely together now, it's bound to slip out if you do. No, my news will have to wait until Holt comes down the mountain. Maybe he'll come for New Year's."

"Well, I should hope so. If he stays away much longer, there won't be any secret left!" Rachel said cheekily, with an envious glance at her friend's stomach. Then she frowned. "Oh, but what will we tell Mother? She'll try to keep you in bed all day!"

"Let me handle her," Angel responded with far more confidence than she felt. "I don't look sick, do I?"

Rachel peered at her closely in the poor light. "Well, you're awfully flushed, but that's to be expected with all the excitement. Maybe if we go downstairs together I can distract her. She's in a terrible state over Mr. Brindle coming. She thinks he's going to propose today."

Angel smiled with genuine pleasure. "How wonderful!"

"Yes, it is. He certainly keeps Mother occupied. Do you know she didn't even say a word about that brooch Neal gave me? Normally she'd refuse to let me accept anything from a young man."

"Well, you two are engaged now," Angel reasoned.

"That doesn't stop Mother from trying to orchestrate everything," Rachel replied wryly. Then she glanced at the ormolu clock on her bedstand. "Heavens! It's after seven. I've got to get dressed! Which dress should I wear, Angel? My brown calico or my gray muslin?"

Angel considered the two choices poor at best, but happily thought that Rachel would soon have some lovely yard goods in order to make a new dress.

"The gray, I think," she said at last. "It has a finer patina that will reflect the tinsel on the tree."

"Of course!" Rachel cried. "Whatever would I do without you, Angel? Will you help me dress my hair? I have a red velvet ribbon left over from wrapping my presents for everyone, and it would be the perfect touch!"

As Rachel chattered on and on, Angel forced herself to be caught up in the excitement and magic of Christmas morning, deliberately ignoring the small well of loneliness deep in her soul, where those still waters reflected the face of Holt, so far away.

Rachel was right; Mrs. Maxwell barely noticed Angel, except to say primly that she hoped her home would not be turned into a hospital ward by the end of the day. As the hired cook presided over bubbling kettles and baked ham in the kitchen, Angel and Rachel volunteered to trim pies and set out a colorful array of preserves and relishes for the guests.

Neal arrived first, bearing gifts and a bevy of hugs for all the women, along with a whispered apology to Angel for Holt's absence.

Her smile frozen in place, Angel nodded understanding although her heart plummeted to her toes. She knew Holt had said he couldn't come, but she had foolishly hoped . . .

Before noon a number of widowed ladies from the church congregation arrived, and a few single older men Prudence considered respectable enough to grace her table. It was obvious she intended to play matchmaker during the holidays, and wanted to force her own happy fate on everyone else. Angel wondered if poor Mr. Brindle had any notion of what was in store for him. According to Rachel, he had just moved to Oro, and already he was to be subjected to the terrifying combined scrutiny of the townsfolk. Well, Angel decided philosophically, she had survived the initiation herself, so this would merely be a test of Mr. Brindle's mettle.

But when noon arrived and the mysterious Mr. Brindle had not yet made his grand appearance, Mrs. Maxwell was overcome, almost rabid with worry. She insisted he must have met with a dreadful accident, or at the very least a horrendous delay, for he was far too chivalrous a fellow to disappoint her. Her reputation was clearly on the line, and she made endless excuses for the man as the ham slowly dried up and the hired cook began to made snide remarks about widows putting the cart before the horse.

Finally Prudence Maxwell miserably accepted defeat and stiffly joined the others at the table. But she wouldn't eat, wouldn't talk, and looked on the verge of noisy tears. Finally Rachel caught Neal's eye, and the young minister reluctantly abandoned his pursuit of a piece of mince pie.

"Prudence," he asked, "would you feel better if I rode across town and checked on Mr. Brindle?"

Mrs. Maxwell's blush was instantaneous. "Preacher Murphy, that's so kind of you to offer, but I really couldn't ask you to go out of your way . . ." Prudence began halfheartedly.

With a nudge from Rachel, Neal began to insist, just as halfheartedly. "Really, it's no trouble, ma'am. Won't take but a minute, in fact. I brought the wagon, so I'll just hitch up the team again and head out."

"I'll go with you," Rachel chimed in quickly. It was obvious she was eager to steal some time alone with her fiancé.

Prudence was too distracted to protest. "Very well," she said primly, touching a napkin to her lips. "I'll give you the directions to his house."

As the other three momentarily left the table, Angel chatted desultorily with the ladies on either side of her, pleased to feel their approval surrounding her like a warm cloak. At long last she had found acceptance and, except for Holt's absence, this was one of the most delightful Christmases she could recall. Here among friends and the only family she had, Angel had been made to feel truly welcome and loved. In fact, she had even taken to calling Clara Maxwell "Aunt," and the spritely little English lady enjoyed it as much as Angel did.

When Prudence invited everyone to visit in the parlor after the meal Angel joined Aunt Clara on a velvet settee before the fire, and they shared stories and laughed softly over the surprising similarities in their lives.

Clara Maxwell confessed that her James had been a bit of a rogue in his day and, like Holt, had courted his share of trouble before their wedding. Angel suspected Aunt Clara was minimizing the "trouble" to some extent when she mildly referred to several of James's gunfights in the middle of town, and the fact that he'd been known as "Quick-Draw Jim" in his younger days.

But it was wonderful to share the happy memories of this spry old lady, and since nearly all of them revolved around James it was clear he had been the love of her life. Aunt Clara even dabbed away a tear or two as she told Angel of her husband's last Christmas.

"James was feeling under the weather, but I wasn't too concerned since it was a frightful winter," Clara recalled. "I kept him bundled before the fire with hot toddies and his medicine, and I thought we'd weather that one as we had all the ones before." She smiled a little sadly. "I should have known the moment I left the room he would throw off his blankets and hobble outside to check on the horses. My James always saw to the animals. Said a man had a God-given duty to look after the lesser creatures of the earth."

When she fell silent Angel said gently, "My father was the same way. So good with children and animals."

Clara nodded, too choked up for a moment. Then she went on, "James caught a chill that day. It went to his lungs and he coughed for days, weeks, slowly losing strength. I'm not ashamed to say I begged the good Lord to let him live. Offered myself and everything I had if only he would spare my dear husband. But our Heavenly Father knows best. I guess he needed my James more than I did."

Tears slid down the wrinkles on Aunt Clara's crepelike cheeks, and Angel swallowed past the lump in her own throat. She took a small hand in her own and squeezed it gently.

"I'm sorry," she murmured to the older woman.

Clara Maxwell smiled through her tears. "Oh, my dear, don't be. I've had a good life, even without my James. I see you are missing your own husband now. Take comfort in the fact that he is still here, even if a mountain away. My greatest regret is that I can no longer watch the doorways with the anticipation that is written all over your lovely face."

Angel blushed. "Is it so obvious?"

"My dear child, love is always obvious to those who have been so blessed themselves," Clara wisely replied. It was her turn to pat Angel's hand comfortingly. "How fortunate you are, my dear. To be rich in love rather than worldly goods, and to look forward to each day knowing that, sooner or later, your man will come home to you."

"Are you sure?" Angel whispered, looking into Aunt Clara's suddenly twinkling eyes.

"I'm rarely known to be wrong, child. And if I'm not

mistaken now, I think your Christmas present has just arrived." Angel turned slightly on the settee, and her face lit up with a glow that had nothing to do with the blaze crackling merrily in the hearth.

"Holt!"

He stood in the doorway, all but hidden in his bulky furs behind a mound of glistening packages. His teeth gleamed white when he announced, "Special delivery for Mrs. Murphy from Father Christmas!"

Angel launched herself across the room, throwing her arms around him with a cry of pure happiness. She didn't care that everyone was staring, and that Prudence saw fit to give one of her little sniffs. She nearly knocked Holt back into the hall with the enthusiasm of her welcome.

"You came!" Her voice was almost accusing, and she wished he'd dump those packages where he stood and hug her back instead. "You missed Christmas dinner," she added a bit petulantly.

"Who says?" Holt murmured, eyeing his beautiful wife as he might a juicy steak. Angel smiled up at him a little saucily and helped him with the gifts and his coat. As he shrugged off the fur and hung it up, he revealed a pair of dark trousers and a clean white shirt, slightly wrinkled but certainly an improvement over gamy buckskins. Angel realized he must have stopped at the parsonage first to bathe in an effort to please her and perhaps placate Mrs. Maxwell.

Holt's dark hair had grown out slightly but was still an acceptable length by fashionable standards. He looked, Angel thought, positively wonderful. There was still a faintly mysterious air about him as he smiled and greeted the other guests in the parlor, and she studied his proud profile for a moment.

Rachel's mother moved forward and invited Holt to partake of whatever remained of the Christmas goodies, but he could hardly tear his own eyes from Angel. She was even more beautiful than he remembered, somehow softer and a little fuller in the face. The good life must agree with her, Holt decided. He was glad he hadn't allowed her to wheedle him into letting her live up on the mountain this winter.

A mischievous smile teased at Angel's lips as she tugged at his shirtsleeve. "Are all of those presents for me, Holt?"

"Greedy woman," he growled with a smack on her shapely bottom that clearly scandalized Prudence and the other matrons. All except for Clara Maxwell, who observed their exchange with a knowing twinkle in her eyes.

Holt moved to the parlor table, where Angel was now looking over the gaily wrapped packages. She picked up a small one and sniffed at it, and her blue eyes sparkled triumphantly.

"English lavender!"

"Irish whiskey," he shot back.

She chose another little box and, unable to pick up a scent on that one, shook it gently and heard a satisfying rattle.

"Jewelry! A necklace or earrings."

"A box of ha'penny nails," Holt tossed back.

Angel set down the gift and linked her hands behind her back. She pointedly looked up at the threshold under which Holt stood.

"Mistletoe," she casually observed.

Holt glanced up and sighed. "You win."

But it was obvious by the way his hands gripped her waist and pulled her within the range of his hungry mouth that Holt didn't mind losing this game. Angel's soft gasp of surrender was drowned out by Prudence Maxwell's louder sniff and Aunt Clara's delighted chuckling, but Holt delightedly heard his wife's sigh of surrender and greedily claimed his own little victory.

When he finally released Angel her mind was whirling and her eyes shone with something besides the rum punch Aunt Clara had been indulging in all afternoon.

"Merry Christmas," Holt said, kissing her again on the temple. "And happy birthday, too."

"Who told you?" Angel demanded with mock outrage. She didn't have to wonder much longer. There was only one other person who knew her birthday was on Christmas Day.

"I promised to protect my informant," Holt said as he lifted his right hand in a mock pledge. "But may I say you certainly don't look a minute older than when I kissed you last?"

"Rogue," Angel muttered, but she couldn't hold back a smile when his gray eyes twinkled down at her.

"It makes sense now," Holt mused. "I always wondered why your parents named you after something so sweet and innocent . . ."

"Ooh!" Angel stuck out her tongue, then started to whirl away. Her stomach tightened with anticipation when he caught her by the wrist and slowly tugged her, step by step, back into his arms.

"Come back here, wife," he growled.

As Holt enfolded her in his warm embrace, Angel's conscience cried, Tell him! It was a perfect moment, with everyone watching them expectantly, that was shattered abruptly when the front door opened and another couple blew in with a gust of snow and wind.

"Neal." Holt immediately sensed something was wrong, even though he still didn't know his half-brother that well.

Prudence Maxwell rushed forward expectantly. "Mr. Brindle?"

Neal Murphy shook his head. "Sorry, ma'am. He wasn't home." Then he looked at Holt and reported gently, "There's been an accident. Miss Valentine has been hurt."

"Lily?" Holt ignored the room-wide gasp at his use of the singer's first name, as well as Angel's chagrin. In fact, Angel noted bitterly, she might as well have dropped through the floor. He abruptly released her, strode over to Neal, and demanded, "What happened?"

With a glance to the curious crowd in the parlor, Neal drew his brother aside, just out of listening range. Angel moved after them. She was determined not to miss anything.

"Apparently Miss Valentine set out last night with the intention of reaching the mine," Neal reported grimly.

"What the hell for?" Holt demanded angrily.

Neal shrugged. "The story's a bit garbled. We heard it secondhand from Joe Tripper on the way back. Anyway, she's been hurt."

"How bad?"

"I don't know that either. All I know is that when Lily was still missing this morning one of her girls reported it to Mr. Tripper, and the old man set out after her. Found her halfway up the mountain, he said. Alone."

"Where is she now?"

"Back at Valentine's."

Holt's tone was curt as he said, "Get my coat, Angel."

When she didn't move he looked at her and saw the rebellious shimmer of tears in her eyes.

"Not Christmas, too, Holt," she begged softly.

Without answering, he went to snatch up the coat himself, yanking it on almost angrily. Then he strode directly for the door, without a backward glance.

Suddenly Angel saw her chance slipping away. If she lost him to Lily now, it would be forever. She would fight for him. She would!

"Wait!" she called out, before the door had slammed shut again. "I'm coming, too."

Holt didn't reply. He didn't even turn around. But, to her relief, he did wait for her, and together they set off for Valentine's.

Angel had expected a sprained ankle, scraped palms, frostbite at the worst. Heaven knew Lily Valentine was a tough customer, and nobody could imagine that tart-tongued lady laid low. But the couple had their first inkling of the depth of the trouble when they saw that the lights were all turned down low in Valentine's, and none of the girls had taken Lily up on her offer to take the day off. The saloon was open, but it was ominously quiet as ladies of the evening and customers alike waited for news with bated breath.

Holt crashed into the place like a hurricane. "Lily?" he bellowed, his eyes immediately seizing on old Joe.

The barkeep just shook his head. "Upstairs, Holt.

Doc's there. T'ain't nothin' more we can do. Up't God now."

"The hell it is," Holt snarled, taking the stairs two at a time. Angel couldn't keep up. She picked up her skirts and moved at a slower pace, conscious of the slippery steps and her wet shoes. When she arrived at the bedroom Lily occupied her first uncharitable thought was to wonder if Holt had ever been there before. The room was beautifully done in muted blue tones and was surprisingly tasteful, in contrast with the rest of the house. Angel saw her husband bending over a form in the velvet-canopied bed. The doctor's chunky frame blocked her view as he bent over to speak softly with Holt. Whatever he said apparently wasn't acceptable, for Holt made a strangled sound, curiously like a sob, and then unexpectedly raged at the woman in the bed.

"Damn you, Lil! Don't give up on me now!"

He reached down, as if to shake the patient, and the doctor quickly intervened, grabbing Holt's shirtsleeve and hauling him aside.

"Gently, now," Angel heard him chastise Holt. "She's in no pain, thanks to the laudanum, but you mustn't wake her."

As the two men argued in low, bitter tones, Angel moved forward toward the bed. Lily had obviously been shot and the area of her chest where the bullet had penetrated had been hastily and clumsily bandaged. Her breathing was so shallow, Angel had to strain to make out any signs of life. Ironically, her red hair was as perfectly coiffed as when she had ridden out the night before. There was even a shiny strand of tinsel still caught in the auburn tresses. She saw Lily's head move slightly against the stark white pillows. As she leaned closer, the green eyes suddenly opened.

"Hello, chick." Lily's eyes were glazed from the drug and her voice was slightly slurred, but she was lucid enough to recognize Angel. "Not a . . . very merry Christmas for me."

Angel felt pity wash over her and reached to take the woman's hand. It was ice-cold and drained of all color. She could almost see Lily fading before her eyes.

"What happened?" she asked the woman softly. "Who did this to you?"

Lily closed her eyes a moment, swallowing painfully. A single tear seeped out and rolled down her pale cheek. Instead of answering Angel's question, she rasped, "Take care . . . of Holt. Always in some sort of . . . trouble."

"No, Lily." Angel could feel the hot tears sliding down her own cheeks now, and she held the other woman's cold hand protectively in her own. "Holt is counting on you to pull through. We both are. You can't let one measly little bullet knock you down."

Lily smiled faintly but didn't reply. Holt's angry voice suddenly rang throughout the room.

"Get out. Out!"

His order was almost feral, and the country doctor looked as if he might argue but then thought the better of it. With a snap of his black bag, he sniffed loudly and disapprovingly and hurried out.

Angel released Lily's hand and stepped away. Holt was too immersed in his own agony to even see her. Pushing past Angel, he knelt beside the bed. His balled fists pounded the mattress, where Lily's blood had already stained the sheets bright red. Holt cradled her head with a big palm, heedless of death staring him in the face. "Lil," he begged, "don't leave me!"

Suddenly Angel couldn't see his agony for her own. Blinded by tears, she blundered to the window and stood there, staring unseeing at the remains of a perfect Christmas, the leagues of sparkling snow, the occasional twinkle of a tree through the window of a nearby home.

Then she heard the shallow rasp. "Mine . . ."

Angel stiffened and heard her husband scold the woman gently, "No, love, save your strength. You've got a big battle ahead . . . don't waste it trying to talk."

"Love," Lily whispered wryly, for a moment sounding just like her old ironic self. "Don't I . . . wish."

Unwillingly, Angel glanced over her shoulder, in time to see Holt tenderly kiss the other woman's forehead.

"You're going to be fine, Lily."

"Mine . . ." Lily said again, and made a faint gagging noise. Angel realized with a chill that she must be choking on her own blood. After a noisy swallow, the woman doggedly continued. ". . . you . . . mine, Holt . . ."

Angel felt an icy tendril of fear grip her. Was Lily trying to say that Holt had always been hers?

". . . not red . . ."

"Lily, stop. Please. You need to rest." Holt's tone was ragged as he pleaded with the woman. Their lips were just a breath apart.

Exhausted from her efforts, Lily gave up trying to make him understand and had one simple request. "Kiss me . . . ?"

"Of course." Holt made as if to peck her cheek again and she weakly shook her head.

"Real kiss . . . like you love me . . ."

"Of course I love you. God, Lil, don't be such a fool. I've always loved you—"

Angel could stand no more. Clapping a hand to her mouth, she rushed from the room, hearing the pounding of her own footsteps in her head. Blindly, she pushed into the first private refuge she could find, the garish little parlor Lily had first taken her to when Holt had been hurt.

Everything was just as she remembered it. Even the cut-crystal decanter still sparkled beside a glass imprinted with bright red lipstick. Outside, the snow beat silently and mercilessly against the window.

Angel was trembling so hard, she had to sit down on a red velvet chaise longue before the cold hearth. She huddled there, her arms hugging herself in a poor show of self-pity. Tears poured down her cheeks, tears of betrayal, anger, and yes, even grief, for herself as well as Lily.

Then she heard the cry upstairs. It rose in intensity, a dark, keening sound of the most heart-wrenching despair. Angel looked to the ceiling for the source. The hearth in this room would always be cold now, she realized with a sudden pang.

Chapter Seventeen

At Neal's silent cue, Angel moved forward to scatter the customary fistful of dirt over the pine casket in the grave, and tried not to wince as the sound echoed dully throughout the churchyard. Moving back into place, she banished the memories of Lily's death and Holt's disappearance and concentrated instead upon the service.

Neal had agreed to perform the sermon, against the advice of all the town matrons. But if he had been expecting an empty graveside, Neal was surely surprised when almost all of the menfolk of Oro and Clear Creek showed up. Even Sheriff Garrett was there, hat in hand and his head low as he paid his respects to Oro's well-loved madam.

Only Holt was absent. Angel didn't have to wonder why. Something told her he considered such affairs a mockery of the dead, though she couldn't say exactly what made her believe that. She supposed he wanted to remember Lily as they'd all known her; snappy and vibrant and too full of life to be dead. Angel wiped away a stray tear. She had worried so much about losing Holt to

Lily when it was obvious she'd never even had him in the first place.

After the service Rachel moved up beside Angel in a show of quiet comfort. In direct defiance of her mother's orders, she had come to the funeral with Angel.

"She was a remarkable woman," Rachel said seriously.

"Yes, she was. I won't ever forget when she rode with us up to the mine. It seems so long ago now . . ."

Rachel nodded. "A lifetime, at least." She looked with satisfaction at the little corner of the churchyard where Lily would rest in peace. Though the snow was still deep, a willow tree curved gracefully over the mound. In the spring the tree's fronds would feather out beautifully. It was a spot Lily probably would have chosen for herself.

Rachel had been the one to fight the church committee on burying Lily Valentine in consecrated ground. They had all maintained that a madam, no matter how good her heart, didn't merit a burial on blessed property. But Rachel's sensitive soul had told her otherwise. She rather pointedly reminded each of the men involved that they all had, at one time or another, partaken of Lily's generous hospitality themselves.

Valentine's was closed now, though in her will Lily had left the saloon to Joe Tripper. The old man had declared he didn't have the heart to run it, and he left town even before the funeral. The windows were boarded up now, the girls disbanded to other towns in the region. But many had returned for Lily's service on this cold December day.

The marker was simple and somewhat crude: *Here Lies Lily Valentine, a Mighty Generous Woman . . . generous of Heart, Soul, and most especially Body.*

Neal hadn't found the epitaph amusing, Angel recalled.

But the men who knew Lily best had thought it up them-selves, and Angel was sure Lily herself would have ap-preciated the risqué humor of it.

As she linked arms with Rachel and they made their slow progress from the gravesite back to the waiting sleigh, Angel said, "Thank you for coming, Rachel. It meant a lot to me."

"I wanted to. Even though Neal is angry at me now." Rachel glanced over her shoulder at her fiancé, who was now supervising the filling of the grave with a grim expres-sion. She sighed and returned her attention to breaking a path through the heavy snow. "Sometimes I don't under-stand how he can be so self-righteous. I know Miss Valen-tine chose the wrong path in life, but she was still a good woman. She was always giving to the poor and taking in hungry travelers. Isn't that what counts?"

"I think so," Angel replied thoughtfully. "Lily was cer-tainly more honest than many people I've known."

"Exactly. She always said what she thought, even if she knew it was going to make someone mad. I wish I was like that."

Angel smiled and said a little teasingly, "But Rachel, you are. You told both your mother and Neal that you were coming to this service, come hell or high water or the 'last great blizzard from Hades.'"

Rachel looked surprised. "I didn't, did I?" She released a quiet giggle into her fur muff, glancing around to make sure nobody heard. "I know you're not supposed to laugh in a churchyard. I feel awful."

"Somehow I suspect Miss Valentine would approve," Angel said wryly as she joined her friend in the sleigh. They waited there bundled beneath the blankets until

Neal joined them a short time later. He looked cold and cross and was obviously irritated.

"Neal, can you drive the long way through the church-yard so we can stop at the grave again?" Rachel asked.

"We're going straight back," he replied briskly as he picked up the reins and whistled sharply to the team.

"I forgot to put these silk flowers on the grave—" Rachel began.

"Come back in the spring, then. We're leaving."

He was definitely rattled about something, Angel thought. Probably the fact that Lily was buried in holy ground, right between the town's former minister and his own mother. Angel wondered then where Holt's mother was buried. She thought her body must have been returned to her people for a native burial ceremony.

During the service Angel had surreptitiously studied Virginia Murphy's grave. There was nothing on the eloquently worded headstone to indicate anything unusual about Neal's mother or her son. It was a bit odd, though, that Arthur Murphy's marker was not anywhere to be found in the little churchyard.

Angel asked, "Where's your father buried, Neal?"

He shot her a quick and startled glance, then obviously collected himself. His tone razor-sharp and even, he replied, "Arthur's buried up on the mountain, with her."

"Her?" Rachel blurted in confusion.

Neal compressed his lips for a moment. "Arthur's Indian squaw," he finally said.

"Oh!" Rachel was clearly enlightened by this piece of news, and so was Angel, when she began to analyze the tone of his voice. Angry. Hard. Every bit as resentful as

Holt in his own way. Was all his talk of brotherly love merely an act?

As if sensing his mistake, Neal apologized abruptly. "I'm sorry, ladies. This has been a tiring day. I guess I'm a bit put out that Holt didn't come to the service. After all, Miss Valentine was supposedly an old and dear friend."

Angel sensed the unspoken implication and tried not to let it wound her too deeply. Where was Holt now? Consoling himself with a cold bottle, or a warm woman?

She shook herself free of pointless fears and fancies. Holt had made it quite clear that there was only one love in his life, and Lily Valentine had just been laid to rest. So Angel wondered why she didn't feel any better now that the competition was gone.

Holt hadn't gone to Lily's funeral for a different reason than Angel and the others suspected. Though it was in the back of his mind on this blustery winter day, there was much more to be done than shedding a few tears over a grave. Lily was gone and he couldn't help her now, but other lives were at stake. As always, he would pull through for his people, no matter the danger to himself.

He offered a faint smile to the man sitting across the fire from him. "Been a long time, Kaga."

The gray-haired Indian gravely inclined his head. "It is so, Igasho," Kaga agreed. He addressed Holt by his Arapaho birth name, rather than the English one that felt strange on his old tongue. The name meant "wanderer," an appropriate description of the younger man, especially considering his activity during the last few years.

Holt had offered the old Indian a cheroot earlier, and

for a while they smoked in comfortable silence as the blue cloud of smoke filled the teepee and drifted lazily through the vent. Words were not as important as tradition, nor did Holt make any move to speak until Kaga had finished the tobacco and smacked his lips with approval.

"Maybe one white man knows his pipe," he grudgingly said, in an indirect compliment.

Holt's gray eyes twinkled, but he maintained a serious mien. "You have come for more than tobacco, old friend. Do the People need more guns?"

The Indian's expression never changed. "There will never be enough firesticks to drive away the greedy ones. When one white man falls another will always take his place. This I have seen in my dreams."

"Dreams have been known to be wrong."

Kaga looked at him shrewdly. "Will you never learn to trust in the old ways, Igasho?"

Holt shrugged, the fur robe bundled around his figure momentarily rising to brush against his face. His eyes shifted to the fire and moodily fixed on the glowing coals.

"You deny yourself," Kaga said quietly. "As you have always denied the People."

At this criticism Holt's gaze shot back to the old man. "I have helped the tribe many times, Kaga. I have put myself at great risk."

"It is so," the other man agreed pleasantly. "But there is no heart in what you do."

Holt blinked, feeling the smoke from the fire stinging his eyes. He had always felt indebted to his mother's people for accepting him so easily, as the whites had never done. He had even considered joining the tribe for a time. He knew he would have blended in easily enough. But

Holt had too much Murphy blood to be content with living quietly in a village. Even fighting the cavalry in hand-to-hand combat alongside the other warriors didn't appeal to him. He would rather remain an ally to his mother's people, helping them in the one way only a white man could.

"If you have come for more guns and ammunition," Holt finally said, "I have hidden them in the usual place."

Kaga made an absent gesture. "There is more to be done. The hard winter has kept the soldiers in their forts. They are too soft. Now is the People's chance to move swiftly."

Holt looked at the old man. "I don't understand."

"You will." Kaga made a move to rise, his long gray braids swinging and settling in place against his fur robes. Though thin and wiry, he had great presence, and his dark eyes were inscrutable as he waited for Holt to join him.

Silently, the two men left the teepee and began to walk toward the mine. Holt assumed Kaga wished to inspect the boxes of guns and ammunition he had hidden away in the shaft. He was surprised when the Indian suddenly stopped and raised his hand.

"This time I must ask much more," Kaga said as he looked toward the forest. Holt's keen eyes tracked the source of the other man's gaze. He soon saw the handful of huddled figures standing just within the protective circle of the trees.

Holt exhaled a cloud of frosty air. "How many?"

"Six."

"It will be difficult," Holt warned the other man.

"Maska only asks that you try."

Maska was the chief of the Langundo Arapaho, and he trusted the tribe's medicine man, Kaga, to make arrangements for the safety of his people. Holt did not need to ask who the six were or why they needed shelter. They were fugitives seeking to escape the white man's law for one reason or another. Most likely they were the survivors of the recent uprising down south that had dealt the U.S. Army a crippling blow.

Holt sensed Kaga keenly observing him from the corner of his eye, and he sighed. "It will be very hard up here, old friend. Food is scarce even in the summer months."

"Are they not of the People?" Kaga's voice was proud. "They can hunt for themselves. You need not nurse them at your breast."

Holt considered the six young braves watching them from the trees. "They are still children, Kaga. Is this the best Maska can find to defend the tribe?"

"All the warriors are gone," the Indian said abruptly.

"All?" Holt was shocked.

The silence confirmed his question. It also assured Holt's answer.

"They can stay here until spring. Then they must go north."

Kaga didn't reply. He merely nodded and continued gazing into the distance. Holt placed his hand urgently on the other man's arm. He said firmly, "The women and children must be protected, too, Kaga. You can smuggle them up here to me in small groups during the winter, before the fighting resumes."

Finally Kaga turned his attention to the younger man. Holt was surprised to see the old man's onyx eyes glittering with tears.

"You may have a white man's heart, Igasho," he said in a low voice filled with pride, "but you have an Indian soul."

Holt knew his plan was risky, but as far as he was concerned, there was no choice. Before Kaga left he saw the young braves settled in the mine. They would have a rough go of it at best. Campfires were too risky and game was scarce. The winter cold was numbing, and though the six young men had dressed appropriately for the weather, frostbite and exposure were always waiting for the unwary. Holt would visit as often as he dared with food and extra provisions like wool blankets. But his latest secret was a deadly one. He could not share it with anyone, least of all Angel or his half-brother.

Holt knew he would need to go back to Oro and discourage Neal's return before the holidays ended. He would have to think on the way of some plausible reason for refusing his brother's help. It was true he hadn't found much to complain about when he and Neal had worked the mine. Holt had expected his brother to be a whiner, but Neal had taken up the challenge with surprising enthusiasm. He had even agreed to help Holt build a new cabin as soon as the ground thawed in the spring.

The spring would bring more changes for all of them, Holt thought, as he carefully made his way down the mountain. He paused respectfully for a moment at the spot where Lily had been found. He forged on without looking back. Holt was relieved when it began to snow again, adding a fresh layer over old memories, starting the healing process sooner than he'd expected and bringing his mind back to the living.

Angel. Was she still angry with him for deserting her on Christmas Day? Holt wondered how he could ever explain the relationship he and Lily had shared. More than friends, less than lovers. It was unthinkable to him that Angel might have asked him to abandon Lily on her deathbed. But he was afraid that was exactly what she had wanted. And he had to admit that if Angel had forced him to choose between them that day, she wouldn't have liked the result. But she hadn't asked him to choose. She had come along in the end, lending quiet words of comfort and support to Lily even though it had obviously hurt her to do so.

Holt sighed. He owed Angel an explanation. But he also owed it to her to send her back to Missouri as soon as possible. This was no life for a woman. Even a hardened one like Lily had finally met her match. She had died trying to warn Holt, and he wasn't sure he could ever forgive himself for that. There was no doubt in his mind that Garrett and his cronies had killed her. The problem was finding proof and making it stick. Judge Felton Garrett certainly wouldn't look twice at a case involving his brother. And Holt knew it was only a matter of time before they started looking to blame him for any number of crimes in the Territory, whether or not he was guilty.

It was a fact that he was breaking the law now by aiding and abetting fugitive Indians. But Holt thought that paled in insignificance beside murder. He felt obliged to justify his actions only to himself. And maybe to Angel, but he couldn't involve the woman he loved in any more danger. Because he loved Angel so much, he would let her go— and never let her suspect how much she truly meant to him.

* * *

When she heard the parsonage door open quietly Angel called out from the kitchen, "You're just in time for dinner."

She finished wiping her floury hands on the apron tied to her waist and brushed back a loose strand of hair before she turned toward the door to welcome Neal back from his rounds.

She faltered and the smile faded from her face. "Holt. I wasn't expecting you."

"Obviously." His voice was tense as he removed his hat, and his snow-flecked dark hair sparkled in the light. He set down a hastily wrapped package on the wooden counter.

Holt surreptitiously studied Angel as he turned to face her. She was flushed from the heat of the cookstove, and tendrils of her hair had curled around her face like a golden halo. Even flustered as she was, she was the most beautiful thing he could ever recall seeing.

She gestured nervously at the package. "What's that for?"

"Venison. I had it cut and wrapped down at Caxton's."

"Oh. Thank you." Angel picked up the meat and opened the icebox. Once she had disposed of it, she rinsed her hands and quickly busied herself over the stove, unsuccessfully trying to calm the pounding of her heart.

Without an invitation, Holt tossed his hat on the dinner table, then pulled out a chair and straddled it, watching her closely as she tried to maintain a cool that was anything but genuine.

"I imagine you're hungry," Angel began, fiercely

scrubbing with a rag at a crusty spot on the stove in order to occupy her trembling hands.

"Very."

Holt's casual reply sent a unexpected shiver up Angel's spine. She recognized that lazy drawl, but she was determined to ignore the unspoken meaning hanging heavy in that single word.

"Well, as soon as Neal returns from the Maxwells', we can eat." Angel kept her tone falsely bright and cheerful.

"I believe he's staying there for dinner. I saw his horse still there when I passed their house."

"Oh, surely he wouldn't be so inconsiderate . . . would he?" Angel half turned and caught Holt's ironic look out of the corner of her eye. She stiffened. "I'd better serve this up before it burns."

"If it's any consolation, I'm sure it won't all go to waste," Holt drawled. "I'm ravenous."

Angel nodded stiffly and picked up a clean platter on which she dished up generous portions of stewed potatoes and meat, along with side servings of beans and vegetables. She poured hot fresh coffee and served the meal in silence, not even looking up when Holt rose and moved his chair to join her at the small table.

With a fork halfway to his mouth Holt paused and inquired casually, "Are you still interested in the mine?"

Angel swiftly glanced at him and wondered what he was getting at. His gray eyes were unusually dark, almost smoldering. "Of course I am. I need the gold for Belle Montagne, and . . . other things." She waited hopefully for him to inquire about the mysterious "other things," thinking it might provide an opening to tell him about the baby. But Holt let it go without so much as a flicker of curiosity in his eyes. A feeling of dread began to rise in her tight throat. For a time they ate in silence, and then Holt sat back and wiped his mouth with a napkin.

"You're quite a cook, Angel. I imagine you could even make your living in a fancy French restaurant if you had to."

Angel felt a pang of misgiving. Was Holt so devastated by Lily's death that he was warning her their marriage was over? Was he politely suggesting she find a way to support herself? Questions spun in her mind while she fumbled to find words.

"Is there something you want to tell me, Holt?"

"No. I do have something to ask you, though. Would you consider selling out?"

At her shocked expression he added quietly, "It's been eating at me, knowing you've got all your hopes and dreams wrapped up in that old mine."

Not all, Angel corrected him silently, but she could only sit and regard Holt with a look of frozen apprehension. He sighed and shoved his plate away, then leaned back and hooked a boot heel in the brace of his chair.

"There's no easy way to tell you this. I don't think the Lucky Angel will be your salvation. Not now, not ever."

His brutal prediction brought only a murmur from Angel.

"Do you understand me, woman?" he asked almost roughly. "I don't think there will be any pay dirt, for either of us."

Her blue eyes rose and fixed on him accusingly. "What about the gold you've been finding?"

Holt snorted softly and shook his head. "Four years' worth of dust and inferior nuggets. Most mines produce more than that in the first six months. Give me a little credit for brains, woman. If there was any hope, do you think I'd be telling you all this?"

"Yes, if you wanted it all for yourself," Angel replied coldly.

"I'm not the one who wants to buy you out. I'm trying to help you make a wise decision."

She regarded him mulishly. Holt sighed again and rubbed the back of his neck as he spoke.

"I can't stand to see you wasting your time up here waiting for the mother lode when you could be getting on with your life. There's a new start waiting for you somewhere, Angel. I've received a respectable offer from someone here in town, and I think you'd be wise to take it."

"Who?" she asked.

"Fellow by the name of Brindle. I don't know the man, but he's new in town, and that probably explains his gullibility."

"Mrs. Maxwell's beau," Angel said with surprise. "I wouldn't feel right trying to deceive Rachel's future step-father!"

"From what I hear the man has money. This will be just a temporary setback for him. It's your whole life at stake, Angel."

She shook her head almost fiercely and suddenly rose from the table. "I don't believe you, Holt Murphy. There's far more to this than meets the eye!"

Angel rushed out of the kitchen. Holt followed her and found the young woman facing the fireplace in the parlor, her body shaking with silent sobs. He walked up behind her and gently laid his hands on her shoulders. "I wouldn't lie to you, Angel," he said huskily. "You mean too much to me."

Slowly she turned in the circle of his arms and raised hopeful, tear-filled eyes to his face. Would Holt declare his love for her now? Because if he did, she would no longer worry about the mine or anything else except their marriage. She was determined to make it work. Perhaps in time he could come to forget Lily and love her just as deeply. Besides, now there was the child to think of. Holt would surely feel an obligation to try and make their marriage work.

Holt softly kissed her brow. "Just consider it, all right? Brindle's made a good offer. You could live comfortably on the money for the rest of your days."

"What about you?" she whispered.

He gave a wry grin. "I'll make do like I always have. I've been thinking of heading west anyway and trying my luck in the California goldfields."

Angel swallowed past the hard lump in her throat. He hadn't mentioned a shared future for the two of them. She said at last, "I want to think about this for a while."

"I'd advise you not to stall too long. Otherwise Brindle's likely to get cold feet."

Abruptly, Angel pulled free of his arms and turned to face the fire. She was cold, so cold. Her future with Holt was crumbling right before her eyes. She didn't think she could stand much more.

"Holt, I want to give the mine a chance," she rasped through her tears. "Time; that's all it needs. Time . . ."

Behind her, Holt made a weary sound. "Well, it's up to you, of course. I have to admire your stubbornness, Angel, but I hope you aren't making a mistake. Don't wait past spring to give Brindle your answer." He was silent for a moment. "In fact, I think we should use the springtime as a goal for other things too."

"Wh—what do you mean?"

"I mean if the mine doesn't come through by the first of spring, I want you to sell and go home."

Angel was silent, the pain too intense for her to speak. Didn't Holt realize she had no home now? Belle Montagne is a beautiful place, she thought, but that's all it is to me now—a place. Home was where the heart was, and hers was here with Holt.

"Give me your promise, Angel," he said almost harshly. "If the mine doesn't deliver by the first of March, you'll go back to Missouri. This is no life for a woman. Least of all one like you."

What did he mean by that? Angel was too hurt and angry to think before she spoke.

"I suppose Lily Valentine fit in just fine!"

"Lily was different," Holt said roughly. "She had a hard life and was used to disappointment. You're not."

"Oh, I don't know about that," Angel said bitterly. "I've had plenty of disappointment in the last few months!"

When Holt stayed silent she turned to face him again and said with icy composure, "All right, you want my word. You have it. If the mine doesn't produce by March, I'll sell."

"And go home," Holt added firmly.

Angel nodded. She didn't feel it necessary to add that "home" was a matter of definition. And as far as she was concerned, Colorado Territory was as close to that definition as she could ever hope to get. That was, as long as

Holt Murphy still lived there. She had three months to change his mind. It was as simple as that.

She firmly wiped away the last of her tears. "Will you stay the night?"

He shook his head. "I've been away from the mine longer than I should have."

"If it's a worthless claim, why bother guarding it anymore?"

He smiled a little ironically. "We don't want Brindle thinking that, do we?" His smile faded as he saw the look in Angel's eyes. "I'll be back down next week for supplies. Keep the home fires burning till then, all right?"

She nodded, too tired and dispirited to point out that he'd just said her home was in Missouri, not here. She had briefly considered telling Holt about the baby, but she didn't want to influence his decision now. If he came to love her on his own during the long winter ahead, then and only then would she share the most precious secret of all. If not, she would carry the price of her love in painful silence all the way back to Belle Montagne and never look back again.

Chapter Eighteen

"A ball!"

Rachel Maxwell's delighted voice carried all the way to Aunt Clara's kitchen, where Angel was arranging pastries to accompany the ladies' afternoon tea. She hastily picked up the silver tray and hurried back into the drawing room to join the rest of the conversation.

"Angel, did you hear that?" Rachel cried. "Auntie wants to hold a New Year's ball in honor of my engagement."

"How exciting," Angel said uncertainly, not sure whether she should encourage the idea or not, since she couldn't readily imagine who would be invited in such a small community or, more importantly, who would even come.

Aunt Clara seemed to read Angel's mind. Her dark eyes twinkled mischievously as she said, "I shall call upon you, my dear Mrs. Murphy, to help me with the arrangements. I'm certain you can provide me with a list of suitable young people for the event." After a disarming smile at Angel, she gestured to a mahogany table arranged before her and Rachel's chairs. "Will you pour, my dear?"

"Of course," Angel murmured, still a bit overcome by the suddenness of the idea and a trifle bemused by what her role was to be in the scheme of things.

". . . my gray muslin, I suppose," Rachel was saying as Angel's attention drifted back to the conversation and each of the ladies had appropriated one of the delicate china cups. There was a distinctly woebegone note to Rachel's tone as she realized the unsuitability of all of her gowns for a ball.

Aunt Clara said pertly, "Nonsense, child. I won't have my niece wearing such a dreadful concoction at a formal function held in her own honor! No, my wedding gift to you shall be nothing less than a new ensemble . . . a complete trousseau, if you will."

"Oh, Auntie!" Rachel breathed, nearly spilling her tea as she set down her cup and saucer with a hasty rattle and crossed the room to fling herself into the old woman's arms.

"Now, now, none of that," Clara said sternly, but a smile tugged at the corners of her mouth as she patted Rachel's back and met Angel's approving gaze. "We have much to do and so little time, girls! Invitations must be issued at once; of course we shall miss New Year's proper, but I'll wager our little community will forgive us."

"Why, yes, it will be quite the event of the new year!" Rachel exclaimed as she straightened up and patted her hair back in place.

"In my day, dear, we would have said it would be the 'highlight of the season,' " Aunt Clara reminisced lightly. "I shall never fully understand American expressions, I fear, but it is enough that you appear pleased."

"Pleased? I'm overcome, Auntie!"

"Exactly so," Clara said. She turned to Angel with a distinctly playful glint in her eyes. "And what do you think of our grand little scheme, Mrs. Murphy?"

"I think it's a wonderful idea," Angel enthused.

"Good. Then I also insist you allow me the favor of outfitting you for the ball."

"Oh, Mrs. Maxwell, how kind of you, but I couldn't possibly—"

Aunt Clara cut her off in midsentence with a sniff. "I shall accept nothing less, and you would do well to take me up on the offer, since I intend to presume quite fully upon your good nature in the days to come. In other words, my dear, I'm going to work your delicate little fingers to the bone. . . . I'm too old for such nonsense myself, and Dulcibel shall have her own hands quite full with making your gowns."

"Very well," Angel said, but she intended to take Aunt Clara's maid aside at the first opportunity and insist that her ball gown, if she must have one, should be plain and of the most inexpensive material available.

Aunt Clara looked very pleased with herself. "I daresay that if we put our heads together, my girls, we can quite set this complacent little community on its ear!"

"O-h-h," Rachel breathed, dreamily studying her own reflection in the cheval glass. She turned very slowly so she could examine herself from every angle. Taffeta rustled softly in the enclosed room. The skirt of the gown was pink silk, matching the bloom in her cheeks, and the two overskirts of white taffeta were short at the front and longer in the back, ending with four pleated frills. The small bustle was drawn back into a flowing train several feet behind her. It was the absolute height of fashion.

Rachel wore her hair in a soft coil, though she had tied a white silk bow in the back for an accent. She looked up with surprise when Angel moved forward with a rope of creamy pearls and fastened the jewelry around her friend's neck.

"My wedding gift to you, dear Rachel," Angel said quietly before she stepped away. The pearls had been a gift from her father on her sixteenth birthday, but Angel had rarely worn them. They better complemented Rachel's gown and complexion, and she felt no sense of loss, only a warm glow of pleasure as she parted with them.

"Oh, Angel!"

The two young women embraced, then stepped apart so as not to crush their respective gowns. Rachel eyed her best friend with approval. "Your gown is beautiful, too," she said loyally. "I'm glad Aunt Clara insisted you have a new dress for the evening."

Angel smiled, catching a glimpse of herself in the mirror as she moved across the room. Dulcibel had surprised them both with her considerable skill with needle and thread. If the maid was not such a dour soul, Angel would have suspected Dulcibel had dressed them as lovingly as she would her own daughters. Angel had insisted her gown be plain and practical, but in a mark of defiance the wizened little woman had crafted a masterpiece.

Angel's dress was made from two materials, cream silk and claret velvet, and trimmed with English Midlands lace. The cuirass bodice sleekly hugged her slender frame, and the draped panniers descended in a waterfall train to the floor.

The gown rivaled anything Angel had ever owned, and she could only marvel over where Dulcibel had found the material. There had not been time to order anything from Denver, and the stage line was still closed due to the inclement weather. The only thing her new outfit lacked was matching jewelry. She was not unduly surprised when Clara Maxwell soon appeared to make amends for that, as well.

After exclaiming her approval over Rachel's new pearls, Aunt Clara proceeded to open a velvet case, revealing a magnificent garnet necklace, bracelet, and earrings. While the younger women made admiring comments, Aunt Clara lifted the necklace from its case and lovingly ran the sparkling stones through her age-spotted hands.

"A gift from my James," she said simply, and then, unexpectedly, her eyes rose to find Angel's. "You will wear them tonight."

"Me? But Rachel is your niece—"

"And she shall inherit the more valuable family jewelry, of course. But these stones are special, my dear. James gave them to me on our first wedding anniversary. I've always considered them more precious than rubies."

"Mrs. Maxwell, I simply can't—" Angel began.

"Of course you can. Can't she, Rachel?"

Angel found herself outnumbered, and she relented with a sigh. "All right, you two. But I'm wearing them this one night only."

The twinkle in Aunt Clara's eyes indicated otherwise, but she deferred the argument for later as she fastened the clasp for Angel and then handed her the matching ear-bobs and bracelet. The dark red stones were a perfect color match to the velvet in Angel's gown, and they all agreed that the simple chignon in which she had styled her hair was most flattering for the wearing of jewelry.

"I should be going downstairs and checking on things," Angel said as she glanced at the ormolu clock on the mantel. "Dulcibel will need help setting out the refreshments."

"Dulcie is quite capable of handling things from here on out," Aunt Clara said complacently. "I hired a pair of young girls from town to help her with the serving line, and you've certainly done your part in the past few weeks, my dear. I insist you rest now before the ball. You're looking a bit peaked, you know."

Before Clara could suggest one of her tonics, Angel said hastily, "Perhaps I will take a brief respite. Will you two ladies excuse me?"

Angel escaped Rachel's room with the apparent notion of retiring to her own room for a time, but she had no intention of doing so. She merely wished for a moment of peace and privacy before the ball. Most of all she wished for Holt, although that was, of course, an idle and futile wish. She'd seen him only twice since he delivered his ultimatum at Christmas. Both times they had been frigidly polite to one another, but nothing had been said about the mine or their future.

With a quiet sigh, Angel went downstairs and entered the conservatory. Idly she ran her fingers over the ivory keys of the piano. She was picking out the notes to "Clare de Lune" when a soft cough sounded in the doorway.

"Neal!" She forced pleasure to mask the disappointment in her voice as the young minister entered the room, looking very dashing in his black evening coat and trousers.

"Angel," he said, giving her a bow. "May I say you are looking very . . . angelic," he finished, with a merry twinkle in his eyes.

"Thank you," she replied as she closed the piano lid and moved to greet him. "You're early, you know. The ball isn't set to begin for another two hours."

"Zounds, Aunt Clara will have my hide for this!" Neal exclaimed, mimicking their hostess's English accent. Then he switched back to a Clear Creek drawl as he said, "Actually, I needed to visit with Rachel before the festivities begin. Is she still upstairs?"

Angel nodded and said playfully, "You know we ladies can't descend until every last hair has been pasted in place."

"That's what I was afraid of. And it's very important I speak with her . . ."

"Is there something I can help you with?"

Neal considered her offer for a moment. "Actually, I suppose you could. I heard about a last-minute cancellation before I left Oro. You'll be short a male guest on the dance floor."

Angel sighed. "Let me guess. Mr. Brindle?"

Neal looked surprised. "How did you know?"

"Because the elusive Mr. Brindle has successfully managed to evade every party, social, or holiday season event since he arrived. Heaven only knows how he ever managed to meet Rachel's mother in the first place. The man has never so much as darkened a doorway in my presence."

"You've never seen him at all?"

"No, nor am I certain I wish to after the way he treats Mrs. Maxwell. He rudely cuts her at every opportunity. I can't imagine why she puts up with him."

"From what I hear he's generous with his money," Neal said. "And Prudence has been alone a long time."

"Yes, but it doesn't excuse his behavior. Now Mrs. Maxwell will be overset, and everyone's evening will quite likely be ruined."

"That's why I wanted you to know what had happened. Maybe it's not too late to find another gentleman to round out the numbers."

"Whom do you suggest?" Angel asked wryly. "Blackjack Tate or Willy Benson?" Both were notorious town drunks. And those two were likely the only men left, as she and Rachel had already snatched every last marginally eligible male from both the streets of Clear Creek and Oro.

Neal choked and turned it into a cough. "Surely it's not that bad?"

"Well Neal . . . there are far more single ladies than men here. Most of the decent men are either up at the mines or already dead. I can safely say were you not engaged to Rachel, you would be considered fair game tonight, by young girls and widows alike."

He blanched and mumbled about something he had forgotten back at the parsonage, then scurried out of the conservatory. Angel shook her head and smiled after him. Neal was such an innocent, really. He was still embarrassed by the notion of marriage, and half the time he didn't seem to know what to do with a woman. She remembered Holt once calling his brother a womanizer, and she laughed aloud now. Neal Murphy was as far from that particular animal as they came.

Aunt Clara's huge drawing room had been rendered into quite an acceptable ballroom for the evening of the ball, and everything from the mahogany sideboard to the polished wood floor shone with a high gloss from the attention it had received. Dulcibel and the two hired girls had kept up with the demands of the guests comfortably at first, but after everyone had arrived they were hard-pressed to keep the glasses and the pastry trays full.

Angel volunteered to help out at the refreshment table, doling out the punch, since she was not interested in dancing or socializing. Her position was that of a married woman without an escort, and as such she stayed in the background and was content to watch Rachel shine.

The dancing had just opened to the tinny strains of a lively quadrille when Angel looked up from serving one of the church ladies, a polite smile still pasted on her lips, when her gaze met Holt's in the doorway across the room.

An intake of breath was the only sign Angel gave of being surprised. She quickly forced a cool look to her face, deliberately turning away to serve another person in the line as Holt entered the room. But with Holt Murphy she was faced with a wild card, and things were suddenly not so simple.

Angel wished she could keep her gaze from straying to the man, but she was too surprised by the sight of Holt in a suit to pretend indifference. She had seen him well-dressed before, but the transition never ceased to amaze her. She had to admit the trim cut of Holt's black evening coat and wool trousers showed his lean, muscular frame to advantage. Tonight he wore a waistcoat of cream-figured silk, which was so similar to the silk in her gown, she almost could have accused Dulcibel of having cut both from the same swatch of cloth. The loosely knotted tie Holt wore gave him an air of casual elegance, and with his black hair combed back he might have passed for a gentleman. Which was about as far from reality as it came, Angel thought, watching him approach a little knot of young ladies and dazzle them with his easy charm.

To her annoyance, she saw several of the younger, single women eyeing her husband speculatively as he talked to them. Little wonder, though. Holt Murphy evidenced a blend of sophistication and barely concealed savagery obvious to even the most puritanical of women. This was brought home when Prudence Maxwell glided up to the refreshment table in a crackle of brown bombazine and hissed at Angel, "What a scoundrel he is, my dear! You really must bring him to heel at once!"

Prudence's present outrage was only outdone by the scandalized look on her face when she had first seen Rachel's gown. Now, however, she was apparently content to find fault with others. Angel forced a smile and said evenly, "I don't presume to order my husband about, Mrs. Maxwell."

"Well! I should hope not! What I meant, dear, was merely that you should ah—politely discourage his obvious interest in the innocent young women of the town!"

"Innocent" was hardly the word Angel would have used to describe Josie Baxter's coy smiles and coquettish giggles as she chatted with Holt, or Emma Drake's love-struck expression, but she set her jaw and departed from the table to interrupt the cozy little scene across the room.

"If you please, ladies, I would like a word with my husband," Angel began, unconsciously stressing the last two words, and when Holt glanced at her with those dark gray eyes she realized he had heard the possessive note in her voice and was amused by it.

The cluster of disappointed females drifted away, and Angel was left alone with Holt, her cheeks burning.

"What an unexpected surprise," she continued as steadily as she could. "I assumed the endless fascination of the mine would pale in comparison to what we mere mortals do down here."

"Are you implying I'm a god of some sort?" Holt lazily inquired. "Like Zeus upon Olympus perhaps, gazing down on his subjects and forever finding fault?"

She looked at him with surprise.

"Don't act so shocked, Angel. Did I forget to mention I'm a relatively educated man among my many other talents?" Holt's chuckle was mirthless as he continued to regard her with a cool, silvery gaze. "Arthur sent me back east for a few years, hoping to pound some brains into my head."

"Did it work?" Angel asked spitefully, but Holt only laughed.

"You're beautiful when you're angry. In fact, I'd almost forgotten how beautiful . . ."

"Don't waste my time with meaningless flattery, Holt. Why are you here?"

Angel hadn't intended to sound so sharp, but his very presence made her quiver inwardly with feelings she was afraid to identify. It was better to chase him off, before further words were exchanged or her heart was hopelessly entangled in her common sense. But she soon found he was intent on staying, just like a barnacle cleaved to a rock.

He gave her a disarming smile. "I heard you were organizing a dance for the Maxwells. You've done very well."

"Thank you," Angel gritted out, but got no further than that when Aunt Clara suddenly drifted up to them in a cloud of patchouli scent.

"My dear Mr. Murphy, I'm so glad you could come after all," the old lady said with real pleasure. Clara looked fragile but beautiful in a blue brocade gown, and she glittered with the sapphires with which her husband had presented her on their tenth anniversary.

Angel suddenly saw the two were exchanging conspiratorial looks, and she understood that Clara Maxwell was behind Holt's appearance and, no doubt, his finery, as well. But however she felt about Holt, Angel couldn't be angry with Rachel's aunt. She gave Clara a warm smile when the little old lady held out her hands.

"We've had such fun, haven't we, my dear?" Clara asked as she squeezed Angel's fingers in her own. "You've become just like my own daughter to me in the past few weeks. Do you realize what a lucky man you are, Mr. Murphy?"

"Of course," Holt said, but his eyes were hooded and unreadable as he looked at Angel.

"There's the 'Missouri Waltz' now," Clara said with satisfaction as the dreamy strains began to steal across the room. "I insist you two young people entertain an old woman's whims and open the floor. Go on with you, now!"

The couple looked at each other uncertainly, but Clara Maxwell's desires were not to be brooked. She almost shoved Angel into Holt's arms, and as his strong hand settled possessively into the small of Angel's back, the younger woman felt a traitorous tingle of pleasure too powerful to ignore.

"Shall we?" Holt asked, tilting his head toward the space that had been cleared for the dancing. Without waiting for a reply, he turned around with Angel in his arms, spinning carefully through the crowd, rendering her breathless with excitement and anticipation. Never in her wildest dreams had she imagined Holt could dance! And not just dance, but waltz as if he had been born with a silver spoon in his mouth and practiced nothing more strenuous than the three-step turn with a woman in his arms. And not just any woman—her. Angel wondered why she felt so giddy and schoolmissish, just because her husband was paying attention to her. But one glance at a beaming Aunt Clara and the group of disgruntled young women Holt had greeted earlier told Angel that she was indeed a lucky woman.

"I've missed you, Angel," Holt said suddenly, huskily, and her eyes flew up to his face as if to test the sincerity of his words by his expression. "It gets pretty lonesome up there on the mountain. Pretty darn cold, too."

His gray eyes were sober. Angel saw he was serious. "Come down to the valley more often," she suggested lightly, with just a hint of warm promise in her voice.

"I'll do that. If you'll have me."

He sounded hesitant, unsure. Angel responded with a coy smile. "You know you're always welcome in my arms."

The carnival tempo of the waltz suddenly quickened, as did Angel's heart, when Holt lowered his head and discreetly nuzzled her neck in full view of everyone there. They were spinning faster and faster, the room a blur of faces and colorful fabrics, but all Angel could feel was the warmth of his lips on her skin, his wonderfully possessive grip on her waist. Around and around the room they went, the few other dancers making way for the obviously distracted couple.

"Shocking!" Prudence Maxwell declared behind her fan to whomever would listen. "Absolutely scandalous!"

Rachel appeared beside her mother in a rustle of white taffeta. "And absolutely romantic," she happily agreed.

The waltz came to an abrupt halt, and for a moment Holt and Angel stood in the center of the floor, looking at each other in a mixture of faint surprise and fascination. For a long moment they didn't so much as move.

Holt took her by the hand. "Have you had enough dancing yet, Mrs. Murphy?" he inquired with a twinkle in his eye as he raised her hand to his lips and gently showered her knuckles with kisses.

"Quite so, Mr. Murphy!" Angel readily agreed, and eyes locked to each other, they slowly left the room together, completely oblivious to the envious stares and whispers that trailed them down the hall.

Chapter Nineteen

"We were very rude, you know."

Angel spoke softly as Holt shut the bedroom door behind them, loosening his tie with his other hand.

"I don't care," he rasped. "I've waited too damn long to have you again."

He shrugged off his jacket and took her in his arms, drinking long and deeply of the sweetness of her lips. Pins rained to the floor as Holt unfastened her hair, spreading her golden tresses down around her shoulders in a shimmering veil. His long fingers moved to unfasten the many buttons and ties on her bodice, and when he gave up with a soft oath Angel chuckled and nimbly finished the job.

The creamy silk of her gown parted to reveal skin of the same color and texture. Holt sighed with longing as he cupped the full breasts in his hands, worrying the dusky pink nipples with the callused pads of his thumbs.

"Lord, woman," he said in a low voice, "I still can't believe how beautiful you are."

Angel tilted back her head and smiled up at him. "Does that mean you've missed me these past few weeks?"

"Do you have to ask?" He bent his head and captured the bud of a breast between his teeth, nipping gently and then soothing the inflamed peak with his tongue. Like an artist, he slowly painted every inch of her exposed flesh, pausing only to tug impatiently at the waistband of her skirt.

"Off," Holt ordered, then promptly resumed kissing Angel until she was gasping for breath, her fingers shaking as she fumbled with the ties of her gown. Moments later he stopped and spun her around, and the lace and silk slid to a heap at her feet as he tore the tapes with brute force.

Angel clung to Holt's broad shoulders as he carried her to the bed and deposited her gently upon the counterpane. Her blue eyes widened as he quickly divested himself of his snowy white shirt and trousers. By the single lamp burning in her room, his shadowed body gleamed with occasional bronze lights. She raised her hand to stroke his smooth, hairless chest and arms, and Holt murmured encouragement as he joined her on the bed.

"I've wanted this for so long," he whispered, gently carrying Angel with him back against the bolsters. He parted the golden curtain of the hair hiding her breasts, and gazed hungrily upon her luscious form as she snuggled close against him.

As if by instinct his big hand moved to cover her belly, and Angel froze. Could he feel the flutter of life there? Of course not, she chided herself. She hadn't felt it yet herself. But her breasts were visibly fuller and her body was changing. Surely Holt could not be blind to all of the signs. She parted her lips to speak, and he swept his down like a hawk to silence her.

"Tonight," he whispered, "no talk . . . just love. Just the two of us."

Angel couldn't find breath enough to challenge him. Her body was aching, almost in pain with the force and depth of her need. It had been so long that when he rose above her and sank deeply into her willing warmth, she released a sob of pure relief.

He moved slowly at first, then harder and faster as he coaxed her to respond. Angel clung to Holt's shoulders, letting her body absorb the impact of their mutual need, as she cried out with quiet joy at what she had lost and found again.

Don't ever leave me, she wanted to say, but though her inner voice shouted, her lips remained still. He said it all in his touch, his kiss. She didn't need promises. She would trust in love, and pray it was enough.

Later, they lay snuggled together beneath the counterpane after the sounds of merrymaking below had faded to silence. Angel slept a little, but her mind was too lively, her hopes too intense for her to rest quietly.

For a while she lay, fingering the garnet necklace she still wore, remembering what it meant to Clara, and hoping it would have the same precious significance to her one day.

"Holt?" she finally whispered. "Are you awake?"

"Hmm?" he murmured, half asleep.

She reached over to stroke the black silk of his hair. "Holt, I have something to tell you, it's—"

A soft snore cut her off in midsentence. With an exasperated sigh, she threw herself back against the pillows, telling herself that she would have to be content with the moment at hand, and let tomorrow take care of itself.

* * *

Sunlight sprinkled through the lace curtains at the window, softly lighting Angel's face. Holt sat propped up on one elbow, studying his young wife as she slept. She was too beautiful to be real, he thought for the hundredth time. It was hard to believe he was deserving of such a woman.

He bent and softly kissed her cheek. Her sleepy blue eyes opened on him, and she stretched with catlike pleasure.

"Good morning," she said, but Holt's only reply was to kiss her until she was fully awake and warm with passion.

After they made love once more Angel reluctantly moved to get dressed, realizing the day was stealthily intruding on them. It was hard not to resent every moment they lost while she was getting dressed and smoothing her hair. Holt watched her the entire time, gray eyes slitted against the sunlight that now dappled the entire bed.

Angel put on the first thing she grabbed, a yellow cashmere gown trimmed with blond lace. When she finished her morning toilette she turned to discover Holt had dressed as well. For some reason she was disappointed. His magnificent body was completely hidden from view.

Holt finished lacing his boots, rose, and approached her. "How do you feel this morning, Mrs. Murphy?" he inquired with a mischievous glint in his eye.

"Perfectly restored, thank you," Angel replied primly. "I must admit you dance divinely, Mr. Murphy."

Holt threw back his head and laughed. "I'd give almost anything to see you dishing out such ditties to the lovestruck fellows back in Independence!"

"Well, that will never happen, will it?"

He suddenly sobered. "No, I suppose not. I'm going to miss you, Angel."

Her startled eyes rose to his serious face. "I . . . I meant it would never happen because I'm not going back to Missouri." She tried to quell the queasy knot that had suddenly seized her insides.

"Not going back?" He frowned down at her. "What about your promise?"

Angel's hands clenched together as she fought the threat of tears. "I thought last night might have . . . changed things," she whispered, stricken.

Holt swore, loud and long, staring at her with outright amazement. "Then it was just a ploy so I would let you stay?"

"No, of course not! Holt, you don't understand—"

"Oh, I understand plenty, lady. I understand you can't keep your word, and one thing I can't abide is a liar." Holt raked a hand furiously through his hair, turning to pace the bedroom. "You continue to amaze me, Angel. A man could come to believe anything in your arms."

Tears began to leak from her eyes. "You're wrong—"

"No, lady, you are." He whirled and pinned her with a hard silver gaze. "In two months' time you're going back to Missouri, if I have to tie you up myself and throw you on the eastbound stage. Is that understood?"

Angel faced him down, her expression a stony mask that carefully hid all the churning emotions beneath.

"Yes," she replied. "I don't think even Lily Valentine could have said it any plainer."

"What's that supposed to mean?"

"Whatever you think it does. I won't take up any more

of your time," Angel said with chilly dignity as she swept up her shawl and started to leave the room.

"Just a damn minute," Holt growled. "There's something we need to straighten out here. About Lily—"

"I don't care to hear the details of your relationship with that woman, thank you," Angel said crisply before she stormed out of the room, slamming the door shut.

Holt stared after her, fists balled at his sides. Here he had been ready and willing to explain everything about him and Lily, and Angel had cut him off cold. Fine. Damn fine, in fact. For all he cared, she could just stew in her own jealous juices until she was broiled a deep, lobster red!

Angel barely glanced up from the letter she was writing to Elsa Loring when Rachel entered the study.

"Holt's gone?" her friend asked, trying not to make an issue of it even though she was obviously concerned.

Angel merely nodded, trying to think of a way to word her peculiar circumstances on paper so Elsa wouldn't be more worried than she already was. She'd received several hysterical letters from Belle Montagne's former housekeeper and her old nursemaid, and Angel had spent the better part of three months trying to convince poor Elsa that she was not only alive but surviving as best she could.

Rachel put in tentatively, "You know the stage won't make a run again till spring. Your letter will have to wait."

Angel sighed and set the pen aside. "Unless I can pay someone to take it to Denver for me."

"Not very likely. Is it important?"

Angel smiled wanly. "Only to an old woman back east and a young fool like me."

Rachel's expression was transformed to one of sympathy. "You miss your home in Missouri, don't you?"

"Sometimes," Angel admitted. "But less and less as time goes on."

"What's it like there?"

"Mostly green."

"Like the pine trees here?"

"Oh, no. Entirely different. There are walnut and maple and oak trees. What they call a mountain in Missouri wouldn't even register on the scale out here. Except for the Ozarks, of course."

Rachel was glad to be able to distract her friend for a while, and she kept asking polite questions until the subjects of Missouri and Belle Montagne were completely exhausted. Then there was no avoiding the inevitable, not when Rachel realized Angel was waiting for advice.

"I don't know what to say," Rachel admitted. "But if it's any consolation, Holt told Neal not to bother coming back up to the mine this week. He's on the outs with nearly everyone in town."

"I've never met such a moody man," Angel snapped, and then sighed and apologized a moment later. "I'm sorry, Rachel. I'm just tired and overwrought after last night."

Her friend hesitated. "Did you tell him . . . ?"

Angel shook her head. "No. There wasn't time—actually, there just wasn't the right moment at all. And now I'm glad I didn't bother."

"Angel!"

"You don't understand." With another sigh, Angel

rose from the chair before the desk and began to pace the blue Persian carpet. "I haven't been completely honest with you, Rachel. And Neal, either, though he knows more than you do."

Briefly, she explained about the proxy marriage back in Independence, and as Rachel's eyes grew wider and wider, Angel finished her tale on a wry note. "You see why I'm not certain of Holt's position. He never actually proposed to me. And I don't want him feeling obligated now. He's made it clear where his first—and only—love lies. Six feet under the snows right now."

"Not Miss Valentine?" At Rachel's horrified gasp of disbelief, Angel nodded, but her friend was unable to accept that so readily. "If he loved her, why wouldn't he have married her long before you arrived?"

Angel shrugged. "Maybe he asked her. Lily had a pretty low opinion of herself as a marriage prospect; she might have refused him."

"Oh, I know Holt is a regular scoundrel sometimes, but he does love you, Angel! I've seen it in his eyes; the way he looks at you when you're not aware of it."

"Please, Rachel, don't try to soften the blow for me. I know my place in Holt's life now is nothing more than it was six months ago."

"I think you're wrong. Don't make a decision you'll come to regret. You said he's given you till spring. If I were you, I'd use every minute of that time to try and change his mind."

"Before last night I thought that way, too. But you didn't see the way he acted toward me this morning, Rachel! I'm nothing more than a—a convenience to him, a body to warm his sheets!"

Rachel shook her head. "You're his legal wife, even according to Neal, and that's all that matters. Holt owes you—and the baby—a chance. I think you should tell him, Angel. If it gives you the trump card so you can stay, who will know the difference?"

"I will. I won't stay in a loveless marriage, not even for the child's sake," Angel stated firmly. "Besides, Holt would come to hate me for deceiving him that way. He might even accuse me of trying to trap him."

Rachel sighed and walked over to her friend, stopping Angel's pacing in order to embrace her.

"Promise me, dear, you won't make any rash decisions today, or even tomorrow. So much could happen before spring; you'd be selling both yourself and Holt short if you didn't give your marriage every last chance."

Angel gazed into her friend's sober hazel eyes and realized that Rachel Maxwell had grown up considerably in the past few months. She thought seriously about the suggestion and then nodded.

"All right," she agreed quietly. "I'll try to stick it out, Rachel. But you'd better pray that nothing else happens to kill my trust in Holt Murphy. There's precious little left of it now."

Angel stayed another week at Clara Maxwell's house; Rachel's aunt insisted on it, and Angel found herself too weary to even consider the long drive back to Oro. Rachel departed only after extracting Angel's promise to stay put, and for a few days all was peaceful and serene in the snowbound town of Clear Creek.

With nothing on her hands but time, Angel discreetly

began to knit baby clothes, planning for the day when she would be forced to make a living for herself and items such as clothing would be scarce. She supposed she could always return to Missouri, but the thought of Will Craddock lurking about still gave her the shudders. Elsa and Hans Loring had been sincere in their offer to take her in, but would they really appreciate having a penniless young woman and another hungry baby on their hands?

As she considered her few options, Angel became more and more discouraged. She considered confiding in Clara, who was indeed like an aunt to her now, but she suspected the old lady would seek to put things right, even if it meant interfering as she had the night of the ball. Clara Maxwell meant well, but she didn't know all the facts about Angel's marriage. If worse came to worst, Angel supposed she could sell the garnet jewelry Clara had insisted she keep, but it would be nothing short of thoughtless to part with such a priceless heirloom.

So Angel made her plans for the future, though they were vague and unsatisfactory at best. As Holt had so coldly pointed out, she was a passable cook; perhaps one of the restaurants in Denver would give her a chance. She could take in laundry or sewing for the many miners who filled the frontier town. Why, she could probably even stay in Clear Creek, though Holt would hear rumors about the child, and she would not risk the possibility of him taking her son or daughter away.

A light snowfall began at the start of her second week at Clara's home, and Angel was considering returning to the parsonage before it worsened when there came a muffled pounding at the door.

Dulcibel answered it, and the grizzled little maid was

nearly knocked over by the figure of Neal Murphy as he burst into the hall.

"Angel!" he shouted urgently, and she hurried out from the adjoining parlor, her heart already beginning to pound at the ominous tone of his voice.

"Thank goodness you're here!" the young pastor cried. "A terrible thing happened over in Oro—Sheriff Garrett was found dead last night."

"Dead?" Angel gasped. "How?"

"Shot twice in the back after he left Jake's saloon." Neal's face was pale and very grim. "That's not all, I'm afraid. Holt has been arrested on suspicion of committing the murder."

"Holt! But surely he was up at the mine!"

Neal shook his head. "Witnesses say he left the saloon just before Garrett did. They'd apparently exchanged words that night, and Holt stormed out."

Angel fumbled for the back of a chair in the hallway, and she sank down on the seat with trembling legs. Dulcibel had already hurried off to spread the news, and within moments Clara Maxwell arrived and took charge.

"What's all this nonsense about a murder?"

Neal faced the older woman with regret. "I'm sorry, ma'am, but I came to inform Angel of Holt's whereabouts."

"The Oro jail, I presume?" At Neal's affirmative reply, Clara sniffed and said briskly, "We'll see about that. I'll have a lawyer brought in from Denver if I have to."

"But, ma'am, the stage is closed down until spring—"

"Bosh and twaddle!" Clara said emphatically. "Money has worked miracles before this, and I daresay it can do so again!"

Angel listened gratefully as Clara rapped out orders, and after Neal had been curtly dismissed the elderly woman turned to her guest and remarked, "That boy has no backbone! He should have thought of all those things himself before he came."

"I'm sure Neal is as upset by all this as I am." Angel automatically defended her brother-in-law. "And maybe he believes the worst of Holt."

"Do you?" Clara inquired shrewdly.

Angel didn't hesitate as she shook her head. "No. Holt does have a hot temper, but he'd never kill someone in cold blood, and especially not by shooting them in the back."

Rachel's aunt nodded with satisfaction. "Then that's all that matters, child. I trust your judgment. After all, who knows a husband better than his own wife?"

Probably half of Oro City, Angel wanted to say, but instead she replied, "I appreciate all you're doing, Clara. I can hardly keep my head on straight."

"It was thoughtless of Neal to upset you," Clara stated with disapproval. "A woman in your condition doesn't need a shock like that."

"My condition?" Angel looked up with surprise.

"Surely, my dear, you didn't think you could hide such a thing from a wise old owl like me?" Clara gave a merry little laugh. "Even a childless woman knows something is up when the food can't stay down!"

Angel blushed violently, and the older lady was quick to take her hands and squeeze them comfortingly. "Never fear, my dear; I want only the best for you and the little one. In fact, I should be very honored if you would stay on with me until the babe is born . . . late summer, wouldn't you say?"

Still stunned, Angel could only manage a nod.

"And after that we shall see, of course. Right now the important thing is to find some good food and plenty of rest for you, and the best lawyer in the Territory for that rascal Holt."

"Oh, Clara, I can't thank you enough."

"Nonsense, child. The only thanks I want is to see you safe and happy. You've brought a light into my life that I should heartily regret to lose." The elderly lady bent and fondly kissed Angel's cheek. "Now, I think we should start by unraveling this wild rumor about your husband, don't you?"

Holt sprang to his feet the moment the outer door leading to the jail cell opened.

"I demand to see the judge!" he said to the deputy who entered and approached his cell carrying a tray in his hands.

The man was taken aback by the fury in Holt's voice and paused to consider whether or not he should risk handing a meal to the prisoner.

"Yu'll see 'em," he said at last, his small piggy eyes dancing with laughter as he spoke. "Don't worry, yu'll git ta see 'em all, Injun. The witnesses, the barkeep, an' 'specially the hangin' judge, the Honorable Felton Garrett."

"Honorable, eh? Sounds like a case of skewed justice to me," Holt said bitterly. "Everyone knows he's the sheriff's brother!"

The deputy grinned, exposing rotted yellow teeth. "Yep, so's everyone knows yur gonna swing, Injun."

"Everyone also knows I didn't shoot Red."

"Tell that ta the judge," the deputy said with an ugly curl to his lip. He decided against feeding the prisoner, looking over the plates on the tray with obvious greed. Holt watched in disgust as the man chose a chicken leg and ate it right in front of him, chewing noisily and smacking his greasy lips.

"Good vittles," the man grunted, and picked over the rest of the tray until only scraps and bones were left. Then he laughed and shoved the remnants under the bars to Holt. "Eat up, Injun. It's better'n ya deserve anyway!"

Holt just stared at the deputy with cold gray eyes until the other man backed away uncomfortably and turned to hurry from the room. Once the outer door had swung shut and was securely locked again, Holt returned to the hard wooden bench in his cell and sat with his head in his hands. It was hard to believe he was going to be tried for murder. He'd expected Red Garrett and his cronies to try something, all right, but he'd never dreamed the sheriff himself would wind up dead, unknowingly framing Holt for the deed.

Garrett had enemies; that much was obvious. Who and why didn't matter as long as Holt could be absolved of the crime. But as Holt ran over the events of the previous night in his head, he couldn't believe how neatly he'd been set up. He and Garrett had quarreled publicly in Jake's when Red had made an ungentlemanly remark about Angel and Holt had taken quick offense. Holt sighed now. It seemed that woman could always get him into hot water, even when she wasn't there!

The bar fight had erupted into a downright brawl, and for a few minutes Holt had enjoyed cracking heads with chairs and smashing his fist into faces. But he'd never drawn his gun or knife like the yellow-livered boys in Garrett's employ always did. In fact, he'd narrowly missed being gutted by Garrett himself, and only after Jake threatened to kick them all out did Holt gather up what was left of his dignity and leave. It was true he'd briefly considered waiting for Garrett in the shadows of the alley . . .

"Holt?"

A soft female voice startled him from his brooding thoughts and he looked up sharply.

"Angel. You shouldn't be here."

His tone was harsher than he'd intended, but he couldn't take back the words. She clutched the bars of his cell and swayed slightly as she spoke.

"I . . . I had to come. I had to let you know that we're doing all we can to get you out of here. Clara Maxwell is hiring an attorney from Denver, and—"

Holt shook his head, cutting her off. "It'll be too late by then, sweetheart. They intend to rush this one right through the courts."

"They?"

He almost smiled at her innocence. "Judge Garrett and his friends. Guess I've been a burr under their saddles for a mite too long. Who else was the obvious man to take the fall for Red's death?"

"Don't say things like that," Angel whispered, tears making her blue eyes very bright. "I don't believe you killed Garrett, and neither will anyone else when this goes to trial."

"Trial? 'Fraid they aren't so formal here, Angel. It'll be a rope on a tree by Sunday noon, mark my words."

"Damn you, Holt Murphy!" she suddenly cried. "How can you be so calm?"

"Because," he said flatly, "I've seen it too many times before. Now get out of here, before they start thinking you had something to do with this, too. Better yet, have Mrs. Maxwell pay someone to take you to Denver. If my brother was half a man, I'd ask him to do it."

"Don't talk badly about Neal. He's doing everything he can to convince the townspeople of your innocence."

"Tell him not to preach any extra sermons on my account," Holt snapped. He turned his head aside, refusing to look any longer at Angel's tear-streaked, pleading face. "Go on, woman. I don't have time for your tears. Get out of Oro while there's still time."

"No. I won't leave you, Holt."

"Don't you understand?" His voice was harsh. "I don't want you here. I don't want you around at all."

The cold words echoed off the stone walls. She opened her mouth to speak, but nothing escaped her except a faint, strangled sound. She turned and blundered through her tears to find the exit from this nightmare. She collapsed against the outer door and pounded on it weakly until the deputy unlocked it, and she nearly fell into his arms.

"Easy there, lil' lady!"

With a sob, Angel shoved past his groping, sweaty hands and dashed through the office and out into the street. Grinning after her with a touch of disappointment, the fat deputy turned back to lock the door and was met by Holt's murderous, level stare from the jail cell.

With a shiver, the deputy hastily slammed and locked the door again, taking care to listen for the reassuring click of the bolt sliding into place. Then he wiped the sweat from his brow and quickly returned his attention to the half-devoured plate left on the dead sheriff's desk.

Chapter Twenty

Neal Murphy heard a soft sound and looked up from the desk where he was working on some papers in the rectory. He was surprised to see his fiancée standing in the doorway, even more so because her normally merry face was splotched with tears.

"Oh, Neal!" Rachel cried, rushing into the room in a sudden burst of emotion. She clutched a linen handkerchief in one hand while the other held up the skirts of a peach lutestring dress. It was the first gown of her new trousseau, painstakingly copied from the pages of *Leslie's Weekly* and reproduced with considerable skill by the redoubtable Dulcibel. But at the moment Rachel cared little for her new finery, as evidenced when she flung herself into Neal's arms, crushing the bows and frills bedecking the dress.

The young minister was taken aback and removed himself somewhat hastily from her person. "Rachel, what are you doing here alone?" he inquired uneasily. "Don't you have an escort?"

"Don't be foolish, Neal. We're engaged, aren't we?

Nobody saw me come in. And besides, something terrible has happened."

He sighed and shook his head. "What now?"

"Please don't look so annoyed with me. I had to come. It's about Angel. I'm terribly worried about her. She went to see Holt yesterday, and since she returned Aunt Clara's said she's acting very strange. Something happened when she saw Holt in prison. She's even refused to see me, and that's not like Angel."

"What were you doing in Clear Creek?" Neal demanded.

Rachel was startled by his curt question. "I left several things there the night of the ball. I went back to retrieve them today, and that's when Auntie told me what had happened."

"I'm afraid I'm missing something here," Neal said dryly. "Of course Angel is upset. What woman wouldn't be if her husband was arrested for murder?"

Rachel grew increasingly agitated. For some reason Neal seemed too calm and unshakable. She wanted him to hold her, comfort her; as if he read the longing in her eyes, he quickly stepped out of reach.

Returning to his desk, Neal murmured, "It's a tragedy, of course, but there's little we can do until the trial. Then, if we're called upon to testify in Holt's defense, we can try to paint a better portrait of my brother."

Rachel was vexed beyond endurance. "Oh, don't you understand?" she cried. "He's not going to get a trial in this town! Auntie sent for a lawyer, but it's probably too late. She confided in me that there's little she can do for Holt, and if Auntie can't do it, nobody can!"

Neal's pale blue eyes rose from his desk and regarded

her almost frostily. "Then I fail to see, Rachel, what you or I can do to rectify the situation."

She stared at him for a moment. "You're the minister here," she said. "People respect that. They'll listen to you. You could delay the trial—"

Neal abruptly cut her off. "I won't interfere with the justice system, even if Holt is my brother. People would talk, and no doubt speculate that I arranged to divert due process or some such nonsense. Our father's position always gave him special consideration. Arthur thought he was above the law. I won't have the same said of me."

"For heaven's sake, Neal, this is Holt's life we're talking about!" Rachel said with exasperation. "Nothing is more important than that, not even your damned pride!"

"Rachel!" he exclaimed, scandalized by her language.

She tossed her head. "I don't care to be lectured any further today, thank you! Mother was furious enough when I borrowed the sleigh to go to Clear Creek. I had to listen to her whine and complain for nearly an hour. It drove me quite mad."

"You've been around Angel and that batty aunt of yours too much," Neal growled, slapping papers around on his desk. "First arranging to have Lily Valentine buried in consecrated ground, then resorting to foul language to promote a lost cause. You're hardly the demure young lady whom I thought would make a proper preacher's wife."

Rachel regarded him with shock for a second. "Is that a threat, Neal?" she asked softly, the sparks in her hazel eyes betraying the simmering anger just beneath the surface.

"Call it what you will. I can't afford to marry a young

woman who chooses to adopt such coarse mannerisms. And who has the audacity to question the judgment of her future husband in such important matters!"

"So it is important?" Rachel triumphantly pounced on his words. "You will grant me that much?"

He shot her a harried, angry look. "I never denied it. But I'm telling you for the last time, Rachel, it isn't my place to interfere with justice."

"You call putting a man on trial without even allowing him to obtain a lawyer 'justice'?" she scoffed. "Everyone knows who the judge will be, and yet nobody in this town has the nerve to question it. Well, I do, and I shall!"

Neal regarded her grimly. "Do as you will, Rachel," he said at last, "but be warned. If you make a laughingstock of me, I shall wash my hands of both you and our forthcoming marriage."

Rachel saw the cold glint in his eyes and realized he meant every word of his soft threat. Neal knew how much she loved him, and yet he was turning his back on her at the very moment she most needed him.

"I don't understand," she whispered, shaking her head in disbelief. "You always preach about helping others in their hour of need, and not judging them. Yet now I see that you, like your father, apparently are exempt from God's law."

Neal whitened at her quiet observation, looking at his fiancée with something akin to amazement. Rachel kept her head high, her gaze evenly locked with his until at last Neal sighed and looked away.

"What would you have me do?" he asked in a low voice as he toyed with a pen on his desk.

"Speak to the townsfolk before it's too late. Force everyone to realize the grave injustice that's about to be committed. Don't let anyone turn away from the truth. Oh, Neal, don't you see the power you have to stop this charade?"

She was pleading with him now, her bold manners replaced by the winsomeness of the young woman he remembered. "I know you and Holt have had your differences," she continued gently, "but if not for Holt's sake, think of Angel. What would she do if the worst happened?"

Neal looked thoughtful for a moment. "Why, I suppose she'd go back to Missouri."

Rachel shook her head. "No, I don't think so. Not for a while, anyway."

"What makes you say that?"

She smiled secretively. "I can't tell you, Neal. I gave my word not to, until . . . well, I just can't, that's all."

He seemed annoyed. "More secrets, Rachel?"

" 'More'? What do you mean?"

"I'm well aware you've been hiding something from me for quite some time," Neal said as he considered her suddenly nervous demeanor. "I also have no doubt it is something of which you know I would greatly disapprove."

Rachel paled but tried to brazen it out. "What a silly notion, Neal!"

"Is it?" he mused. "I wager I could have you falling all over yourself to confess in the right circumstances. But I'm willing to be Christian about it and say no more . . . if you tell me Angel's secret instead."

Rachel's eyes went round with dismay. "But, Neal, I couldn't! I gave my word!"

"Not sworn, I hope," he said with unusual severity. "I should hate to think my future wife had used the Lord's name in vain."

"Well, of course I didn't, but . . ." Rachel was completely flustered for a moment and then reasoned that Angel's little "secret," such as it was, could quite possibly make all the difference in saving Holt's life. Surely Neal would not continue to refuse to help his brother if he knew the full story.

"Very well," she said, wringing the tear-stained handkerchief in her freckled hands as she spoke. "I'll tell you if you promise to speak with the deputies first thing."

Neal nodded tersely. Rachel had to accept that as his word.

"Angel is with child," she said quietly.

He had apparently expected something entirely different, for he was visibly shocked.

"Does Holt know?" Neal asked.

"She wanted to tell him, but the opportunity never arose. That's why she made me agree not to tell anyone else. Of course she wants to break the news herself."

"Of course," Neal murmured, seeming suddenly preoccupied. "This throws a whole different light on things, doesn't it? In all good conscience I cannot sit back and watch Holt go to the gallows."

"Oh, I knew you would understand!" Rachel cried with relief. "That's why I love you so much." She hurried across the room to embrace him in a sudden show of affection, too overcome to notice that Neal did not return the gesture. "Will you speak out on Holt's behalf now?"

"I shall do everything I can, Rachel," Neal responded

quietly, his hands closing at long last around her waist. "You may rest assured of that."

Angel was only slightly heartened when Clara Maxwell found a man willing to brave the inclement weather and treacherous winter passes in order to head east and find a lawyer. It was scant comfort when she learned that the man was Gil Martin, the burly stage driver who had originally taken her and Holt to Denver, but it did assure her he was unlikely to abscond with Clara's money, and that he would do his best to complete the mission.

Since Holt's abrupt refusal of her help, Angel had been searching for something to occupy her time and delay the inevitable return of her thoughts to the grim situation at hand. She tried to content herself with knitting more baby clothes and taking care of Clara, though it seemed the old lady had neatly reversed their roles and was looking after Angel herself. Nothing would do but for Angel to move permanently into Clara's home, and since she was no longer a mere guest but considered family, Angel was given a large, sunny bedroom on the south side of the house, overlooking the English garden. Though the garden was, of course, presently buried by several feet of snow, Clara assured the younger woman that the view would be well worth the long winter wait. It was no accident, Angel soon discovered, that her new bedroom opened up into a smaller chamber, the unused nursery that Clara and James Maxwell had longed to fill with babies and never had.

There was even a handcrafted wooden cradle and rocker in the room that James had carved lovingly many years ago, and while Clara's eyes filled with tears when she saw them again, she insisted that Dulcibel dust the baby furniture and set the room to rights.

"Dear Clara, I wouldn't cause you any heartache for the world," Angel said gently as she toured the nursery with her adopted aunt. She paused to buss the older lady's cheek affectionately. "If seeing these things makes you sad, I'll have Dulcibel put them away . . ."

"Nonsense," Clara replied sharply. "What this old house needs most of all is to ring with childrens' laughter. For too long it's been the stuffy domain of an ancient crone with the dubious reputation of having the sharpest tongue in the Territory."

Angel had to laugh. "Surely not you!"

"Well, of course, child. Who else would have had the temerity to tell Prudence Maxwell to mind her manners when she was browbeating poor Rachel about her new ball gown?"

"Oh, I would have dearly loved to hear that!"

"You were a wee bit preoccupied at the time, as I recall," Clara said cheekily. She viewed the sunny little nursery with satisfaction. "I've no doubt you and Holt shall manage to adequately fill this room, and perhaps overflow into a few others, as well."

At the mention of her husband, Angel instantly sobered, which did not escape the shrewd English lady.

"Buck up, my girl," Clara said stoutly. "The war's not over yet. I've been called many different things in this part of the Territory, but one thing I've never lost is the townspeople's respect. If Clara Maxwell says there ought to be pause for thought, then there is, and I intend to make those puerile little deputies think twice before they put Holt Murphy on trial."

Angel couldn't contain her tears or her gratitude. She turned and embraced the little woman fiercely.

"I don't know what I'd do without you, Aunt Clara," she confessed brokenly.

"Rot!" came the crisp retort, but over Angel's shoulder Clara Maxwell's eyes had suddenly misted.

On the morning Gil Martin was to leave for Denver, Angel received an unexpected summons to the Oro jail. The note was delivered by one of the deputies, a different fellow than the fat, leering one she remembered from her visit, a wiry man who actually had manners and tipped his hat politely to her as he presented the message. Even more surprising was the note itself. It was from Holt, written in a bold, slashing hand she did not doubt belonged to the man she loved.

> I need to talk to you. It's important. Don't let Gil leave until you see me.

He had signed it simply "Holt." Angel quickly found Clara and showed her the note, receiving the older lady's promise to delay Gil Martin's departure until Angel returned.

Clara insisted that Angel ride to Oro in her English-style brougham, along with a hired man who would see to her safety and comfort. Since it was bitterly cold and the drive was rather long, Angel agreed, and she quickly adapted to the European custom of wrapping hot bricks in flannel to warm the passenger's feet. She had donned a light blue wool gown with a matching flared cape that completely concealed her figure, and she was relieved to find Holt only gave her a cursory glance as she was shown into the inner hold of the prison.

"We only have a few minutes," Holt said, with a dark look after the broad back of the departing deputy. "I don't have time to argue with you, and I especially don't have time to explain. Do you understand?"

His eyes were gray as flint and just as hard. Angel nodded a little stiffly. She had assumed he was going to apologize for his rudeness the other day. Instead, she was apparently expected to listen to more warnings to leave town.

Annoyed as she was, Angel couldn't help but ache at the sight of Holt looking so unkempt and thin. He had lost weight since her first visit, and she worried that he was being mistreated. She had no chance to ask, though, before he launched into a request that took her completely by surprise.

"I need you to go up to the mine," Holt said, an urgent tone to his otherwise quiet voice. "Take as many blankets and as much food as you can find or steal without causing an uproar."

As her eyes widened, he added curtly, "And whatever you do, Angel, don't tell anyone else or take anyone with you." She had been about to suggest Neal, and Holt obviously knew it. "This is too important. Lives are at stake. Do you understand?"

He spoke as if to a particularly slow child. Angel's hackles rose, and she fought the bit of silent obedience he was trying to force into her mouth.

"No, I don't understand," she retorted testily. "The only life I see at stake right now, and the only one that matters, is yours! Why are you trying to distract me from the real issue?"

"Real?" Holt snorted and raked his hand through his tangled black hair, then turned to pace impatiently like a caged panther in his cell. "I'll give you more 'real' issues than you can handle, Angel, if you'd just do as I ask. I wouldn't ask you at all, but there's nobody else I can trust."

Angel doubted he intended that as a compliment and didn't take it as one. "What's up at the mine that's so all-fired important?" she demanded. "Why should I help you?"

He stopped pacing and regarded her through the bars with a look that chilled her to the bone. "Maybe I was wrong," he growled softly. "Maybe you don't have what it takes to survive up here. Maybe you don't even want to try."

Holt expected Angel to rise to the challenge, and she didn't disappoint him. With an angry toss of her head she stated, "Tell me what to do. I won't ask you any more questions."

He smiled faintly, ironically. "Good. First of all, it's important for you to speak to Gil on my behalf before he leaves. You remember Jean-Claude and his wife?"

"Of course."

"I need Gil to find the Frenchman and tell him what's happening now. And also to retrieve some things I left at the cabin when we were passing through on our way to Denver."

Angel was puzzled, but she remembered her word and nodded. "All right. And when should I go to the mine?"

"As soon as you speak to Gil. Today, if possible." Holt

paused, seeing the questions flooding her beautiful blue eyes, wanting to confide in his young wife but uncertain if he dared to. "And," he finally added, "remember to be careful. I've seen you handle a gun before. You must find one and take it with you. Promise me."

"I will. It's too bad Lily isn't around to go with me," Angel said, a genuine note of regret in her voice.

"Yes. I'd have asked her if she was here. But I still hate having to depend on others to help me."

"You're too proud, Holt Murphy," Angel said softly as she raised a gloved hand to lightly touch the sun-bronzed fingers curled around the iron bars. "When will you open your eyes and see that I'm here for you?"

"Guess I'm a slow learner," he confessed, a ghost of a smile curving his lips. "But if you keep pounding it into my thick head hard enough, maybe I'll start to see the writing on the wall."

Angel watched the last flurry of snow settle into place after Gil's departing horse and turned to trudge back into the house. Halfway there she paused at the sight of Jack Miller, Clara Maxwell's hired man, outfitting sleigh runners to the buckboard wagon he used when he obtained supplies in Oro.

A sudden idea occurred to Angel as she watched the man working on the wagon. She walked carefully down the path Jack had cleared to the barn and greeted the older man in a friendly tone. Expressing interest in his work, Angel encouraged Jack to explain how the buckboard would smoothly and easily traverse the deep snows.

" 'Course, you still need two good, sturdy mounts to

pull a load, 'specially when it's full up," Jack finished as he nailed the last runner in place.

"Oh?" Angel inquired innocently, glancing past him at the stables he was responsible for overseeing. "Which horses are the strongest, Mr. Miller?"

He rose and brushed off his snowy canvas trousers as he seriously considered her question. "Well, the missus keeps a mighty fine stable, considerin' the cost an' all, and most of her horses are big-like, rough-an'-ready types. 'Cept fer Mercury, o'course, and he's some fancy mount, useless fer pullin' carts or anythin'."

Angel had to smile at the disapproval readily apparent in the man's voice. "The dark gray gelding? I believe he's a Thoroughbred."

Jack only snorted and shook his head. "Waste o' feed, if you ask me. 'Course, I'm not paid to give my opinion."

"Maybe not, but who knows these horses better than you do?" Angel reasoned, and he preened at her flattery.

"Would you like to see the horses, missus?" the grizzled old man suddenly offered, a rare treat indeed, for Jack seldom warmed to strangers.

"I'd love to," Angel replied with a winsome smile and followed him into the stable, which was kept warm and dry. There she shook out her damp wool skirts and then quickly turned her attention to Jack Miller's monologue.

"This mare here, this is Juno," he began as he reached out to stroke the Roman nose of a big piebald.

Angel joined him, letting the mare snuffle her scent as she made friends with the animal. "She's draft, isn't she?"

Jack nodded, surprised by her knowledge. "Shires, the missus calls 'em, but all I know is, they're mighty strong. She had 'em imported from England nigh five years back."

"This must be Juno's mate," Angel guessed, moving on to the next stall, where a nearly identical horse thrust its head over the door and eyed her curiously.

"Yep, that's Jupiter. For all he's a stallion, he's gentle 'nough."

"A good thing, since they're so huge," Angel murmured, wondering as she scratched the horse behind the ears if she could handle the pair of them. She had quickly ascertained that these two were the strongest in the stable, and Jack confirmed her suspicions with a disparaging glance at the high-strung gray stamping in his stall.

"That's Mercury, o' course. Crazy names the missus picked out, but then, I'm not paid to name 'em, either."

"I had no idea Mrs. Maxwell was so fond of mythology," Angel said. "Perhaps I'll buy her a book on the subject for her birthday."

Jack merely shrugged at this information, eager to get on with the tour and show her the rest of the horses and the fine leather tack he so carefully maintained. By the end of the hour, Angel had learned her way around the stable and knew enough about the horses' individual temperaments to risk the next phase of her plan. She had also made a new friend in the lonely old man most people considered gruff and unfriendly.

It would be hard betraying Jack's trust, but Angel had given her promise to Holt to go up to the mine. Giving Jack another warm smile and her thanks, Angel left the stable and returned to the house. The hour was growing late. Soon she would have to put her plan into motion, but she couldn't move until Jack Miller had left for the day. He lived in a little one-room cabin about a mile away, he had told her. Angel didn't want to travel in the dark, but it seemed she had little choice. She would spend the rest of her time upstairs, getting ready for the long, cold journey.

Leaving a message for Clara by way of Dulcibel, saying she had a terrible headache and was retiring early, Angel hurried up to her room and began to assemble a variety of warm winter clothes. She then took all the blankets off her bed and off those in the adjoining guest rooms. She would raid the pantry later, after the others were abed.

Glancing over and catching her reflection in the cheval glass across her room, Angel raised a startled hand to her face. Her cheeks were flushed rosy with excitement and her neat chignon had come undone, spilling tiny golden curls around her brow. She was actually enjoying this! She, the sensible and proper Angel McCloud-Murphy, was about to rob a larder, steal some horses, and ride off into the dark night like some lowly desperado. A soft gurgle of laughter escaped her lips. She could only pray Clara Maxwell would understand. Somehow Angel had the feeling that her tart little hostess would not only understand, but quite heartily approve.

Chapter Twenty-one

Even the creak of leather seemed to echo too loudly in the night as Angel finished securing the horses in the wagon tracings and carefully climbed up into the driver's seat. A quick glance over her shoulder revealed her hidden hoard in the buckboard, safely covered by waterproof oilskins, and she reached down to touch the reassuring barrel of the long rifle hidden beneath the blankets covering her lap.

It was too risky to light a lantern so close to the house, so Angel had to maneuver the wagon by memory down the rutted snowy lane. There was just a thin sliver of moon, which only served to highlight the clumps of firs around the house, changing the dark trees into eerie, gnarled shapes. For a moment she was sorely tempted to stop this foolishness, return the sleepy Juno and Jupiter to their stalls, and sensibly retire to the warmth and safety of her bed. But Angel knew she'd never forgive herself if she backed out now. Holt had asked her to do this, a precious sign of his growing trust, and though she realized he'd never have asked her if Lily was alive or he knew about the child growing beneath her heart, Angel was too determined to validate his faith in her to consider the risks she was taking.

If she went slow, if she kept herself from becoming chilled, if she took the good road up to the mine . . . why, it would be as easy as slicing a hot knife through butter, Angel reasoned. She had dressed in half-a-dozen layers of wool clothing, not counting two horsehair petticoats and the fur wrap she had "borrowed" from Clara's coat rack, and in view of the brisk temperature she had worn three pairs of gloves and wrapped a woolen scarf around her face beneath a hat so only her eyes showed. Angel estimated it would take her at least two hours to get up to the mine, maybe three if she was forced to rest the horses. But the draft animals seemed hale and hearty now, pulling their burden swiftly along as if it weighed little more than a thimble.

Everything seemed to favor her cause by the time Angel reached the main road, branching north and south. There was no wind and she still felt comfortably warm. She stopped the wagon to light the lantern she had brought and hung it securely above the driver's awning to light the way. The horses waited patiently until she was ready to set off again, then smoothly turned the wagon in the direction of the mine. They hardly seemed strained by the gradual ascent, and Angel was heartened enough to urge them faster.

For a long time they simply plowed through the new snow, the runners hissing softly as they broke a fresh trail. Once or twice Angel thought she heard the low, distant howl of a coyote or dog; surely there were no wolves left, she reassured herself. The horses' ears flicked in the direction of the sound, but they continued their steady, plodding gait up the trail.

Angel gradually relaxed when she no longer heard anything except the crunching of the horses' hooves breaking through the thin crust of the snow. She relaxed so much, she even fell asleep for an undetermined time, awakening with a start when the horses suddenly stopped in their tracks.

Angel blinked her lashes free of the snow that had fallen from tree branches as they'd passed beneath the tall pines. She was surprised and a little worried to find herself cold and numb, her joints aching in silent protest as she fumbled for the reins she had dropped. She clicked to the horses and tried to urge them on, but neither of them so much as moved a muscle. Their ears were tilted forward and they jingled the harness as they shifted nervously in place.

Angel finally turned her attention forward, trusting the animals' instincts. She saw nothing, heard nothing, but by the wavering light of the lantern she recognized the dip in the road descending to the mine shaft.

"I made it," she said to herself with quiet jubilation, but her optimism was quickly snuffed out when she heard Juno snort with surprise and take a step backward. Angel looked over just in time to see a hand snag the mare's bridle and hold her fast. Another hand reached out from the darkness and seized Jupiter's lead as well, and before Angel could grab for her gun she found herself surrounded by a dozen disembodied faces, all of them watching her with glittering dark eyes.

* * *

As if in a dream, Angel saw a man step forward from the shadows of the nearby trees, most of his body hidden by a heavy fur robe, but his angular, leatherlike face clearly visible beneath the lantern's feeble glow.

Soon she made out long gray braids hanging on either side of his lean cheeks, and she realized that he and his friends were Indians. Curiously, she felt no fear; just a calm sense of something about to happen before he spoke.

His low voice rumbled a question, but she shook her head to indicate that she did not understand. Reluctantly, he repeated the phrase, this time in broken English.

"You are Igasho's woman?"

Angel shook her head again. "No, I'm Holt's wife . . . Holt Murphy. Do you know him?"

The old Indian's teeth gleamed in a sudden smile. "To us, he is known as Igasho."

Suddenly Angel understood. She did not doubt that these people were the ones Holt had intended her to find, the ones who desperately needed the blankets and food, as evidenced by their pinched faces and shabby, moth-eaten buffalo robes. Her eyes had adjusted to the poor light now, and she saw that those with the older man were hardly more than children, young braves with hostile expressions, waiting for their leader to translate her words.

"Holt sent me to find you and bring you these things," Angel said, gesturing to the buckboard. She managed to keep her voice from trembling. She did not think these people would hurt her, not when she was given a chance to explain.

The elderly Indian nodded almost regally at her. "I

am called Kaga, medicine man of the Langundo Arapaho. The man you call Holt—Igasho—is the child of my *natane* . . . you white ones would say 'daughter.' "

Angel could not conceal her shock. "You are his grandfather?"

Kaga nodded again, almost sadly. "When he chooses to honor me as such."

Angel was moved by his quiet words, and surprisingly angry with Holt when she understood the implication that he had rejected the older man's relationship to him for some reason.

"Kaga," she said hesitantly, "I do not pretend to know Holt's—Igasho's—mind, but he sent me up here even in the deep snows to help you. He knew you would need blankets and food to survive the winter. He cares about you a great deal."

"Then why did Igasho not come himself?" Kaga asked with a shadow of the stubbornness reflected in his face that she saw so often in Holt's.

"He could not come. He has been put in prison—a white man's jail."

"I know of prison," Kaga said, his dark eyes grave as he swept a hand to indicate the younger braves around him. "All the Langundo know of the white man's punishment box."

Angel's heart went out to the old man and the others. Quietly, she said, "I have a great many questions, but I'm sure you and your people are very hungry and cold. Please, take the supplies now."

Kaga agreed and then turned to speak to the waiting braves. When he was finished they regarded Angel with mild curiosity, but none of the hostility they formerly had displayed. They moved quickly and quietly to unload the wagon, carrying the goods toward the mine shaft, where the other Arapaho, the young and the old and the ill, were hidden, unknowingly awaiting the bounty of this precious cargo.

Angel did not hesitate when Kaga invited her down from the wagon. "We must talk," he said simply, inclining his head toward the shadowy outline of a teepee in the distance. "What are you called?"

"My name is Angel," she told him as she retrieved the lantern, cautiously dismounted, and picked her way through the deep snow after Kaga's retreating figure.

"Huh," Kaga grunted thoughtfully as she reached his side. "I have heard of this white man's 'angel' before, on the reservation. But my head is old now, and I have forgotten. Does an angel bring life, or death?"

His innocent query sent a tremor of emotion through the young woman, but she kept her voice steady as she replied, "This Angel brings nothing but mercy, Kaga. I can promise you that." When the old man paused to regard her with sober brown eyes Angel spontaneously reached out and touched his wrinkled hand. "I will help your people by bringing more supplies," she announced. "This will be my way of bringing life to the Langundo."

"It is good," Kaga replied, regarding the young woman with a puzzled, surprised expression. "It is very good. But why do you wish to do this?"

"Because," Angel replied, "I want to. But also, I owe it to your great-grandchild."

"Ah," Kaga said softly, and for a moment she thought she saw a twinkle of laughter in the old Indian's eyes before he looked ahead and resumed walking. "Come with me, Angel-of-the-Mountain. There is much we must talk of before the sun eats the darkness again."

Angel was surprised by the fire and warmth that awaited her inside the teepee. She recognized many of Holt's possessions strewn about inside the buckskin enclosure, and she looked at Kaga with a question in her eyes.

"Igasho spent many moons with the Langundo," the Indian explained as he settled down his old bones amid the buffalo throws. He gestured for Angel to do the same, and then continued speaking in a quiet, measured way. "My only *natane*—daughter—chose to be a white man's woman. But Istas was always foolish as a child, more so as a woman." Kaga shook his gray head sorrowfully. "Istas was young, and—how do you say?—good for men to look upon."

"Beautiful," Angel murmured, absently tracing the soft lining of a beaver pelt beneath her, not surprised at all to discover Holt's Arapaho mother had been fair of form and face.

"Istas," she repeated when the old man fell silent. "What does that mean?"

"In your tongue, 'snow.'" Kaga groped for words and made the motion of falling snow with his hands. "Not just snow, but 'snow that melts fast under the sun.'"

"Soft Snow," Angel supplied, suddenly remembering Holt's English name for his mother.

"Yes, Soft Snow." Kaga sighed deeply at the memory of his beloved daughter. "She was a white man's second wife. This you knew?"

By his shrewd look he obviously expected surprise on Angel's part, but she merely nodded.

"The first wife was jealous," Kaga recalled as his old hands kneaded the warm robe across his lap. "White women are always jealous of other wives for some reason." He shrugged, perplexed by such things. "The first wife was very angry. She hated Istas with all her strength. She hated Istas more when my daughter bore Ar-thur a son."

"Holt," Angel whispered into the moment of silence.

Kaga nodded. "The white woman also had a son, a seed of her bad blood. She wanted no other sons by Ar-thur to live."

Angel felt a chill sweep over her at Kaga's matter-of-fact words. Unconsciously, she reached out and drew a warm fur blanket up to her chin, watching the old man's face by the light of the glowing coals.

"Ar-thur's first wife told a story," Kaga continued softly, his onyx eyes affixed to the leaping flames, "a story of wanting to forgive Istas and live together in one big teepee, like sisters, and raise their sons to be true brothers. Istas believed the white snake's words. I did not."

Angel swallowed hard, her voice a mere whisper when she finally asked, "What happened?"

"Ar-thur's first wife said she needed to know where Istas lived, so she could send presents and food. Ar-thur had kept my daughter and grandson hidden, up here at the mine. He was wise then."

Kaga sighed at the painful memory. "Istas came to me and I told her, 'Do not tell the white snake where you live.' But she had a good heart. She wanted to believe; she wanted to have a sister who shared her love for Ar-thur.

So I made her give me Igasho, just until I saw the wounds between the women were healed."

"Where did you take Igasho?" Even Angel was beginning to think of Holt by his Indian name now.

"Back to the People. There were women there who cared for him. But back here the white snake sent men to find Istas. The men and the first wife went to the cabin, and there the first wife made her first son watch as Istas was hurt and killed."

Angel gasped. Neal had been forced to watch Holt's mother tortured and murdered! By his own mother's hand! What a terrible burden to place upon a child. She shook her head in horror and disbelief, but Kaga was not finished.

"The white snake was very clever. She made it look as if Istas had killed herself, and her body was left in the cabin so Ar-thur would find it. He was a white man, a foolish man, but he loved Istas very much. He became very ill in his heart after that."

"How do you know all this happened?" Angel asked.

Kaga was silent for a long moment. "When Igasho came back to the white men years later he met his brother-by-the-snake. There was a fight. The snake's son told Igasho he had seen Istas die, and that he had not helped her. Igasho was very angry. He said he would never forgive his brother."

"But Neal was just a child, like him," Angel exclaimed. "He couldn't stop grown men, and it wasn't his fault if his mother forced him to watch that . . . that monstrous act take place!"

Kaga looked across the fire and regarded her soberly. "The one called Ne-al also told Igasho he had become a man that day, with Igasho's mother beneath him."

Angel feared she might retch. She felt her head spinning and pressed a hand hard across her lips as she choked back a cry of outrage. Had Neal truly participated in a gruesome rape? He had only been thirteen at the time! Old enough to know better, but also old enough to join in the torture of Holt's mother if he thought it would gain him Virginia's twisted, sick approval.

Oh, dear God, she thought, was this the source of Holt's seemingly "unreasonable" hatred toward Neal? Didn't it make sense now? And Angel had been lecturing Holt for nothing, not having a true picture of what had happened! She did not doubt Kaga and believed the story, and a soft moan escaped her lips as she realized that, if it was true, the hell Holt had endured all these years was staggering, especially if he felt obliged to be civil to Neal, considering his half-brother's sudden "turn around" as a man of God.

Why Holt had not killed Neal in cold blood was a mystery to her, but she suspected it was because Holt wasn't sure whether to believe the awful story himself. Perhaps he thought he had only imagined it now, or he didn't really believe Neal capable of such an act. But the fact that Neal had refused to help Istas at all, even by running to alert the sheriff or calling his own mother to account for the heinous deed was almost as terrible.

Tears slipped down Angel's soft cheeks as she asked Kaga in a trembling voice, "Why have you told me this story?"

The old Indian considered her words for a long time. "There is only one thing to remember," he said at last. "The child of a snake is still a snake, no matter the robe he wears."

She shivered at the words. She had heard Holt say something similar once. "Then you think Neal is evil, like his mother."

"I think a snake should be made to shed its skin," Kaga replied. "I do not think it should be left to hide until spring."

His words were troubling, and as Angel studied the old man's glistening black eyes, she realized Kaga still was mourning the daughter he had lost. It was natural of him to want revenge, but what if he was wrong? What if Neal had had no part in Istas's unfortunate death? All whites were not evil. Angel was determined to prove this much herself.

"I have to think about what you've said," she told Kaga gently. "It's hard for me to accept such a story, since I know a far different Neal than you do. But I promise I will look and listen very carefully from now on."

Kaga nodded at her words. It was enough for now. But he feared that Igasho's Angel-of-the-Mountain might be made to suffer, too, if the white snake's son ever learned of her visit here, or of the child she carried beneath her heart.

Angel's eyelashes fluttered against her skin, and as she came awake she heard a crochety voice exclaim, "About time!"

She opened her eyes on Clara's worried face, dazed and confused for a moment when she realized she was back at the house, but with no recollection of having arrived there. Had she dreamed everything? Had she fallen asleep instead of taking the supplies up to the mine as she'd promised Holt? Had Kaga and the others been a figment of her imagination?

As Angel groped for answers, she had a sudden, intense memory of the interior of a warm teepee, the smell of damp skins and of the mellow tobacco that Kaga had smoked, and of her own eyelids growing heavier and heavier as the medicine man sang softly in his hypnotic voice, his eyes like fathomless black pools as he gazed knowingly at her across the fire.

She looked up now at Clara Maxwell, saw another pair of knowing eyes, and knew she had not dreamed her adventure. She also saw the questions coming, and she laughed weakly as Clara helped her to sit up against the fluffy pillows in her bed.

"Where did you find the extra blankets?" Angel asked, knowing there would be no use denying that she had stripped nearly all of her hostess' upstairs beds.

"I'm well stocked for the hard winters here, and it's apparently a good thing, too," Clara replied in a scolding tone as she handed Angel a cup and saucer. "Now, drink all of this down, dear, and then I'll send Dulcie to prepare a dinner tray for you."

"Aren't you going to ask what I did with all the blankets and food?"

Clara sniffed. "Certainly not. If you wanted me to know, you'd have involved me in your little drama in the first place. I won't deny you frightened the tar out of all of us, child, turning up like that early this morning, but as long as you're no worse for wear, I'll content myself with knowing you're safe."

Suddenly Angel had another vivid memory, this time of her drowsy, fur-bundled figure being handed up into the wagon by several hands, and of someone driving her back down the mountain, then disappearing into the snow-flecked trees just as dawn had broken across the pearly sky.

"What time is it?" she asked Clara urgently.

"Late afternoon. You slept most of the day, dear. You were exhausted."

Angel set down the untouched tea on the bureau beside the bed and threw back the covers. "I have to see Holt!"

Clara was alarmed. "Not until you've recovered completely. I won't hear of it!" She picked up the saucer again and thrust it at the younger woman firmly. "Drink this. It will help you regain your strength."

Reluctantly, Angel accepted the cup again and sniffed suspiciously at the flower-scented contents. "What's in it?"

"A nerve tonic and a restorant, both guaranteed to put the roses back in your cheeks. And neither one will hurt the babe, I promise."

Angel sampled the hot brew and, finding it surprisingly delicious, finished the cup, to Clara's clucks of approval. Within minutes she felt unaccountably sleepy again, and as she struggled to keep her eyes open, she looked up at Rachel's aunt with a look of hurt betrayal.

"But Aunt Clara, I have . . . to . . . have to . . . see Holt," she murmured between huge yawns.

"Tomorrow, my dear," Clara replied, smoothing Angel's golden hair back from her face with a loving hand. "Today the only thing you have to do is get some much-needed rest."

* * *

For the first time in months Holt Murphy hadn't any extra time to think about Angel or his mixed feelings for her. Instead, he was torn between overwhelming relief and a sense of deeper dread as he overheard the heated conversation taking place in the front room of the jail.

"T'ain't right," the fat deputy, whose name Holt had learned was Elijah Perry, whined to an invisible party standing on the other side of the sheriff's desk. "The judge'll hear 'bout this, and then we'll see who'll git ta hang the Injun!"

There was a tense silence, and then another man's voice, lower-pitched and crisp with authority, said, "I can appreciate your position, Mr. Perry, but I'm afraid the federal government has a prior claim on Mr. Murphy. He must be tried in federal court first, for the charges listed here, and only then can he be returned to the Territory to stand trial."

Holt heard a rustling of paper. Just as if Perry had not heard a word the other man had said, he grumbled, "That half-breed done kilt our sheriff, and he ain't leavin' here alive."

The visitor responded coolly, "While I dislike pulling rank, sir, I'm afraid you leave me little choice. As United States Marshal for this region, I must insist you release the aforesaid prisoner to my custody."

Holt heard Perry's fat fist pound the desk impotently. "I'm the law here now!" he wheezed.

"You are the newly deputized sheriff?" the other man inquired skeptically.

"Well, naw . . . not yet. But I will be!" Perry's voice was belligerent as he scrutinized the federal marshal with equal disdain. " 'Sides, Mr. . . . Ree-nalt—what kind of a bloomin' name is that, anyways?—I don't see no proof of yer 'dentity, an' I sure as hell won't release nobody without askin' more questions."

"Very wise of you, I'm sure," replied the second man dryly. "And by the way, Mr. Perry, the name is correctly pronounced 'Renault.' It's French."

Perry gave a snort that effectively indicated his opinion of the French, U.S. Marshals, and Fabien Renault in particular.

Marshal Renault continued smoothly, "I trust I have made myself clear that the prisoner is not to be put on trial or moved before I have made adequate arrangements to transfer him to Denver."

Perry answered sullenly, "I s'pose not."

"Very good, Mr. Perry, though I hope you will not take it amiss if I ask for your word in writing?"

There was a tense silence, after which Perry admitted grudgingly, " 'Fraid I c'ain't do that."

"Are you refusing to cooperate?"

"Nope. Just c'ain't, that's all."

Comprehension slowly dawned on Renault. He inquired almost kindly, "You don't know how to write?"

"Never learnt. Hell, what need's a man got way out here for all that fancy book-learnin'? Shee-it, Elijah Perry's word's as good as gold!"

"I see," Renault murmured. "Well then, I suppose your word will have to do." As he left the front room and came toward the open door leading to the prisoner's cell, Holt overheard the marshal mutter sarcastically, "Elijah! What kind of a name is that, anyway?"

* * *

Much to his own dismay, Holt found he liked Fabien Renault. The marshal was witty, cool in his approach, but undeniably fair. He questioned Holt over the matter of the Indian uprising several times, obviously trying to elicit an unguarded response from the prisoner, but after a while he stepped away from the cell and regarded Holt with admiration.

"I must admit, Mr. Murphy, that you are sticking to your story quite well. But I have to ask, are there any witnesses as to your apparently harmless activities in the fall?"

"One. My wife, Angel." Reluctantly, Holt brought her into the picture. "We were just married then, living up at the mine."

"Where is Mrs. Murphy now?"

"Staying with a friend until this blows over. If it ever does," he added wryly.

Renault scratched a few more notes on the pad he held, then inquired, "Would you have any objections to my speaking with your wife?"

Holt's silver eyes narrowed slightly. "Do you intend to bully her into a false confession, Renault? Because if you even so much as try, I guarantee you'll regret it."

The marshal's dark eyes locked with Holt's momentarily, but he was the first to look away. Renault was a handsome devil, a ladies' man if Holt didn't miss his guess, and his uniform was crisply creased and pressed, not a speck of lint or soil to be seen. His curly black hair gave him a boyish look, but his face was weathered with experience—experience Holt did not underestimate.

"You have my word as a gentleman, sir," Renault responded at last, clicking his heels and bowing slightly in a European fashion. "Your lady will not be harassed by me or any of my men."

Holt relaxed imperceptibly. "She's staying with Mrs. Clara Maxwell, over in Clear Creek."

"Thank you," the captain said quietly. "You will not regret your cooperation."

"Anything to postpone the stretching of my neck," Holt jested, but there was no real humor in his voice, and Renault did not laugh.

"These are some very serious charges, Mr. Murphy. Aiding and abetting fugitive Indians is a serious crime in the Territories."

"Show me the proof and I'll gladly pay the price," Holt replied boldly, meeting Renault's gaze with unflinching calm.

"You doubtless know we have no proof . . . as yet. But I am most thorough in my research, sir, and I can guarantee that if there is anything to be found, I shall find it."

Holt nodded curtly, accepting the challenge. "You have my permission to try," he said.

Chapter Twenty-two

"Absolutely not," Clara Maxwell said sharply, blocking the doorway with her small, rigid frame. "It is out of the question for you to see Mrs. Murphy now, or at any other time!"

With only the greatest admiration for the little woman's spirit, Renault bowed low and said quietly, "I'm afraid I must insist, ma'am."

As Clara began to argue again, she was interrupted by a clear, feminine voice inquiring from the stairway, "Who is it, Auntie?"

"Some man . . ." Clara began angrily, helplessly, but before she could order Angel to go back to her room the younger woman had descended the stairs and moved forward from the shadows.

Angel wore a rose-pink gown simply trimmed with black Chantilly lace. The color enhanced the faint pink glow to her fair skin, and her hair was drawn to one side and tied with a black velvet bow. The long ringlets cascaded over her shoulder and down to her waist like a golden waterfall. She regarded their visitor with curiosity for a moment, and then demanded in a surprisingly crisp tone, "Who are you, sir, to be upsetting Mrs. Maxwell so?"

"I regret if my arrival has upset you, ma'am," Fabien murmured to Clara as he fumbled awkwardly, his hat in his hands. He was stunned by Angel's beauty and almost forgot his manners.

Swiftly recovering himself, he finally apologized to Clara, "It was certainly not my intention to disrupt your household." He bowed once again, this time in Angel's direction. "Captain Renault, ma'am, at your service."

"What do you want?" Angel asked flatly.

"A word with you, ma'am, regarding your husband."

He saw the wariness spring to life in her sky-blue eyes. "Indeed? Then you have come to the wrong place. Holt is in the Oro jail, not here."

"I know. I have already spoken to him myself. It was he who gave me permission to visit with you concerning the charges brought against him."

Angel glanced at Clara, who was still livid, and said gently, "I need to speak with this man, Auntie. May we use the little parlor?"

"You don't have to tell him anything," the woman insisted. She looked Renault up and down with a sniff and then announced, as if he could not hear her, "French! They're not to be trusted, my dear!"

Renault's dark eyes were laughing as he informed Clara gravely, "The war in the colonies was over long ago, ma'am. I am an American now, as was my father."

Clara sniffed again, but Angel persuaded her to allow the captain to enter, and told the older woman soothingly, "Go upstairs, Auntie, and take your tonic, as you usually do. I'll have Dulcibel call you when we're finished."

After Clara Maxwell had reluctantly departed, with one final warning glare at the captain, Angel invited Renault into the sunny little parlor reserved for entertaining guests and motioned for him to take a seat on the red velvet settee. He gingerly complied, obviously fearing that his weight would break the spindly legs.

"I am sorry to have distressed your aunt so," he began in a truly regretful tone.

Angel's eyes were twinkling as she said, "Clara Maxwell is not my real aunt, but she is very dear to me, and I won't abide anyone upsetting her." Angel briefly turned to busy herself at the sideboard, while Renault watched her graceful movements with admiring eyes.

"Will you take tea, monsieur?" she inquired in French.

Renault was so delighted, he almost forgot his manners all over again. "No, thank you . . . but I must confess to being most curious as to where you learned French."

Angel smiled mysteriously as she finally chose a sugared comfit from a tray on the table and sat down in a chair facing him. "My mother was of French descent, and where I grew up it was considered only proper for young girls to know a Romance language or two."

"Ah." He nodded. "But education in a woman is still considered a dangerous thing in the old country, I think."

"My father was more enlightened than most. But we are not here to speak of me. You came about Holt." She bit into the comfit and waited for him to explain himself.

Renault had to admire the way Angel got down to brass tacks. She was no-nonsense now, their pleasantries having concluded, and her blue eyes were keen on his face as she listened to him speak. He informed her of the serious charges against Holt, and began questioning her gently about her husband's activities in the past few months.

Aware that Holt's life was at stake, Angel kept calm throughout the inquiry, even though her heart was pounding rapidly. Renault was a shrewd man, and he watched her every gesture and expression like a hawk. The only way she could disarm him was with a little laugh or smile, and then, like any other man, he would briefly lose his composure and gaze at her admiringly.

But for all his fascination with Angel, Renault did not forget his mission for a single minute. He was aware of Angel's intelligence and suspected her coy simpering was just an attempt to divert him from his pursuit of the truth.

"So you know nothing about your husband's involvement with these renegade Indians?" he persisted in what seemed to Angel to be the thousandth time, and she made her eyes very wide and pressed a fluttering white hand to her throat.

"Mercy, no! I haven't seen so much as a bead around Holt, much less any red men! Do you still call them red men, Captain? Or is there another term now? Savages, perhaps?"

Her voice held a faint sarcasm the captain did not miss. "We call them Indians, ma'am, and these particular ones are very dangerous indeed. Surely you've heard of the massacre down at Fort Lyons?"

"I don't believe so," Angel replied, a distinct chill creeping into her voice. "At any rate, I can assure you that Holt would have nothing to do with such riffraff."

"Not directly, but perhaps by supplying arms and ammunition to the war parties?"

Angel sighed. "Your persistence is most fatiguing, Captain. I can only tell you yet again, for what is surely the hundredth time, that I knew nothing then and still know nothing of Holt's supposed activities with these outlaw Indians. What will it take to satisfy you, sir?"

"The truth, Mrs. Murphy," Renault said gently, aware that she was growing weary of his questions, and also knowing that she was at her most vulnerable now. "The truth is always the easiest course, is it not, and when you tell me the truth I shall quickly and gladly release you from this interview."

She pressed a hand to her aching temple. "I've told you before, we were up at the mine most of the time. There was never any chance for Holt to smuggle arms or anything else down south!"

"Ah, yes. The mine." Renault flipped back several pages in his notebook and reviewed his previous notes. "This gold mine of yours; where is it located?"

She made a vague gesture. "Up on the mountain."

"Which one?"

"Mount Elbert, of course." Seeing his patient, waiting expression, still tinged with suspicion, she cried, "Oh, please, enough!" In her sudden agitation Angel rose abruptly from the chair, aware that she had almost slipped. Renault had been there only an hour, but he was an expert at pulling and pushing witnesses, and she was confused and hardly knew what to say anymore.

Forcibly calming herself, she said, "I will repeat for the last time, Captain, I know nothing. Nothing!"

Renault reluctantly rose as well, aware that she did not intend to endure his presence a moment longer. "Very well, ma'am," he said gravely, "I shall leave you now, but

if you wish to reconsider any portion of your story, you
can leave word for me at the Oro Hotel."

Angel looked across the room at him with flaming blue
eyes. "There is nothing to reconsider, sir."

"Of course," Renault murmured. Without another
word he donned his military hat, nodded with excruciat-
ing politeness in her direction, and left.

The moment the captain was gone, Angel flew upstairs
to find Clara. Her heart was still pounding and her mouth
was cotton-dry from the long interview. She realized with
a keen instinct of her own that Renault intended to search
the mine, and somehow she must beat him there in order
to hide Kaga and his people.

She found Clara in her bedroom dozing fitfully in her
rocker before a warm fire, but the old woman came
awake and alert immediately when she felt Angel's kiss on
her cheek.

"Oh, dear me, I didn't mean to fall asleep," Clara said
crossly as she sat upright in the chair. "I must say, that
particular tonic packs a wallop!" She eyed Angel's pale
face with concern. "Did that bossy Frenchie leave yet?"
she demanded.

"Yes, Clara, but I'm afraid I must also depart again.
And I have a great deal to ask of you. I need to borrow
the horses and wagon again."

Without asking a single question the pert old lady replied, "Of course! But I do wish you'd take Jack along for
company and protection; he's grown very fond of you,
you know."

Angel smiled. "I didn't think he'd ever forgive me for

stealing his favorite horses right out from under his nose."

"Pooh! I think he was proud of you, the old coot! Funny soul, that Jack . . . never quite figured him out." With a sigh, Clara added unexpectedly, "Asked me to marry him once, you know."

"Jack did?" Angel was surprised and then had to laugh. "Oh, Clara, why didn't you say yes?"

"Because he didn't call me anything but 'missus'!" she retorted crisply. "What kind of a man can't even bring himself to speak a woman's first name?"

"A very timid one, I think," Angel replied as she drew the hand-knitted afghan snugly around the little woman. "You just stay here, Auntie, and rest. I'll be back before you know it."

Clara's age-spotted hand caught Angel's once before she left. "Oh, child, do be careful," she begged. "There's the little one to think of now."

"I know, Clara," Angel said as she gently pried her fingers free. "And that's the very reason why I must do this now."

Angel intended to take the back roads to the mine this time, since it was daylight and she didn't want to encounter Captain Renault by accident. She headed out with far more confidence than she soon felt, for as she drew near the outskirts of town, she caught a glimpse of a red sleigh headed into Clear Creek, and its heavy-set occupant.

Craddock! Her lips formed the name, a silent cry of denial, and then Angel blinked and the sleigh was gone. There was no possibility Craddock could be here right under her nose, was there? Of course, she was overwrought and nervous over the role she was called upon to play in order to save Holt's grandfather and the rest of the renegade Arapaho. She had lied to Renault, an uncomfortable if harmless enough action, but now she was going to warn the Indians of the marshal's arrival. If she was caught, she would be guilty of treason against the government by aiding the fugitives. But these same fugitives were the relatives of her unborn child!

Her thoughts would drive her wild at this rate, Angel decided, and she cut them off as she turned the wagon and headed south. She was as warmly wrapped as the last time she had traveled, and nothing would keep her from her goal: not fear of Craddock or Renault, or the very real possibility that she would be caught. Even Clara Maxwell wouldn't be able to help her then.

Angel thought she had headed out unobserved, for she didn't notice the single horseman hidden in a clump of pines, watching her disappear behind the plume of snow that was plowed up by the wagon. The man nudged his mount forward, and the winter sunlight cast his brooding, thoughtful features in harsh relief.

Neal Murphy wondered where his sister-in-law was going in such a hurry. He wondered, too, why she had seemed so furtive as she left the Maxwell house, and why Jack Miller's face had been pinched with worry as he'd helped her harness the two big draft horses.

Angel was headed in the opposite direction from Oro. She could only be going up to the mine then. But why? Neal didn't wonder overlong. He kicked his horse into a canter, following the smooth tracks left from the wagon runners, knowing that he dared not pass up this chance of discovering more evidence that would finally frame Holt for both treason and murder, beyond a shadow of a doubt.

For once, Rachel Maxwell was entirely immune to her mother's orders.

"I'm going to the jail," she repeated firmly as she finished fastening the frog clasps on the fashionable mauve cape that matched her gown. "I have to speak to Holt."

"It isn't proper!" Prudence gasped, her cheeks reddening as she imagined the other church ladies getting wind of her daughter's activities.

"Bosh and twaddle!" Rachel snapped, in direct imitation of her vinegary aunt, and proceeded to storm down the stairs.

Prudence trailed after her, puffing with indignation. "If you disobey me again, Rachel Esther, you'd better not darken this door again!"

Rachel paused at the dramatic announcement, then turned to face her mother and said wearily, "Very well, Mama. I'll go to live with Auntie Clara until the wedding."

Mrs. Maxwell's mouth opened and shut like a fish for several moments, and then, abruptly, she whirled and stomped back upstairs, her bombazine skirts crackling with outrage.

With a sigh, Rachel gathered up her reticule at the door and prepared to leave. She was just walking down the front steps when she looked up and saw her mother's beau coming up the walk.

"Good morning, Mr. Brindle," Rachel said coolly. She, for one, disliked the man, though why that was, she couldn't really say. He wasn't handsome in the remotest sense of the word, being inclined to fat and slovenliness, but Rachel wouldn't have held either against him if she thought he was sincere about winning her mother's hand.

"Miss Maxwell," he returned, giving her a bow as low as his great girth would allow. For the first time Rachel noticed he had a slight lisp, though she was too preoccupied to care.

"Forgive me for not stopping to visit with you, but I am in a great hurry," she informed the gentleman. "My mother is inside, and I am sure you have come to call upon her."

"Actually," Brindle said, "I also came to see you, my dear. I wished to convey my best wishes on your engagement, and express my sincere apologies that I could not attend your betrothal ball. Gout, you know." He coughed delicately behind one plump gloved hand.

"Oh, of course. It's quite all right, Mr. Brindle." Rachel was chafing with impatience to be gone. "Do ring at the door and I'm sure Mother will be delighted to see you."

"Dear Prudence," he sighed, deliberately ignoring Rachel's attempts to politely brush him off. "I fear I am doomed to disappoint her in the end. I have come here to break it off, you see."

"Oh." Rachel didn't know quite what to say.

"Indeed, I'm afraid I have somewhat misled the lady with my feeble attempts at courtship . . . I was merely amusing myself, you see, until I could catch the stage back home in the spring."

Rachel's jaw was definitely beginning to ache from her forced smile. "I see. How unfortunate for Mother. Now, if you will excuse me . . ."

"Of course, my dear, of course." He fumbled to execute another bow. "And do proffer my humblest apologies to your friend Angel McCloud, as well, won't you? She has invited me to many gatherings this winter, all of which I was obliged to decline, due to my ah—er—gout."

"Yes. Goodbye, Mr. Brindle." Rachel hurried off before he could delay her any longer. She was halfway to the jail before she realized what had disturbed her most about Brindle's smooth speech. He had referred to Angel by her maiden name, which he couldn't have possibly known, unless . . .

"Good heavens!" Rachel gasped, and leaned forward to pound the surprised driver on the shoulder. "Drive faster, Tully! It may be a matter of life and death!"

"Craddock is here?" Holt's skin was white with tension where his hands clenched the iron bars separating him from the world. "Are you sure?"

Rachel nodded almost wildly. "It makes sense, but I never put the facts together before! As Mr. Brindle, he was always careful to avoid any gatherings where he would meet Angel, but everyone just thought he was a rich recluse. Now I see he must have used Mother to find out more about Angel, and to track her movements, though to what end I can't dare say."

"I can," Holt said grimly, remembering Craddock's aborted attempt to cheat at cards in Denver and win Angel's lissome body in the bargain. He frowned with frustration and anger as he spun away from the bars and began to stalk his cell.

"What are we going to do?" Rachel cried.

"We?" Holt gave a short laugh. "I'm afraid it's going to be up to you, Rachel, until I can get out of here. The first thing you need to do, of course, is warn Angel."

"Thank heavens she's safe with Aunt Clara," the young woman sighed.

"Make sure she stays there, at least until I'm out of here," Holt instructed. "Tell your aunt not to let Angel out of her sight! Craddock is a dangerous man, completely unpredictable. I never dreamed his obsession with my wife would go this far."

"I'll ask Neal to watch Craddock's every move in town," Rachel decided. "He knows where the man lives, and as a minister he has a perfect excuse to drive around town, checking on people during these hard winter months."

Holt nodded absent agreement, frustrated by his imprisonment and the utter helplessness he felt to help the woman he loved. For he had discovered during these long days and nights, which offered nothing but time for introspection, that he loved Angel with all his heart and soul, and that he would give anything to make up for the wrongs he had done her. He knew he had hurt her, though she was, in her own way, every bit as proud as he, and would never let her wounded heart reflect back to him in her beautiful eyes.

Damn! What a fool he had been. If they had only stayed in Denver, made a new start . . . Now he was dragging the very woman he loved into a dangerous mire, and she could only suffer for it. At least, he thought, it was some small consolation that she was with Clara Maxwell now, and Craddock couldn't easily get at her.

"I'll go to Clear Creek first thing," Rachel told him,

then paused to add, "Don't lose faith, Holt. That marshal coming here was Providence, after all; Perry has had to stay your trial until this silly matter of supposed treason is settled to the captain's satisfaction."

"Which could take months," Holt said wryly. "How long, do you suppose, before they install a fireplace back here?"

He was shivering even beneath the warm blankets Rachel had brought, and she made a mental note to bring more of her father's clothes, even if Prudence screamed to high heaven. Those things would better serve the living now, Rachel decided firmly, as she bade Holt goodbye and hurried back outside to the waiting sleigh.

Angel drew the horses to a halt, peering around the clearing uncertainly, searching for any sign of the Indians. The teepee was gone, and the mine shaft appeared deserted as well. Only a number of tracks in the snow, headed north, indicated there had ever been anyone there.

They had gone! She felt almost dizzy with relief, and carefully dismounted from the wagon to approach the mine and check to be sure no one had been left behind. She felt a familiar fear begin to steal over her at the sight of that huge, dark hole yawning into the earth but, shaking herself mentally, she forced her cold feet on.

"Hello?" Angel called out softly when she reached the mine itself, and she leaned as close to the entrance as she could without actually going in. A puff of snow plopped down from the roof of the mine at her voice, and she heard the word echoing endlessly into the darkness below.

The wind sighed, stirring the trees, and gusts of fine snow blew across her face as she turned back to the wagon. Angel paused when she saw a rider break from the trees and automatically groped for her pistol, only to realize she had left it in the wagon.

Her knees went weak with relief when she recognized Neal on his dark bay gelding. She waved and called out to him, slogging slowly through the deep snow to meet him.

She noticed the strange way he looked down at her, almost feverish in the light of the noon sun, and she asked, "Neal? Are you all right?"

"Is it true?" he blurted. "Are you—with child?"

Angel nodded with surprise, wondering why his usually calm voice sounded so high-pitched and thin. "Is that why you followed me up here? To make sure I was safe?"

For a moment he stared at her, his pale blue eyes cold and curiously detached, and then he let out a short bark of laughter. "Oh, no, Mrs. Murphy. You've got it all backward."

Something in his chilly laughter frightened her, but Angel didn't immediately sense anything seriously amiss. "Then you . . . you must know about . . ."

"The Indians? Of course I do," he said contemptuously. "Holt's been helping those filthy savages for years, even giving them weapons so they can kill God-fearing Christians! Do you see what sort of man you married, Angel? What a low-down cur Holt really is?"

She took an inadvertent step backward at the venom in his voice. "I . . . I didn't really marry Holt," she reminded him. "There was the mix-up with the proxy wedding—"

"Oh, yes." Unexpectedly, Neal smiled down at her, his

teeth bared in a savage grin. "Clever of me, wasn't it, to arrange that handy little marriage in order to get you out here? I must admit you disappointed me at first, Angel. You didn't seem at all eager to get on with finding the gold up here, and you were much, much too attracted to Holt for my liking."

"Holt is your brother!" Angel exclaimed.

"Half," Neal reminded her with a snarl. "His mother was nothing more than Arthur's squaw, his Indian whore. Arthur shamed my mother, flaunting that redskin in her face at every opportunity. Everyone knew he kept his Indian slut hidden away somewhere, but only my mother was clever enough to figure out how to flush out the woman!"

Alarmed by his raving, Angel took another step away, but Neal saw her slowly retreating and suddenly swung down from the saddle.

"Do you understand now?" he hissed, but there was almost a plea of sorts behind his maddened words. "It had to be done! Arthur had told Virginia he was leaving her for that . . . that filthy squaw of his. He had even claimed Holt as his own! He would have thrown my mother aside and made *me* the bastard in the end!"

Angel shook her head and spoke softly, trying in vain to reason with Neal as he came closer, a crazed look in his eyes. Kaga had tried to warn her, but she hadn't really listened, and now she would pay the terrible price.

"Neal, why?" she pleaded unexpectedly, throwing him briefly off guard. "Why did you arrange a marriage by proxy and send me that letter supposedly from Holt? What did it gain?"

He paused to regard her in amazement. "The mine, of

course! After Arthur's death I went to claim my share and learned that he had signed everything over to your father. I tried to contact Royce and discovered he, too, had died. But in the process I learned about the debts you had incurred—folks tell ministers everything, you know—and I reasoned you'd be looking for an easy way out pretty soon. The mine was yours, but I gambled you didn't know its true worth, and that Holt hadn't been finding consistent signs of a strike. The only way I could get you out west was by a trick of that magnitude. Clever of me, wasn't it?"

She countered his question with one of her own. "Why involve Holt at all?"

Neal looked at her with a puzzled shake of his head. "I had to keep him in one place, of course, until I could spring my trap. What better way than to saddle him with an unexpected and unwanted wife?"

Trying to ignore the painful sting of Neal's words, Angel continued, "What trap, Neal?"

Suddenly he was angry. "It wasn't always easy, you know! I didn't plan to kill that Valentine woman, but she got in the way—"

Angel made a sharp little cry. "You killed Lily? For heaven's sake, Neal, why?"

"It was an accident," Neal said abruptly. "I heard the sheriff was going to ambush Holt up at the mine, and do all the dirty work for me, so you can imagine how relieved I was. Then I saw Lily riding out of town, headed up the trail to warn Holt. I didn't know he wasn't up there then, and neither did she. It was a real shock to come back down after killing her to find out Holt was in Oro the whole time."

"You played your part very well," Angel said coldly. "I

never would have guessed you had just murdered Lily when you were there wooing Rachel and caroling along with the rest of us!"

He almost preened at her accusation. "I did what I had to do, and though Holt wasn't accused of Lily's murder, as I hoped, it was easy enough to dispose of that braggart of a sheriff when he was in his cups. I knew the charge would stick on that one."

Angel observed quietly, "Then what Kaga said was true. You didn't try to stop your mother from killing poor Istas, either."

"Why should I?" Neal said belligerently. "She was just an Indian."

"And Lily was just a prostitute, and Red Garrett just a drunk," Angel finished for him in a furious tone. "You'll always find an excuse for whatever you do, won't you?"

"I don't need excuses," Neal snarled, reaching out and seizing her by the arm. "I need justice! And since nobody will give it to me I'll damn well take it for myself."

He sounded like a petulant little boy, Angel thought. Neal Murphy had never grown up. Whatever twisted sense of justice his mother's terrible act had instilled in him, he would never value another human life. His pale eyes glittered coldly as he looked down on her without emotion.

"I'm truly sorry it had to end this way, Angel," he rasped as he began to drag her toward the open mine shaft. "It would have been so much easier if you'd sold the mine to Brindle and gone back to Missouri as I planned. I gave you every chance in the world."

"Please, Neal!" she cried, trying to brace herself against his chest. "I'm going to have a baby! Holt's child—your nephew or niece!"

"No!" he denied, shaking his head furiously as she struggled against his maddened strength. "It all stops here, now!" He paused to shake her, and as her head snapped painfully back, he cried, "Don't you understand? I don't have any choice now!"

"There is always a choice," Angel whispered through her tears, but Neal wasn't listening. He thrust her roughly toward the open mine, directly into the semidarkness of the shaft.

"I'm sorry, Angel," he said yet again in a curiously quiet voice. Before she could cry out he pulled a gun from his coat, and the world as she knew it exploded into darkness.

Chapter Twenty-three

Rachel Maxwell brushed past the sputtering deputy at the door. "I must see Holt Murphy. Now!" she said over her shoulder as she pushed past the second man, Captain Renault, and entered the prison area.

Before they could stop her, Rachel saw Holt and cried, "Angel is gone!"

"Gone? What do you mean?" His gray eyes almost wild with worry, he demanded, "Craddock?"

Rachel shook her head. "I don't know!" she cried. "I can't find him or Neal or anyone else to help me!"

"What's going on?" Fabien Renault asked. He had followed Rachel into the corridor after he overheard their urgent exchange.

Holt turned to the marshal. "My wife is missing. We think she may have been abducted. I need to get out of here now, Captain!"

Renault shook his head regretfully. "I'm sorry; it isn't possible. Perhaps if the young lady here could explain the circumstances to one of the deputies—"

"Those worthless pigs!" Rachel exclaimed.

Elijah Perry appeared in the doorway. "Here, now, missy—" he began indignantly.

"Angel could be halfway back to Missouri by now," Holt snapped. "I promise I'll come straight back to the jail, but this is much more involved than either of you gentleman can realize. This Craddock is a madman—"

"Craddock?" Renault repeated patiently, drawing out his infamous pad and pencil. "How do you spell that? Is he one of the other men involved in the supplying of arms?"

"Dear God, no!" Holt exploded, briefly clutching his throbbing head between his hands. "Rachel, will you kindly explain all of this to the good captain's satisfaction before I knock out his teeth?"

Renault quickly stepped back from Holt's cell as Rachel began to sketch the events of the last few months. The marshal didn't quite grasp everything, as evidenced by his many questions, but eventually he waved a hand and said, "That's quite enough, Miss . . ."

"Maxwell," Rachel supplied, surprised and a little embarrassed to find herself noticing how handsome the captain was under such circumstances.

"It's terribly unfortunate, of course," the captain began, "but there is no way I can possibly release you until you have been cleared of all charges—"

"Now why did I expect that?" Holt drawled sarcastically. "You're too damn obsessed with not letting a petty criminal slip away to give another thought to a possible murder taking place!"

"It doesn't sound as if this Craddock person intends to harm Mrs. Murphy," Renault replied coolly. "It sounds more as if he is trying to woo her away from you."

" 'Woo'?" Holt echoed. "Woo? You damned Frog, is that all you Frenchmen can think of? My wife's life is at stake!"

"You have my sympathies," Renault said frostily before turning to instruct Perry to lock the outer door at all times. Then he firmly escorted Rachel to the door, fortunately too late to notice the iron file she had slipped through the bars into Holt's clenched fist while the captain was looking the other way.

The late-afternoon shadows provided momentary cover for Holt as he slipped the last of the bars free and set it gently down on the hard-packed floor. The spot he had opened up was barely wide enough for him to squeeze through, but there wasn't time to risk another bar before Perry or Renault appeared to bring him his evening meal.

Carefully, Holt began to thread his lean frame through the narrow opening, wincing as the sharp edges of the cut iron caught on his shirt and trousers and skin. He was halfway through when he heard voices coming in his direction from the other room. He swore softly and reentered his cell, turning his back to the gaping hole just as the outer door was unlocked and swung open.

"I don't like it, not one durn bit," Holt heard Deputy Perry grumble, but then another man stepped forward from the shadows and Holt couldn't restrain a grin.

"Jean-Claude! So you lived after all! And here I did my best to kill you."

"And nearly did," the Frenchman replied, a huge grin splitting his swarthy, bearded face as he came forward to survey Holt's mean quarters. "Not much of a hotel here eh, *mon ami?*"

Perry waited just long enough to make sure the two were up to no apparent mischief, then relocked the door behind Holt's visitor and quickly returned to his half eaten supper. The moment the heavy door closed, Jean Claude's twinkling eyes shifted to the man-sized hole Holt had uncovered.

"Why did you send for me, eh? You are doing just fine!"

Holt shrugged. "It's a tight fit, but I reckon I'll be out of here shortly. Your timing couldn't be better, Duvet. need your help."

"*Tiens!* What now?" the fur trapper demanded good naturedly. "Was it not enough to involve me in you dealings with Maska?"

"It was too obvious for me to smuggle the arms to the tribe directly and you know it," Holt growled beneath his breath. "Besides, you got a fat cut of the profits . . enough to keep yourself in fine furs, I see."

Jean-Claude accepted the rebuke with good grace. "Do you like my coat?" He stroked the rich brown fur he wore with loving fingers. "I can find you another just like it— for a price, of course."

"Of course," Holt chuckled, finding he still liked the irrepressible Frenchman, almost against his better judgment. He and Duvet had done a brisk business for years, and though Holt had never let on to Angel that he already knew Jean-Claude and his family, it hadn't been easy to maintain an impersonal air when Duvet had been so seriously injured.

"How's the head?" he asked the other man, tapping his own temple as he spoke.

Jean-Claude winced at the memory, then sighed, "Better, *mon ami,* but I still have strange dreams and visions of a beautiful angel bending down to earth to claim my soul—a golden-haired beauty with sky-blue eyes."

"That angel you speak of is my wife," Holt interrupted tersely. "She wet-nursed you all the way to Denver and held your hand while you were ranting about Anne-Marie!"

Jean-Claude laughed at his friend's obvious irritation. "But of course! Okoka told me of your lovely little bride; why didn't I figure it out myself? A girl with yellow hair, Okoka said, and eyes like Zuni stones."

Holt's expression was thunderous, but he forced himself to ask, "Is Okoka with you?"

"*Oui,* she and the bébé are staying in a boardinghouse. *Le Grand Hôtel* would not take us in; they said they do not cater to squaws and Indian-lovers!" Jean-Claude chuckled, apparently not offended, but he didn't miss Holt's low growl.

"The people of this town have a lot to learn," Holt muttered as he positioned himself to slip between the bars once again.

Duvet looked alarmed. "What are you doing, Murphy?"

"Making a break for it." Moments later, Holt stood beside the other man, a wry grin on his face. "Now comes your part, Duvet. Angel—*my* angel—is in danger. I need you to distract the deputies while I slip out the back way. Then I want you to meet me behind the building. Do you have a horse, or a wagon?"

"A dog sled," Duvet replied proudly. "I thought you might want some speed and agility in the snow."

"How well you know me, old friend," Holt said, and then began to instruct the other man in the final details of his plan.

Neal Murphy's hand trembled as he poured a shot of amber whiskey into a glass and then hurled it down his throat in one stiff movement. He was still shaking from the close call he'd had, when the unstable mine shaft had collapsed after the gunshot and sent tons of rock and silt pouring down on him and Angel. The memory of the muffled roar still echoed in his head, as did Angel's cries, until the thundering earth had finally snuffed out her life.

He wiped his perspiring brow with the back of his dusty sleeve, yanking open his clerical collar to get more air. God, how close he'd come to dying himself! The realization sent a cold chill through his body. It was merely Providence that he'd been able to find a pocket of air that lasted until he was able to paw through the rubble and crawl free.

He glanced down at his clothes with chagrin. His black trousers were torn and stained, his usually immaculate shirt and hair peppered with dirt as well. He would have to get rid of the evidence before anyone suspected—

A sharp knock at the door startled Neal from his musings and he looked up, panicked, to assure himself that the parsonage door was locked. It was, but he could hear Rachel's muffled voice on the other side, demanding that he answer her.

"Neal! I know you're in there. Please, I have to talk to you!"

His momentary hysteria subsided when he realized

here was no way she could know of his activities. Quickly, Neal looked for a way to cover his soiled clothing. He found a dressing gown behind his bedroom door and shrugged it on, kicking his shoes and stockings under the bed. Barefoot, he hastily combed his fingers through his hair to dislodge any dirt clods and went to answer the door. He forced a thin smile to his lips and managed to say, evenly enough, "Rachel. I just finished my bath. I'm sorry; I didn't hear you at the door at first."

"Oh, Neal, it's the most awful thing," Rachel burst out, pushing past him before he could block her at the door. "I've been looking for you all day!"

"Well, I had my calls to make," he mumbled, wishing she would leave. But she was distraught and had come to him for succor.

"Angel is missing," she began, and Neal congratulated himself on looking appropriately shocked at the announcement.

"Is there any sign of foul play?" Neal asked, and when she shook her head he smiled with relief, which he knew Rachel would misinterpret, and suggested, "Perhaps she went back to Missouri, after all."

"That's ridiculous! She never would have left Holt."

"He's—not out of prison, is he?" Neal asked uneasily. She shook her head. "No, not yet, but I'm sure he's working on it right now." She didn't tell Neal about the file, because she knew he'd disapprove of her tampering with justice and she didn't have the heart to argue with him or anyone else right now. She was too worried about her friend.

"There's a horrible man named Craddock who is surely behind all this," Rachel started to explain, and

after she finished the story Neal could hardly believe hi
luck. William Brindle . . . Will Craddock . . . yes, yes, o
course! It made sense now, and what a fool he'd been no
to question that old lecher's obvious interest in Ange
before this. But Craddock was the perfect dupe to take the
blame for the crime. Nothing the old man could say
would keep him from hanging.

Suppressing a wild urge to laugh, Neal gladly offered to
escort Rachel back to her mother's house and then look
for Angel and Craddock himself.

"I want to go with you," she countered promptly.

"It wouldn't be wise, Rachel. I insist on taking you
home, where you will be safe."

"Angel is my friend," she answered him, softly but
firmly, and her hazel eyes sparkled with tears. "I can't rest
until I know she is safe, Neal! Surely you can understand
that?"

"Of course," he soothed, reaching out and briefly taking her hands to pat them. "I need but a moment more
to dress . . ."

He hurried off and Rachel sighed, wiping her tears
away on the back of her glove. For a moment she couldn't
figure out what was bothering her so, other than Angel's
disappearance, but there was something about the room
or Neal himself . . . something definitely amiss. Rachel
remembered that she had glanced at Neal's hands when
he had taken hold of hers a moment ago, and her brow
puckered in confusion.

His nails were dirty. Black. Caked with dirt. Besides the
fact that Neal was such a fastidious person, he had told
her he had just finished bathing. Then . . . he had lied. But
why?

Rachel's sharp gaze eventually singled out something else out of place in the little parlor. An unstoppered liquor bottle sat on the sideboard, an empty glass beside it. She knew Neal kept a few spirits, ostensibly for wounds and such, but he had always preached that liquor was the devil's nectar. She stared at the half-empty bottle, her thoughts whirling wildly.

"Ready to go, Rachel?"

His crisp voice spun her around.

"Oh—of course," she stammered guiltily, her cheeks reddening when she felt Neal's pale blue eyes taking close measure of her as she hurried to the door. She caught the faint whiff of liquor on Neal's breath as she passed him, and nearly stumbled. Something was wrong here, she thought. Something very wrong, indeed.

Holt grabbed the man by the lapels and spun him around, slamming Will Craddock against the outer wall of the town smithy.

"You bastard!" he snarled, battering Craddock's head against the bricks, "Where is she? So help me, if you've hurt her—"

Craddock wheezed for breath, struggling against Holt. He finally managed to whimper, "For God's sake, man, I'm leaving town today! Don't kill me!"

"Killing's too good for you," Holt replied with a snarl, releasing the old man just long enough for Craddock to clutch his collar and hack and gasp for air. Holt watched impassively, half wishing Craddock would crumple up and die before his eyes and half wishing he could have the pleasure of throttling the old reprobate.

Jean-Claude was watching out for him at the other end of the alley, but he hadn't liked the idea of Holt pummeling someone in full view of the public, particularly considering the fact that Holt was supposed to be in prison, not wandering the streets and making such a noisy spectacle.

"*Mon ami!*" he hissed in warning a moment later. "There are men in uniform coming, on horseback!"

Holt grabbed Craddock by the collar, literally dragging the man after him into a tiny doorway, where their faces were forced but inches apart. Holt smelled the rank scent of fear on the whimpering old man and grinned wolfishly into Craddock's fat, perspiring face.

"I ought to gut you right here and now, like the swine you are," Holt growled under his breath.

"Please," Craddock wheezed again, "please! I haven't touched Angel, I swear . . ."

"Why should I believe you, Craddock?" Holt inquired in a dangerous, silky-soft voice. "Angel is missing and you're the only one with any reason to do her harm. Don't deny you followed us here from Denver!"

"All right, all right!" the old man sputtered. "I did follow you, but not for the reason you think. I would never hurt Angel . . . she was everything to me, everything!"

"Then we have one thing in common," Holt snarled. "If you've touched a single hair on her head, by God—"

"No! I swear it!" Craddock babbled. "I was leaving today; I've had enough of this godforsaken wilderness and the people who live here . . . s-savages like you!"

Holt threw back his head and laughed softly. "I'll take that as a compliment, Craddock!" His silver eyes narrowed on the man again, who shriveled in his fierce grasp. "You know what, mister? I almost believe you . . . almost, but not quite."

"Oh, God," Craddock whimpered, sagging in Holt's grasp as he saw the murderous rage filling his adversary's eyes.

"Save your breath! I think even He's forsaken a fat slug like you," Holt murmured as he slid his strong hands to press into the folds of fat jiggling around the old man's neck.

Suddenly Duvet was there, tugging urgently on Holt's sleeve. "Murphy, we must go! They have discovered you are gone. There is no time!"

"Damn!" Holt cursed, releasing Craddock, who slid to a sorry, gurgling heap at his feet. "This bastard knows more than he's telling!"

"Maybe so, but it is more important to keep you hidden now! They will be searching the streets soon, and there are dozens of them and only two of us!"

Holt swore roundly. "You're lucky this time, Craddock," he told the sniveling man at his feet, before he turned to follow Jean-Claude to safety. "Next time I'll cut your throat and leave your innards for the dogs!"

"Hurry!" Jean-Claude's voice urged, as he and Holt stepped off the sled and ran past the team of panting huskies toward Clara Maxwell's home. It was dark now, and the lights within the house cast the men's haggard, weary faces in sharp relief as they approached a window.

Tapping quietly on the pane, Holt waited until a light flickered on on the porch, and then he nodded to Duvet and slipped from the cover of darkness onto the doorstep.

"You devil!" Clara scolded Holt when she opened the door wide enough to admit him and his friend. "You scared half a dozen years off me!"

"Then that's why you look so young tonight," Holt said mischievously as he planted a quick kiss on the old woman's cheek. Then he became serious. "Clara, this is Jean-Claude. He's my friend from Denver."

"Hmmph!" was the response, as Clara stood with two little fists on her hips and looked the grinning trapper up and down. "Another Frenchie! What's this world coming to?"

Turning to Duvet, Holt said with amusement, "Clara here thinks the French are solely responsible for all the evils in the world."

"An unfortunate shortsightedness in one so lovely," Jean-Claude replied, bowing low over Clara's hand and bringing two spots of high color to her cheeks.

"Smooth, isn't he?" the old lady quipped tartly, withdrawing her hand with a sniff of not-quite-so-forbidding disapproval. "Have you found our Angel yet?" she demanded.

Holt shook his head. "I found the man I think is responsible for her abduction, but he wouldn't talk. And Duvet and I have been too busy trying to outsmart Renault and his men to look for her anywhere else."

"I have a terrible feeling," Clara said, wringing her hands as she spoke, "a dreadful feeling that she is in dire trouble! And that you must find her very soon . . ." Tears welled in the old woman's eyes, and Holt moved to hug her reassuringly.

"I'll find Angel," he vowed. "You have my word. I

won't rest until she has been returned to us, safe and sound! And if she isn't . . ."

Clara swallowed hard in the momentary silence. "Yes?"

"If she isn't," he finished quietly, "then so help me God, I shall personally see to the man who did this, and he will wish a thousand times over that he had died earlier, when he had the chance!"

She crawled weakly, desperately, after the tiny shaft of light, her lungs bursting with the effort of holding her breath to make each precious inch of air last. Bit by bit, hour by hour, she moved as if swimming against the crushing tide of dirt and rock, slowly inching her body free of the rubble. She no longer remembered who she was, or where she was; only the primal instinct for survival kept her legs and arms churning toward the light, away from the black hole that threatened to suck her down into its gaping maw.

Her bloody fingers clawed through yet another pile of sharp rocks and silt, and she felt the dirt pouring back over her arms, into her mouth and eyes and nose, and then the entire wall suddenly gave way, spilling a wave of winter sunlight across her gasping face.

Cold air poured through the hole she had dug; blessed, fresh, sweet air! She gulped it in greedily, her lungs still burning painfully from all the dust she had inhaled, and then, exhausted, she lay down her head and knew no more.

* * *

Hours later, as Holt and Jean-Claude sifted fruitlessly through the rubble, the Frenchman was the first to spy a lock of golden hair mixed into the dirt.

"Merde!" he cried, pointing. Holt scrambled across the pile of debris, carrying the lantern, and an anguished cry escaped his lips as he set the light aside and began to dig feverishly, his big hands sending the dirt flying in every direction.

"My God . . . Angel . . . no!"

Holt's broken cry echoed through the shaft as he finally uncovered his wife and wiped the dirt from her nose and mouth, his fingers shaking uncontrollably.

Jean-Claude moved forward and gently tried to pry his friend away from her battered, broken body. "It is too late, *mon ami . . .*"

"No! No-o-o!" Furiously, Holt batted away Duvet's hands, returning his attentions to the golden head cradled in his lap. "Angel, Angel, oh God, why?" He groaned, rocking back and forth in agony as tears ran down his grimy cheeks.

"S'il vous plait, Murphy—" Jean-Claude was agonized by the sight of his friend, but he stayed back, knowing better than to disturb the grieving man again.

For a long time Holt just bent over the body, his quiet moans muffled in Angel's hair. Then a keening cry suddenly broke from his lips, and he threw back his head and howled, raising the hairs on the Frenchman's neck.

But a moment later the woman in Holt's arms made a small, choking sound, and both men froze and stared down at the still figure. Angel coughed again, weakly but distinctly, and, shooting a wild look at Duvet, Holt bent

over her once more, this time to murmur words of hope
and encouragement in her ear.

"Yes, Angel, yes! Come to me!"

"The light . . ." she murmured faintly, wonderingly,
"it's so beautiful . . ."

"No," Holt begged her softly, tears staining his lean
brown cheeks, "don't follow the light, sweetheart . . .
follow my voice, the voice of the man who loves you."

He pleaded, coaxed, even scolded her, until finally she
whispered a single, frail word that gave him hope.

"Holt . . . ?"

"Oh, my God. You've come back to me." And he
buried his face in her silken mane and sobbed without the
slightest shame.

Chapter Twenty-four

The swirling mist before Angel's eyes cleared long enough for her to see Holt bending over her, his handsome features a study in fear. Her body was feverish and racked with pain, but she managed to make her bruised lips form the all-important question.

"How . . . ?"

He understood at once what she meant. "Jack Miller saw you head off in the direction of the mine," Holt explained. "He also saw a man following you, but the fellow was too far away for Jack to tell who it was. By the time Jack got word to us, we'd nearly given up. I never expected to find you alive, Angel." He closed his eyes, and when he opened them again she saw the tears of a man in love.

"Holt," she rasped, "are we . . . safe?"

"Yes, for the time being. I don't think anyone will think to look for us here. Just rest, sweetheart. The doctor's coming; he'll be here soon."

Angel could make out the confines of the room in which she lay, but it was too dim for her to distinguish any features. Surely she was safe in Aunt Clara's house, and with that comforting thought she began to speak again, surprised to find her words slurring to the point of being indistinguishable.

"Holt, the m-man . . . it w-was . . ." Angel felt a fog rolling in over her thoughts, and with a sigh of frustration she drifted off again, saving her strength for what was to come, when she must tell Holt of his brother's deceit.

Gently, Holt tucked up the covers around his wife and departed after dropping a tender kiss upon her feverish brow. Dammit, what was keeping the doctor? Angel had lapsed in and out of consciousness during the long trip down the mountain, and if not for Jean-Claude's steady hand on the reins, Holt knew she would be in worse condition now. They were lucky they had found the wagon intact, and the horses still there. But he could only wonder why Angel had felt the need to go up to the mine since the Indians were long gone.

With a weary sigh, Holt left the small bedroom where his wife was resting and met Neal in the main room.

"Thank you for taking us in," Holt said. "I know it's dangerous for you."

"This is a house of refuge," Neal replied, camoflauging his nervousness with his usual piety. He had barely been able to contain his terror when Holt had first turned up on his doorstep, carrying Angel in his arms. Only after several heart-stopping minutes was Neal able to determine that Holt knew nothing of what had happened at the mine . . . yet.

"Was Angel able to tell you anything?" he asked as he anxiously fiddled with the well-worn Bible in his hand.

Holt shook his head. "She's still delirious, and while the

audanum you suggested seems to have eased her pain, 's made her too sleepy to talk."

"Sleep is a healing process," Neal murmured.

Holt didn't hear him. He had already turned and narched toward the parsonage window, where he flicked back the curtains and gazed impatiently into the wintery norning. "Where the hell is Jean-Claude with the doctor?"

"Your friend may have encountered bad roads," Neal suggested, pleased with himself for having had the foresight to send the Frenchman on a wild-goose chase to Clear Creek, adding many miles and hours to what would otherwise have been a simple procedure, for the good doctor was presently just down the street.

"Maybe I should go after him," Holt muttered distractedly, obviously loathe to leave Angel but worried about her health as well.

"That wouldn't be wise," Neal countered quickly. "I'm sure Deputy Perry and the others are still looking for you, and it's best if you stay out of sight. It makes much more sense for me to go." As he spoke, he reached for his outerwear, hung on a nearby peg, and almost smiled with relief when Holt made no move to stop him.

As he shrugged on his heavy coat, Neal said, "I'll come back as quickly as I can." With the deputies and a U.S. Marshal, you stupid Indian, he added with a silent laugh.

Before he departed Neal gave his brother the bottle of audanum and instructed him to give Angel another spoonful in a half hour. Neal had doubled the dose, knowing the powerful opium would keep Angel safely unconscious until Holt could be taken back to jail.

After Neal had gone Holt tried to occupy himself with

a plan of escape, but he was too worried about Angel
care about himself anymore. How could he have bee
such a fool? He hadn't even realized he'd been living li
on the edge, day after day, without any joy or satisfactio
until he'd met that impossible Missouri woman. A ha
smile curved his lips as he remembered the day he
confronted her in Clear Creek, called his alleged "wife
every name in the book, and then challenged her to t
her hand at mining.

Well, Angel had called his bluff—more than onc
She was a stubborn little thing, but Holt realized th
was one of the reasons he loved her so much. An
dammit, the thought of her dying now was too much
bear. He returned to the bedroom with the bottle
laundanum.

Angel still lay motionless, but when Holt perched o
the edge of the bed she moved slightly and opened h
drug-glazed eyes. A dreamy smile was the only sign th
she recognized him, and Holt felt an incredible surge
protectiveness and love as he bent over his wife.

Smoothing back the golden wisps from her forehea
he said softly, "I'm going to take care of you, sweethea
Today and always."

He spoke to her in a steady, gentle voice for a long tim
until Angel finally roused herself enough to reply.

"Is that a . . . promise, Mr. Murphy?" she whispere
a spark of the old teasing in her eyes.

"Damned right it is, woman. As soon as you get we
we're going to start over, just you and me."

Angel shook her head weakly against the pillows. "N
just us, Holt . . ." Her right hand dropped to smooth th
covers over her stomach, and she gave him a falterir

smile. "There's someone else now who'll likely have something to say about that."

Holt stared at her for a moment, and then an incredulous look of mixed joy and apprehension spread over his face. "You mean a baby? A real, honest-to-goodness, ornery little Murphy?"

"Is there any other kind?" she murmured sleepily, the smile on her face transformed to one of pure satisfaction before she drifted off again.

Holt rose slowly and stared down at her, the unused bottle clutched tightly in his fist. My God, a baby! His own son or daughter! For a moment he stood there shaking, and then he let out a quiet whoop of delight and spun around three times.

"You did the right thing," Captain Renault assured Neal Murphy as he checked his six-shooter and slid it into the army-issue holster strapped to his waist. "Your brother is a dangerous fugitive, and a lot of people could have been hurt if you hadn't turned him in."

"I'm a man of God," Neal replied piously. "I could do no less."

Privately, the marshal disliked Neal's cool, superior mien, but he couldn't fault the man's judgment. Holt Murphy might be his brother, but the preacher obviously knew when justice must be served.

"We'll go in quickly and take him as quietly as we can," Renault said as he turned to face the waiting deputies. "Perry, has the street been closed off?"

"Yep," the acting sheriff said abruptly, returning his attention to the thick wad of chewing tobacco in his cheek.

"Good. Hawkins, you and I will take the alley leading to the parsonage, and the rest of you men can guard the remaining entrances. Pastor Murphy, is there a back entrance to the house?"

"Through the chapel," Neal said. "It's kept unlocked."

Renault nodded thoughtfully. "Murphy won't be expecting this—the other Murphy, I mean—so with any luck we can lasso him before anyone gets hurt. Any chance of him taking the woman hostage?"

"Possibly," Neal said. "I can go in first and distract him if you like, and after he's safely rounded up I'll stay with her until the doctor comes. She's seriously ill."

Renault nodded again, a little troubled by the idea of the beautiful young lady he had met being put into such danger. Well, there was no choice. Murphy must stand trial for his crimes, and it was up to him to see that it was done.

Holt heard the rear door leading from the chapel click open and pivoted smoothly with his knife in hand. Seeing Neal standing there, he relaxed, and it was then that Captain Renault and his men burst into the rectory.

"Drop the weapon, Murphy," Renault ordered quietly, regret in his voice as he leveled his Colt directly at Holt's heart.

To everyone's surprise, Holt did exactly that, opening his white-knuckled fist to let the knife fall with a soft thud to the rug. Renault stepped forward cautiously to kick the knife out of Holt's reach, then relaxed as two of his men moved in to restrain the fugitive.

"I'm disappointed in you, Murphy," Renault said.

"You would have been given a fair trial, at least in federal court. Now we have to add the charge of escaping the law to your growing list of criminal offenses."

"I'll take my chances in Denver," Holt replied mildly, "as long as you see to my wife. She's badly hurt, and Doc's not bothering to show up."

"Someone will see to her," Renault promised, nodding to Neal as he approached the prisoner. "I'm sorry, but we'll have to escort you back to the jail. Do I have your word not to try to escape?"

"My word's as good as any Indian's, I guess," Holt answered coolly, and his flint-gray eyes met and locked with the young captain's in a surprising display of defiance.

Angel heard the noises in the other room, penetrating her hazy mind like little scurrying insects, just irritating enough to coax her awake. She struggled to raise her eyelids, but they were like lead weights keeping her down, and she gasped with the effort of trying to sit up. Her heart pounded horribly, and there was an awful metallic taste in her mouth. She tried to call out for Holt, but nothing emerged from her lips except a silent moan of agony.

Her body burned and ached, now that she was coming out of the drugged state, and she glanced down to find her many weals and cuts had been carefully tended and wrapped. Holt's work, no doubt, and she wanted to thank him for it, but where was he?

A short time later the noises stopped and the bedroom door opened slowly, admitting a stream of sunlight that fell on the bed. Angel blinked against the glare, barely able to make out the dark figure silhouetted against the light.

"Holt?" she whispered uncertainly, struggling to sit up against the pillows.

"He's gone, Angel. And he won't be coming back."

Oh, my God! The terrified scream was choked in her throat as Angel tried to scramble from the bed, Neal's laughter ringing in her ears. How could he be here, in Aunt Clara's home? If she cried out loudly, surely someone would come . . .

As if reading her mind, Neal chuckled sadistically. "Not this time, my dear." Almost savagely, he kicked the door shut behind them. In his hand he held Holt's huge knife, and it flashed silver where the sunlight caught it.

"Don't make it difficult this time," Neal advised, his voice cracking like a horsewhip in the small room. "There's nobody to hear you now. I'll make it so quick and easy, no pain . . ."

His low, coaxing voice was almost hypnotic, and Angel whimpered as she slid to the floor and struggled to gain her feet. But her legs were numb and refused to bear her weight, so she gripped the edge of the bureau and the headboard of the bed instead, and slowly pulled herself up. She found she wore only a brief chemise and her pantalets, but there was no cowering in her stance or her gaze as she confronted the madman yet again.

"What have you done to Holt?" she demanded.

Neal seemed surprised by her verbal attack. He knew she had to be reeling on her feet, but her voice was surprisingly strong and angry.

"I didn't have to do anything to your half-breed husband," he snarled, his lip curling back like a cur's. "He made his own bed and now he'll lie in it. They've just taken him away to hang!"

"No!" Angel cried, almost doubling over as his hateful words penetrated her dazed mind. Too late she realized that Neal had only been waiting for her to falter. When he rushed her and knocked her back against the bureau she was too stunned to fight back. The jarring impact nearly broke her already badly bruised ribs.

In a flash, Neal held the razor-sharp edge of the big blade to her throat, pinning her in place with a single arm. "Now," he growled, "it all ends here—"

The bedroom door slammed open against the wall, and they both jumped at the sound, the knife lightly nicking Angel's skin. Several drops of blood stained the blade.

"Rachel," Angel whispered at the sight of her friend, standing alone and courageously wielding her father's Confederate revolver one last time.

"Let her go, Neal," Rachel said tonelessly, her finger snug on the trigger. "It isn't worth dying for."

The young minister stared at his fiancée in obvious shock for a moment, but then his pale eyes cleared and took on a fanatical gleam as he said, "You're wrong, Rachel. So very wrong! Gold is worth dying for—a thousand times over! And you could share it with me . . . if you'd only see reason."

Angel saw her friend's aim begin to waver slightly, but Rachel didn't lower the gun. "I'm sorry, Neal," Rachel said firmly, "but it's wrong, and I won't let you hurt Angel or anyone else. You're a very sick man—"

"And you're a pathetic, sniveling ninny!" Neal exploded as he briefly forgot about Angel and squared off with the other woman. "Do you think I ever loved you, Rachel? Then you are as stupid as you are ugly!" At her hurt, startled look, he pressed on ruthlessly, "It's true! The only reason I asked you to marry me was so I could have a good excuse to keep an eye on Holt and his sweet wife! After all, you and Angel were such good— little—friends!" He punctuated each word with a poke of the knife in Angel's ribs, but she didn't cry out, knowing it would distract Rachel and put them both in even greater danger.

Tears began to leak from Rachel's hazel eyes, but she didn't bother to wipe them and she kept her gaze trained on Neal's rapidly heaving chest.

"I don't believe you," she murmured, giving a little shake of her head. "You loved me, Neal, I know you did . . ."

"I could no more love you than I could my horse," he retorted cruelly, and as Rachel gave a little cry, he snicked the blade of the knife across Angel's side, leaving a torn chemise and a bloody trail in its wake.

Angel saw Rachel lower the gun with trembling hands, and as she prepared to meet her end she thought wildly, desperately, of Holt and their unborn child, and a cry of pure rage rose in her throat.

"No-o-o!"

Angel's mouth finally opened, but she realized the sound had not come from her but from Rachel. As if in slow motion Angel watched the gun rising again, and a deafening roar slammed her back against the wall as the room filled with acrid smoke.

*   *   *

Holt heard the gunshot ricocheting off the buildings behind them, and he grabbed the knotted reins of his mount with his loosely bound hands and wheeled the horse about, tearing back down the road the way they had come.

"Gosh-durned Injun!" Perry swore, trying to bring around his strawberry roan to pursue the fleeing man. But the plump mare spied a juicy clump of bunchgrass poking through the snow instead and lurched in the opposite direction. As he struggled with his horse, Deputy Perry yelled loud enough and gestured wildly enough to attract the attention of the other riders at the fore, and Renault turned in his saddle in time to see Holt vanishing around a corner. He felt a familiar sinking sensation, and a leaden resolve took hold of him.

"Knew we shouldn't have taken him at his word," the captain muttered, but his tone was almost admiring as he wearily ordered his men about and they set off at a gallop back to the parsonage, thundering past the cursing, red-faced Perry along the way.

Holt knew he didn't have much time, but something in his gut told him Angel was in danger, that the gunshot had come not from any of the saloons in Oro but from the parsonage itself. He saw he was right as he tore past a crowd of gawking people, all of them staring in the direction of the church. A desperate fury seized Holt, so intense he didn't even feel the pain when he vaulted from the saddle with his hands still tied in front of him and landed with a jarring impact on the ground.

Tearing at the rawhide knots with his teeth as he ran, Holt paused only to hurl himself bodily against the locked doors of the church. Gritting his teeth, he slammed his bruised shoulder again and again at the barred door until he heard a splintering crack and the entrance suddenly gave way.

Holt stumbled through the broken door, tossing aside the rawhide as he freed his hands. "Angel!" he shouted, rage giving way to fear when he heard the quiet sobbing at the rear of the parsonage. He also heard the pounding of hooves and the snorting of horses as Renault and his men drew up outside the building, but without a pause he dashed through the main room to the tiny bedroom where he had left his wife sleeping peacefully.

When he stepped into the room Holt had eyes only for the blond woman slumped against the wall, blood dotting her snow-white chemise.

"Angel!" he cried again, and when her tear-filled blue eyes flickered open and she attempted a smile, Holt felt a dazed sense of relief wash over him. Slowly, he took in the rest of the room—his half-brother on the floor, motionless; a shaking Rachel Maxwell still holding the smoking gun in a death grip. Moving past them both, he took Angel into his arms, soothing her trembling body until she dissolved into deep, wracking sobs, her tangled golden hair spilling across his chest.

Holt thought Neal was dead, but he found that he was wrong when the man on the floor groaned softly and began to move. Startled, Rachel uttered a whimpering sound and dropped the gun, backing away with her hands clapped to her mouth until she was flush against the wall.

As Neal stirred again, Holt saw the minister had merely sustained a flesh wound to his right leg. Moments later, Neal was able to open his eyes and look around, apparently as surprised as they were to find himself still alive.

Seeing Holt holding Angel protectively, a bitter smile curved the young minister's mouth. "So . . . it comes to this. You'll be the one to carry on the Murphy name with your dirty Indian blood."

Holt's eyes flashed, but he said evenly, "You're not going to die, Neal, much to my regret. I wonder why I didn't figure it out before. It was you who killed Garrett and tried to frame me for it. You were the one who followed Angel to the mine and tried to kill her, weren't you?"

"Bravo!" Neal laughed weakly, coming up on his elbows and staring at Holt with hate-filled eyes. "You're smarter than you look, little brother! But that mine belongs to me, and you know it. Father was tricked into changing his will by that Indian mistress of his."

"That isn't true, but even if it was, it's a moot point now, and as worthless as the mine itself. There's never been any gold up there, Neal. I salted the mine myself, in hopes of tempting a prospective buyer."

"You lie!" Neal burst out, his pale eyes nearly popping from his head. "You're as much a liar as that Indian whore you called your mother!"

Holt couldn't restrain a low growl, and he gently set Angel aside as he confronted his brother. "Soft Snow was my mother, and a damn sight more motherly than that snake who spawned you! She loved Arthur with all her heart and soul, and Virginia Murphy's way of repaying her was to kill my mother in cold blood!"

Neal released a shrill sound, almost like a hysterical laugh. "But you're wrong, little brother! Virginia didn't kill Istas. Oh, you're right, it was her idea to waylay the little Indian slut up at the cabin and threaten her, but that's all she was going to do. Until I convinced Mother she and I would never be safe until Istas was dead . . ."

"Damn you for a liar!"

"Am I, Holt? Or don't you want to admit the thought of a thirteen-year-old raping and killing your precious whore of a mother is too fantastic to be believed?"

Releasing a feral howl, Holt charged for Neal, just as Captain Renault and his men flooded the room, and the marshal himself grabbed Holt by the collar and spun him around.

"Don't do it, man! I overheard everything. Justice can be served now, Murphy—"

"The hell it will," Holt said hoarsely, wildly. "That bastard killed my mother . . . he'll pay for it . . . don't stop me, damn you!" His hard silver eyes pleaded with Renault, but the captain was adamant in his restraint.

"As of now you're a free man, Murphy. Don't risk it. My men found the arms stashed in your brother's rectory; it's all over now."

Holt suppressed a wild urge to laugh. Renault had found the guns and ammunition Jean-Claude had brought here on his request; until now, he'd forgotten they had hidden them temporarily in Neal's parsonage, knowing it would be the last place the law would look for supplies being funneled to the renegade Arapaho.

Renault was saying gently, "Your wife needs you, Murphy. As for this one—" Renault's own eyes hardened as they swept with disgust over Neal, "he'll be dealt with as harshly as the law permits. Now, let's see about getting your wife and Miss Maxwell to the doctor."

Reluctantly, Holt turned away from Neal to tend his wife, tenderly wrapping the half-conscious Angel in several blankets while the captain saw to Rachel. A pair of deputies were left behind to guard Neal until the doctor could be sent to look at his leg, but none of the men saw the dropped pistol Neal managed to slide under his sleeve.

As Holt carried his wife down the street, a curious crowd trailing them at a distance, a second shot rang out, echoing loudly in the winter air. Holt faltered for only a moment when he realized it came from the parsonage. Then, with a look of steely resolve settling over his handsome features, he left the past behind and strode firmly into the future.

Epilogue

An unexpected chinook wind swept through the high mountain passes, the last vestige of fall before winter would once again clench the new state of Colorado in its iron grip.

As she momentarily stopped scrubbing on the washboard to raise her sun-kissed face to the warmth of the wind, Angel Murphy sighed with contentment for herself and regret for a few friends who were no longer there to share her life with her.

She had received a letter from Rachel just a week earlier, and while she was happy for her friend and Fabien, and excited at their news that they would soon be adding to their family, Angel couldn't help but feel a tiny twinge of longing to see Belle Montagne again. The house had seemed the perfect wedding gift for the couple when Fabien had proposed to Rachel in the spring and then announced his impending transfer back east, but now Angel wished she had taken the baby and visited the Renaults earlier in the fall when they had invited her.

But Holt had been the one to cancel that plan, worried

that such a long trip would be draining or even dangerous to his wife or their newborn son, Matthew. For being such a fearless man himself, Holt treated his little family as if they were made of porcelain, and Angel had to chuckle as she remembered how he had hovered over her during her long but uneventful pregnancy.

Her other regret was that Kaga was no longer there to teach Matthew the way of the Langundo Arapaho. Holt's grandfather had died in September, shortly after Matthew had made his appearance. Fortunately, Angel and Holt had made a trip to the reservation to show Kaga his only great-grandson just days before the old man had passed away.

Angel's eyes misted now as she remembered how gently Kaga had placed his withered hands on the baby's head and solemnly christened him Mingan—Gray Wolf—either for the color of his eyes, which were gray like Holt's, or the way Matthew howled when anyone other than his mother held him, Angel wasn't sure.

Chuckling a little at the memory, Angel looked down at the cradleboard propped beside her, to look at her precious son, snuggled sleeping in his blankets, his tiny fists clenched. Little Matthew resembled Holt strongly, with his gray eyes and dark hair, but he had the McCloud nose and temperament, too, the latter loudly evidenced whenever the baby decided he was ready to eat.

Of course, Clara had served as Matt's godmother, though she herself was Mrs. Miller now, since Jack had gotten over his shyness after all those years. The older couple was as deliriously happy as any pair of newlyweds, and just as inseparable. It had definitely been a year for love.

Angel was so absorbed in these precious memories, she didn't hear Holt sneaking up behind her until he caught her around the waist and swung her in the bright fall sunshine.

"Penny for your thoughts," he said, pecking her nose and pulling her flush against his broad chest.

"I was thinking I'm a very lucky woman," Angel replied with a mischievous grin. "Lately I seem to be thinking that a great deal."

"Good." Holt sounded as content as she was, and though he was dirty and sweaty from a day working in the mine, she didn't have the slightest hesitation about wrapping her arms around his neck and kissing him soundly.

Laughing, Holt asked, "And what was that for, Mrs. Murphy?"

"For building me the cabin."

"Jean-Claude helped with that," he reminded her.

After a short pause Angel kissed him again.

"Mmm. And that one?"

"For making the beautiful cradleboard for Matt."

"Okoka showed me how, remember?"

Angel sighed and thought a moment, then brightened and kissed him once more, this time even more emphatically.

"Well?" Holt asked.

"That's for giving me Matthew. Nobody else could help with that!"

"And nobody'll help with Lillian, either," Holt growled under his breath as he playfully nipped at her ear. They had both agreed that their first daughter, whenever she was born, would be named after the woman who had meant so much to Holt as a friend,

and who had given her life for the very special friend
ship they had shared.

"I think," Holt said, a hint of a dimple appearing in hi
left cheek, "that it's time for us to both take a break fron
work and enjoy one of the last warm days before winte
sets in. What do you think, Mrs. Murphy?"

Gazing around at her little home in the wilderness, a
the mine shaft that had unexpectedly and ironicall
begun to produce gold beyond their wildest dreams, a
her delightful, sleeping son and the man she loved with al
her heart, Angel didn't have to think twice.

"Well, what are we waiting for?" she retorted, and
dissolved into laughter when Holt suddenly swung her
into his arms and charged like a wild bear for their bedroom, just inside the cabin door.

Kaga had been right; Life was good. It was very good,
indeed.

ABOUT THE AUTHOR

Patricia McAllister lives in the cozy community of Gooding, Idaho, bordered by mountains on one side and desert on the other. Her interests are as varied as the landscape: classical music, "Star Trek" reruns, and chocolate!

With a journalism degree in hand, Patricia first worked in the exciting fields of radio and newspaper before settling down to pursue her one true love—historical fiction. Her previous Zebra Heartfire was *Gypsy Jewel*.

Sea Raven, Patricia's third book, will be released in February '96. She enjoys hearing from readers. You can write to her at: P.O. Box 304, Gooding, ID 83330.

WHAT'S LOVE GOT TO DO WITH IT?

Everything . . . Just ask Kathleen Drymon . . . and Zebra Books

CASTAWAY ANGEL	(3569-1, $4.50/$5.50)
GENTLE SAVAGE	(3888-7, $4.50/$5.50)
MIDNIGHT BRIDE	(3265-X, $4.50/$5.50)
VELVET SAVAGE	(3886-0, $4.50/$5.50)
TEXAS BLOSSOM	(3887-9, $4.50/$5.50)
WARRIOR OF THE SUN	(3924-7, $4.99/$5.99)

Available wherever paperbacks are sold, or order direct from the Publisher. Send cover price plus 50¢ per copy for mailing and handling to Penguin USA, P.O. Box 999, c/o Dept. 17109, Bergenfield, NJ 07621. Residents of New York and Tennessee must include sales tax. DO NOT SEND CASH.